MW01134444

THE DEMON OF RAVEN'S BACK

A Novel by Patty Bowman

This is a work of fiction. Names, characters, places, events and incidents are either the product of the author's imagination or used in a fictitious manner. Any resemblance to actual persons, living or dead, locations or actual events is purely coincidental.

Copyright (c) 2017 by Patty Bowman. All rights reserved.

ISBN-13: 978-1975607449

ISBN-10: 1975607449

For

Miss Tobey
and
Nellie Pumpkin

and for those on the front lines
of protecting endangered species.
You are my heroes.

"To know is nothing at all; to imagine is everything."
-Anatole France

"Until one has loved an animal, a part of one's soul remains
unawakened."
-Anatole France

Other books by Patty Bowman

Valley Village Vampires

Chapter I: Madness By The Sea

Innis Kilbride grew up near the coast with the sea whispering to him as he slept, surprised on awakening not to find himself wrapped blissfully in thick green seaweed strands and floating weightlessly in the depths of the waves as he'd been in his dreams. Even as a boy he often pondered the difference between waking and sleeping dreams and loved hearing the Irish mythologies his grandfather passed down. One particular myth remained in Innis's memory: The Voyage of Mael Duin. This was the tale of a sea voyage during which amazing and fabulous islands were encountered, each holding its own unique beauties and terror. The Island of Ants, The Island of Horses and Demons, The Island of Black & White Sheep (where the sheep changed color). And The Island of Murderers.

Innis was disappointed that such places didn't actually exist, though he wondered if perhaps they had at some time, so far back in history that no living person could still remember. Surely, he reasoned, there must be some kernels of truth to be found in myths, otherwise how could they have come to be invented?

The everyday reality of being a child in the fishing village of Glenraven, on the Antrim coast of Northern Ireland, was conducive to belief in magic, for the natural beauty of the area was stunning and its relative isolation from the outside world served as a cocoon of protection. Innis knew little of matters beyond his small town, family and neighbors despite his mother's ambitions for him to venture from his birthplace and make his mark in the world. She recognized the boy's intelligence and inquisitive nature early in his development, and since she herself had secretly longed to escape the confines of Glenraven, lovely as they were, she imagined such a possibility for her son.

Innis was her firstborn with his brother Dalton, a boy of a completely different temperament from his older sibling, following three years later. Where Innis was like quicksilver, seeking small adventures and keen for his books and the sea, Dalton was a steady flame, tied closely to the land with a penchant for manual work instead of mental agility. Their mother, Irene, loved her sons equally, celebrating and cherishing their differences and encouraging each boy in his own inherent strengths and inclinations. There would be no more children for Irene after a series of miscarriages convinced her of the physical danger in persisting with such attempts. Her husband, Abbot, was satisfied with the two boys, but Irene had wished for a daughter and hid her disappointment while concentrating on her sons.

The family Kilbride held its own mysteries, including Irene's sister Bridget whose insanity had never been properly treated, diagnosed or acknowledged. As a boy, Innis was drawn to his Aunt Bridget's strangeness, though he'd never been told exactly what ailment caused her bizarre, and at times threatening, behavior. Bridget lived alone, nearby in a section of Glenraven known as Raven's Back. Her history was a tragic one as her beloved young man, Gage, had been lost to the sea before they could be married and the young Bridget, then only twenty years old, had never recovered.

Gage was one of the local fishermen, a dark and charming wastrel of whom Irene and Bridget Bahane's parents had never approved. His death in a fierce, sudden squall that overturned his small boat, drowning him along with two other fishermen who'd been with him, was considered a sad blessing by the family but Bridget was undone by the loss of her wild and beautiful boy. At first her expected grief and devastation at the tragic turn of events was understandable and ordinary enough, but recovery failed to occur. The young girl withdrew into a private world of mourning and deep depression, settling into the small fishing shack in Raven's Back where Gage had lived, refusing attempts by family and Gage's fellow fishermen to remove her from the ramshackle dwelling. She ceased communicating with the outside world except for daily walks to the sea where she gazed at the water for hours, sometimes wading into the waves as though moving toward some invisible beckoning presence, oblivious to the soaking of her shoes and clothes until some fisherman or passerby pulled her from the waves.

Bridget dressed exclusively in black for the rest of her days, and the sight of the small, ebony haired girl striding along the shore became an eerie, familiar one in Raven's Back. The area had always held a certain sense of dread for the locals since tales of destructive, vengeful ghosts and the history of several murders cast a dark pall on the small, secluded neighborhood. Bridget's family rallied around her in her grief, especially her older sister Irene who saw the seeds of destruction in her sibling's extended mourning. It was impossible to determine or foresee at what point the bereft girl's sorrow and loss slipped into madness, especially when Bridget began to avoid her family and withdraw even further into silence and isolation.

Irene frequently visited the ramshackle fishing shack in Raven's Back, knocking and calling at the door and windows to no avail. Sometimes she could see her sister inside the shack, moving as though in a dream, oblivious to Irene's entreaties. Once, when Irene ventured to the dwelling in the dead of night, hoping to perhaps surprise her sister or gain access, she heard the sound of Bridget's voice before she'd even reached the place. It was an otherworldly voice, declaiming loudly in tongues with an angry intonation that was both surprising and frightening. Irene had never known her sister to contain such fury but she recognized the disturbing otherness of the tirade, as though the words coming from within the shack were spoken by a creature who was not quite human.

Rushing to the door, Irene shouted her sister's name, rattling the locked door handle and begging for entry. Bridget went quiet, creeping to the window to pull the thin, tattered curtains closed then speaking calmly and firmly through the door in her normal tone.

"Go away, Irene. You're not needed here."

Irene leaned her forehead against the door, struggling to find an approach that might allow her to reach the sister she knew, now hidden within the mad woman. In a deep despair she realized the task was beyond her and turned slowly, trudging away from the shack and its tragic occupant.

Determined not to abandon Bridget to her demons, Irene began to follow her at a discreet distance whenever she made her treks to the sea. Usually Bridget would merely stand and gaze at the waves and the horizon for hours while Irene struggled to maintain patience. At other times, Bridget called out Gage's name or raised her hands to the sky, pleading in a broken voice for a sign, a signal of the spirit, some gesture of acknowledgment from the dead or the water itself, then falling on her knees to the rocky shore, burying her face in her hands and sobbing with an animal intensity that broke Irene's heart.

After weeks of secret surveillance, Irene decided something must be done before her sister became completely unreachable. She consulted her parents, who had adopted an attitude of denial, refusing to concede the severity of the problem. After several intense and futile arguments, the family had reached no consensus and Irene realized she would need to proceed on her own.

The isolated, bucolic location of Glenraven allowed for minimal interference from the outside world. Among the gloriously green fields, tangled ravines and bubbling brooks there was little room for stark realities such as insanity. Citizens of the area co-existed in close physical proximity, each familiar with the families, histories and difficulties of those around them yet seldom directly confronting the problems of others. In that unspoken, respectful way of a small, close-knit community, they kept their opinions to themselves but were quick to offer assistance should it be requested. Of course there was always gossip, and word had circulated throughout all of Glenraven about the crazy young girl who occupied the deserted fishing shack in Raven's Back. At first everyone had felt solicitous toward the grieving Bridget, particularly the relatives and loved ones of the two other fishermen who'd perished at sea along with Gage. Bridget had refused any assistance from the beginning, brusquely dismissing all efforts at comfort or commiseration and alienating the widow of one of the deceased fishermen to the point of hostility.

Even before the tragedy at sea, Bridget had been reluctant to socialize with the other fishermen and their spouses or families, devoting herself to Gage with a singularity that was its own form of strangeness. Gage had been popular in his community, full of fun and charm with a wicked sense of humor and a way with the ladies. Some had been surprised when he selected Bridget Bahane as his special love. Despite her wild beauty, which matched Gage's own, there was about her an otherworldly removal from her surroundings, a distance many found off-putting. When she was in Gage's presence, her black eyes laughed and danced with joy, her rare smile dazzled, making her lovely face even more beautiful. Her ownership of Gage, however, made itself known in disturbing ways. Any female who flirted with the handsome young fisherman became Bridget's enemy as she watched and waited for opportunities for revenge. It might be merely the spilling of red wine on a new dress at the pub or the theft of money from a purse, but inevitably Bridget would punish her rivals in some small way. Her fierce jealousy was intimidating and eventually the girls of Glenraven conceded defeat. Gage and Bridget made a stunning couple, both of them excellent dancers with a sense of style that belied their small-town origins. It was rumored that the pair had become secretly engaged just before the tragedy, but no diamond ring was ever spotted on Bridget's hand and no formal announcement was forthcoming.

Irene knew she would receive little assistance in trying to

8

rehabilitate her sister due to the hard feelings Bridget had engendered from the locals, so she set to the task on her own. The greatest fear was the possibility of Bridget doing physical harm to herself or someone else. During one of Bridget's solitary sojourns at the sea, Irene crept back to the fishing shack and found an unlocked window, allowing her to enter her sister's abode for the first time. She immediately set about inspecting the premises, looking into drawers, cupboards, closets and various boxes, struggling to go quickly before her sister returned but stymied by the jumbled mess inside the small shack. The extent to which Bridget had let her life lapse into chaos became disturbingly apparent with rotten food in the cupboard, unwashed dishes on the table and soiled clothing tossed to the floor. The dirty windows barely allowed any light to enter while the threadbare rugs displayed clumps of mud and seaweed from Bridget's daily seaside visits. The shack reeked of rot, fish and despair, and Irene forced herself to keep her mind on her task instead of collapsing in sorrow. What she sought, however, she scarcely knew and the only item of any value or interest she discovered was a beautiful, surprisingly expensive looking diamond ring tucked away in a small brocade box on a nightstand by the bed. She sat on the bed briefly, staring at the ring with tears streaming down her face, astonished that her sister had indeed been betrothed to Gage yet had never mentioned it to anyone. Replacing the ring carefully in its box she left the shack, soberly aware of the frightening extent of her sister's downfall.

Irene drove to Belfast the next day to meet with a psychologist she'd read about in a newspaper article and knew she couldn't afford, yet was determined to seek out as a first step in saving Bridget. Perhaps the man would take pity on her with her desperate situation. The city had always held great appeal for Irene, whose excitement at entering its crowded streets was tempered this time by her sad mission. Luck was with her since the psychologist agreed to see her without an appointment, confirming his specialty in grief counseling but referring her to a more reasonably priced therapist in Belfast. As she navigated the unfamiliar streets, her steps slowed while her plan for helping her sister began to disintegrate in her mind. Glenraven was a provincial little town, she knew, rife with gossip and ignorant of many of the ways of the outside world. To the fishermen, merchants and farmers of the area, insanity was seen as a curse, something to be avoided or whispered about, hardly anything to be openly discussed or treated as a form of illness. Irene had acknowledged that her parents' reluctance to accept Bridget's condition was probably due to the bad light in which it would cast their family, the way in which blame might find its way to their doorstep. Fear was a factor as well. Her own terror at discovering the state of the shack in Raven's Back and hearing Bridget's shouting in tongues could not be denied. The country of madness was a terrain she'd never thought to enter, but now she must explore it, ready or not, in order to save her sister. She found a bench and sat for a long while, barely aware of the vehicles and people passing by, of the noise and bustle surrounding her. How could she ever convince Bridget, who barely spoke to her or anyone, to travel to Belfast and lay bare her soul to a stranger? It would never work. Nor would the possibility of taking a psychologist to Bridget, provided that one might even be willing to travel to Glenraven.

Irene sighed deeply and rose to her feet, allowing herself to drift aimlessly along with the crowd, glancing occasionally into storefront windows, disheartened that she'd wasted a trip and couldn't bring herself to enjoy a rare visit to Belfast. It wasn't realistic that she should continue following and spying on Bridget forever, perpetually worried that her sister might one day simply walk into the sea the moment Irene had abandoned her vigil. At the same time, it was unacceptable to her, giving up as everyone else seemed to have done, resigning herself to the inevitability of Bridget's madness. Her heart would not allow it. Nothing in Irene's young life had prepared her for such a dilemma, and she grew weak at the thought of failure.

Continuing on her way, distracted and jostled by the busy crowds around her, she found herself by the Belfast City Hall and paused to gaze at the old Belfast Coat of Arms displayed there in a large stained glass window. She'd seen it before during one of her previous visits to the city, but now examined it with keener eyes, taking in its details with a desperate focus. Trying not to break down, she concentrated on the Coat of Arms depicting a shield supported by two creatures, one a chained wolf, the other a gray seahorse, along with a sailing ship with full white sails on a sea of green waves. Irene smiled for the first time that day, thinking of all the sea meant in her family's life, wondering if perhaps Bridget might be distracted by a token from Belfast. She returned to an area of the city where tourist items were sold and found a postcard featuring the very Coat of Arms at which she'd been gazing. Purchasing two of the cards, she hurried back to her car, spending the entire return trip with her mind in turmoil, attempting to manufacture a solution to her sister's situation.

After briefly settling herself at home in Glenraven, she took off again, rushing to the shack in Raven's Back to find it locked with no response from within. She slipped the postcard from Belfast, which she'd addressed to Bridget and signed with a cheery greeting, under the front door and once again found her way down to the nearby sea where the familiar sight of her sister looking out at the water brought her much relief. Watching the forlorn figure in black, whose long ebony hair was whipped fiercely by the wind, Irene then returned home and went to bed in the late afternoon, despondent and longing only for the oblivion of sleep.

Despite her emotional exhaustion, Irene slept badly and was up in time to see her parents off to work the next morning, her father to his duties at the fish processing plant and her mother to a teaching post at the community secondary school. Irene had taken two days off from her own job as a cook at one of the local restaurants and paled at the thought of an empty day ahead with no results from the previous day's excursion and no one in whom to confide her troubles. She was surprised by a knock on the door and peered out the window to see her sister standing there with postcard in hand.

Throwing open the door, Irene embraced Bridget in a fierce hug before she could even consider her impulse. Although Bridget didn't return the spontaneous gesture of affection, she stood silently and at least allowed it. Irene broke the embrace, keeping one arm around her sister's shoulders and gently persuading her into the house. It was the first time Bridget had entered there since the loss of Gage, and she appeared dazed, gazing around as though trying to identify her surroundings, still clutching the postcard. She wandered to the nearby couch and sat, her eyes ablaze with a fierce wildness tinged with fear. Irene sat beside her, afraid to make a move or a sound but Bridget turned to her, a sudden smile lighting up her face as she held the postcard toward Irene, pointing to the figure of the gray seahorse on the Coat of Arms.

"This is a sign," she whispered to Irene, her voice holding a breathless excitement. "This creature was sent to me by Gage. Don't you see, at last a sign! I've waited so long, praying for some message from beyond and this is it. Look!"

She held the card out to Irene who took it hesitantly, staring at the creature on it as intently as she could. It was shown in profile, dark gray in color with a spiked mane, a red tongue and a crown-like item around its neck. Instead of hooves the front legs were webbed flippers and the tail, in mermaid/hippocampus style, curled under its body. A smaller version of the seahorse stood atop the shield and a banner, stretched across the bottom of the shield, was inscribed with the Latin words "Pro Tanto Quid Retribuamus." Irene, who'd studied Latin in school, translated it as "What shall we give in return for so much." She smiled and handed the card back to Bridget, who'd been peering at her in a slightly unsettling manner.

"It's a lovely Coat of Arms," she nodded to Bridget. "I've read that the ship and the seahorse are a reference to Belfast's long maritime history."

"Exactly! But this seahorse, it speaks to me." Bridget clutched the card to her heart. "Or rather, Gage speaks to me through it. They met, you know, when he went beneath the waves. This sea creature rescued him, took him to a safe haven under the sea, and not until now was he able to let me know. It will no longer be necessary for me to visit the beach every day because I can talk to Gage whenever I choose, through this."

She once again tapped the gray seahorse with her finger, her eyes shining with delight.

"Oh, Irene, I was so lost, looking and listening and waiting at the wrong spot for some sign from Gage, a communication with his spirit, and at last I found it. You found it for me, my beloved sister. How can I ever thank you enough?"

At a loss for words or any appropriate response, Irene smiled and took her sister's hands, holding them briefly and looking into the smiling face she hadn't seen for more than six months. Bridget's eyes still showed the glaze of madness and her face was slightly dirty, but Irene secretly breathed a sigh of relief. Perhaps she could work with this, as long as the girl in black sitting beside her was communicating and relatively happy. It seemed a fragile thread on which to hang her hopes, yet she seized it with joy. Releasing Bridget's hands, she measured her options carefully. She could play along, knowing it might be encouraging the delusions Bridget was clearly embracing or she could seize this opportunity of somehow keeping her sister here in the family home in order to try treating her mental disorder, whatever it might be. Irene decided to play along.

"I found this in Belfast, my dear," she announced to her sister. "Something about it spoke to me and, yes, especially the seahorse. And I instantly thought of you."

It wasn't a complete fabrication and the joy which instantly filled Bridget's eyes reassured Irene that she had chosen the right path. I may have gotten this all wrong to this point, she thought. Instead of attempting to cure the madness perhaps I should have been trying to understand it, even to adopt aspects of it. Whatever works.

Bridget had moved a bit closer to Irene on the couch and Irene could feel a kind of electric current coursing through her sister's body. It frightened her but she pushed aside her trepidation.

"It seems both of us were meant to meet this creature who channels Gage, don't you think, Bridget?"

"Indeed! I almost lost my faith, you know, wondering why I couldn't reach him. Gage, that is. We promised each other, should something ever happen to one of us, that the other would receive a sign. Some communication from beyond to make it known there was indeed another place to which the lost loved one had safely arrived. And Gage has already told me so much since I found this picture by the door last night. There are wonders below the sea, Irene, did you know? Amazing, magical wonders."

Bridget's eyes shone with such happiness that Irene fought to keep back her own tears. Why should she question this strange yet miraculous form of cure? She recalled their father's tales from The Voyage of Mael Duin and how she and Bridget had warmed to their fanciful thrills as children. Surely here was a way out of the tunnel of madness.

"Would you like some tea, Bridget?"

There was a slight hesitation and Irene held her breath, hoping she could keep her sister here as long as possible, wondering if the grieving girl was even eating properly as she was visibly thinner.

"I wouldn't say no," Bridget replied with a fleeting smile, settling back on the couch and carefully holding the postcard like a cherished treasure.

From that day forward, Irene and Bridget tentatively found their way back to a form of normalcy, though their shared secret of the gray seahorse remained hidden from outsiders, including their parents. Bridget's trips to the sea were greatly reduced and Irene finally ceased following and spying, accepting that her sister was no longer in jeopardy of harm from her madness. The ability to communicate with Gage from the underwater realm in which Bridget believed he was dwelling had vanquished her restless desperation, replacing it with a comforting peace that relieved both sisters. Irene continued to check on Bridget at the shack frequently and one evening heard her speaking to Gage in a normal tone as though having a conversation with a living human who was in the room with her.

Bridget's detailed descriptions of Gage's underwater realm were vibrantly alive with the colors, textures and sense of the sea. That first day when Bridget had re-entered Irene's life with postcard in hand, they'd sat on the couch with their tea for hours, Irene continually refilling their cups as Bridget spoke of the images she'd received from Gage.

The most astonishing thing, to Bridget, was the discovery that the gray seahorse on the Coat of Arms was, in fact, actually a living creature who ruled the watery kingdom beneath the waves; hence, the crown-like accessory it wore around its neck. According to Bridget, it was only Gage who'd gone to dwell beneath the waves. The other two fishermen who'd drowned along with him were not there and Bridget regretted that she would not be able to bring good news to their families and loved ones. Still, it was exciting to become acquainted with Gage's new world, though he'd made it clear to Bridget that she was not to join him there until it was her natural time to leave the world of the living. This was a big relief to Irene as she'd consistently worried about the possibility of suicide for her sister.

While Bridget spoke of fantastical underwater caves and sea creatures, giant floating fronds of seaweed in pink, purple and orange and the amazing ways in which the light struck the bubbles beneath the sea, all detailed for her by Gage, Irene watched the genuine wonder dancing in her sister's eyes and almost envied her. It was a magical form of insanity, so much kinder than the harsh realities of everyday life. At times Irene worried that she was making a grave error by encouraging her sister in her delusions, but they were conspirators again as they'd been as children when they'd plotted against their parents' commands or gone on secret adventures that felt more dangerous than they actually were. Irene cherished those memories and clung to the belief that Bridget had turned a certain corner with her madness and it would be more manageable in the future. The magical seahorse remained their own private realm, though Irene reported to her parents with pleasure that Bridget's condition had improved.

Irene visited the shack in Raven's Back on a regular basis, helping Bridget restore a semblance of order to the home, bringing her nourishing food, making certain she took care of basic hygiene and, most of all, enjoying her stories. Gage's underwater kingdom was spun out in all its glory as Irene listened well into the evening while Bridget told her all the latest. How Gage explored miles and miles of the seabed aboard the gray seahorse's back, encountering other lost kingdoms and their strange citizens: deep purple fish with orange ringed eyes and fins, small sea dragons who spat fire even under the waves, sheep with gills and magical wool which changed into all the colors of the rainbow, sea plants towering over the ocean floor with tendrils that reached out and caressed Gage's face and hands. There were whole worlds beneath the waves where an octopus might really have a garden as in the old Beatles song. Bridget's daily life, and that of her sister, was conveyed to Gage as well, despite its lack of color and excitement. It was important to let him know that things were going well enough, Bridget insisted to her sister, so he wouldn't worry.

Gradually, the blazing madness that had filled Bridget's eyes softened to a bright, perpetual gleam of excitement, her face wearing an expression of childlike anticipation. Months would go by without a visit to the sea, and Bridget occasionally ventured forth into the village to buy produce at the market or browse in the shops. She wore the beautiful diamond ring which Gage had given her but continued to dress exclusively in black. The citizens of Glenraven were polite and solicitous when they encountered her but refrained from too much familiarity or conversation. They could sense her otherness, the whisper of insanity when they looked into her face, the sense of an implied threat or danger. Secretly, many who'd known her were disturbed by her countenance and she came to be known as The Mad Widow of Raven's Back despite the fact that she and Gage had never formally married.

There were a few true sea widows in Glenraven though none, save Bridget, were notorious. Irene took care of her sister, providing for her out of her own wages with some assistance from her parents who'd developed a tentative relationship with their younger daughter. Bridget infrequently visited the Bahane family home, where Irene still lived, and would usually spend only an hour or so, leaving her parents concerned yet relieved that progress had clearly been made. The girls' father, in particular, was somewhat embarrassed by Bridget's reputation in the community but kept his own counsel and turned a deaf ear to gossip and speculation. In private moments, however, he mourned the loss of his younger daughter for he scarcely recognized Bridget in this new creature with a faraway look in her eyes.

Irene continued to keep a watch on Bridget as the years progressed, sometimes wondering about the workings of that warped, fanciful mind to which she'd grown accustomed. Bridget developed a fondness for crocheting, advising her sister that her hands easily worked in coordination with her mind as she listened to tales from Gage or pondered those he'd already told her. Her fingers flew as afghans, sweaters, caps and mittens in bright colors and pleasing patterns appeared from her crochet hook. It was obvious that Bridget had a natural talent for the work, and she earned some extra money by selling items to villagers and one of the shops in Glenraven. There were those who resisted purchasing any pieces from Bridget, afraid and superstitious that her malaise might somehow communicate itself to any wearer of a scarf or cap created by the mad woman. Irene encouraged her sister in this new pastime, even speculating that Bridget might show her wares at one of the street fairs which were regularly held in some of the nearby towns. It would be risky, she knew, exposing Bridget to crowds of strangers and she doubted her sister would even be interested in such a proposition.

One day as she waited in the tiny living room area which Bridget had created in the fishing shack, listening contentedly to the sound of tea preparations from Bridget in the kitchen, Irene's glance drifted to a round wooden-legged stool in a corner. Draped over the stool was a small crocheted blanket depicting the Belfast Coat of Arms. The gray seahorse had been given a position of prominence, but Irene marveled at the skill it required to recreate such a complicated pattern with no guidelines. As Bridget entered the room with the tea service, Irene pointed to the crocheted blanket.

"My God, Bridget, that's fantastic! When did you make this and however did you do it?"

Bridget smiled and set the tea tray down on the rickety table, settling herself beside Irene with a casual shrug.

"It just came to me, easy enough. One morning I simply felt

the need to do it, like something told me. No doubt it was the sea creature, working my fingers and the yarn, that's all. I'm glad you like it. I've plenty more if you want one."

Irene stared at her sister in astonishment while Bridget motioned to the bedroom.

"There's a drawer full of them in that chest in the bedroom. The feeling comes over me sometimes and I have to create the sea king. They're not for sale, of course. They're only for me, a kind of tribute for all he's done for my Gage. I'd allow one to you, though, since you're the one person who knows him here above the water, besides myself. You mustn't let anyone see, it must be private. Otherwise there might be consequences. You understand."

Her brow furrowed, Irene nodded slowly but her thoughts were racing. Perhaps her sister was not as well off as she'd hoped and she'd made a serious error in assuming the best, allowing the madness to continue unaddressed. After tea, Bridget ushered Irene into the bedroom, opening the lid of a wooden chest to reveal dozens of crocheted items featuring the gray seahorse. As Bridget took each folded scarf, baby blanket, hat and tea cosy out of the chest and spread them out over the bed, she beamed proudly at her sister.

"Take whatever you fancy, Irene. You've earned it for all the support you've given me, for still loving me and for bringing salvation to me. For finding the seahorse king. I know I can trust you."

Irene's eyes roved over the items in a kind of frenzy. It was obvious that much time and care had gone into this work and something else, an unnameable channeling of skill and creativity. Blinking back tears at the thought of Bridget's innate talent held captive by her insanity, Irene pointed to one of the scarves.

"I'll have that if it's OK with you, darlin'. Don't worry, I won't wear it out so anyone can see, but it'll be handy to warm my neck just the same when I'm at home this winter. They're all so beautiful."

"Why, thank you, sister. Wear it in health and always be mindful there's a bit of magic from beneath the sea caught in all those little hooks and stitches."

Irene secreted the scarf in a small hope chest she kept for the future, bringing it out during the dead of winter to wrap around her neck, always with the inevitable thoughts of Gage's underwater world and her sister's madness.

As the years progressed, and Irene met Abbot Kilbride, her

future husband, the secrets between her and Bridget remained, along with their bond. Bits of the anger and fierce sorrow about the loss of Gage began to seep back into Bridget's behavior, but Irene remained the keeper of the gate to her sister's madness, allowing no one access to the true extent of Bridget's retreat from the world. Even after Irene and Abbot were married, Irene's visits to the shack in Raven's Back remained her own private affair. Abbot met his sister-in-law and knew the gossip about her since he was a local boy and familiar with the whole sad story. He was pleasant to Bridget yet kept his distance, sensing the disturbing undercurrent there and realizing she preferred minimal contact with others.

After initially questioning Irene about her sister's state of mind, he recognized the wall which continually went up whenever he pushed too hard and retreated from pursuing the issue. Bridget would be welcome in their home, he assured Irene, and although he hoped that one day his new wife might trust him enough to divulge further information about the madness in the family he let it rest. Abbot was a live-and-let-live sort of fellow, precisely what initially drew Irene to him. When their sons, Innis and Dalton, arrived, the boys spent limited time with their Aunt Bridget on the isolated occasions when she visited the young family's home. She was skittish around the babies at first, her eyes taking on a wild and nervous expression that caused Abbot to watch her closely. Eventually, with more exposure to the growing children, Bridget relaxed and seemed to enjoy telling her nephews tales from her own father's repertoire.

During the period following the boys' births, when Irene suffered several miscarriages, Abbot noticed that his wife's visits to the shack in Raven's Back increased, and she would return shaken and distracted, avoiding his offered concern and shutting herself in the bedroom for hours. He listened with frustration and fear to her heartrending sobs but when he knocked softly on the door all went quiet within and he eventually left Irene alone with her pain.

Finally, the pattern began to annoy him and he confronted his wife one night as she returned from a visit with Bridget.

"Look, I know you've always taken care of your sister and whatever goes on between you two over there in Raven's Back is not to be discussed, but every time you come back from seeing Bridget you're a mess. Worse than when you left. I know you're heading over there every time things get to you. What I don't understand is why you keep doing it when it makes you this upset. What gives,

Irene? I'm your husband, don't I have a right to know something?"

Irene sank down onto the couch as though all energy had instantly drained from her body. After a brief silence, while Abbot continued standing nearby and watching her expectantly, she turned her eyes to her husband.

"You'll never understand it, Abbot, even if I were to tell you. Tonight's the last, I promise. Bridget's been helping me this time and just now, this evening, it's become clear to me that I've got to stop trying to have another child. Two miscarriages is enough. Bridget had to make me see that, and in her own peculiar way she finally did. I know you've tried, and you've been more than kind and fair about being content with the two boys as our family. Now so will I. I'm sorry I've been hard on you, shut you out, but please don't blame Bridget. She's made me see the truth."

Abbot rushed to Irene, enfolding her in a warm embrace and the consultations between Irene and Bridget were never discussed again, though Abbot would always wonder what had taken place in that fishing shack.

Chapter II: The Kilbride Boys

Partners in crime. That's how many of the residents of Glen-raven thought of the brothers Kilbride, Innis and Dalton. Innis, the elder, was the mischief maker with Dalton designated as the one man clean-up crew for his brother. In truth, most of the brothers' escapades were a result of conspiracy with Dalton every bit as involved with planning the latest scheme as was Innis, who nevertheless was front and center when it came to carrying it out. The boys never got into serious trouble and, due to their strict Roman Catholic upbringing, were always contrite about any harm caused by their pranks, ready to make amends and admit their guilt. The small fishing town of Glenraven was the main source of income for the area with a fish processing plant and various seafood-related enterprises such as fish markets and restaurants supplying the majority of jobs. The boys' father, Abbot, however, had nothing to do with the fishing industry. He operated a small farm of only a few acres, growing vegetables and managing a herd of sheep that provided wool, comprising an income of modest means on which the family lived. Irene, their mother, continued to work as a cook at one of the local restaurants as she had before marrying and starting a family, though her hours had been greatly reduced due to the time she needed to spend at home with her sons. When they became of school age she returned to a longer work schedule and often brought restaurant surplus food home for the family's dinner.

Innis, like his mother, preferred being out of the house and away from the farm, exploring the surrounding glens and once hitching a ride to Belfast. Dalton, however, loved the farm and from a young age was keen to join his father in the fields, tending the sheep and vegetables. Abbot grew to rely on the boy for assistance with most of the farm tasks, from shearing the sheep to harvesting the crops, and noticed his son had a natural affinity for the land and the world of nature. The family's sheepherding dog, a border collie named Keeley, was Dalton's constant companion, sleeping in his bed at night and rising with him early each morning to begin the work day. Innis adored Keeley as well, though he was much fonder of playing with the dog than working with her. When he was only six, he insisted to his parents that he and Keeley had achieved a meeting of the minds and he was now able to speak to her in her own language. Dalton, then three years old, was mightily impressed by his brother's ability to 'speak dog', but Abbot teased the boys good-naturedly, asking them for the latest news from Keeley. By the time Dalton began working the sheep with Keeley, he was nine and the dog was older, though still spry and adept at controlling the herd. The boy had developed his own form of communication with the dog that far outstripped his brother's imaginary 'dog speak'. Some-times, watching Dalton and Keeley work the sheep together, Abbot marveled that the boy and dog seemed truly of one mind.

Although Innis was more adventuresome than the home lov-ing Dalton, he adored books and was a precocious reader, rejecting the typical cute and cuddly children's books for more esoteric fare. Irene often read to the boys when they were small, but Innis clam-ored for the adults' volumes though they were well beyond his understanding. When Irene's father visited, Innis in particular was keen to hear the Irish myths and fables which were usually told in a dramatic fashion. He favored his Aunt Bridget above any other rela-tives despite the infrequency of her company. She had a fondness for him as well and would usually relent when he begged her for a story. Some of her stories made little sense, but Innis would listen attentively, sometimes adding his own twist to the tale while Bridget frowned and hesitated then often picked up the new thread and con-tinued with the detour Innis had contributed.

One of the brothers' most popular spots for exploration and mischief was Raven's Back. Already familiar with the chilling tales of this secluded and mysterious area of Glenraven, Innis was anxious to discover its secrets. Dalton would accompany his brother with trepidation, though he secretly enjoyed these exciting forays into the unknown. They'd never been inside the fishing shack where their Aunt Bridget lived but knew where it was located and passed it many times, occasionally peering in the windows though never actu-ally disturbing its occupant. There were other fishing shacks scat-tered throughout the area and a couple of old stone houses where a few chickens and sheep were kept, as well as one obstreperous don-key. It was Innis's particular delight to hear the donkey bray, and he became adept at making it happen during the wee hours before even the early rising occupants of the area had left their beds.

Most of the resident of Raven's Back were rugged individual-ists who kept to themselves, operating their own independent small farms or businesses such as repair of fishing gear. There were also many fishermen who left their shacks well before dawn, though

Innis made a point of coaxing the loud vocalizations from the donkey well in advance of the fishermen's breakfast. The donkey, whose name was Malcolm, had bitten and kicked both of the Kilbride boys in the past when they'd tried to take him for a ride without permission from his owners. They'd been warned and threatened about bothering Malcolm, whose temperament was already nasty toward everyone. Dalton had pleaded with his brother to leave the donkey alone, but Innis loved Malcolm's feisty ways and felt sorry for the donkey, who spent his days in a small enclosure in the back yard of the stone house where his owners lived.

Several times Innis had volunteered to exercise the donkey, but the couple who lived in the stone house, a surly pair who resented intrusion from any outsider, refused. Dalton had been persuaded by his brother to sneak over to Malcolm's enclosure early one morning and take the donkey out for a ride. With little more than a rope and their misguided good will, along with a handful of carrots, the boys managed to lead Malcolm away from the stone house and find a tree stump from which Innis leapt onto the donkey's back, gripping the frayed rope for dear life as Malcolm ran, leaped and bucked across acres of sheep pasture. Dalton made a feeble attempt to catch the comical pair but soon gave up and sat watching his brother flying precariously off the donkey's back yet somehow managing to stay aboard. After struggling with his wild ride for what seemed a prolonged period of time, Innis finally got the donkey somewhat under control and come trotting back to Dalton, bouncing around on Malcolm's back like a small sack of potatoes.

"Did ya see?" Innis enthused to his brother, proud of his ability to stay on the donkey. "Have a go, Dalt, he's fun and he loves it!"

Jumping from Malcolm's back, Innis was startled to see the donkey easily slip out of the loose, improvised rope halter and go dashing off over the fields, bucking and farting. The boys took off after Malcolm calling and laughing while the donkey led them on a merry chase. Eventually all three tired of the game, and Dalton was able to recapture the donkey and lead him back to his small corral. This adventure proved irresistible to the boys, and they returned a few days later with Dalton, as well as Innis, getting a thrilling ride aboard Malcolm, who was slightly less wild this time. The third visit to Malcolm, however, proved disastrous as the brothers were greeted with loud brays from the donkey, in anticipation of his carrot treats. The couple came grumbling from the stone house, annoyed at having been awakened at 2 a.m., and lights from a couple of nearby dwellings came on since Malcolm's vocalizations could be heard for miles.

Innis and Dalton were punished by their parents after complaints were received from several residents of Raven's Back, including Malcolm's owners. It seemed the boys had returned a few more times to Malcolm's corral after being chased off and warned by the donkey's owners. The neighbors had also grown weary of being awakened at an ungodly hour. The brothers were thrashed by their father and made to do some light work for Malcolm's owners by clearing their yard of rocks, branches and other debris caused by a recent storm. Dalton and Innis were secretly pleased with this part of the punishment as it gave them additional time around Malcolm and even though there were no more free rides they snuck carrots to the donkey and took every opportunity to pet and talk to him.

Another caper involved the boys' Aunt Bridget. It had now become their habit to visit her when they were in Raven's Back, and although Dalton became a bit nervous around his aunt, Innis was fascinated by her. Her home, to which they were eventually admitted, was kept as tidy as possible by Irene but reverted to a state of chaos in between cleanings. Once the boys were served a plate of strange tasting cookies that clearly contained small black bugs baked into the batter. They kept quiet about the unsavory treat but it became a running joke between them to use bugs as a recipe ingredient. Shortly after the bug cookie experience, they gathered some small beetles they found in the dirt around Bridget's shack and stealthily put them into their mother's flour tin. The exclamations and disgust from Irene when she attempted to make a pie with the buggy flour was worth the punishment meted out to the boys by their father, and after the usual spanking they spent the hours locked in their room as further discipline laughing uproariously at the success of their scheme. Despite being questioned about the motivation behind their actions, the boys kept their secret about Bridget, though they never again accepted any offering of food when visiting her home.

Innis had a talent for art and began drawing at an early age. No one else in the family had ever displayed any creative inclination or ability except for Bridget with her crocheting. Irene was thrilled at her son's artistic bent, encouraging him with as many art supplies as the family could afford. He was particularly fond of painting, gathering various objects from nature to sketch or paint, even doing an impressive portrait of Malcolm. Once, during a visit with Bridget, he discovered a small closet with long strands of varying types of seaweed draped over the pole where clothes would normally hang. He asked Bridget about it and she advised that she put the seaweed in her baths, enabling her to float beneath it while imagining herself to be in the ocean. The nutrients are quite good for your skin, she told the fascinated boy, and left you smelling delightfully of the salty ocean air.

Innis loved the sea almost as much as did his aunt, and created a strange painting of Bridget in the tub with seaweed. At first his parents were puzzled by the meaning of the drawing, but Irene remembered she'd also found the closet of seaweed in Bridget's shack at one time without questioning it and realized now the purpose of the odd custom.

Chapter III: The Curse of Raven's Back

As Innis and Dalton grew older, their paths began to diverge. Dalton concentrated on assisting his father with the farm while Innis began entering local art contests and spending increasingly more time on painting. He'd added sculpting to his creative efforts as well as some wood carving. A propensity toward dark, mysterious and often downright odd depictions of strange creatures, objects or scenes limited his success at the art shows, but everyone was nevertheless impressed by his obvious talent. Like his mother, he enjoyed the city and made frequent trips to Belfast where he visited art galleries and the sites of significant events in the stormy history of that city. Having been raised Catholic, he had a certain respect for the goals of the IRA though not for their methods. He occasionally considered the possibility of someday moving south to Dublin or another spot in the Republic of Ireland but his roots were too firmly planted in the magical green hills and glens of the North. Whenever he returned to Glenraven following a trip to Belfast, he felt himself once again at home, under the spell of the sea, the hidden ravines and the mysteries of the place where he'd been born.

Irene began to urge Innis to apply for a college or art school but he resisted, loathe to leave his community and its familiar comforts. It was clear that Dalton would follow in his father's footsteps, becoming more involved in tending the crops and taking over most of the work with the sheep from Abbot. There was little place in Glenraven for Innis's art, however, and Irene feared he might abandon it for some method of making a living that was less suited to him. The family didn't have funds for an expensive school so Irene concentrated her efforts on the smaller, more affordable art schools in Belfast she'd researched online. She sensed a disturbing ennui from Innis when she mentioned the information she'd gathered and finally sat him down for a serious discussion about his future.

"Darlin', what is it you wish to do for your future?" she began. "I don't see you staying here forever and not doing something with your art. You've God-given talent and it's not to be wasted."

"I know, Ma, but I don't want to go to one of those art schools and be told how everything's supposed to be, what colors and methods and kinds of paintings are correct. It'll ruin art for me."

Irene hesitated, reluctant to puncture his youthful idealism.

"I understand what you're saying, son, but your father and I can't support you forever, you know. You must eventually find your own living and it just seems like art would serve you well. It's what you most enjoy, is it not?"

Innis shrugged.

"I enjoy it, yeah, but how long would I love it once I had to do it for a living?"

"Is there something else then?"

Innis looked away from his mother and seemed to be considering his reply, then returned his gaze to Irene.

"I dunno. I keep feeling like there's something I'm meant to do but I don't know what it is. Dalton's lucky, you know, he's got exactly what he wants right here. I don't, but when I'm in Belfast I don't get any sense that's right for me either."

"Sometimes you have to work to make things right. You need to forge your path or look further before you can follow it."

Nothing was resolved regarding Innis's future, but Irene noticed he was spending more time in Raven's Back, initially to visit his Aunt Bridget and then to hang out with some of the other residents of the area who were renowned for their reclusive ways. Innis had always favored this part of Glenraven above all others with its dark foliage, dense woods, secluded little random brooks and history of nefarious incidents and notorious people. He became friendly with a few of the fishermen who owned shacks similar to the one where Bridget had settled, and he rose before dawn on several occasions to join them on their fishing expeditions. Always drawn to the sea, he also had a healthy respect for it, remembering the stories he'd heard about the squall that took the life of his aunt's true love and those of his fellow fishermen. He'd tried to draw out details from Bridget but she vehemently advised him to desist as the sea held secrets never to be carelessly divulged. His mother was no help, also refusing to provide much information and even some of the fishermen he came to know, who'd worked with the doomed trio taken by the waves, were strangely reluctant to discuss the tragedy.

The first time Innis set out with three of the fishermen from Raven's Back on a clear, dark morning, it was with some trepidation that he noticed the lights of Glenraven growing ever more distant as the small fishing boat in which he rode headed toward the open sea. He knew little about tides or the workings of a fishing boat but was soon at home surrounded by nothing but darkness, water and the occasional squawk of sea birds. It was on his third expedition with the fishermen that one of them told him about the curse of Raven's Back. It seemed that one of the reasons for the almost universal silence on the subject of the squall in which the three fishermen had perished was the unspoken belief it had been caused by the curse. The majority of fishermen who operated out of Glenraven lived in areas other than Raven's Back and for a specific reason. A long series of tragic and disturbing incidents stretching back hundreds of years had been attributed to a curse placed on that area by a sailor who'd washed up on the shore at Glenraven and found his way to Raven's Back in search of assistance. During an unexplained accident at sea, he'd lost his bearings and his mind, arriving in Glenraven with little memory of his past or what had happened to him. Bedraggled, dehydrated and wild-eyed from an indeterminate time at sea adrift and alone, the babbling man frightened the locals who turned on him, refusing to provide help and eventually forcing him back to his boat to disappear forever. The curse he'd levied on Raven's Back for his ill treatment and rejection, however, remained.

Since that time, the stories went, one tragedy after another had visited the area, from vicious murders to numerous deaths at sea. There was rampant speculation as to why those who died or were harmed by events related to the curse had been chosen, but the accumulation of tragic incidents made it difficult to deny the reality of the curse itself.

Innis wondered if his Aunt Bridget was a victim of the curse or if she was even aware of it, but knew better than to mention it to her. It turned out that those who made their living at sea were accustomed to dealing with the vagaries of fate as they were consistently subject to the whims of Mother Nature. Nothing could have been done to anticipate or avoid the freak squall which had taken the lives of Gage and his fellow fishermen. Perhaps using the curse as an explanation for such unpredictable tragedies made them somehow more acceptable, Innis reasoned, regardless of how unlikely the reality of an ancient hex on the area might be. He eventually put it out of his mind when he was out with the fishermen, though he noticed specific rituals performed by certain of their group before setting out to the open sea. Innis's fishing skills were not equal to his artistic ones, but the fishermen came to accept him for his enthusiasm and respect for their profession. He never tired of witnessing the dawn of a new day from out on the water or the comforting lull of the sea's sounds, motion and scent.

To Irene's chagrin, her eldest son's artistic inclinations began to drift away from painting toward woodworking and carpentry. Through his association with the fishermen he'd met a man named Oren who was a shipwright. Innis began spending time observing his work, questioning him about his profession and expressing keen interest in learning from him. About a month after their previous conversation concerning his future, Innis asked his mother if they could speak in private. Worried about the outcome, Irene quickly agreed, preparing some of her son's favorite apple tarts for their afternoon meeting. Innis seemed nervous as he sat beside her on the couch, complimenting her on the bakery treat and downing several of them before he spoke.

"Ma, you might not be too happy about what I want to say, but I've thought about what you said, about my future. I know you want me to pursue the art and all, but I've decided I'd rather be a carpenter. It'll be a living and I won't have to go away to school to learn it. I can apprentice with Oren, the bloke I've been talking to in town. He's agreed to take me on as a shipwright and woodworker, although I think I'd rather build houses maybe. Anyway, I can apprentice with him for now until I figure out the rest. He'll pay me something. It won't be much, but he's gonna help me build my own place over in Raven's Back so at least I'll be outta you and Da's hair."

Irene sighed.

"Darlin', it was never about you bein' out of our hair. I hope you know that. You're welcome to stay her for awhile. You're young yet. It's not like you're taking advantage."

"I'm drawn to Raven's Back, Ma. That's the bottom line. Have been ever since I started visiting Aunt Bridget as a wee lad. It's where I want to make my home."

"But why, Innis? I don't know that I want you living there."

"Is it the curse you're thinking about? I know all about that, the fishermen told me."

"And it doesn't bother you?"

"Not a bit. Don't know if I even believe in it. Besides, sometimes where there's a curse there's bound to be magic too. I might have already found some. Am I sounding a bit much like an Irishman?"

His dark eyes twinkling with mischief, Innis offered the irrepressible, impish smile his mother had found impossible to resist from the time he was an infant.

"You know I'm not about to refuse you, Innis. Besides, you're of age now and can take your own decision, which you've obviously decided to do. But what about your art? Please don't just let it go. It's a gift, you know, and its own form of magic."

"I'll still do my art, don't worry, Ma. Raven's Back brings out the art in me, I swear."

Irene raised an eyebrow.

"Indeed? And what's this magic you claim you've already found?"

"Not yet, it's too early to say for sure. I'll let you know when the time is right."

"I'll be waiting on it. One thing, Innis. You'll be near your Aunt Bridget living out there, but promise me you'll not become too frequent a visitor with her. I know you've always been fond of her, but there are some lines it's better not to cross. Madness is a power-ful, but also a delicate, thing and needs to be respected."

Innis stood and leaned down to kiss his mother's forehead.

"Always, Ma. I'll bear it in mind."

Chapter IV: The Grove of Purple Trees

The magic which Innis had mentioned to his mother had arrived in the form of a tree. It was his common practice to use the wood of crab apple or chestnut trees for his carving. Early one morning, while exploring into the denser woods on the far edge of Raven's Back, he'd discovered a type of tree he'd never encountered. At first, he thought it must be a trick of the light that the small tree's bark appeared to have a purplish hue, but on closer inspection it proved to be true. Even the undersides of the tree's large, thick leaves displayed the same coloring. Its branches were twisted in places while its trunk featured long, visible roots stretching out above ground and reaching into the soil like bony fingers.

Walking slowly around the tree, Innis marveled at its glorious strangeness, almost afraid to approach it but finally reaching a hand out to feel the rough, purplish bark. It was surprisingly soft to the touch and a small piece broke off into his grasp. He closed his fingers around the bark and felt a slight warmth. Looking up into the tree's foliage, he felt a sudden disorientation, as though he'd lost his bearings, and quickly turned his attention away to survey the rest of the surrounding woods. He'd never come quite this far into the thick of the Raven's Back forest and began inspecting the area for additional trees matching the anomaly he'd just encountered. Prowling among the woods, he sensed himself an intruder in this dark, hushed world of trees and paused to listen to the dense silence. Not a trace of bird song, leaves rustling or branches creaking broke the stillness.

"It's almost eerie," he whispered aloud, glancing around with nervousness. He'd always felt at home in the woods, especially in Raven's Back, but now there was some sense of threat in the air. A small distance away he spotted another tree with the purplish hue. Rushing to it he examined its trunk and leaves, thrilled that it was identical to the first one he'd seen but slightly taller and larger in circumference. Breaking off a small piece of bark again, he compared it to the original one which he still clasped. They appeared to be the same, and closing his hand over them he felt again the warmth and vibrancy of a living thing.

Pushing farther into the densest part of the forest, he found an area where the purplish trees grew in abundance, a grove of them that caused him to catch his breath. He walked among them, gazing in astonishment at their strange beauty, amazed that some trees displayed a rich, royal purple hue while others were a lighter shade approaching lavender. For some reason, the tale of the curse of Raven's Back sprang to mind and he wondered if the trees might be harmful in some way, perhaps even poisonous. His hand showed no rash or ill effect from holding the bark and he reached up to touch the leaves on one of the trees, carefully pulling one from its branch. Turning the leaf over in his hand he thrilled to its sheen and thickness, its alternating shades of dark green on the visible side and deep purple on the underside. This is like a waking dream, he told himself, but the leaves and bark were solid and real.

Determined to find the origin and name of these marvelous trees, he hurried back to Glenraven, wondering if he might use the wood of such trees for carving purposes. The thought of cutting down even one of them, however, was unbearable. Still, he sat down at the computer at once to research his discovery. No one in Glenraven or Raven's Back had ever spoken to him of such trees, and he kept this newfound knowledge to himself. He had no success in finding anything like the trees on the Web despite spending several hours attempting to do so, and finally gave up, worrying that perhaps he'd hallucinated the whole phenomenon.

The apprenticeship he'd begun with Oren, the shipwright, took precedence over Innis's obsession with the strange trees, and it was several days until he could return to the hidden grove. During this interim a storm had passed through the area and Innis was anxious to see what effect it might have had on the purple trees. Much to his relief, he found the smaller tree he'd discovered first still standing, but as he inspected the grove he was sad to see one of the larger trees had toppled to the ground. Oddly enough, the roots of the tree remained attached to the soil; only the trunk had snapped off midway, leaving a stump that displayed a rich purple interior, much darker and more pronounced in color than the bark. Although he was sorry for the loss of even one of these exquisite trees, he assumed it might grow again since it had not been uprooted. The idea that such a beautiful, unique tree would simply lay on the forest floor to rot away was unacceptable so he decided to salvage as much wood from it as possible and try using it for carving. Imagining the amazing items he could create with the purple hued wood, he immediately gathered tools for cutting up the trunk and branches, keeping a portion of the leaves as well since he found them striking, thrillingly unusual. It was a challenge attempting to retrieve the tree in secret but he was determined to guard his discovery for fear the locals might learn of the purple grove and decimate it.

It took several days of careful, tedious work before Innis managed to gather as much of the wood as he wanted, storing it in a deserted shack in Raven's Back which he'd been using as a workshop. Anxious to begin discovering the properties of this new type of wood and how he could make it work for his carpentry, he was once again frustrated by a delay due to his apprenticeship duties. Eager to learn all he could, however, he concentrated on his lessons, storing them away for application to his secret project. He had no intention of using the purple wood for building a boat but rather some fanciful item or piece of furniture he might use away from the prying eyes of others who would surely clamor for information about the unusual wood coloring. There was no guarantee the wood from the tree would even be conducive to fine carving, though Innis was optimistic, noticing the softness of the bark he'd originally gathered and the relative ease with which he'd been able to cut up the tree.

Finally, one evening after finishing his other duties, Innis went to the shack to begin work on carving the purple wood. He first examined the grain of the wood, noticing its many peculiar patterns that made it difficult to determine the best method for working with it. He'd already somewhat sanded it down during earlier, sporadic visits, and he now tried applying a gouge to scoop away some of the rough edges. The wood proved amazingly pliable and he could tell it would be a delight to carve. His excitement increased as he continued to shape the wood which seemed to bend to his every idea and whim. He remained in the workshop well into the night, unable to break away from the wonderful ease with which one lovely creation after another materialized from the purple wood.

By early the next morning, Innis, exhausted but happy, sat back to survey his work. It was as though the wood itself had given him inspiration. He cast his gaze over an impressive array of items: a small sheep figurine (which he planned to give to Dalton), a jewelry box, a bowl, a corner table. His favorite carving was one which had come to him almost unbidden, not so much planned as simply imagined, channeled by some unknown source. It was a baby dragon emerging from the shell of an egg, its head and two front legs having broken free while its claws gripped the sides of the egg as though about to pull itself free. The dragon's mouth was closed in a sweet smile, its scales wonderfully detailed, its ears flattened onto its

32

head, its wings not fully visible but poking up a bit through the broken eggshell. Innis stared at it in wonderment, amazed at his own skill and the beauty of the purple wood. It was the most sophisticated and imaginative carving he'd ever created. As expected, the purple wood had proven amazingly malleable, more so than any other material with which he'd ever worked, and he longed to show his creations to someone. The only person he felt he could trust to keep the secret of the purple wood was his Aunt Bridget. Perhaps Dalton might also be willing to honor his wishes for secrecy if he was given the sheep figurine.

Exhausted from his marathon carving session, Innis fell asleep in the workshop, oblivious to the cold and discomfort of stretching out on his work bench. Dreams immediately came to him. In one, he was wandering in the grove of purple trees in desperate search of something he could not identify. The wind came up and he felt a surge of fear, then suddenly found himself on the beach, scanning the horizon for boats but finding only the dark water, tinted in a purplish hue. In another he had awakened in his workshop to see disembodied eyes staring in at him from the darkness. They were a gold amber in color, almost like a cat's eyes but otherworldly, holding some droll secret in their expression, partially amused and partially threatening. He attempted to speak but fell back onto the work bench, closing his eyes to avoid the unrelenting gaze of the entity outside the window.

Innis awoke in the early afternoon, pocketed the sheep and dragon carvings and hurried to his family's house. Dalton was out with the sheep so Innis tucked the sheep figurine into one of his brother's coat pockets with a brief note asking him not to show the figurine to anyone until they'd spoken together. He then returned to Raven's Back, lingering by Bridget's door, uncertain whether to share the dragon carving with her or keep it to himself. Recalling his mother's words about the qualities of madness, he turned away, afraid of altering his aunt's delicate balance despite longing to share the creature with her. She seemed the only person who might appreciate and understand his own joy in its strangeness and inexplicable creation, but he resolved to keep it with him, secluding it from all eyes but his own.

Chapter V: Tryst in Belfast

Oren and Innis had begun to renovate a small cabin in Raven's Back where Innis would live. It was some distance from any of the other structures in the area, as Innis had requested, and not much larger than the fishing shacks dotting Raven's Back. The cost of materials was partially deducted from Innis's apprenticeship wages with Oren covering some of the expenses himself. He explained to his apprentice that the work was part of Innis's school-ing, thus the extra consideration from his mentor. Oren had located the deserted, partially dilapidated structure, its foundation still sturdy, mitigating some of the expense and effort to restore it and add onto it a bit. While building on the house proceeded, Innis returned to the purple grove several times as it was now closer and more easily accessible to him. He'd decided to attempt selling the few items he'd created from the purple wood to one of the shops in Belfast, where no locals from Glenraven would have cause to see them or question him.

On the first free day he had, he drove to the city, carrying with him the jewelry box, bowl and corner table he'd carved. He'd done some online research to locate a small art shop specializing in wood items and catering to an eclectic clientele, then spoken with the proprietor on the phone, impressed by her kind manner and will-ingness to look at the offerings of an unknown woodcarver from the north.

The shop was tucked away down a small alley featuring sev-eral other craft enterprises including a jewelry shop, an art gallery and purveyors of stained glass and quilts. The Forestry, the shop he sought, was the last one at the end of the alleyway. He'd brought a small cart with him and trundled it to the door of the shop, hesitating before entering. The confidence and enthusiasm with which he'd left Raven's Back plummeted. These items in the cart were really rather rudimentary with the exception of the music box, to which he'd added a rather detailed front panel of a forest scene complete with deer and a fox. Why would a professional dealer in fine items of wood even consider such merchandise? Steeling himself for rejec-tion, he opened the door, pulling the cart in behind him.

The space was small but well organized with wood items of all kinds displayed on shelves, in cases and on tables. There was a rustic feel to The Forestry and Innis was pleased to spot a few carvings of animals that suited his taste. It was clear that all of the items in the shop were professionally made, most of them with a polish and craftsmanship Innis could only dream about. Propping the cart against a wall, he approached the counter where a tiny, dark haired woman was speaking to someone on a cell phone. She held up one finger and nodded to Innis, who noticed she was speaking Gaelic but couldn't understand a word she was saying. She disconnected from the call and turned her attention to Innis with a smile.

"Good day, sir. Are you Innis Kilbride?"

"Indeed."

Innis offered his hand and the woman shook with him. He noticed her fingers were covered with silver rings, one in the shape of a frog, another a swan. A thin bracelet of silver, its links consisting of interlocking trees, hung from her right wrist. She nodded toward the cart against the wall.

"Are those the items you called me about? Oh, I'm Finola, as I mentioned on the phone. Finola O'Brian. Please call me Fin."

Innis smiled, startled by the charm of her dancing blue eyes and gamin-like face.

"Yeah, those are the things I wanted to show you. There's only three of them, but I've never actually sold any of my stuff to a shop in Belfast before so guess I should start small."

He pulled the cart over to the counter, lifting out the jewelry box and placing it in front of Finola. He added the bowl then took the corner table and set it on the floor. Fin's eyes widened at the sight of the purple wood objects and she turned to Innis with astonishment.

"Why, my God, this wood is so beautiful! Or is it only a purple you've stained it with?"

Running a finger over the box and bowl, she held the bowl closer and examined it carefully, scrutinizing every inch of it.

"This is truly purple wood, is it not?"

Innis nodded, grinning at her amazement.

"Yeah, it truly is. I don't even know the name of the tree it came from. Seems odd, I can tell you, but there it is."

Fin came out from behind the counter to inspect the table. She laughed with delight.

"The grain of this wood is even unusual. Was it difficult to work with?"

"Not at all. It's a very soft wood and the items I've carved from it didn't so much need to be on the grain, if you know what I mean."

Fin nodded.

"I do. These are simply exquisite, Mr. Kilbride. I've never seen their like, nor has anyone else I'm sure."

"I'm glad you like them. You've got some lovely things in here."

He looked around the shop, pleased that nothing in it rivaled his own creations in eye-catching, dramatic effect.

"Yes," Fin placed a hand on the table. "I gather wooden crafts from all over Ireland, but nothing as unusual as what you've got right here. Am I mistaken, or could it be there's actually a warmth to this wood?"

She removed her hand from the table top and Innis smiled and nodded.

"Yeah, there actually is. Incredible, isn't it?"

"More like magical."

Innis grinned, excited by the confirmation of his expectations for the effect this wood might have on others.

"What sort of wood is this, Mr. Kilbride, you really don't know?"

"No, I don't, haven't been able to figure it out. I found it in--"

He cut himself short, reluctant to divulge the precise location of the purple grove.

"Well, up north," he finished. "The Antrim Coast area. It doesn't seem to be indigenous to that part of Ireland, or anywhere really, so...it's a bit of a mystery, I guess."

Fin narrowed her eyes and examined the face before her. The man appeared to be honest enough but what sort of craziness allowed for wood from an unidentifiable tree? Was he trying to trick her? She wished he wasn't quite so appealing to her.

"And you carved these yourself?"

Innis nodded, suddenly embarrassed by her attention.

"I'm just beginning as a professional woodworker, but this wood is unusually pliable. It allows for plenty of detailing if you've a mind to go that way. I've preferred things simpler for the most part, so these are fairly plain as you can see, but the wood speaks for itself, does it not?"

"Indeed. And in volumes."

Fin smiled, running her fingers gently over the smooth surface of the wooden bowl, marveling again at the slight warmth it projected.

"How much are you wanting for them, Mr. Kilbride?"

Flustered, as he had only a vague idea of the prices that might be appropriate, Innis shifted and hesitated. He decided to be honest with this stranger since she was clearly an expert on woodcraft and would know the best cost far better than he.

"What do you think, Ms. O'Brian?"

"Please call me Fin, remember? Well, usually I bargain for pieces that are brought in, but these are so unusual. There's really no comparisons I can make. And you spoke of being a relative new-comer to woodworking, but this music box is rather detailed for a novice. The other items are also very well crafted."

She picked up the music box and examined it carefully with an amused expression. Why did she suddenly have the wish to keep this dark-eyed, intriguing stranger from leaving her shop? Turning her attention back to Innis, she saw that he was staring at her but quickly averted his gaze.

"Well, thank you for the compliments, Fin. To be honest, my wood carving went up a notch, so to speak, when I started working with this wood. I honestly don't know how, but it truly granted me new skill. I suppose I'll leave it to your discretion as far as setting prices. I trust you, and profit isn't my greatest motivator. I just couldn't help wanting to share this beautiful wood with others."

"That's easily understood, who wouldn't? Why don't I draw up a bill of sale for you, suggesting prices, and see what you think."

"Brilliant, that's perfect. Thanks for your consideration. I'm an utter novice at this, guess I don't need to tell you. How long have you had the shop? Assuming you're the owner."

"Yes, I am. It's been about three years. Not a tremendous living in it, but I get by. More tourists than locals, actually, although I have a few regular buyers who operate in other parts of Ireland."

"Have you always been interested in wood objects, or wood?"

"Pretty much. My da was a cabinetmaker in Galway, so I grew up around it. He considered crafty items like the ones I sell a bit frivolous, of course. What about you, have you worked in wood carving for awhile? You said you're new to it but your work is clearly not amateur."

"I started out loving to paint, actually, and I still do that but I needed a practical trade and I haven't the salesmanship to become a professional painter. It seems quite competitive. You're from Galway, then? Ah, the wild west."

Fin laughed.

"Don't know how wild it is," she remarked, "but yeah, I grew up there. And you're a native of the north?"

Innis nodded.

"I refer to it as the magical north," he laughed. "When I was a lad I had names, well adjectives really, for the four areas of Ireland. It was the magical north, the exciting east, the charming south and the wild west. Not sure where I got those terms since I've never been farther away from home than Belfast. Probably from looking at pictures. My ma's big on knowing as much as possible about the wide world."

Fin found her gaze wandering to Innis's ring finger, feeling foolish yet relieved not to see a wedding ring. How silly and old-fashioned, she scolded herself. It doesn't necessarily reveal any status after all. She nodded to Innis.

"If you don't mind waiting for a short bit, I'll draw up your bill of sale and see what you think. Perhaps have a look around the shop?"

"Happy to. And thanks again, Fin. I wasn't sure anyone would even want these so I'm most grateful you've been so kind."

"Kind has little to do with it. They're quite lovely and will fetch a pretty penny. You are aware that once customers have seen or purchased these items they'll be looking for more."

Innis's brows furrowed.

"Huh, hadn't really thought of that, no. Could be a problem. You see, I believe there's a very limited access to this type of wood. I can't imagine being able to make much more from it, only a few small things perhaps. I've only one tree to work with."

Fin stopped on her way to the back room where she kept her office and turned to face Innis.

"Are you telling me there's only the one tree?"

"No, there's a small grove but only the one tree was felled in a storm. I'd never cut them down just to use them for wood carving, you know. Since the one was already down, from natural causes, I used it for carving, otherwise never. For all I know it's the only grove of tress like it in the world. Crucial to preserve it, don't you think?"

38

Fin returned to the counter and leaned against it, shaking her head and offering Innis a wry smile.

"You're full of surprises, Innis. Are you certain you want me to display these items in my shop? As I said before, people will want to know about this unusual wood, its origins, how they can purchase more of it. If it's going to be only a one-off, then..."

Innis joined her at the counter, picking up the music box to run a finger over its surface.

"You're right, Fin. I can't very well sell these or even let people see them, I suppose. Don't know what I was thinking. It just seems a waste, having them sit in my workshop with no one to see them but me."

"I'd buy this bowl from you." Fin picked up the purple wood bowl and held it to her heart. "I adore it and honestly can't bear the thought of it going back out the door with you. I'd keep it for my own personal use so no one could question it."

Innis looked at the small woman opposite him and felt a surge of elation and warmth. She was not only an obviously kind and lovely person but a woodworking expert and fan of his own creations as well. He lost all sense of decorum and reached across the counter to attempt an awkward embrace of Fin, crushing the bowl between them as they both laughed with embarrassment. Innis broke away and sputtered an apology but Fin's beaming smile reassured him it was unnecessary. She set the bowl back onto the counter, put her hand on one hip and tilted her head, eying Innis with delight.

"So, Mr. Innis Kilbride, shall I make an offer for this beautiful bowl or will you name your price?"

Innis grinned, folded his arms and pretended to study his options.

"I believe, Fin O'Brian, I will allow the lady to set her bid."

"It's hardly fair, you know, seeing as I've already let you know how much I love this and want it."

She held up the bowl again, turning it over and wondering how she could possibly persuade this adorable Antrim coast fellow to stay a little longer. He appeared to be slightly younger than she was, probably only by five or six years, if she was in luck, but absolutely irresistible. What were the odds of a handsome, rather rustic, talented wood-carver walking into her shop again? No, she could not simply ignore her instincts and allow him to disappear back to the north without at least attempting to make a further connection.

"I trust you'll set a fair price," Innis cut into her reverie. "Of course, considering it's an extremely rare sort of wood, possibly one of a kind..."

His eyes dancing with mischief, Innis leaned against the counter, smiling in a teasing way. Fin smiled back, barely resisting the urge to lean across the counter and kiss him. She cocked her head and began counting up on her fingers as if adding invisible sums, then burst out laughing and named a very generous amount. Innis looked startled, shaking his head.

"Ah, no, I couldn't possibly take that from you. I was only joking about the wood being rare and all--"

"But it is! Usually, you know, the buyer bargains down and the seller up, Innis. It's a fair price, believe me, and worth every bit. I do know a thing or two about setting prices, it's my business. Are we settled then?"

Innis offered his hand and they shook.

"It'll be my pleasure knowing the bowl's in such good hands, luv, with someone who genuinely cherishes it."

"I'll just write you up a bill of sale."

Fin headed back toward her office again but paused and turned back to Innis.

"I wonder if you might consider having lunch with me since you're in Belfast and it'll be that time in about an hour."

Innis's undisguised expression of astonishment made Fin laugh.

"I'm sorry, a bit too forward?" she ventured. "You don't have to agree to go."

"No, no, I'd love to have lunch with you."

He began digging in his pockets and looked up at Fin with embarrassment.

"I'm truly sorry, it's just that I haven't that much money and--"

"You silly goose. I'm paying you for the bowl, don't forget. Besides, you won't need any money. I usually take my lunch in the park nearby, just some things I bring from home, and you're wel-come to share if you don't mind a simple meal. Bread, cheese, and apple and a couple of cookies."

"Sounds terrific," Innis beamed. "It's lovely of you to share but I don't want to take too much of your meager lunch. I've enough to pop into one of the markets or shops and get a little something extra to add to it."

A customer entered the shop and Fin nodded to Innis, holding up a hand for him to wait. She greeted the man, who spoke briefly with her then began to browse around the shop. Fin returned to Innis at the counter.

"Sorry about the interruption. Well, if you don't mind that sounds fine. Shall we meet here at The Forestry about an hour from now? Oh, your bill of sale, I almost forgot!"

"Don't worry, I'll pick it up when I come back. Till lunch, then."

He gathered up the table and jewelry box, placing them back in his cart and leaving the bowl on the counter. What just happened, he asked himself. Is this darling lady just being polite or could she actually fancy me? And Fin, struggling to keep her focus on attending to the customer who'd entered her shop, was asking herself a similar question. Did the fabulous man who'd just accepted her lunch invitation merely wish to avoid hurting her feelings or could he actually fancy her?

The answers to their questions became clear while they shared a park bench and a lunch consisting of the provisions Fin had brought to work and a few extra items Innis had purchased after leaving the shop. Both a bit shy and awkward at first, their reticence slowly vanished as they discovered a surprising number of things in common and conversation began to flow quite naturally. In addition to their common background in woodworking, it was revealed that some of Fin's family were sheepherders and farmers in western Ireland. Like Innis, she was fond of the folk tales and myths of their native land and familiar with the tales from The Voyage of Mael Duin which Innis had heard from his grandfather. Her taste in art, though more sophisticated than was Innis's, ran to the weird and dark, and her love of the sea rivaled his own.

The overcast skies of Belfast seemed to Fin to be glowing with sun as she continued her animated conversation with Innis, catching his smiling eyes as often as possible, occasionally lightly touching his arm as they laughed and joked. His teasing, wry sense of humor pleased her, suited her in a way she'd never experienced with anyone else, and she felt almost alone with him even as the busy motion of Belfast rushed around them.

An hour seemed to vanish and although Fin could have lingered for the rest of the afternoon her obligation to the shop tugged at her and she reluctantly gathered up the remnants of lunch, preparing with a sense of panic to bid Innis farewell. Before she could decide what to say or how to bring herself to take leave of him, Innis cleared his throat.

"It was a lovely lunch," he began, looking at his feet shyly then back up at Fin's expectant face. "Shall we do it again sometime? I can arrange to get down to Belfast now and then if you'd like. At least, I'd like to."

Fin dropped the brown paper bag holding the trash from lunch onto the park bench and threw her arms around Innis in a rush, savoring his warm hug in return.

"Yes!" she beamed, releasing him from her embrace. "It would be my joy."

An unplanned tryst, a connection made. As Innis returned to Glenraven he offered a silent thanks to the fates for putting Fin in his path. As Fin stood in her shop admiring the purple wood bowl she'd purchased, she felt its magic and that of the man who'd created it dancing around in her heart.

Chapter VI: The Shepherd

The green fields of Glenraven, covered in early morning rain or dew with the sea as backdrop, were Dalton's natural home. As he and Keeley took the sheep out to their pastures, which were criss-crossed by low stone walls, the sea air and calling of gulls greeted him like the closest of friends, welcoming him back to the place he most loved. There was never the same comfort to be found among people or even his own room in the old house he still shared with his parents. It was only in nature that he truly felt himself, at ease and in his element. The narrow dirt paths leading out to the sheep pastures were usually deserted early in the morning with only the occasional donkey cart trundling vegetables to market with a brief nod of acknowledgment from the driver. Otherwise, the quiet of the sur-rounding hills and fields held Dalton in their protective embrace as he and Keeley guided the flock to the designated pasture for their day's grazing. He considered the sheep to be his true family and knew each of the thirty-five as an individual with its own history, temperament and habits. Keeley practically read his thoughts when it came to managing the sheep, collecting strays and guiding the flock smoothly and efficiently. She also savored the trek out to the fields, Dalton could tell, as every fiber of her being came alive once they left the house. Alert and ever vigilant, she would sometimes push her nose against Dalton's leg as they left for the day, her eyes shining with purpose, urging him to begin their day's tasks.

It wasn't only the herding of the sheep that appealed to Dal-ton. Every aspect of their care and tending, from shearing to feeding to assisting with lambing, was dear to his heart, cherished and enjoyed despite the hard work and often harsh weather it involved. He'd read that shearing of sheep was being done by machines now, sometimes even by robots, and it disheartened him to know such methods were being used for something he considered to be extremely important, requiring great skill and patience. When shear-ing time came on the farm, both Dalton and his father worked care-fully with the sheep, ensuring there were no problems or struggles with the flock. Dalton had assumed the bulk of the shearing since he was so familiar with the sheep and adept at handling them. During bad weather, those who'd been sheared were kept in sheltered pens until their wool grew back sufficiently to offer protection from the elements. Dalton was particularly fond of caring for the indoor

43

dwellers as it afforded him individual, direct contact with the sheep, which he treasured. The thought of robots or machines processing the shearing of sheep like a conveyor belt horrified him, making him even more grateful for the small community where he lived, sheltered from the modern world. He'd recently heard of drones being used for sheepherding, an unfathomable abomination. Dalton had no interest in straying from the boundaries of Glenraven and listened to Innis's stories of Belfast with polite indifference.

The family raised Cheviot sheep even though the breed produced less wool of a lower quality than those breeds used primarily for wool production. The breed had been on the farm for as long as Abbot could remember and although they were also used for meat, Dalton in particular resisted selling many of them for such purposes or slaughtering them for the family's food. Abbot had attempted to lecture his younger son against becoming sentimental about the sheep, reminding him frequently that the animals were their livelihood and must be treated as such. His advice fell on deaf ears, however, as Dalton attached himself to the flock from the time he began working them as a boy and only became fonder of them as time went on. His knowledge of the sheep and natural ability in handling them soon made Abbot abandon his efforts to retrain his son. It was clear that, despite some of Dalton's more unorthodox methods of dealing with sheep, the flock was well cared for, unusually healthy and productive with a minimum of problems arising. Dalton considered them superior to any others in the vicinity and their bare white faces, the high carriage of their heads and absence of horns did provide an aristocratic appearance. The sheep were hardy with compact, sturdy bodies and roman noses which were especially pronounced in the rams. Alert and lively, they were sometimes challenging to handle but Dalton and Keeley made a formidable team whose success with their flock became well-known in the area around Glenraven.

Dalton was particular about providing the sheep with the best in feed and bedding when they were in the barn and conscientious about ensuring they received their vaccines and any veterinary care that was needed. Income from wool, combined with crops, was sufficient for the family's needs but still they struggled at times to get ahead. It was a hard scrabble life in many ways and one to which Dalton was especially suited. He considered himself a shepherd above all else and eventually spent as little time as possible on the raising of crops. Lambing, usually taking place in the spring, was one of the highlights of his job and he was always thrilled when a lamb was born in the barn instead of in the field. The first time he witnessed the event, as a child beside his father, it seemed an unimaginable, if slightly frightening, miracle and it never ceased to offer him genuine amazement and joy regardless of how often he participated in the blessed event. Twins had been born at his first lambing experience and, ignorant of the frequency of such an occurrence, he took it as an especially fortuitous sign, declaring to his father that surely their flock was blessed.

It was a relief to Dalton that Abbot had always preferred a process of natural weaning of the lambs from their mothers rather than an enforced separation. Once Dalton had heard the pitiful bleating of lambs and ewes who'd been manually separated for weaning purposes at another farm. The stress and forlorn desperation obviously being experienced by the sheep was something he never forgot. It amused and gratified him observing the gradual, off-handed way in which the ewes would naturally wean their lambs, walking away from them when they attempted to nurse. The fact that this process usually occurred in late summer or early fall, when the diminishing nutrition of the grass allowed the ewes' milk to dry up, was a confirmation to Dalton of the perfect harmony in which nature worked, a system that operated in synch so unlike many of the workings of the human species.

On one occasion, however, the symbiosis of nature's plan failed and Dalton became concerned about an overly aggressive lamb which would not leave its mother alone. Despite the ewe's determined efforts to avoid nursing it, the lamb would relentlessly follow her, sometimes lifting her off the ground as it butted at her udder. It was a tough decision for him, but Dalton finally chose to put the lamb in the barn to wean it in order to avoid further stress or any damage to the ewe. Once again he heard the loud, mournful bleating of the separated pair, although this time it was tempered by his experience, knowledge and understanding of the necessity of the process. He was able to filter out any emotion and sympathy toward the sheep involved and soon enough his efforts were rewarded.

Abbot, who'd worried about his son's failure to develop a thicker skin when it came to handling the flock, was gratified by Dalton's actions and relaxed a bit in conceding the responsibility of the sheep to Dalton.

One spring, a black lamb was born to the flock. Dalton, startled and confused at first and wondering if this might be a bad omen, was assured by his father that this was not uncommon despite both parents of the lamb being white. From that point forward, the black lamb became Dalton's favorite. He knew the lamb's wool would not be as valuable on the market since white wool was preferable as it can be dyed any color. Therefore, the lamb became a kind of pet to him despite Abbot's disapproval. Dalton resisted naming the little ram, but secretly thought of him as Kieran, meaning black or dark. He took a special interest in the lamb, closely observing his interactions with his mother and the rest of the flock, gratified to see the feisty but sweet personality the lamb displayed.

At times Kieran reminded Dalton of Innis with his dark, charming appearance and quick learning abilities. Dalton had always enjoyed observing how the lambs were taught by their mothers how to locate water and shelter, the way in which the pecking order of the flock was established. His favorite lamb rapidly learned his life lessons, outdistancing many of the other lambs close in age and insinuating himself into an advantageous position in the flock without too much aggression. Since Dalton found as many opportunities as possible for interaction with Kieran the lamb became affectionate and more acclimated to people than usual.

"He's not a pet, Dalton," Abbot admonished his son more than once. "This is a working sheep farm, not a bloomin' zoo."

Dalton, properly chastised, would mumble an apology to his father and for a short while make a special effort to refrain from cuddling or playing with Kieran, but eventually he'd revert to his usual familiarity with the lamb and be warned by his father again. The softhearted shepherd had even considered taking Kieran into the house with him on cold nights but drew the line at such foolishness. He knew it was unprofessional to become so attached to a sheep but Dalton found himself always watching carefully when he and Keeley gathered the flock at the end of the day to make sure the dark wool of Kieran was still to be seen among the rest of the white flock. Predators weren't a severe problem in Glenraven, but the occasional ewe or lamb had been taken by a wild dog or other creature and Dalton could scarcely bear the thought. Sheep were sometimes lost as well, wandering off or escaping their pasture to become caught in thick brush or a fence. Keeley excelled in locating any strays and Dalton was proud they'd seldom lost a sheep to anything except illness or old age.

Innis was also fond of Kieran, teasing his brother about the resemblance between himself and the lamb since Innis's hair was dark and curly like his mother's and aunt's. Dalton favored his father's side of the family with fairer hair and complexion, gray eyes and a smattering of light freckles that gave him a boyish sweetness. Several of the local girls were interested in Dalton but soon became discouraged when he failed to respond to their overtures or avoided them altogether. His mother tried to draw him out about his discomfort around the female gender, only succeeding in embarrassing him further without a clue as to the problem. She sometimes wondered if he might be gay but didn't really believe he was. The truth of the matter, which Dalton kept to himself, was his inability to imagine the sort of life the majority of Glenraven residents led, a puzzling routine of courtship, marriage and children. He had no interest in such a life and felt ashamed to acknowledge to himself that his time with the sheep meant more to him than he could ever imagine a girlfriend, wife or children meaning. His sex drive was minimal, another facet of his person he was certain would never be accepted or understood by anyone else.

At times he considered discussing things with Innis but couldn't bring himself to confess such personal deficiencies even to his beloved brother. He knew Innis had met a lady in Belfast with whom he'd begun a long distance relationship and encouraged him, setting aside his own loneliness as an intrinsic part of himself, like an appendage he could not amputate for fear of becoming warped, unlike his true self. When he was heading out to the pastures in the morning with Keeley and the flock, he felt his full, natural self in an exhilarating way that never occurred at any other time.

Innis had sketched a picture of Kieran and given it to Dalton along with the sheep figure carved from purple wood. The sketch had been received first and Dalton was quite fond of it, setting it in a frame on the nightstand beside his bed. The black lamb was a perfect subject and Innis had captured him in impressive accuracy from the pronounced Roman nose typical of Cheviot rams to the alert, saucy stance and expression of warm curiosity in the eyes. When Dalton spoke his prayers before bed he always mentioned Kieran, requesting safe and happy passage through life for the beloved lamb.

Abbot was reluctant to use Kieran as a breeding ram as he grew older but since the gene for black wool was unpredictable and just as likely to originate in the ewe, it was decided to breed him.

Kieran proved a prolific sire with Dalton suppressing his pride at the black sheep's progeny and his secret wishes for a black offspring. Kieran remained the only black sheep in the flock, however, and Dalton's special favorite who still allowed attention from humans, especially Dalton.

On finding the purple wood sheep carving in his coat pocket, Dalton was astonished at its detail and accuracy. In addition to the unusual beauty of the wood, he was pleased at the resemblance to Kieran and anxious to speak with his brother about the gift. He and Innis found themselves together with increasing infrequency and Dalton missed his charming, high energy sibling. Not one to seek others out, he waited to hear from Innis and one evening, after a rare dinner at the family home with everyone present, the brothers retired to Dalton's bedroom for a private chat. Innis was pleased to see the sheep carving sitting on the nightstand beside his sketch of Kieran. After expressing his gratitude and fondness for the carving, Dalton earnestly looked into his brother's face.

"I sometimes wish I was more like you, Innis. I know I'm the farthest thing from it, but I think Ma in particular would be happier if I was."

"What rubbish!" Innis blurted. "I'm surprised to hear you say that. What's brought this on?"

Knowing his brother, Innis figured something specific had triggered these remarks since Dalton had always seemed content with his way of life and with himself. Perhaps he'd misread his normally stoical brother all along.

"Well, she's been asking me about my lack of interest in the ladies." Dalton's voice had dropped to almost a whisper, his unease painfully apparent. "I've told her I'm just as happy with my sheep and she's let it go, but she must find it bothersome. I suppose many people do, see it as strange, that is. Honestly, I don't really know why. I've seen the couples and the families in Glenraven and many of them don't seem as glad of their lot as I do of mine."

It was a lengthy speech for Dalton and Innis felt a surge of gratitude toward his brother for this obvious trust. He knew the young man before him seldom talked to anyone aside from Keeley and the sheep. To Innis's surprise, Dalton continued.

"I know you've got Fin you're seeing in Belfast, and I'm glad about that. She seems to make you happy. It's not for me, though, these connections with people, be they men or women. It's not what

I'm after."

"And you shouldn't apologize for that." Innis put a hand on his brother's shoulder. "I am fond of Fin but who knows what'll happen. You're right about love or marriage or whatever, it's often not a terrific outcome. Just think about our Aunt Bridget. Her life's been completely undone by it. Then again, Ma and Da have a wonderful thing together. Don't be ashamed of who you are, Dalt. You have to do what's right for you, and only you can know what that is."

Dalton smiled at Innis and nodded, relieved to have finally unburdened himself of his concerns. He picked up the purple sheep figure and showed it to Innis.

"This is what works for me, Innis, sheep. Nothing makes me as happy as watching Kieran play around in the pasture, teasing the others and making mischief."

"Then hang your hat on that, brother. And don't let anyone make you feel wrong about it. Not even Ma. Besides, she'll come around. Don't think she's gonna bother you for long, she'll let it go. Not sure she's wild about my Belfast girl either, so see. You can never win."

The brothers embraced warmly and Innis listened while Dalton related several amusing stories about Kieran, Keeley and the flock, the words tripping off his tongue as though he'd been saving them up for months. Innis recognized the loneliness that Dalton refused to acknowledge but also the joy in the life of a shepherd that his own labors as a woodworker could not come close to approaching. He'd never allowed himself to consider how much it had cost him, leaving his painting behind. Despite his fondness for Fin and the good times they'd been sharing, he suspected it wouldn't end in anything as permanent as marriage. When he thought of the almost completed house in Raven's Back where he intended to live, he always imagined himself alone there and knew it suited him. Visiting the purple grove to walk among its beautiful trees in wonder, savoring the quiet and seclusion of his Raven's Back shack, painting in secret in the dead of night, listening for the nocturnal creatures who reclaimed the forest after dark. These were the things he cherished. Perhaps he wasn't so different from his brother the shepherd after all.

Chapter VII: Connla

Innis completed preparation of his home in Raven's Back with the help of Oren and settled into his new abode with pleasure and a certain sense of accomplishment. He hadn't anticipated leaving his childhood home and having a place of his own by the time he reached his twenties but here he was. The move from Glenraven had been more emotional than he was prepared for but he knew he had the full support of his parents and brother who promised to give him time to acclimate before coming for a visit. He'd done little in the way of furnishings and immediately missed his mother's excellent cooking, taking most of his meals in the restaurants and pubs of Glenraven or stopping by for dinner with his family at the house he'd recently left.

The wonders of Raven's Back and being on his own were more than enough compensation for home-cooked food, however, and he quickly grew fond of his new, independent life. The cawing and chortling of the many crows which inhabited Raven's Back, the comforting proximity of the wooded glens and the purple grove, the soft rushing of a nearby stream that had replaced the sound of the ocean waves all became comfortingly familiar to him, whispering 'home'. His Aunt Bridget was also close by and he began to visit her more frequently, often walking to her shack in the early evening with a pie in hand from one of Glenraven's best bakeries. He knew she'd always had a sweet tooth and a particular fondness for pies, and he worried about the quality of her diet as he was aware throughout his childhood that Irene had tried to make sure her sister ate properly.

Visitation was sporadic, however, and subject to Bridget's ever fluctuating, unpredictable moods and frame of mind. At times, Innis would arrive at his aunt's shack to find his knock on the door ignored despite the fact that Bridget was clearly at home and could be glimpsed through the window. He would then leave the boxed pie at the door, calling to her that he'd done so and retreating to a safe distance to observe her opening the door and retrieving the treat. On other occasions, Innis would be welcomed and spend a pleasant few hours with his aunt, sharing the pie along with her strong, delicious tea and listening to stories of Gage and the underwater kingdom where he dwelled. Bridget's face would come alive with vitality and joy as she described the creatures with whom her beloved communicated and swam, the entity she referred to as Connla who was the ruler of the sea kingdom and the many secrets of life beneath the waves. She'd eventually included Innis in the secret of the magical seahorse, showing him the chest where the many crocheted items she'd created featuring the creature were kept. This was Connla, she explained, and he was the conduit through which she was able to communicate with Gage.

Despite Innis's familiarity with many of the myths of his native land, he wasn't aware of the origin of the name Connla, but Bridget was glad to expound on this theme, making certain to explain first that the name was something she'd decided to call the underwater ruler, not necessarily his actual name. Mere earth dwellers were not usually allowed the privilege of hearing the proper names by which those in the underwater kingdom were known. Connla, Bridget explained, from early Irish lore had given his name to a well which bestowed great wisdom on all who drank from its waters. Magical salmon swam in the well and transported its knowledge to all the rivers of Ireland. Somehow that wisdom and knowledge had also permeated the sea near Glenraven and therefore Bridget had chosen this name for the seahorse.

Innis suddenly remembered the story of Connla and the Fairy Maiden from Irish mythology which his grandfather had told him when he was a child. However, it bore no resemblance to the one Bridget had mentioned. In this tale, Connla was a character summoned from Scotland to Ireland by his father. There were three conditions to his journey: that he could not turn back once he began, that he must not refuse any challenge and that he never tell his name to anyone. Once in Ireland, a maiden appeared to him, advising she was from the Hill Folk who made their home in the round green hills. She called to Connla to come away with her in a crystal canoe which he did, leaping into the canoe which glided away over the sea, never to be seen again, its destination unknown. Innis wondered if elements of this story had been incorporated into Bridget's tale or if she was even familiar with the fable of Connla and the Fairy Maiden. It seemed to apply to her own situation in a strange way.

These stories also reminded Innis of another told to him by Fin about the origins of her own name, Finola. It was connected with the tale of The Children of Lir which involved the character Finola and her three brothers who were all transformed into swans by a jealous stepmother. They remained trapped in that form for nine hundred years before being freed by a hermit. Innis assumed this explained the delicate silver swan ring Fin often wore as well as the silver necklace with a small swan he'd occasionally seen around her neck. He enjoyed these mystical meanings and histories of names and complimented his Aunt Bridget on her excellent choice of Connla for the seahorse. She cut him short with a hint of anger, as she often unexpectedly did.

"I didn't name him, boy," Bridget narrowed her eyes at Innis as though she hadn't just told him exactly that. "He told me to refer to him by that name. I would never presume to bestow my own idea of a name on one so powerful."

"Of course not, Auntie. I didn't mean to imply--"

Bridget waved one hand dismissively.

"It's of no consequence, my dear Innis. The important thing is that Connla, as you know, has become my master as well as Gage's. When I die, I too will descend into the depths of the sea and you must make sure it happens. I've not even told your mother about this requirement. It's to be our secret. Connla will make certain of it, but I also need you to prevent my burial in the earth. It must be in the sea so that I may be reunited with Gage."

Innis, taken aback by this revelation and concerned about his aunt's always fragile state of mind, hesitated then decided to probe further.

"Of course, Auntie, but first won't you tell me more about Connla? Or aren't you allowed?"

Bridget smiled and settled back into the small sofa on which they sat, sipping her tea with a strange light dancing in her eyes.

"Connla will only divulge so many secrets to those on the land, Innis. He has told me many things, though most of them I cannot say to you. I will tell you of his kingdom and the other creatures who inhabit it, but I cannot let you know of Connla's plans for me."

Still worried about the implications of the mysterious connection between Bridget and Connla, Innis resisted questioning his aunt further for fear of losing her trust. He would try to be subtle and patient with her, hoping more information might emerge.

"Tell me of Connla's kingdom, Auntie."

Bridget set down her teacup and curled up on her corner of the couch as though settling in for a long spell. She was silent for a few minutes while Innis drank his tea, watching her face which took on a faraway expression.

"Connla's kingdom is vast, Innis, so I've only been given

52

glimpses of certain portions of it but they are truly beautiful. There are caverns of coral in the most amazing colors, purple and royal blue and the deepest green. Creatures of all sorts live among the coral. Octopus nests are there, filled with small and giant ones of fantastical design, some of them with hands like humans instead of suction cups. Fish of every imaginable type and monstrous eels with razor sharp teeth who are really harmless, only frightening to look at until you know their gentle nature. Of course seahorses abound but none as large, magnificent or powerful as Connla. All the creatures are aware of Connla as their ruler, but he communicates with each one individually according to its own species and language.

"Gage is not the only human who dwells in the undersea kingdom, there are others. Connla's told me about them, though not in detail, and he's never allowed me to see them. He's shown me Gage only a couple of times but not at first. Connla is an intermediary between me and Gage. For a long time he relayed messages from one of us to the other, and I made no request of him. I knew I didn't dare ask anything of Connla. He would give me what he chose and I was only too happy to accept it. I respect his place as ruler and would never question him."

"He did allow you to see Gage?"

"Yes, only recently."

Bridget stopped speaking and put her hand over her mouth as though trying to suppress an intense emotion Innis couldn't quite read. Was it joy or sorrow? Then Bridget raised her eyes to his and he saw that tears of happiness had filled them.

"Oh, Innis, I can't describe how lovely it was, seeing the face of my beautiful boy after all this time, after thinking I'd never see him again. He didn't speak to me but he smiled, that smile I remember from when he was here with me. His eyes too were the same, those laughing eyes."

Innis had never known his aunt to display such intense emotion and it touched him but also gave him pause to consider the extent to which she believed in this alternate universe of Connla. Bridget continued, her eyes shining with joy.

"That first time, after I'd seen Gage, Connla told me that I would join him in their kingdom when my time on earth is done. That's why it's so important for me to be buried in the sea."

"I see that, but why haven't you told this to my mother? Surely she should be the one to make such arrangements."

"No, Innis. It must be you. My sister will want a place where she can go to be near me once I've passed, a place where she can kneel and place flowers and talk to me. The sea won't do for her. Trust me, I know this about her. You are a child of the sea, I can tell. You must promise to fulfill my wishes."

"I do, Auntie. Hopefully it will be a long time yet until such plans must be carried out."

Bridget offered an enigmatic smile.

"We are not given to know that time. For me, it will be the day of true freedom for me and I look forward to it with joy."

Like his mother before him, Innis grappled with the struggle between worrying about his aunt's state of mind and simply accepting it. And like Irene, he chose to accept Bridget's madness for what it was, a sad yet strangely soothing form of salvation.

Although he no longer headed out to sea in the early morning with the fishermen, Innis had become accustomed to rising early and sometimes stood looking out over the ocean's expanse just before dawn. He thought of Connla and his aunt's imaginings of the underwater kingdom he ruled, letting the sound of the waves and the smell of the sea wash over him. It was a form of blessing and he felt it during each visit. Unlike his Aunt Bridget, there was no voice from Connla talking to him from the ocean's depths, but the sea undeniably spoke to him in other ways and, unbeknownst to Innis, was soon to offer up to him a singular magic that would change his life.

Chapter VIII: A Stranger From Madagascar

As Innis settled into his new home and life as a woodworker, he became aware of disturbing aspects of the small fishing village where he'd grown up. Human beings behaving in their typical manner was nothing new, so gossip, family disagreements and drunken misconduct went with the territory regardless of the place you called home. Innis had never been one for gossip, nor drinking too heavily in the local pubs, though he enjoyed a few bottles of Guinness and sometimes found camaraderie in the pub atmosphere. His exposure to his Aunt Bridget, however, had made him realize there could be an edge to the discomfort with which people often approached anything or anyone alien to their understanding. The group dynamic that made life in Glenraven pleasantly familiar could also be cruel, and he'd witnessed this first-hand in regard to his aunt.

Once, as a young boy, he'd found his mother crying in the kitchen while she prepared a beef stew for dinner. It startled him since he'd never seen her cry and could tell by the way she quickly brushed away her tears and dried her hands on her apron, turning away from him, that she wished to hide her sorrow. Innis remained in the doorway, afraid to speak yet reluctant to leave her alone.

"Ma," he finally ventured hesitantly, "what is it?"

Irene put both hands on the kitchen table and lowered her head, causing Innis to rush to her and gently put an arm around her shoulder. The face she turned to him was once again tear streaked and he saw a pain in her eyes that made him feel like crying himself.

"Oh, Innis. It's not for you to know at such a young age, but people can be so cold and cruel. Your poor Aunt Bridget. And your Da."

"What's happened?"

Innis couldn't keep the alarm out of his voice and guided his mother to one of the chairs where she seemed to collapse, burying her face in her apron and sobbing. Quickly pulling herself together while Innis stood by with a stricken expression, she smiled tearfully and put one hand on his cheek.

"I'm sorry, my darlin' boy. You look as though you've seen a ghost. I didn't meant to frighten you, come here and sit down with me."

She pulled out one of the other kitchen chairs and Innis sat, pushing the chair next to his mother who glanced at the dinner preparations which remained partially finished on the table.

"I must get back to that," Irene indicated the beef stew ingredients, "but first we'll have a small talk. Don't worry, Innis, there's nothing dreadful happened nor anyone in danger, at least I hope not."

"What did you mean about Da and Aunt Bridget? And why are you so upset? What can I do, Ma?"

"Not a thing, lad. That's the hell of it. There's nothing can be done about human nature. I've tried to protect you boys from some of the cruel things in this world, the ways in which people can be hurtful, but you're bound to know sooner or later."

Innis lowered his head and his voice, loathe to speak the truths he already knew but feeling he must.

"I know people talk about Aunt Bridget, Ma. I've heard 'em. And sometimes at school I get the odd look. I've overheard people talking about our family and the crazy lady. Is that it?"

Irene shook her head sorrowfully and hugged her son, holding him close for a moment and kissing the top of his head.

"Yes, darlin', that's part of it. I'm sorry that's happened to you. What have you done when you hear those things?"

Innis shrugged.

"I try to ignore them. I pretend I don't hear but it hurts. Sometimes I get really mad and want to fight, but what good would it do?"

"You're right, son. Not a bit of good would it do. I've never been able to figure out why otherwise decent people will sometimes act in such indecent ways. It's like a devil in them that suddenly escapes and they become mean and scared. Your aunt is a bit mad, yes, but she's never hurt anyone and stays away from others for the most part. It's the difference in her that bothers them, Innis. She's not like them and so they reject her and anything to do with her.

"You might as well know that someone's written 'lunatic' on the side of her shack in Raven's Back, painted it right onto the wood in big, bold red letters. She discovered it herself and now she's so afraid and upset, terrified in her own home. It's a big setback, after all my careful work with her--"

Irene broke down, burying her face in her hands as Innis patted her lightly on the shoulder, uncertain what to do. He was seething inside, ready to go in to town and confront everyone until he found the culprit, but he was only a boy and knew he'd never hold his own with some of the larger, rougher lads. As his mother had confirmed, it wouldn't change anything and the damage was done. It was several minutes until his mother stopped crying, hugging him then abruptly standing up and going to the sink to wash her hands and face. She resumed work on the beef stew, chopping carrots and potatoes almost robotically while Innis watched in puzzlement. Finally he could hold his silence no longer.

"So, what now, Ma? What's to be done about it?"

Irene continued her dinner preparations as she spoke.

"Try not to worry, darlin'. We've already taken care of the shack, the word's been painted over by your father. The damage done to your aunt will take much longer to fix, but I'm working with her and eventually we'll see our way clear."

She stopped and looked at Innis, anger blazing from her eyes.

"I want you to promise me, son, that you will never be cruel in that way. There are those among us, your Aunt Bridget being one, who are fragile. They're to be protected, treasured and cared for, not ridiculed. Your words and actions impact others, Innis, always remember that. There's no revenge to be taken, only the damage control now and I'll see to that. I believe Bridget will recover. It's only a long, thorny road we've got to walk. Not to worry, darlin', we'll walk it."

His mother's words stayed with him as he grew older, and Innis increasingly noticed the small, petty ways in which people could be carelessly cruel and rude. He knew there was a certain judgment toward his family in some circles in Glenraven but he tried to ignore it. When he was with his Aunt Bridget he sometimes wondered what land it was that she inhabited, what were its rules, if any, its laws and parameters. Occasionally he wished she could become more understandable, that the veil of madness might be lifted from her so she could be clearly seen, yet he had to acknowledge she was one of the more interesting characters in the area. Accustomed to her unpredictable ways and mysterious moods, he was puzzled that others could find her objectionable, a subject for scorn and avoidance.

As a resident of Raven's Back, it took longer for Innis to walk to the sea than when he'd lived with his family in Glenraven, but sometimes he missed its comforting presence and made the trek to stand by the waves, breathing in the bracing ocean air. Early one morning, as he wandered along the shore, he noticed a dark pile of what appeared at first to be a large clump of seaweed on the sand a short distance from him. He sensed movement in it and walked closer, realizing as he approached that the object resembled some sort of furred creature.

Suddenly a dark hand with long, black, bony fingers reached out from the pile of darkness to clutch at the sand. Innis froze in place, his heart racing. He was reluctant to get any closer and watched in horror as the dark object pulled itself along the shore, leaving a small, wet trail in its wake. An eerie sound came from the creature and it turned its face to Innis. His breath caught in a soft gasp as he realized that here before him was surely an alien. Never in his life had he seen such a face, one which verged on monstrous yet featured such mesmerizing eyes. Those eyes, of a deep amber gold with tiny black pupils resembling a cat's, held a desperate yet almost threatening expression, with two large, bat-like ears completing the unsettling picture.

What the hell was this thing? Innis was afraid of it but could see it was struggling, possibly partially drowned as its path seemed to lead from the sea. He moved slightly closer and could see the creature had a long tail, soaked in seawater, and appeared to be covered in dark fur which was also drenched. It was the strange hands of the creature that especially disturbed Innis and he couldn't recall ever seeing a picture of such an animal. There were five long, bony fingers on each of the creature's front hands but the middle finger was elongated in such a way as to appear almost comical as well as vaguely threatening.

The creature had stopped moving and dropped its face into the wet sand. Innis took off his coat and rushed to the animal, throwing the coat over it then scooping it up into his arms and carrying it from the beach toward Raven's Back. There was a brief struggle from the creature when Innis first picked it up, but then all movement ceased as it lay silently bundled up in the coat. It took some time for Innis to walk back to his home and he wondered if the creature was even still alive. It weighed only a few pounds, the size of a cat, and his mind was racing as to what he should do with the strange being or whether it might be dangerous, poisonous in some way. He walked as quickly as he could and laid the bundle on the wooden table on which he normally ate, carefully unfolding the coat and stepping back to wait for a response from the wet pile of fur.

For a moment all was still, then the creature stirred and gave a slight cough, slowly sitting up and shaking itself off like a dog.

Once again the weird eyes confronted Innis, this time with an amused expression in them as though the creature was chuckling at him. Still afraid to approach it, Innis waited and watched. The creature appeared to be shivering so Innis started a fire in the small fireplace he used for heating the shack. The animal ignored his movements, brushing over its face with its long fingers and wobbling a bit before burrowing back into the coat.

Once the fire was going, Innis carefully picked up the coat and carried the creature to the fireplace, setting it near the warmth of the fire's heat. He stepped back and watched again, hoping the strange being would revive despite his grave concerns about exactly what he'd just brought into his home. After a few minutes by the fire, the creature emerged from the wet coat and moved closer to the heat, shaking off more moisture from its fur and closing its eyes in obvious pleasure at the warmth in which it was basking. Innis sat on a nearby chair, keeping his distance but examining the creature more carefully as it dried and began to take on what he assumed was its usual appearance.

The ears were those of a bat, the eyes those of a cat, the tail that of a lemur, the body that of a monkey and the teeth, which Innis had briefly glimpsed while the animal cleaned itself, were distinctly rodent-like. It was as though a bizarre collection of mismatched parts had been arranged to create a being straight out of a fantastical tale or a picture from a children's book, perhaps a horror film. As the creature's fur dried by the fire, Innis could distinguish a dark brown color interspersed with white hairs and white around the face. While the odd beast slept, exhausted from its ordeal in the sea, Innis got his laptop and began attempting to identity the strange being. Covered with fur as it was, he assumed it was not a naturally sea dwelling animal so he first searched for mammals indigenous to Ireland. After finding nothing even vaguely resembling his new housemate, he switched to primates since the animal appeared monkey-like in some aspects. It was unlikely that any primates were normally found in Ireland, however, and he enlarged his investigation to include an international scope. He was amazed at the number of apes, monkeys and lemur species and decided to narrow things down to lemurs. The eyes of these primates reminded him of those he'd marveled at in the creature he'd rescued.

Scrolling through pictures of lemurs, he came to a halt. Here, unmistakably, was the animal who now rested by his fireplace. An aye-aye. He'd never heard of such a beast and quickly opened several articles with information about this critically endangered member of the lemur family. It wasn't surprising to discover that there had been some difficulty in properly categorizing the aye-aye, even for scientists, but what shocked Innis was the puzzling detail that the animal was found only on the island of Madagascar and in a few captive breeding facilities, none of them within any proximity to the Antrim coast. What the hell had happened here? The likelihood of an aye-aye making its way from Madagascar to the northern coast of Ireland was non-existent. Perhaps someone in the vicinity had kept the creature as a pet, but why had it then come out of the sea?

Innis began taking notes about the fascinating animal, including its diet which consisted of fruit, insects and insect larvae, seeds and fungi. They were also known to eat eggs and nectar. The aye-aye was nocturnal, spending its life in treetops where it ate, slept and even mated. It was solitary, believed to be the most intelligent of the lemur family with teeth that never stopped growing, and the only primate to use echolocation to search for its food. The disturbing elongated middle finger was for digging beneath tree bark to extract insect larvae as well as for scooping out the flesh of coconuts and mangoes that supplemented its diet.

The fact about the aye-aye that stopped Innis in his tracks, however, was the way in which the animal was perceived as a harbinger of doom, bad luck and even death in its native land. To many Madagascar citizens, if the aye-aye was seen near a village it foretold a death and the animals were often killed on sight due to their strange appearance and ominous reputation. They were sometimes used for meat as well and since their natural habitat was threatened with destruction the aye-aye population was in danger of extinction in the near future. This made Innis's situation more dire and he decided, rather than attempting to determine how the strange visitor had appeared on the beach, he'd better go about making certain it survived.

The diet of fruit, seeds, insects and fungi would be easily enough obtained, and he laughed to himself that perhaps he'd even give the creature mushrooms. The aye-aye's natural habitat, however, would be harder to duplicate but Innis decided to gather as many leaves, small branches and sticks as possible, hoping they might be fashioned into a reasonable facsimile of a nest. He wouldn't dare release the thing to wander into the woods to create its own accommodations in the treetops, he knew, for fear of someone spotting it. The process by which an aye-aye taps a tree or branch, listening for sounds within then scooping out larvae and insects had intrigued Innis when he read about it, and he thought about the grove of purple trees. Might a branch from one of them serve as a tester? Unsure about the nature of these unidentifiable trees he chose to delay such an experiment, knowing if harm came to the rare aye-aye it would weigh heavily on him. He asked himself why so many mysteries were presenting themselves but cast the question aside and planned a course of action.

The aye-aye slept a bit restlessly, shifting and muttering in its sleep, drying slowly by the fire as Innis watched. The fur of the animal was coarse, he could now tell, but rather pretty, as opposed to the elongated fingers which occasionally twitched as though trying to grasp something. Innis wondered how the creature walked with such cumbersome appendages on its front feet but figured he'd learn soon enough. Once the aye-aye woke up, he'd begin foraging for something to feed it and gathering material for its nest. How would he ever keep it here, especially with no one knowing of its presence? How might the creature behave? It didn't seem dangerous or poisonous according to the reading he'd done, but it was in a strange place and circumstances well outside its comfort zone. He wished he had someone to confide in, but, like the grove of purple trees, the aye-aye must remain a secret. True, he'd shared the phenomenon of the purple wood with Fin and no one else the wiser. The aye-aye would be a different matter and Innis could think of no one who might be in the least knowledgeable about such an animal. Before his own research, he hadn't even been certain where Madagascar was located.

The thought of his Aunt Bridget suddenly crossed his mind and he felt a surge of sympathy for the disturbingly odd aye-aye. Surely it was feared, shunned and punished in similar ways to his aunt with her madness. At least she hadn't been killed, but the similarities were clear to him. There were many citizens of Glenraven who viewed Bridget and her family as a certain form of outsider, to be avoided for fear of some vague doom or dire outcome, a guilt by association. He remembered his mother's words about protecting the fragile and the creature he was now watching soak up the heat of the fire was the very definition of fragile. Reluctant to leave the aye-aye alone, Innis continued to monitor it while he prepared a simple meal for himself, setting aside a few of the raw mushrooms he'd mixed with his scrambled eggs since the aye-aye's diet included fungi. Eating his quick breakfast while he watched the creature sleep, he wished he could mention his new house guest to Aunt Bridget but knew he didn't dare. Would the aye-aye try to escape when it awoke and realized it was in an unfamiliar place and in near proximity to a human? Might it attack him? Could the cold, rainy climate of Ireland be too much for the creature after the environment of its native land near Africa?

Questions tumbled around Innis's mind but he had little time to consider them as the aye-aye had awakened and sat up to look around, calmly assessing its surroundings, its incredible eyes meeting those of Innis who smiled at the creature, feeling foolish. The aye-aye yawned, displaying long, rodent-like teeth that made Innis nervous. He'd read in his research that aye-ayes were singularly unintimidated by humans, fearlessly rubbing against the legs and shoes of researchers in the field, and he hoped this one was equally friendly. The aye-aye slowly left its place by the fire, raising its long fingers so they did not touch the ground as it walked, thus creating a weird and awkward gait. Innis remained at the table while the aye-aye made its way to the small kitchen, its bushy tail dragging behind and leaving a slight trail of wetness as it was still damp from the ocean. The creature's ears were focused forward as though listening for any slight sound or trying to pick up vibrations to guide it.

Innis quickly retrieved the handful of mushrooms from the kitchen counter and set them on the floor near the aye-aye, then returned to his place at the table. The creature had frozen in place while Innis was in motion but now calmly proceeded toward the mushroom offering, picking up one of the pieces with its long, black fingers to investigate it and then quickly eat it. The aye-aye finished the rest of the mushrooms with surprising speed, continuing farther into the kitchen and gazing up at the surrounding cupboards and stove. Uncertain of whether to whistle, cluck or remain silent, Innis began to talk to the visitor as if it was a human friend come for a surprise visit.

"I'm glad you liked the mushrooms, aye-aye. We've got more and I'll go out and get some of the other things you eat as soon as you've settled. You're in Northern Ireland, I'm afraid, far from home, poor thing. Whatever happened to you?"

The aye-aye ignored Innis's words and turned back toward

the fireplace, brushing softly against Innis's leg in passing. It paused then left the fireplace area and headed toward the front door of the shack. Its long, bony fingers explored the small gap beneath the door where the slightest cold breeze from outside filtered through, then it lowered its head to smell at the fresh air. Gazing up toward the ceiling and lowering its eyes to the doorknob, it seemed to be gauging the manner of this obstacle before it. Turning away it began to wander around the remainder of the small living room, its clumsy movement causing Innis to chuckle in spite of himself. He knew the aye-aye was nocturnal and hoped it would sleep for the better part of the day, allowing him to gather some provisions for it. The creature, however, seemed to have different plans and made its way to the bedroom with Innis following at a respectful distance. It frequently looked up toward the ceiling or the tops of cabinets and dressers, probably searching for a treetop, Innis assumed. Poor thing, so utterly out of its element. How would it ever survive?

Making its way to the bed, it glanced up at the top surface where a quilt made by Innis's mother covered the other blankets and hung down almost to the floor. The aye-aye burrowed past the over-hanging quilt and disappeared under the bed without a sound. Innis waited a few minutes, hoping the animal would settle there in secluded darkness to hibernate. Lying down on the floor, he peered under the bed and was gratified to see the creature sleeping, its strange hands somehow even creepier in repose. Innis's Internet reading had revealed that aye-ayes enjoy grooming and could sit meditating for hours. He hadn't seen this behavior from his visitor yet but only a few hours had passed since it had crawled out of the sea. The female of the species had two nipples located in the groin area, he'd learned, though whether he'd ever be allowed close enough to examine the animal in this way was doubtful.

Innis returned to the kitchen to clean up his breakfast dishes, filling a porcelain bowl with water and setting it on the floor near the bed. Checking on the aye-aye, which was still asleep, he gathered some tools and headed out after securing all windows and doors in the shack. Fortunately, he had no job for the day and spent the next few hours in the woods collecting material for a nest, along with a few insects and some dirt which he put into a small wooden box he'd brought with him. He'd decided perhaps the aye-aye might feel more at home with some dirt to play in and laughed to himself at the idea of an aye-aye litter box. Worth a try nevertheless since none of his research had revealed the potty habits of the creature. Hesitating as he reached the outskirts of the forest, he saw the purple grove ahead and longed to retrieve a branch for the aye-aye. He didn't dare, he knew as he turned away, and walked back to the shack. The properties of the purple trees were unknowable and therefore too much of a risk when it came to a member of an endangered species like the one waiting for him at home. He trundled the nest materials, glass jars of insects and box of dirt to his front door in a wheelbarrow, relieved that no one had seen him. Opening the door cautiously, he found the aye-aye nowhere in sight and hauled the wheelbarrow into his living room.

After checking under the bed to find his primate visitor still curled up asleep, he went to work fashioning a nest out of the leaves and branches he'd gathered, trying his best to shape the materials into a ball with a single hole as an entry opening as he'd learned from his research was the way of aye-ayes. The nests were usually situated in the fork of a tree, which would be difficult for Innis to duplicate. Glancing around his small cabin, he saw no possibilities but returned to the bedroom and noticed the old armoire which his mother had given him as a housewarming gift. It was from a distant cousin of Irene's and had been in storage before being willed to her then passed on to Innis. Worn, slightly unsteady and made of some nondescript, dark wood, unadorned with any decoration or detail, the piece was too bulky and slightly depressing for Innis's taste though he'd used it to store his clothes and a few items he hadn't the room for anywhere else. Now he thought of a possible alternative use for the monstrosity: a home for the aye-aye.

The top of the armoire reached close to the low ceiling of the shack but there was enough room for the nest and the aye-aye, especially if the creature slept curled up in its spherical nest. He'd read that the animals were prone to moving nests every few days, which would be a problem. Still, he had to begin somewhere and stood staring at the armoire, trying to determine how the creature would reach the nest. The aye-aye used its claws to cling to tree trunks and branches in the wild, sometimes hanging upside down from thin branches with its claws acting as hooks. Innis retrieved one of the more sizable branches he'd gathered and propped it against the armoire. A bit precarious, he thought as he pushed against it to test its stability. The aye-aye wasn't large, but would it be able to navigate this branch and would it even attempt to do so?

Innis returned to the wheelbarrow and removed the box of dirt, placing it on the floor of the bedroom, comforted by its earthy smell. This room would obviously become the aye-aye's home if the creature cooperated, so Innis would concentrate his efforts here. Turning the dirt over with his hands, Innis glanced up to find the aye-aye staring at him from the foot of the bed. The animal had partially emerged from beneath the overhanging quilt and the amused expression in its eyes made Innis laugh out loud.

"You're a sly one, aren't you my friend. Are you laughing at me?"

The aye-aye came toward Innis cautiously, its ears pricked forward, its nostrils sniffing out the dirt and the human, its weird fingers held off the ground as it moved along in its awkward way. Innis remained perfectly still as the aye-aye approached, astonished that it showed no fear, only curiosity. Immediately noticing the branch propped against the armoire, it bypassed Innis and made for the branch, increasing its speed. Innis was glad he'd already wedged the improvised nest on top of the armoire and watched as the aye-aye deftly climbed onto the branch, making its way adeptly up toward the top despite a slight wobbling of the branch. Upon reaching the top, the creature immediately began to investigate the nest, smelling and pushing it then using its long fingers to unwedge it from the spot where Innis had placed it and roll it a short distance along the top of the armoire. Reaching into the entry hole Innis had created, the aye-aye felt around inside the nest then suddenly squeezed into it with a small squeak that made Innis smile. Settling into the nest, the creature soon slept and Innis sat on the bed, exhausted yet pleased that so far his amateur efforts seemed to be paying off. He'd wanted to offer the animal some of the insects he'd collected but obviously sleep was what the creature craved.

All sorts of problems, questions and misgivings began to make their way into Innis's thoughts. Was it realistic to expect that he would keep this strange animal as a pet, especially without anyone discovering it? Obviously not. Was there any way for him to ascertain exactly how it had come to arrive in Glenraven, or it if had an owner to whom it might be returned? Clearly not. He chuckled at the thought of posting a "Lost" notice around town, or even in Belfast, with a picture of the aye-aye. How would he ever care for the thing? It needed a forest in which to live, a natural setting which Raven's Back could never satisfy. The more Innis pondered these unanswerable questions, the more discouraged he became. There was already something about the aye-aye that tugged at his heart, silly as it seemed. He'd practically saved the creature's life and felt an obligation to it as well as sympathy for its sad plight as an endangered species partially reviled in its native land merely because of its odd appearance and an undoubtedly undeserved reputation. He shook his head, thinking of the ostracism his Aunt Bridget, and the rest of his family by association, had experienced. He would not surrender to such foolish and ignorant superstition. And yet the thought hovered in the back of his mind: a harbinger of death.

Chapter IX: Life With An Alien

Everyday life at Innis's cottage in Raven's Back became an adventure, the routine which he'd barely established in his new home completely shattered by the arrival of the aye-aye. In order to set things up for the creature, Innis took a few days off work, advising Oren there were some personal matters he needed to attend to. True to its nature in the wild, the animal would come alive when the sun went down, causing Innis to lose sleep as he tried to adjust to the nighttime schedule and observe the aye-aye in order to determine its needs and habits. The first night following its rescue, the creature climbed from its nest atop the armoire and found the box of dirt, digging a hole to do its business then covering it much like a cat, just as Innis had hoped. Innis, who'd barely closed his eyes to sleep when the aye-aye made its way down the branch to the floor, leaped from the bed and rushed to the jar of insects in the kitchen, dumping them onto the bedroom floor for the aye-aye. They scattered with some running and others hopping, but the aye-aye quickly collected them, making short work of the improvised meal. The creature then began to wander around the bedroom, occasionally glancing up, obviously in search of the mangrove trees which were its natural habitat. Feeling a bit silly, Innis nevertheless spoke to the aye-aye.

"I'm really sorry you've come to this strange place, macushla," he used the Celtic word for darling, "but there's not much I can do about it. I'd love to set you free out there in the forest where you'd have some trees at least, but you wouldn't last a day. Somebody'd kill you for sure and there's so few of you left in the world. You'll just have to adjust, do the best you can. Both of us will. God, I wish you could talk."

The aye-aye watched Innis as he spoke, its eyes gazing at him in that disconcerting, direct way that made him slightly uncomfortable yet also delighted. Turning away then, the creature proceeded to investigate the bedroom, finding the water bowl Innis had put out and having a brief drink. It explored the living room and kitchen, once again investigating the bottom edge of the front door with its long fingers. Innis, standing in the bedroom doorway watching, sighed. This will never do, he thought. The animal longs to be outside and it must be. This is not a house pet, it will never work for the poor thing.

Turning its head to look at Innis, the aye-aye made a small

sound that tugged at Innis's heart then came over to him. A shock ran through him as the creature began to climb up his leg but he forced himself to remain perfectly still, barely breathing. When the aye-aye reached Innis's waist and clutched at the material of his pajamas to haul itself higher, Innis folded his arms beneath it in an attempt to hold it like a cat. The creature allowed itself to be held, to Innis's surprise, and cuddled into his arms, its slightly earthy smell and warmth radiating a comfort that reminded Innis of the purple wood. He held the aye-aye for several minutes, wondering if he might risk simply carrying it outside since few of his neighbors would be out and about at this time of night. It would be easy for the creature to escape, though, and he added a leash and harness to the mental list of items he was accumulating for his housemate. Whether the animal would even allow itself to be strapped into a harness was another question, but so far it was proving to be surprisingly amenable to human contact and handling, at least with Innis. The idea of leading a wild animal from Madagascar on a leash into the woods was hilarious and he was determined to try.

Like his Aunt Bridget's secret about Connla, the seahorse king, the presence of the aye-aye in Innis's cabin became a closely guarded component of his life. After a tricky period of time when the creature caused an upheaval inside Innis's home, the two housemates settled into a precarious but compatible routine. The aye-aye proved adept at opening cupboard and closet doors with its long fingers, and Innis returned from work several times to find clothes, cooking utensils and wooden items on which he'd been carving scattered around. His bed clothes were sometimes on the floor, shaped into a nest for the aye-aye, who favored a position by the fire during the cold evenings. It had continued using the nest atop the armoire as a sleeping space but also created spots for itself on top of the kitchen cupboards and even on a floor lamp where it had somehow fashioned a nest out of a few of Innis's clothes. Innis frequently brought leaves and small branches in from the woods and loved watching the aye-aye create a nest with an effortless dexterity. Over the short period of time they'd been together, Innis had learned the aye-aye's favorite foods and was pleased by its ease and consistency with using the box of dirt as a litter box.

The unfortunate timing in their schedules, however, created some problems. Innis was gone at work during the day while his housemate slept; then, at night, as the nocturnal aye-aye became active, sleep was at a premium for the human. Keeping the presence of the aye-aye in his home a secret proved taxing as well, and as the days passed Innis sensed a growing despondency in the creature he'd become inordinately fond of sharing his home with. He purchased a harness and leash in Belfast during one of his visits with Fin, and one night managed to put it on the aye-aye, carrying the creature in his arms until they reached the edge of the woods where the purple grove began.

Though the aye-aye had remained fairly still in Innis's arms while they walked, it continually lifted its head to sniff the air, its ears swiveling to take in the night sounds, its eyes closing in contentment as it sensed itself returning to its element. After looking around to make sure there were no humans or other distractions nearby, Innis set the aye-aye on the ground near a tree, suddenly realizing it wouldn't work with the leash attached to the harness if the aye-aye attempted to climb to the top of a tree. Cursing his own stupidity, he scooped the animal back up and returned to the cabin. What the hell was he thinking, trying to control such an animal on a harness and leash like a domesticated pet? It was almost an insult to the poor creature. How could he risk losing the aye-aye, or allowing harm to come to it, without using the restraints?

The futile excursion weighed on Innis as he kept remembering the aye-aye's euphoric reaction to being outdoors. It seemed inhumane, keeping this primate in a residence, especially one as small and unsuitable as his cabin. The animal was eating well enough, didn't appear to be losing weight or having any physical problems, but at times he noticed a despondent expression in its eyes. He decided a rope attached to the harness might work if he used a long enough length of it. True, there was no elasticity to a rope but it would allow the creature more freedom of movement. It was easy enough to get some rope and once again Innis and the aye-aye set out toward the purple grove, this time with an exceedingly long rope attached to the harness. As before, the aye-aye enjoyed the walk, obviously luxuriating in the night air and forest smells but remaining quietly in Innis's arms until they reached the edge of the woods.

Placing the aye-aye on the ground, Innis allowed plenty of slack on the rope and watched the creature. It briefly explored the area at the base of a purple tree, whuffling among leaves and stray twigs then cautiously smelling the bark of the tree. Innis was startled to see the aye-aye jump back away from the tree, scurrying a short distance then turning to stare at the tree as though it had somehow offended the creature. Innis laughed but couldn't help wondering if the animal sensed something he could not. He let the aye-aye explore a bit on the ground and it headed back toward the woods through which they'd come, away from the purple grove. With Innis following at a short distance, the aye-aye covered a considerable amount of ground, foraging for insects and finding quite a few which it devoured with gusto. It also began collecting leaves and small branches which Innis assumed it wanted for a nest. He picked up the materials the aye-aye had gathered, putting them into a canvas bag he'd brought with him.

The creature looked up at him with a droll expression, each of them holding the other's gaze for a moment, a kind of understanding passing between them. Then the aye-aye proceeded to find more nest materials, waiting for Innis to secure them in the bag each time before continuing on to the next spot. Amused by the ritual, Innis followed the creature with delight, forgetting his surroundings until they'd traveled a fair distance back to where fishing shacks and cabins began to sporadically appear. Suddenly he noticed the light in the window of a nearby cabin and realized that he and the aye-aye had wandered too close to civilization such as it was in sparsely populated Raven's Back. He'd barely gathered the slightly protesting aye-aye into his arms when a vaguely familiar voice called out into the darkness.

"Who's out there? Is that you, Innis?"

He recognized the caller as one of his neighbors, Charlie Halloran, with whom he'd shared a few conversations as well as the occasional visit in Charlie's cabin for coffee or ale. He couldn't simply pretend not to hear the greeting and turned slightly away in order to conceal the aye-aye, wishing they could both simply disappear into the night.

"Yeah, it's me, Charlie!" Innis shouted, continuing to move away from the cabin in the direction of home.

He became aware that the long length of rope by which he'd secured the aye-aye was dragging behind him and struggled to gather it up while moving on and holding the now still aye-aye. Afraid to look in Charlie's direction, he knew by the sound of the voice that his neighbor was probably standing in the back doorway of his cabin and hoped the man couldn't see too much detail through the darkness. A narrow column of light came from the cabin door but Innis and the aye-aye were well beyond its range.

"Too bad, Charlie, but I've gotta run. Didn't mean to disturb you. I was just gathering some materials for a project."

"At night? Haven't you a lantern? And what's with the rope?"

Innis waved and hurried away, calling over his shoulder.

"I'll talk to you later, Charlie. Sorry, gotta get home now."

Cursing his luck and recklessness, Innis quickened his pace, grateful the aye-aye had remained relatively quiet despite shifting around a bit in his arms. Hurrying home, he put the aye-aye down in the bedroom, dumping the bundle of nest materials out of the canvas bag. The animal shook off and groomed itself for a few minutes, the first time Innis had seen it engage in such action and he folded his arms with a smile, watching with amusement. The animal gave off a few chuffs and whuffles as though somewhat insulted and put out then turned to the pile of leaves and branches it had collected with Innis. It began gathering them up in a haphazard fashion. To Innis's astonishment, it didn't take long for the aye-aye to transport every-thing up the branch to the top of the armoire bit by bit.

Innis remained in the bedroom doorway, fascinated by the creature's methodical actions. He observed the aye-aye pulling material from the original nest which Innis had made, adding to the new structure as it fashioned a fresh nest combining the old and new leaves, sticks and pieces of branches. Innis shook his head, once again chuckling at his housemate's antics and breaking into a laugh as the aye-aye pushed the remains of the old nest off the armoire after completing the new one. Retrieving the discarded nest, Innis sighed while the aye-aye settled itself into the new nest. I'm already far too attached to this creature, Innis told himself, and couldn't help believing the animal shared this sentiment a bit after their episode of collecting nest materials together. He knew it was unrealistic to entertain such ideas, but still he wanted the bond between him and the aye-aye to be true.

The foray into the forest with the aye-aye on a harness and rope had been somewhat of a disaster and Innis had to make a con-certed effort to avoid his neighbor Charlie for several days. He found himself also evading his family's requests to visit his new home and see how he was getting on in Raven's Back. It would be impossible to hide the aye-aye and equally impossible to explain it.

He'd considered contacting a zoo to see if the animal might be accepted and cared for, but already the thought of no longer sharing his abode with the creature caused him too much anguish. As their days together advanced, he'd come to discover more intriguing facets of the aye-aye's habits and personality.

Although Innis's research had indicated that aye-ayes might prefer tree sap and vegetables to insects, his housemate loved the insects Innis brought home for him and displayed a decided preference for beetles. The creature marked the branch leading to its nest with its scent by rubbing its cheeks and neck against the bark, much as a cat would do, and had adopted the custom of joining Innis by the fire sometimes in the evening. Once, as the aye-aye rolled over onto its back, enjoying the warmth of the fire, Innis glanced at its underside, noticing the absence of nipples which would have indicated a female. At times he thought of the animal as Indigo or Yaeger, meaning hunter, but resisted giving it a formal name since it would only further cement his growing attachment.

The aye-aye had adjusted to its unfamiliar surroundings with impressive ease and one night, when Innis had fallen asleep by the fire, he awoke to find the creature sitting on his lap and staring into his face. Startled, he jumped and the aye-aye scurried back to the floor, turning to give a withering glance before huffing off to the bedroom as though highly insulted. Innis felt a combination of nerves and pleasure that the animal had come so close to him while fixing him with that unsettling gaze. If he'd been a superstitious person, he might have convinced himself that the aye-aye was casting some spell on him. Innis, however, mainly regretted that he'd been surprised and spoiled the opportunity to cuddle the creature, hoping there would be another chance and amused, as always, by his housemate's droll personality.

He began doing additional research on the Web and in the library in Belfast, this time searching for news stories that might provide a clue to the aye-aye's appearance on the Antrim coast. Perhaps there'd been a shipment that sank or an individual who'd been apprehended trying to profit from trade in endangered species. Finding nothing, Innis had no choice but to accept the mysterious arrival of the creature as some strange stroke of fate, the meaning of which he might never know.

As time passed, Innis and the aye-aye settled into a more or less symbiotic existence, acclimating to one another slowly yet steadily. There were now more frequent trips to the woods in the dead of night with Innis taking a more circuitous route to avoid Charlie's cabin and using extra care in remaining as far removed from civilization as possible. While Innis was friendly enough with his neighbors, and familiar to some of them from his visits to the area as a child, he'd never been one to invite them over or visit their homes, and the citizens of Raven's Back were known for their rugged individualism. The people who were attracted to living in the area did so because of its isolation and sparsely settled, wooded terrain that encouraged privacy over sociability. Now Innis was glad he'd kept to himself for the most part and hoped the secret of the aye-aye would be easily hidden from his neighbors.

Night excursions involved a variety of activities for the aye-aye. Innis had settled on the name of Yaeger for his companion because of the creature's clear preference for hunting. Always keen for a search of the grounds and trees in the forest, Yaeger demonstrated his skill at tapping on trees to locate grubs then gnawing a small hole in the wood into which he inserted his long middle finger to pull out the grubs and eat them with gusto. Innis, fascinated by observing this odd ritual of which he'd read, longed to remove the rope and harness from Yaeger and let him go free to live the natural life of an aye-aye but kept to their routine, giving the animal plenty of rope in an effort to infringe as little as possible on the aye-aye's hunting ritual.

The first time Yaeger scurried up a tree, Innis experienced a moment of panic, worried the creature might settle down to spend the night, leaving the human to stand watch below while foolishly holding the rope. Apparently the tree was not to Yaeger's liking, however, as he soon descended and resumed his hunting.

Gathering material for nests was another activity that Yaeger enjoyed, and Innis was relieved to discover his friend did not attempt to build a nest in a tree as he would normally do in the wild. Instead, he reverted to the search and collect system the two of them had established with Innis gathering the items Yaeger found and putting them into a canvas bag to take back to the shack with them. Had the aye-aye become so quickly domesticated or was there some other strange dynamic at play here? Perhaps the trees in the woods surrounding Raven's Back were too different from the rain forests of the aye-aye's native habitat. Innis considered it a bonus that Yaeger wasn't inclined to climb trees and encouraged him in his hunting and gathering activities during their nocturnal excursions.

Oren had noticed his apprentice's lack of energy and the dark circles beneath Innis's eyes attesting to a lack of sleep and who knows what else. He refrained from questioning Innis at first but finally called him aside.

"Are you not sleeping well, my boy?" Oren made sure to allow his genuine concern to show in his voice. "You don't seem ill, but I've been a bit worried and you've taken off a couple of days."

Embarrassed and unprepared, Innis hesitated.

"If it's something personal, never mind that I asked," Oren quickly added. "I just wanna be sure you're OK or if there's any-thing you want to tell me. Maybe I could help. You've been such a good worker and it's not that you've let your work go at all. It strikes me that something's bothering you."

The idea of confessing to Oren about the aye-aye flashed across Innis's mind but was instantly dismissed.

"Sorry I've worried you, Oren. Truth is, I haven't been get-ting much sleep, you can probably tell. Not sure why but I've had trouble sleeping. Then I had a few personal things to take care of when I took the couple of days off. I appreciate your indulgence. And your patience."

Oren put a hand on Innis's shoulder and smiled in his off-handed way.

"Think nothing of it. Hope you figure out a way to get more sleep though. You look a bit ragged, Innis."

Innis promised to find a way of getting more rest and felt lucky to have escaped without further interrogation. It reminded him, however, that life with Yaeger as a secret from everyone he knew wasn't a realistic option. His neighbor Charlie had shown up at the shack early one morning, anxious to question Innis about their night encounter, wondering why Innis had been prowling around the woods at that hour trailing an extraordinarily lengthy rope and acting nervous. At the risk of rudeness, Innis kept Charlie at the front door, putting him off as best he could with evasive answers and attempts to change the subject. Charlie eventually left, slightly disgruntled, but Innis thought long and hard about the proper course of action. It wouldn't surprise him to find Charlie attempting to spy on the night-time excursions with Yaeger. Sooner or later someone else must know, and Innis knew there was only one person he could trust with this information: his brother.

Dalton, an animal lover, would understand Innis's attachment to the aye-aye and be circumspect in keeping the secret. Perhaps he might even have suggestions or ideas for dealing with the situation. With a large measure of relief, and an equal amount of nerves, Innis invited his brother to the shack for dinner, requesting their parents should not be told. At last the little stranger from Madagascar would emerge from the shadows and meet another member of the family. After this, there could be no turning back and, come what may, at least there would be a partner in crime, his brother, like in their boyhood days. Innis couldn't wait.

Chapter X: The Dinner Guest

Dalton had reluctantly accepted his brother's invitation to dinner, questioning why their parents weren't included and couldn't be told but receiving no answers from Innis. He seldom ventured far from the family farm and developed a case of nerves during the two days prior to the dinner. Should he take a housewarming gift and, if so, what? Having no clue about such situations and no one he could ask, he felt obligated to offer some token of appreciation to his brother after the treasured purple sheep figure and sketch of Kieran he'd received.

Following Kieran's first shearing, Dalton had kept the wool and asked his mother to knit a scarf from it, knowing the dark wool would be less valuable at market but cherished for his own personal use. Irene, unaccustomed to personal requests from her younger son, had obliged with the caveat that she was far from proficient in knitting or crocheting. She considered giving the task to Bridget, whose impressive talent for crocheting would quickly produce a superior result. Instead, she accomplished the task herself, knowing it would mean more to Dalton this way and he wouldn't care about the less than perfect appearance or lack of sophistication in the garment. He'd worn the scarf religiously, offering thanks in his own terse way and showing his gratitude and pleasure by his obvious fondness for the dark garment. It became a kind of talisman for him, but now he wondered if he should offer it to Innis. The thought of giving it up was troublesome yet he could think of nothing else to offer his brother except a few pints of his favorite ale, which seemed too impersonal.

Taking the black scarf from his closet, Dalton cleaned it up as best he could, though it still exuded the scent of sheep and hay. He wrapped it carefully in tissue paper and moved on to the next dilemma he faced: deciding what to wear to the dinner. There was no question of formality but the only clothes he owned were basically those he wore for work on the farm so he felt like a country bumpkin next to his artistic brother. Finally choosing a plaid flannel shirt, a slightly ragged fisherman's sweater and his cleanest pair of jeans, Dalton ventured to Raven's Back carrying the scarf in tissue paper. The requirement of avoiding his parents' involvement bothered him as he wasn't normally given to subterfuge and felt uncomfortable about secrets. Nevertheless, he left the house quietly after they'd gone in to town, positioning a note on the kitchen table explaining he needed to run an evening errand related to supplies for the sheep. He'd have to think of some more detailed story later and felt a stab of resentment toward Innis for putting him in the position of deceiving their parents.

Making his way the short distance to Raven's Back in his old pick-up truck that held remnants of hay and a few tools which rattled around in the truck bed, Dalton parked as near to his brother's cottage as he could. The woods surrounding Raven's Back made access difficult so most residents and visitors parked in a large dirt lot then hiked the rest of the way to the cabins and shacks. Innis's home was one of the more distant ones from the parking area but Dalton was glad of the extra time to prepare himself for the visit. It surprised him to be nervous about visiting his brother, though he'd always felt a certain dread of any social occasion and Innis's success as a woodworker, artist and man of the world, from Dalton's perspective, made things even more intimidating. Along with his nerves, however, was a bit of pride at being the first in the family to visit his brother's new home.

Clutching the gift, he trudged through the woods, passing the occasional residence but reveling in the quiet and isolation of being in nature. It was easy to understand why Innis had chosen this area. The semi-darkness of twilight made the woods a little spooky, though, and Dalton thought of the stories and rumors he'd heard about the curse of Raven's Back. He could see how this area might encourage such legends. The haphazardly spaced residences were oddly numbered with their exact addresses difficult to determine, but Dalton soon found the cottage that Innis had described and saw his brother standing by the front door of his home. He waved and hurried forward with Innis coming to meet him with a big smile and a bear hug.

"Little brother, you found me!" Innis held Dalton at arm's length to look at him. "You're still taller than me, not at all fair."

Dalton smiled, pleased to see his brother looked well with the exception of some darkness under his eyes that must indicate a lack of sleep. Innis headed back to his shack but turned to face Dalton when they reached the front door.

"Look, Dalt, before we go in I have to warn you about something. I have a housemate."

"Finola's moved in, has she?"

"Nope. Not at all. It's quite a different kind of housemate actually. Hard to even describe it to you, you'll have to see for yourself. I just wanted to give you a bit of a warning before you walk in and see Yaeger."

Innis's eyes twinkled with mischief.

"Yaeger?" Dalton hesitated. "Have you gotten a dog? A cat?"

"Come on in, you'll find out. I'm opening the door slowly since I don't know if he's out and about. He doesn't usually hang out by the front door, but sometimes...anyway, wouldn't want him to dart out. Prepare yourself. He's not something you could ever expect."

Dalton's eyes were on the small cabin, however, assessing the excellent craftsmanship that had gone into the refurbishment of a fishing shack into a very livable domicile that verged on charm. He knew Innis was talented with woodworking but still thought of him more often as a painter. Before he could compliment his brother on the building, the front door had been opened and Dalton was welcomed by the warmth of a cozy, if sparsely furnished or decorated, interior with a fire going in the fireplace and the smell of beef stew tantalizingly greeting him. It was easy to take in the majority of the living space in a glance: a small sitting area with an equally small kitchen opening directly off of it with a plain wood kitchen table and four simple chairs. There was a comfortable, though worn, chair arranged by the fireplace, a couch and a corner cabinet in the living room, and an old portable television on a rickety stand.

The kitchen table was set for two places with slightly chipped plates and jam jars as glasses. Dalton laughed inwardly, remembering his trepidation at the dinner invitation and concern about what to wear and how to behave. How had he forgotten that this was his older brother, who was even more of a stranger to protocol than he himself. Relaxing a bit, Dalton handed the tissue paper package to Innis.

"Here's a housewarming gift, Innis. Sorry about the wrapping."

Innis looked surprised but took the offering. The tissue paper easily fell open to reveal the black wool scarf which he quickly recognized as Dalton's signature garment on the farm. He knew his brother practically lived in this scarf during the cold winter months, that it was from the wool of Kieran. Tears sprang to his eyes as he stared at the scarf and he waited until they'd subsided before raising his gaze to his brother.

"This is too much, Dalt. It's your special scarf. I couldn't possibly take this from you, I know how much it means to you."

"No, I want you to have it. I've cleaned it up the best I could, but it probably still smells a bit like sheep. I wouldn't know since I'm around that smell so much. I can always have another made."

Innis shook his head and brought the scarf up to his face, the wool scratching him a little, the smell of sheep filling his senses. If anything would always remind him of his brother, this would be it. Burying his face in the garment, he could almost feel the many cold mornings it had accompanied Dalton out into the fields with his flock. He grinned, throwing his arms around Dalton then wrapping the scarf around his neck with a flourish.

"It's brilliant! What can I say, Dalton. I'm really touched and flattered. I still can't imagine you without this scarf, though."

"It surprised me that I wanted to give it to you, but I just do, can't explain it. Time for me to do without it. I've got Kieran and that's more important to me than a scarf."

Dalton hesitated awkwardly, shifting his weight and lowering his voice to almost a whisper.

"I don't know anyone I'd rather have it," he looked down as he spoke. "That's how much I love you, brother."

Innis embraced him again, then looked around for a sign of the aye-aye. Yaeger was nowhere to be seen. Perhaps company wouldn't be to the creature's liking; time would tell and this was their first experience with a visitor. Dalton too had looked around, puzzled by his brother's comments about his housemate. There was no evidence of this mysterious Yaeger but he had not yet glimpsed the bedroom. After checking on the stew, which was bubbling away in a simmer on the stove, Innis motioned to his brother to take a seat at the kitchen table. Dalton sat but couldn't contain his curiosity.

"So where's this Yaeger? He must be in the bedroom."

Innis brought two bottles of ale from the fridge to the table and sat opposite his brother. Aware that Dalton seldom drank, he surmised that some extra fortitude might be needed for his introduction to an aye-aye. To his surprise, Dalton opened the bottle without hesitation and they clinked bottle necks.

"To the Kilbride boys!" Innis announced.

"And to your new home. I can't believe what you've done, restoring all this. When you first showed it to me it was little more than a rundown fishing shack. Now it looks like a real home. Well done, Innis."

Innis had positioned himself so that he would be able to see Yaeger entering the area before Dalton could and kept an eye out while he cut a few thick slices from the loaf of dark rye bread he'd bought that morning at his favorite bakery. Dishing out the stew, he felt a rush of pleasure at hosting his brother in his own home. The stew had turned out well, especially without any advice or assistance from Irene, who'd been kept in the dark about the visit and thus couldn't be consulted. He'd watched his mother prepare this dish many times and even though his version was missing a few of the extra spices and little ingredients Irene added to make for a savory and satisfying stew, this was good enough and Innis was proud of himself. Now if only that damn Yaeger would appear.

Dalton, never much of a chatter, remarked on the excellence of the stew and ate with focused enthusiasm, dipping the bread into his bowl to scoop up every morsel. As he enjoyed the meal, he wondered why his brother had failed to answer the question about Yaeger but assumed this was a subject for after dinner. Innis did most of the talking, catching up Dalton on his recent trips to Belfast, his slowly progressing woodworking apprenticeship and a brief mention of Fin. He grilled Dalton on all the details of the farm: the health and status of the flock, the vegetable crop and their parents as well as the condition of the family house. Neither Dalton nor Abbot were particularly handy with household repairs, so Innis had always taken care of those chores even after leaving home. There were no projects at present, Dalton reassured his brother, and things were going fine at the farm. He offered a few of the latest stories about Kieran's antics and the topic finally turned to Yaeger.

"You know I mentioned my new housemate when you arrived, Dalt? Before dessert I thought maybe it's better to fill you in a bit so you won't be too startled when you first see him. It was a true shock for me when I first laid eyes on him, I can tell you."

"OK. I assume we're talking about some sort of animal here?"

"Yeah, but not just any animal. Truth is, it's an animal I never even knew existed until now."

"What exactly is it?"

Innis couldn't keep the gleam of mischief out of his eyes. It was seldom that he could have one over his brother when it came to the animal kingdom.

"Yaeger's an aye-aye."

Dalton adopted a quizzical expression.

"A what?"

"An aye-aye. It's a primate, a form of lemur. But here's the best part: native to the island of Madagascar and found only there."

Innis sat back in his chair with satisfaction, watching Dalton take in this revelation. There was only a brief silence until Dalton spoke up.

"Spelled how?"

Innis laughed.

"You're worried about spelling? Classic Dalton. It's a-y-e, with a dash, a-y-e. It's said the name comes from people's reaction when they saw the thing for the first time. Believe me, it's appropriate. Just wait, you can't imagine how weird this creature looks. I swear, it's like looking at an alien."

Dalton folded his arms.

"Is this a trick, Innis? Are you having me on?"

Innis shook his head and chuckled.

"No, trust me. He's right in the bedroom, you'll see. We should probably have some pie first, though. I got it from the posh bakery in town. Apple, your favorite."

Now it was Dalton's turn to laugh.

"OK, you've just finished telling me about some strange alien creature from Madagascar, who's in your bedroom, and now we're taking a break for apple pie? You're too much, Innis. And apple is your favorite, not mine. I want to meet Yaeger."

"And you will." Innis retrieved the pie and began slicing it. "I don't want to disturb him though, and I was hoping he'd come down from his nest and join us on his own. You can't get the full effect until you see him walking."

He slid a plate with a generous slice of pie across the table to Dalton, who shook his head and, with an amused glance at his brother, dug in. Pleased with the success of the dessert, Innis took his own piece of pie and made short work of it, thinking, as he often did when sharing a dessert with Dalton, of the buggy cookies Aunt Bridget had once given the brothers. Finishing first, he watched Dalton enjoy the pie and realized how much he missed his younger brother. Anxious to see how Dalton would react to the aye-aye, he kept an eye on the kitchen doorway, hoping the scent of food might attract the creature, but there was no sign of Yaeger. Just like the caustic little critter to avoid their first visitor.

When Dalton finished his dessert, thanking Innis profusely for the meal, there was a brief silence. Dalton had expected Innis to be full of stories and details about the refurbishing of the shack he now called home, but his brother appeared to have other things on his mind. Innis stood and motioned to the doorway of the kitchen.

"Well, I guess it's time for you to meet Yaeger. Shall we go to the bedroom? That's his territory. Don't worry about the dishes," he waved a hand toward the table, "I'll deal with all that later."

Dalton set down the dessert plate and fork he'd been about to take to the sink to rinse.

"Are you sure? I'm happy to rinse my dishes."

"Nah, I'll get it. Later. Right now it's high time you became acquainted with an aye-aye."

Anxious to finally see the mysterious creature, Dalton followed his brother to the bedroom. He quickly surveyed the few pieces of furniture: a simple bed, a dresser, a chair, a wooden chest and a three-legged stool. All had been made by Innis, he was certain. His attention was immediately drawn to a box of dirt on the floor near the bedroom doorway and a tree branch propped against the old armoire he recognized as his mother's heirloom from her cousin. The room was somewhat dark with only one window which let in limited light from the forest surroundings outside. Innis held out his arm toward the armoire as though presenting an amazing sight.

"Behold, the lair of the aye-aye!" He laughed, indicating an indistinct mass of what looked like twigs and leaves atop the armoire. "That's Yaeger's nest. He's in there right now, obviously asleep. Too bad, I was really hoping he'd be out and about. He's normally coming to life around this time, nocturnal you know. That's why I invited you for dinner. Now, of course, the little bugger decides to hibernate."

Dalton, who hadn't noticed the nest until now, strained to see the odd item but couldn't make out any details. There was an entry hole in the front of the nest and he thought he discerned a bit of dark brown fur protruding from it, but with the sticks and leaves partially obscuring the hole and the darkness at the top of the armoire he couldn't be sure.

"Sorry, I can't quite make him out."

"I know." Innis sighed, clearly disappointed. "Let's give it a minute, he's bound to roust himself at some point."

Innis sat down on the end of the bed and Dalton sat beside him, gazing at the tree branch and box of dirt.

"What's the dirt about?"

"That's his litter box. I know, weird, right? I swear, Dalt, he does his business in there and covers it up just like a cat. He just did it automatically."

"Innis, how in hell did you come upon this thing? Or did he find you?"

"A bit of both, I think. He crawled out of the sea and I found him on the beach early one morning, halfway drowned. I didn't know what the hell it was, of course, but it was something I felt compelled to do, save this animal. I know it's gonna sound crazy, but I can't help feeling like it's some sort of sign, a stroke of fate. I'm sounding like Aunt Bridget, right?"

Dalton smiled as his brother had guessed his precise thoughts as usual.

"Maybe. I'd feel less that way if I could actually see him."

"You think I'm making this up?"

Dalton laughed.

"Of course not. It just all seems so far-fetched, you have to admit."

He went back to the armoire, peering up at the bundle of twigs and leaves and struggling, without success, to discern the shape of an animal inside the nest. Returning to sit beside Innis, he put a hand on his brother's shoulder.

"Why can't Ma and Da know, Innis?"

Innis turned a wry look on his brother.

"Are you kidding? I chose to tell you first for a reason. Look, let's sit here for a few minutes and see if he comes down. Better yet, let's go back to the living room. Maybe he can smell you and since he doesn't recognize the scent he's decided to hide out. He hasn't been here that long, so we're still figuring each other out."

The brothers returned to the living room and settled on the couch with Innis closest to the bedroom doorway in order to keep a look-out for Yaeger. Immediately jumping back up, he headed for the kitchen.

"I'll make us some coffee while we wait. Be right back."

Dalton, pleased at the prospect of Innis's strongly brewed cof-

83

fee, tried to relax, glancing around the cozy room which he was amazed his brother had almost created from scratch. Innis returned with two mugs and the smell of the freshly brewed coffee filling the small space. Sitting beside Dalton and handing him one of the mugs, he grinned.

"It's truly my own home, little brother. Sometimes I still can't believe it."

"You read my mind. I was just sitting here admiring everything you've done. You've a right to be very proud, Innis. I wish you'd let Ma and Da come here and see it. I don't like lying to them, y'know."

Innis sighed and shook his head.

"I know, and I'm sorry about that, but it's the aye-aye. I've gotta keep it as much of a secret as I can and the more people who find out the less control I've got."

"Why does it matter if people know?"

"Oh, you haven't seen Yaeger. He'll scare people and God knows what they might do to him. This is a highly endangered animal, Dalt. I'd never forgive myself if somebody killed him just out of fear. In his native land he's killed from superstition. They believe an aye-aye's appearance near a village signifies death, and that the animal sneaks into houses through the thatched roof to murder the people in their sleep by puncturing their aorta with that long middle finger it's got."

"Good God."

"Yeah, right? I hate to say it, but it's easy to see why there's this fear and suspicion. When I first saw Yaeger I was afraid of him and sometimes he still freaks me out a little bit, but he's only a creature. There's no magical, sinister powers at work here. If somebody was to see him without knowing any of this, though, their first instinct would probably be to kill him. Especially the people living here in Raven's Back. It's not exactly the friendliest place to begin with. More like shoot first and ask questions later."

"Do you think you could get him down from the nest so I could have a look at him? If he doesn't come out on his own, that is."

"Sorry, not really. I've never disturbed him like that when he's sleeping and I don't wanna start. He needs to trust me."

"Is he the reason you're looking a bit ragged, like you haven't slept for weeks?"

Innis gave a sheepish grin.

"You noticed, huh? So did my boss. Guess the aye-aye's nocturnal ways are at odds with my day job. I take him way out in the woods late at night to do his hunting and gathering. You'd die laughing, Dalt. I've got him in a dog harness with a long rope tied to it. So far the only problem's been running into Charlie Halloran once, that's one of my neighbors. He saw the rope but, luckily, he didn't see Yaeger. Anyway, he loves it too much, the aye-aye, going out and being in his element. I can't deny him that. The only thing is it takes away a couple of hours from my sleep time every night. It's worth it."

Dalton stared at his brother, amazed at this uncharacteristic declaration of caregiving. He'd seldom known Innis to put himself second as a young boy and it was obvious he was now exerting extraordinary effort for this odd creature he claimed to have found. Growing up in the shadow of his aunt's madness, however, Dalton couldn't help conjuring a different scenario. What if his brother had lost his mind? An endangered species of animal native to Madagascar washing up on the shore of the Antrim coast was very far-fetched. How could Innis have snapped so suddenly? Unlikely. He hadn't spent much time around his brother recently, but things seemed to be normal enough in his life. Surely the restoring of the shack, the apprenticeship with woodworking and the evolving relationship with Fin could not all be carried out seamlessly by a madman. Innis was going to extreme lengths to care for this creature and keep him hidden. Dalton was puzzled.

"Innis, you can't go on losing sleep because of this aye-aye. It's bound to harm your health sooner or later. What did you tell Oren when he mentioned it?"

"I gave him some malarkey about going through some personal stuff. I certainly didn't tell him the truth."

"Maybe all this secrecy isn't such a good idea. If other people knew about Yaeger they could help you with him. I'm usually busy at the farm but I might spare a little time for taking him out at night once in awhile. It would save one night's rest for you and other people might be willing to do the same."

"That's kind of you, Dalt, but I couldn't ask it. You get up earlier in the morning than I do to be out with the flock. It wouldn't be right. I'm close to the end of my apprenticeship with Oren and once I get my licenses and certificates I can be a freelance woodworker. Then I can build my schedule around Yaeger."

Dalton was silent for a few minutes. It wasn't his custom to comment on anyone else's decisions or lifestyle, nor had he given advice to his older brother on many occasions. This time, however, there was a genuine concern for Innis's physical and mental well-being and he felt obligated to comment.

"It's a bit crazy, though, Innis. I still don't understand why the aye-aye must be a secret. You're only making it more difficult for yourself and you can't go on this way forever. Besides, someone's bound to find out at some point, don't you think? It's unrealistic to expect otherwise."

Unless, the disturbing thought occurred to Dalton, his brother really had gone mad and created the fiction of an aye-aye for God knows what reason.

"Yeah, I know you're right," Innis's response brought Dalton's attention back. "but it's just too tricky. Look, I know you can't stay here too late waiting for Yaeger to make an appearance. Ma and Da will be worried if you get home too late and they'll start grilling you about where you've been. Guess we'll have to try again another time. At least we got to have dinner together. It's been too long."

Innis stood up and Dalton reluctantly did the same, casting a glance back into the bedroom toward the nest which remained still and silent.

"Look, Innis, I've gotta be honest. I don't like lying to Ma and Da and I'm not very good at it."

Innis clapped a hand on his brother's shoulder and grinned, retrieving Dalton's coat from the back of the couch where it had been tossed.

"Sorry to make you lie to them, but please hang in with me just a little more. I promise it won't be too much longer. I know you're right, things have to change with Yaeger but I have to figure out what's best for him and me. I didn't think I could trust anyone but you, hope you understand."

Dalton put on his coat, shoving his hands into the pockets, and looked down at his feet. He couldn't help recalling the many times as boys when Innis's schemes had gotten the two of them into hot water with Dalton being a reluctant participant who couldn't resist his brother's persuasion. Frustrated with Innis, he raised his gaze to his brother's face.

"I'm glad you've trusted me with this secret, but I can't keep it forever. And I can't just accept this crazy idea about building your whole life around an aye-aye."

"But Dalt, I'm surprised hearing you say that. Haven't you built your life around the sheep, and especially Kieran?"

Dalton blushed and lowered his gaze again, but before he could respond Innis continued.

"Don't get me wrong, I'm not saying there's anything wrong with it, that's my point. I think it's great the way you're devoted to the sheep, you know that. So why can't I do everything I can to take care of Yaeger?"

"It's not exactly the same thing. An aye-aye's not a sheep and he's a secret, Innis, who's making you lose sleep. I'd never judge you. I didn't mean it that way. I'm just worried about you. I don't wanna see you run yourself into the ground. That won't do you or him any good."

Innis sighed and shook his head.

"I know you're right, Dalt. I just don't see a way around it. Look, I know he doesn't belong here, but there's no sending him back to Madagascar. I don't even know if there are any laws about endangered species like him. Besides, it might sound crazy but I feel like he came to me for a reason. Don't know what it is yet but I can't ignore this bond I already have with him."

For the first time, Innis recognized the importance of the seahorse king, Connla, to his Aunt Bridget. It was something crucial to her survival, a sacred trust she'd been given that must never be broken. He felt the same way about Yaeger. Although one was real and the other imaginary, who could deny the bond that each had forged with its human. Downplaying the hold Yaeger had on him, Innis now had to acknowledge the true reason for his resistance to finding an alternative situation for the aye-aye. He wanted Yaeger to stay with him. Even his relationship with Fin held less importance for him than that of the strange little creature who shared his home.

Dalton surprised him with a hug.

"You're a million miles away, Innis. You look like you're having some serious thoughts."

"Yeah, guess I am. Hope you enjoyed dinner and I'll think about what you said. Really sorry you didn't get to meet Yaeger. It might have made it easier for you to understand why I'm acting this way. I'd tell you to Google 'aye-aye' but I know you're not much for the computer."

"I'll keep your secret, don't worry. Maybe next time he'll grace us with his presence. I'd best not come back right away, though, or Ma and Da'll start getting very suspicious. Wait a little while until you invite me back and please think about what I said. The dinner was super, by the way, and your house is a work of art. I don't know how you did it, but congratulations."

Innis hugged his brother and touched the dark wool scarf around his neck.

"Thanks for this, it really means a lot to me. It was wonderful having you here. Take care of yourself."

"And you too. Please try to get some sleep."

"You sound like Ma," Innis teased. "I'll try, and I appreciate you keeping the secret. I promise it won't be for too long."

Innis watched his brother walk off into the dark then went to the kitchen to begin clearing away the dinner dishes. Something made him turn and he found Yaeger standing in the kitchen doorway watching him.

"You little bugger, where the hell were you?" Innis laughed and shook his finger at the aye-aye. "You did it on purpose, didn't you? And now my poor brother probably thinks I've lost my mind. All your fault, macushla."

He stopped piling dishes into the sink and went to the spot where he kept Yaeger's supplies, gathering up the harness, rope and canvas bag.

"OK, little devil. Guess it's past due time for our hunting trip. You're spoiled rotten, you know. How could this happen so quickly?"

He smiled as the aye-aye meandered over to him with what Innis would have sworn was laughter dancing in his golden eyes.

Chapter XI: Fin's Advice

The long distance romance between Innis and Finola had proceeded at a slow but steady pace. Visits to Belfast were sporadic at first as Innis was busy with his woodworking apprentice duties and uncertain how to go about becoming closer to the shop owner. There were a few email messages between the two following their initial meeting, and Innis began to devise excuses for visiting the city. A second and third lunch in the park convinced both of the hesitant sweethearts that they were drawn to one another in some mysterious way which only the heart could understand. Fin, better educated than Innis, introduced him to some of her favorite writers while he entertained her with the tales from his grandfather which had enthralled him as a child. They spoke of family and their own ambitions, of places they wished to see and the ones they'd already visited. Again, Fin outstripped Innis in travel experience. She'd been as far as Dublin and Cork and, having grown up in Galway, had seen the north, south, east and west of their native land as well as London and Edinburgh. Innis reminded her of his boyhood descriptions of the four corners of Ireland, which delighted her and she began referring to Galway as "The Wild West." A descriptive conversationalist, Fin spoke of windy Galway Bay and the city with its colorful houses and inns, of lovely, quaint Kinsale near Cork, of the bridges over the River Liffey in Dublin and the lights along the River Thames. A voracious reader, she'd visited the Writers Museum in Dublin and teased Innis with information on the Guinness Brewery as she knew his fondness for ale.

He found himself divulging things to her that he never mentioned to anyone else, not even his family: doubts about his future as a woodworker, his ability to restore the shack he'd found in Raven's Back, his reluctance to accept his neighbors. Since spending time in Raven's Back, he'd realized there were reasons for the selection of that isolated area by its residents. After deciding to create a home for himself there, he'd initially attempted to meet and become friendly with a few of the households nearest his shack. He still remembered the couple who'd owned the donkey Malcolm, how they'd kept the animal restricted to a small enclosure and had resented the antics of Innis and Dalton. Still, in the end they'd allowed a certain amount of time for the boys to spend with the donkey to make amends so Innis envisioned most of the Raven's Back folk in such a way: tough and rough but with kind hearts. His naivete became clear to him, however, almost immediately when he began to introduce himself to his future neighbors.

He discovered that the majority of residents were older, having settled in Raven's Back many years ago and never left. Many of them were suspicious of any newcomers, resentful that their own insulation from the larger world of Glenraven was being infringed upon even to a small degree. Innis was friendly with the few fishermen he'd accompanied out to sea, but there were others who kept to their own counsel, leaving their homes early in the morning and returning late, coming and going almost like ghosts in their community. Charlie was one of these, though he proved more sociable than the average fisherman and inclined to a nosiness that was unusual in Raven's Back. The citizens of the area kept to themselves for the most part but nevertheless seemed to be acutely aware of any changes or unusual events in the vicinity.

Innis had introduced himself to all of his closest neighbors when he'd first decided to purchase and restore the shack he would call home because it had been awhile since he and his brother had spent time in Raven's Back as kids. His main purpose was to avoid disgruntlement at any noise or inconvenience his restoration of the building might cause. Despite these overtures, a few of the neighbors he'd met showed up at his shack during construction, watching the work with a disapproving manner though refraining from any verbal exchange. This bothered Innis, who attempted to placate them with apologies and explanations that fell on deaf ears. The neighbors seemed determined to be disgruntled and Innis eventually despaired of satisfying them. It provided a bothersome glimpse into the stubborn, dour nature of some of his neighbors, however, and made him wonder why anyone inclined toward privacy would infringe on their own neighbors in such a way.

Charlie occasionally enjoyed gossip and tried to recruit Innis as a co-conspirator in this pastime but was soon discouraged by the lack of response. This caused a certain resentment on his part and he became nosier about Innis's activities. It became more and more apparent to Innis that he would need to protect himself from the disappointing habits of his neighbors and he withdrew from most contact with them while maintaining a vigilance about their judgments.

When he was in Belfast visiting Fin, he found it amusing that the hustle and bustle of the city provided a certain anonymity his own small community in Raven's Back had failed to do. He understood why Fin preferred it, but he still missed the beautiful, natural surroundings of his home and was always relieved to return to the glen. For some time he'd been considering inviting Fin to visit him at home, but with the introduction of the aye-aye this had become impossible. After his dinner with Dalton, though, he'd begun thinking more carefully about sharing his secret housemate with Fin as well. It seemed to Innis that secrets ran in the family, what with his Aunt Bridget's Connla fixation, his brother Dalton's Kieran fixation and now his own aye-aye fixation.

Fin and Innis had progressed to a more intimate relationship, and when Innis could arrange time off work he would stay in Fin's small flat in Belfast where their lovemaking usually began awkwardly and tentatively then progressed to fierce abandon. Of course with the arrival of Yaeger these overnight visits had ceased and Innis worried that Fin must be puzzled by the change. He also missed spending the night with her and realized it wasn't fair to continue this way. One afternoon, as they headed back to The Forestry following their usual lunch in the park, he mustered courage and made a start at disclosure.

"How do you feel about secrets, Fin?"

She furrowed her brows and shrugged.

"I suppose it depends on the secret. What an odd question. Did you have something particular in mind?"

"Well, I've been thinking lately about a few of the secrets in my family and I guess everybody's got those but it seems to be a theme with us."

"Huh. I don't think my family's got so much of that, or maybe I just don't know the secrets."

She smiled and put a hand on Innis's arm to stop him as they walked.

"What's this really about, darlin'? Is there something you'd like to reveal?"

"Ah Fin, you know me too well already. OK, yeah, there is, but I just don't know how to even go about it. It's my secret."

"Of course, I figured that. Well?"

Embarrassed and slightly hurt by her curt reply, Innis balked.

"We'll leave it for another time. You don't wanna be late opening the shop back up after lunch. It's probably better if I figure some things out before I go divulging stuff."

"Has it anything to do with why you can't stay with me for a night or two any more?"

Meeting her gaze, Innis was surprised to find angry tears in her eyes. He'd expected her to be worried and possibly hurt but not angry.

"I'm so sorry, Fin. I should have never pretended nothing's going on. I know I've left you in the dark and given the wrong impression."

"Yes, you have. What am I to think? I know when I'm being avoided but it's worse that I don't even know why. Are you disappointed in me? Maybe I'm not sexy enough? Too sexy? It seems like soon after we began sleeping together your trips to Belfast tapered off. What am I to think?"

"Whoa, that's not it at all."

Innis couldn't believe he'd been so oblivious to Fin's perspective and realized with a start the inevitability of revealing the truth about Yaeger to her. Where to even begin?

"I'm terribly sorry, Fin. You're absolutely right, I mean not about the reason but that I've been giving you the short shrift. It may sound strange but it really doesn't have a thing to do with you."

"Of course not," Fin scoffed. "Should have known."

"God, I'm no good at this. What I mean is, I've been keeping a secret from you. Now I see it's got to be told."

Fin looked intently at Innis.

"A secret. OK, let's go back to the shop. No good talking about secrets right on the street."

"I've adopted a strange creature and he's living in my house," Innis burst out with the words before he could prevent them. "Well, actually, I found the creature and saved his life. So, you see, it hasn't been that I've been avoiding you. It's that I've been taking care of him and I haven't told anyone about him except my brother, and now you."

Fin couldn't help being amused as a small smile crept onto her face.

"What sort of creature is it, Innis? And why the big secret?"

"It's a long story and I don't want to make you late opening the shop back up."

"The shop can wait. That's one of the lovely things about being the owner. I don't have to keep strict hours if I don't want to. No, this is more important. I can see you've been keeping this secret for too long already, so spill. Maybe we should go back to the park and sit."

"Great idea. I'll feel a lot more comfortable there."

They returned to the same park bench they'd recently left and the story of the aye-aye spilled from Innis in a torrent while Fin sat quietly, clutching the empty brown bag which had held her lunch. The tale of Yaeger struck her as almost fable-like yet she believed every word. She'd never seen Innis this animated as he warmed to his story, expounding on all the details he'd learned about aye-ayes as well as the odd but special bond he'd developed with the animal over the few weeks they'd been sharing a home. Fin's concern and anger over Innis's avoidance of her vanished, replaced by an intense warmth and fondness toward the kindness of this man who was revealing himself to be even more softhearted than she'd originally thought. What advice could she have for this dear fellow she increasingly adored? His life had clearly been upended by a strange, mystical event and she wanted to help him in any way she could. Feeling foolish for having been hurt and insulted by his lack of atten-tion, she turned full concentration back to Innis's aye-aye stories. She laughed at the image of him and Yaeger out in the woods at night encountering Charlie and at Innis's attempts at building a nest for the creature in his bedroom.

"Does he sleep with you as well?" Fin teased.

"Not yet, but he has sat in my lap once. You must think me insane."

"Yes, and delightfully so."

"What the hell should I do, though?"

"Well, you may not want to hear it but your brother's right. It can't stay a secret forever. Are there any of your neighbors you trust?"

Innis considered her question, weighing the little he knew from his limited exposure to the people he'd met in Raven's Back since moving there. There was an elderly woman who lived on her own in a small cottage fairly near his own. Hers was a ramshackle place, cluttered and rustic, fairly dusty and furnished with worn, dingy furniture that appeared to have been salvaged from a dump or thrift shop. When he'd stopped to introduce himself shortly after moving to Raven's Back, she'd been one of the few neighbors to wel-come him into her home with friendliness and a rough sort of hospi-tality. Despite the disheveled appearance of her cottage, there had been a fire burning in the fireplace and something about the abode exuded a warm, cozy feeling.

The woman, whose name was Sheena, was dressed for the cold with a heavy fisherman's sweater, a plaid wool scarf, a buckskin jacket and a pair of men's trousers several sizes too large for her. A ruddy round face, open-fingered gloves, piercing green eyes and long, wild, mostly gray hair created the image of a pioneer woman. Her sturdy build and generous bosom were partially concealed by her clothing but Innis found her brusque demeanor and general earthiness rather appealing.

She'd offered him an ale and a bit of shepherd's pie, though it had been only mid-morning, but he'd politely declined since she was only one of many stops he intended to make while introducing himself to all of his neighbors. Later, he'd wished he'd taken the time to talk to her, seeing as none of the other residents had appeared as generous or welcoming. Now he thought of her, though he could hardly claim to trust her since he'd only met her the once. Trusting his instincts was one thing when it came to everyday matters, but quite another when it came to Yaeger.

"Nah, not really," he answered Fin. "I barely know them, and they're not a friendly or helpful lot, I can already tell. In fact, that's one of the problems. I'm keeping Yaeger secret mainly because he wouldn't be accepted and might be feared. That's the outcome I'm trying to avoid."

Fin nodded. The situation appeared complicated, not easily resolved.

"I'd offer to help you out on the occasional night," she offered, "so you could get some sleep, but it's just too far with the shop and all."

"Of course, absolutely true. I appreciate the offer. Dalton did the same, but he's got to get up early with the sheep. The only person who's somewhat nearby who I might ask to help is my Aunt Bridget, but what with her mental problems...wouldn't work. Besides, even if I get help from someone with taking Yaeger out at night, I'd still need to keep him secret and that can't last forever. I've looked for some place like a sanctuary I might take him, but the only ones I found were in the States, Africa or the Jersey Zoo. Too far to go."

"Hmm. Perhaps you could at least tell your parents, that way they could visit you and they're hardly going to freak out, right?"

"Well, they'll be puzzled but they'd probably accept it. Yaeger wouldn't come out of his nest when Dalton was there."

"I hate to say this, but you do realize that by keeping all this a big secret you risk more disaster should anyone accidentally see Yaeger somehow. If people knew what they were dealing with at least they wouldn't panic or make false assumptions."

"True. How would I let them know? I can hardly hold an aye-aye seminar explaining everything to everybody in Raven's Back."

"Why not? If it would help keep Yaeger safe--"

"And should I include the part about a harbinger of death?" Innis broke in. "That would be reassuring. Besides, you haven't met my neighbors. Most of them are unwelcoming and suspicious of strangers. They're probably superstitious too, which wouldn't incline them toward acceptance of an aye-aye."

"Still, wouldn't it be better to tell them about him rather than letting them stumble on the truth? When a secret's kept, others usually assume it's for a good reason."

Innis considered the idea of visiting all his neighbors to explain the aye-aye and scoffed at the thought. Most of them had barely been civil when he'd introduced himself. Keeping Yaeger a secret could seriously backfire though. Assuming even one neighbor saw the aye-aye or somehow found out, then began rumors or gossip among the community, disaster would ensue. Fin interrupted his train of thought.

"What about distributing a flyer to your neighbors with a picture of Yaeger and information about him. Perhaps it could mention your nocturnal expeditions but refrain from saying anything about the superstitions connect with aye-ayes. Are many of your neighbors likely to do much Internet research? If not, they'd never know about all that 'harbinger of death' nonsense."

"Not a bad idea." Innis looked at Fin with amazement. "It might work. See why I'm always coming to you for advice? And no, I doubt if many of my neighbors even own a computer. Reception's dreadful in those woods anyway. Fin, you're brilliant!"

He hugged her with the exuberant warmth she'd begun to cherish and she laughed, hugging him back.

"It's not really so unusual an idea. At least you wouldn't have to meet them all face-to-face which doesn't sound as if it went so well. Those who have questions or concerns can come see you.

Who knows, perhaps someone will be interested in meeting Yaeger. I for one would love to."

The words popped out of her mouth before she thought and she inwardly cringed at the presumption of inviting herself to Innis's cabin. He beamed at her, though, and suddenly kissed her, almost toppling both of them from the park bench. Fin, thrilled and swept away in the moment, grabbed Innis's curly hair and drew him closer, returning his kiss with a passion she could barely control and dropping the empty lunch bag she'd been holding. She shook her hair when they finally broke apart and grinned at Innis.

"I suppose that would be a 'yes'?"

"A hundred times yes." Innis held her hands as his smiling eyes met hers. "You're the first person I'd love to have meet Yaeger. I tried with Dalt but maybe Yaeger will be friendlier with you. At any rate, I want you to come up to Raven's Back and visit us. I should have invited you much earlier, but with this secret aye-aye and all...sorry it's taken me so long. I've really no excuse except I guess I'm just a backward farm boy. Hope you'll come see us as soon as you'd like. Actually, first I'd better tell my parents about Yaeger, otherwise Dalton would kill me. You should have a chance to meet Yaeger before they do though, especially since you've asked."

They returned to the shop, chatting excitedly about plans for Fin's visit and the distribution of flyers about Yaeger to the residents of Raven's Back. Before Innis returned home, Fin had a final question for him.

"Innis, I know you're not keen to disclose information about the purple wood you used for those items you brought in here, but I can't help wishing there could be more carving done with it. I've kept the bowl at my place, as you know, and haven't allowed anyone to see it as I promised. Another secret we share. Anyway, I've been wondering if you've ever made anything else with that marvelous wood. Sometimes I'll just hold that bowl and I swear there's a warmth comes from it."

"All the items are like that. I haven't made anything else because I've been too busy with my apprenticeship, building my home and, of course, the aye-aye. I might as well tell you, since we're sharing secrets, that the wood comes from a grove of trees in Raven's Back. I stumbled on it one time when I was exploring the area. It's far beyond the forest that surrounds Raven's Back and not that easy to find. Guess no one else has ever ventured out there or, if they have, they didn't care about a bunch of strange trees. The weirdest thing is Yaeger's reaction to it. I took him out there one time because I thought he might like it, but he didn't. He wanted to get away from it, freaked out a little bit, so I never tried it again. In fact, I've stayed away from it myself after that. Who knows, maybe there's something wrong with it that he senses and I don't."

"Hmm, interesting. There's nothing strange about the bowl I have except its warmth and I like that. Gives a wonderfully comforting feeling."

"I know, I'm the same way with it."

"It could be quite the sensation if you carved from it and sold the items. I know you're not interested in that, I'm just saying..."

"Something to consider, but no. It would be a sensation all right, and next thing you know the entire purple grove has been cut down for profit. Besides, if there is anything mysterious about it, better left alone."

"Does Yaeger react to the purple wood items you kept, the three legged stool and the jewelry box?"

"He avoids them. Once he smelled the legs of the stool and had the same response he did at the grove. He quickly left it, acted annoyed and maybe spooked. I've put those items away anyway so when I have visitors no one will see them and ask questions. God, I never thought about it but I'm becoming a hoarder of secrets. Yikes."

Fin laughed.

"I suppose you are. There's something to be done about that though. You could start by giving one of them away."

"I know. The aye-aye."

"Mm hm." Fin was puzzled. "I sense some reluctance in you about that. It doesn't seem like it has anything to do with other people knowing about Yaeger. Am I imagining that?"

Innis marveled at Fin's insight, reluctant to admit she knew him better than he wanted her to.

"No, I suppose you're not imagining it. You're right, as usual. How is it you've figured me out this quickly? Utterly transparent, am I?"

"Give me some credit. No, you're not transparent at all, Innis Kilbride. Far from. I've studied you over this period of time, that's all. And I believe you have a special bond you've found with Yaeger.

Once you let others in, perhaps it won't be as special you're thinking."

Innis was silent. He didn't want to think her words were true though he knew they were. Why was he resistant to growing closer to Fin yet anxious to have an intense relationship with the aye-aye? In the past, when he'd been unable to understand his motivations, he'd resisted too much self examination, ignoring reasons and concentrating on actions. Was there something warning him about sharing Yaeger with the world? Could an intuition he didn't even completely comprehend be at work? What if it was, and by ignoring it he might cause harm to Yaeger?

"Do you believe in premonitions?" he suddenly asked Fin.

She hesitated, frustrated by his resistance to reason.

"Yes, I suppose I do. I've always been more practical minded, though, and sometimes intuition is little more than knowledge from experience. Don't talk yourself into something, Innis. What's considered intuition can be misinterpreted too, you know."

"I'll sleep on it and let you know."

"If you need my help with the flyers about Yaeger please ask for it. I'd be glad to assist. I have some experience doing that sort of thing for the shop. And I absolutely want to meet Yaeger. You won't back down on that, will you?"

"You're not letting me off the hook here, are you?"

Fin wanted to shake him until his teeth rattled. How hard could it be for him to see that she badly wanted to be part of his life? Stifling her frustration, she was determined to break through his stonewalling.

"Well, after all, it isn't every day one gets to meet an aye-aye. Is it a date?"

Innis nodded.

"Yeah, of course. You let me know when. Just give me a couple of weeks to let my parents and the neighbors in on the secret. Do you think I should tell my Aunt Bridget as well? Really not sure what to do about her knowing. Could be tricky."

"You know your aunt far better than I do. Matter of fact, I wouldn't mind meeting her too when I'm up your way."

Innis shook his head.

"Nah, one bloody thing at a time. Don't be getting ahead of yourself, missy."

"Sorry," Fin laughed. "OK, I'll look forward to seeing

Yaeger. I think I've imparted enough advice for today and I'll leave it to you to figure out what to do regarding your aunt and the aye-aye."

Satisfied with even the vague agreement on a future visit, Fin hated to see Innis return to Raven's Back but kissed him goodbye with more passion than she'd planned. He returned her ardor then held her at arm's length, adopting a teasing, overly serious expression.

"You Belfast girls are maybe too forward for us mere boys from the northern glens. Not that I mind, darlin'. I might even like it."

She loved his teasing and tapped his face in a mock display of insult.

"On your way then, boy from the northern glens. I'll see you soon and no, I'm not letting you off the hook. Not very easily."

That night, after he'd taken Yaeger for their excursion to the woods, Innis thought long and hard about everything Fin had said. He valued her advice but something in him still resisted sharing Yaeger. As he watched the aye-aye digging into the tree branch they'd brought home, dipping its long middle finger rapidly into the hole it had gnawed to collect the grubs and larvae within, he smiled and sang the old traditional Irish song, "Eileen Aroon", he'd learned from his Aunt Bridget to Yaeger.

Chapter XII: Rumors in the Kitchen

Murphy's, the restaurant where Irene worked as a cook, was more of a local place than a tourist or trendy spot, though few tourists spent much time in Glenraven. Despite its scenic beauty and seaside locale, the town had never been developed into much of a destination and offered few amenities or attractions for visitors. It was a working fishing village for the most part and its citizens were wary of outsiders. The occasional tour group, visiting the glens of the Antrim coast, might stop in Glenraven for a few hours, but they would seldom venture into Murphy's. The restaurant's owner, Nolan Murphy, started the place as a revenge move against his wife Shannon, who'd run off ages ago after years of rows between the couple about her cooking. It had always angered the headstrong Shannon that her husband enjoyed cooking much more than she did and excelled at food preparation far beyond his wife's very limited abilities. It wasn't right for a man to be the cook in a household, Shannon firmly believed, and she mightily resented Nolan's renowned skills. It made her look bad in the eyes of others, she felt, and her husband's constant jokes about her substandard culinary talent made matters worse.

There were fights of epic proportions with Shannon occasionally dumping meals Nolan had prepared for them out into the street and Nolan vowing to open his own restaurant in order to get a decent meal. Finally, Shannon stormed out, leaving town for parts unknown, never to be heard from again. Shortly after her departure, Nolan bought an old deserted fishing equipment space near the water, not far from Glenraven's main street, and turned it into Murphy's, a basic, unadorned eatery where seafood, stews and local brews were served to the working citizens of Glenraven in an often boisterous but family oriented atmosphere.

Those sitting in broad wooden booths by the windows were treated to the sight of fishing boats heading out into choppy waters early in the morning when breakfast was served, but it was hardly a panoramic view. The windows of Murphy's, blasted by the sea air, were sometimes grimy and seldom kept spotlessly clean, an effort Nolan found to be unimportant. The locals, accustomed to the sea view, scarcely noticed it anyway and the tasty, hearty meals served in the restaurant more than made up for the slightly dingy interior of the place. The kitchen was always well stocked and maintained, and

Nolan's talent for cooking finally found full flower in a place of his own. His pride and satisfaction in operating Murphy's was clear and the locals, who'd mostly sided with him against Shannon during their domestic disputes, soon provided loyal patronage.

The success of Murphy's brought Nolan a measure of financial comfort he hadn't anticipated and he was able to hire badly needed extra help. The kitchen, always his priority, was especially time consuming but Nolan was protective of his realm and took a long time to select an assistant cook. Irene Kilbride, well-known by her friends and neighbors for her delicious stews, pasties and vegetable rolls, was near the top of his list, though she would only be willing to work part-time due to her family obligations. She'd been working in other Glenraven restaurants since she was a young girl but had taken a break to raise her two sons. Nolan, who didn't know her well, hesitated in selecting her mainly because she was female. The thought of once again clashing with a woman over the kitchen was unacceptable, to be avoided at all costs. He'd heard that Irene was, for the most part, even tempered and easygoing, unlike his fiery and unreasonable ex-wife, yet the specter of a battle over the traditional female terrain of a kitchen gave him pause.

He was aware that once, during one of their particularly vicious shouting matches, Shannon had informed him that Irene Kilbride was in agreement with her about the cooking issue. It surprised him, then, that Irene had expressed interest in working for him. Feeling obligated to at least consider her application for the job as cook's assistant and part-time chef, he interviewed her in the small back office just off the restaurant's kitchen. It was on a Sunday, the one day of the week when Murphy's was closed, so the usual clatter of pans and food preparation wouldn't interrupt.

After a pleasant greeting, the two sat silent for an awkward moment. Nolan, unaccustomed to interviewing prospective employees, decided to cut to the chase. He was not a man given to diplomacy and figured the elephant in the room should be addressed sooner than later, possibly saving him time and effort.

"Look, Irene, I've heard what a good cook you are and even though I've never tasted your food I think I can believe the testimony of our neighbors. I don't have any doubts you would most likely be good for this job. My problem comes with the notion that you knew my wife and agreed with her ideas about a man in the kitchen. Well, obviously I can't live with that."

Irene's eyes widened but she resisted a knee-jerk response, weighing her words carefully.

"I've no objection at all to a man in the kitchen if you must know, Nolan. In fact, I find it a wonderful thing. The meals you prepare here at Murphy's are marvelous. You've probably seen me and my family eating here on occasion. My husband is a disaster in the kitchen, but I have to say there are times when I've wished he could help out a bit."

Nolan wondered if his wife had lied about Irene's support during the matrimonial disputes. Or was she lying now? There was no time for speculation.

"Well, I'm happy to hear that, Irene. I suppose my wife was building up a case for herself then when she told me you agreed with her about me taking her place in the kitchen."

Irene had seen this coming and paused to compose herself. She sometimes marveled at how delicate the male ego could be but nevertheless knew she must find a way to placate this potential employer. Luckily, the truth would do this time. It was simply a matter of couching it in the correct terms.

"Well, Shannon did talk to me a few times about the kitchen issue between the two of you. I've no way to know, of course, truth from fiction, but I could see she was genuinely upset by the situation. It isn't that I sided with her against you, Nolan, not at all. I was more of a sounding board and did more listening than talking. Honestly, it bothered me that she'd taken such pains to prevent you from doing something you love and have a talent for, but I wasn't about to tell the distraught woman that. I find the notion of a woman's place being in the kitchen, and a man's place not, simply ridiculous. I hate that idea. So no, I didn't agree with her about that, though I never told her as such. What I could understand, forgive me for saying so, was the humiliation she felt when you and others made fun of her own cooking efforts. That was cruel and certainly didn't serve your purpose. I believe, frankly, it probably hurt your cause. Did you ever try teaching her what you know about food preparation?"

Nolan, astonished at the cheek of having the problem tossed back onto him, bristled.

"Sounds to me like you're still siding with her now. So this was all my fault, was it?"

"Of course not. I'm only saying perhaps a little sharing and compromise might have worked for you both. It's really none of my concern. I only spoke to Shannon because she sought me out. And I did tell her that I've always found a man who can cook to be my idea of a real man as well as a wonderful asset. She disagreed, of course, but there you have it. Now, should I polish up on my Ulster fry or get my coat and go?"

Irene was hired and Nolan found himself increasingly relying on her presence in the restaurant and expertise in the kitchen. Since his specialty was preparing seafood and hers tended toward stews and breakfast meals, they balanced one another perfectly with each teaching the other more about the areas of cooking in which they lacked. Nolan knew he liked Irene after that first meeting and grew even fonder of her when she served him a breakfast of porridge with a pinch of salt and a dash of Bushmills whiskey before one of their early morning meetings to review her job duties and hours. He'd asked others in Glenraven about her and was satisfied with the almost universal approval rating she received.

The situation with her mad sister Bridget was already known to him, but instead of taking the view of many who were nervous and concerned about this family skeleton, Nolan decided it spoke to Irene's credit that she'd cared for and protected her sister. Abbot, who, like his son Dalton, rarely ventured into town, was more of a mystery though his reputation as a well respected and hard working farmer held no worries.

Occasionally the Kilbride family would dine at Murphy's on nights or mornings when Irene wasn't working, and Nolan was impressed by the two boys' respectful behavior though it was clear that Innis could be a bit of a handful. The restaurant had always specialized in seafood so Nolan maintained a good working relationship with the fishermen in the area who provided fresh salmon, haddock, mussels and shellfish to Murphy's. Irene made an excellent seafood chowder along with her beef or mutton stews and outstanding vegetable rolls with peppery minced beef, fresh leeks, carrots and onion. Her Ulster fry breakfasts were immediately popular with Murphy's customers and there was the added advantage of obtaining fresh vegetables from the Kilbrides' farm at a discount.

Irene had a maternal way about her, but as Nolan continued working with her he noticed a hidden ambitious side to her nature and began to extend her hours at the restaurant, especially as her children grew older and needed her less. She responded with enthusiasm and Nolan realized she wasn't entirely the housewife and mother content to stay at home which he had initially pictured her to be. She had no problem supervising the other, mostly young, employees in Murphy's and eventually Nolan came to rely on her to the extent that he eased off some of his own hours spent working at the restaurant. Over time, the defensive posture he'd adopted when it came to enjoying being in a kitchen, so ingrained in him during his battles with Shannon, fell away and he realized he had nothing to prove to Irene. She valued and appreciated his cooking skills and he learned much from her as well.

Rumors began to circulate among the staff of Murphy's regarding the nature of the relationship between Nolan and Irene. The laughter and teasing that was often present when both of them were in the kitchen working on a new dish or during particularly busy times fueled the gossip, along with the marked change in Nolan's temperament. He'd been blustery and a bit too bossy when he'd first opened Murphy's, intent on having every little thing done his way, rarely satisfied, not only with the efforts of the employees but with his own as well. Even when the success of the restaurant became clear, he persisted in pushing for more, driving himself and everyone else relentlessly to the point where it effected employee morale. As Irene spent more time working as his assistant, however, he relaxed and enjoyed his work more, his insecurities finally being laid to rest.

The employees naturally drifted toward Irene for advice and questions as she always seemed to have time and patience for them. Nolan's happier disposition, obviously brought about by Irene's presence, could be due to more than just professional confidence and ease. Speculation swirled that the two cooks had formed a more than just professional alliance and this explained Nolan's kinder, more relaxed and pleasant attitude. When Murphy's had first opened, fresh on the heels of the break-up with Shannon, Nolan had indulged in an excess of drinking, though he was never drunk on the job. Always a gregarious, life-of-the-party type of man, he couldn't have been more of a contrast with Irene's taciturn husband Abbot.

Irene herself appeared to blossom at Murphy's, becoming lighter hearted, less critical of herself and almost playful in response to Nolan's constant teasing. While Nolan's anger slowly evaporated so did Irene's melancholy and the two shared a common meeting ground of fun and affection for each other along with their love of cooking.

There were those in Glenraven who held a suspicious attitude toward the Kilbride family, mainly due to Bridget's condition but also because of their lack of sociability. The town was small enough to make it noticeable when community functions were avoided by individuals and families, and the Kilbrides tended to keep to themselves for the most part, concentrating on their farm and their own affairs. When Nolan had announced the hiring of Irene as his assistant cook and manager he'd received a visit from an irate customer, the mother of one of the fishermen who'd perished along with Gage in the boating accident. It was her belief that something about Bridget had doomed the men on the fishing boat, bringing about the freak squall in some sort of retribution for evil deeds. Bridget's avoidance and snubbing of the widows and families of the dead fishermen only reinforced the resentment and distrust many of them already felt toward her.

This particular woman, enraged at the thought of Irene Kilbride's insane sister having any connection with Murphy's, confronted Nolan one morning in the restaurant. A regular customer, she often took her breakfast alone, avoiding the windows that looked out onto the sea. Before Nolan could even offer his usual morning greeting as she entered the restaurant heading for her usual spot, she turned to him, stabbing a finger toward his surprised face.

"Shame on you, Nolan Murphy!" she shouted, causing a few of the customers to glance her way. "I'll not be eating any food prepared by Irene Kilbride nor patronizing this place ever again. How could you take on that woman, knowing her family's history? I'm telling you, there'll be dire consequences. Wouldn't be surprised if she poisoned the food or maybe hexed your patrons in some way. It'll be on you if she does. I've loved eating here, but no more."

Startled at the outburst, Nolan froze in place as the woman brushed past him, slamming out the front door before he could react. He quickly turned and rushed after her, catching her marching along the sidewalk toward a nearby pub. His pleas and apologies fell on deaf ears as she angrily proclaimed her intention of warning her friends and neighbors away from Murphy's then continued on her way. Nolan, returning to the restaurant to find the morning diners enjoying their breakfast as though nothing had happened, dismissed the tirade from his mind. He'd once been considered somewhat of an outsider himself and knew he and Shannon had been the subject of much gossip so he set little store in the opinions of others.

As he grew to know Irene, it touched him that she and her family were shunned by some of their neighbors yet managed to carry on in a civil and even pleasant way, ignoring the rude treatment and speculation. His fondness for his assistant cook crossed the threshold into something close to love at some indefinable point and although he kept his feelings to himself there were occasional telltale signs his employees and patrons were bound to notice.

Nolan, who'd never been a particularly affectionate man with Shannon, would touch Irene in a friendly manner, a hand on her shoulder or arm, a warm hug for a job well done, a light guiding hand on her lower back when he held a door for her. He was oblivious to the fact that others noticed these gestures and, in the usually non-physical Nolan, interpreted them as something more than friendship. Abiding by the rules against intimate involvement between employer and employee, he was careful to hide his growing affection for Irene but it nevertheless continued and increased, making it difficult at times for him to refrain from expressing it to her. The fact that he was fairly certain his feelings were not reciprocated prevented him from a confession. Irene laughed at his jokes and teasing, enjoyed his company, taught him new recipes and proved to be an ideal, dependable and popular employee and business partner, but she clearly loved her husband.

Sometimes Nolan wondered what she saw in the rather somber, stoical Abbot who seldom spoke and dressed like the farmer that he was. Yet when the Kilbride family ate at Murphy's, Nolan couldn't help noticing the unspoken affection between Irene and Abbot. The way both of them watched their two boys with pride and indulgence, the comfortable manner in which Abbot always helped Irene off with her coat and pulled out her chair, the conspiratorial way in which they occasionally leaned their heads toward each other to whisper something cut at Nolan's heart like a knife. He knew there was no future for him and Irene except as co-workers and eventually accepted this fate. Unfortunately, gossip had already begun about the two of them and Nolan sensed it, trying to ignore it, hoping it would die down without any fuel to fan the flames. He didn't figure on the superstitions and avoidance toward the Kilbride family as a component in the scenario, however, nor that, because of it, the gossip and rumors would turn not against him but against Irene.

A couple of the waiters and waitresses at Murphy's had heard a strange story from Charlie Halloran, who occasionally ate dinner in the restaurant. He claimed to have caught Innis Kilbride lurking about in the woods of Raven's Back late one night, trailing a long length of rope and hiding something in his coat. There had been a quick, awkward exchange of words, he related, but Innis had obviously been in a hurry and determined to avoid Charlie. Later, when Charlie attempted to get clarification about the encounter, he'd once again been met with evasion and nervousness. Innis clearly was hiding something and Charlie was determined to discover the secret.

After that he'd stayed up late a few nights despite the havoc it played with his schedule, watching for Innis to appear in the woods but the bloke had probably decided to try a different path and couldn't be spotted. Not giving up, Charlie expanded his vigil, wandering into the woods himself in search of any sight or sound that might illuminate Innis's location. Following several futile trips in the dark he'd given up, though he refrained from implying as much to the servers at Murphy's who were keen for a good story, a juicy morsel of gossip. Charlie decided to give them one.

He spoke of seeing Innis far out in the woods, wrapping the long rope around a tree branch and using it to climb up into the tree where he settled among the leaves, partially obscured from sight. Due to his distance from the tree, the surrounding darkness and the leafy cover, Charlie couldn't be precise about what he saw next. He told his rapt audience that Innis had pulled a small figurine from inside his coat, a totem of some sort, and begun chanting to it. Disturbed by the strange incantations, Charlie had retreated and ceased his investigation, too upset by the implications of this bizarre behavior to put himself in harm's way.

Since that time, he advised the waiter and waitress who stood by his table listening intently, he'd been in a quandary as to his best course of action. It appeared to him that Innis Kilbride may have followed his Aunt Bridget into madness, but was it Charlie's responsibility to take action? Did the Kilbrides know what was going on with their eldest son? Was Innis a danger to himself or his neighbors? So many thorny questions to agonize over, and what's to be done?

Charlie's story spread quickly through the restaurant, passed along by employees and customers while morphing gradually until Nolan finally heard through one of his seafood suppliers that Innis Kilbride was suspected of devil worship. The tale had been carefully kept from Irene, of course, but by the time it reached Nolan there was a substantial rumor mill at work. In the small, hard working fishing village of Glenraven, there had already been some uneasiness toward Innis due to his artistic inclinations. The village was largely composed of fishermen, farmers and merchants so creative endeavors, while somewhat appreciated by the smattering of crafts people in the town, were suspect, viewed as play and not as a proper means of making a living. Innis's skill as a woodworker was impressive, more acceptable, yet still he presented the vague sense of an outsider with his numerous visits to Belfast, his wild, curly hair which never seemed to be properly brushed or kept clean and his habit of visiting the shoreline in a solitary way early in the morning as his mad Aunt Bridget had frequently done. He was pleasant enough, charming and often full of fun and mischief, well-liked by his neighbors, but somehow the idea of him secretly being a devil worshiper or indulging in odd, secret practices in the woods at night could be readily accepted.

When the gossip about Innis landed with Nolan Murphy, he immediately dismissed it, familiar with the ways in which such tales spread through small communities like Glenraven. He'd heard a few of the far-fetched rumors about himself and Shannon and although initially angered by them had eventually learned to ignore them. Now he gave little credence to the idea of Innis's devil worship but, as usual, was unable to determine how such gossip had originated. The thing that bothered him most was the thought of Irene somehow hearing the bizarre tale or being ostracized due to the belief in such rumors. He knew he must tell her. He'd already noticed suspicious glances at her from other restaurant staff and delayed only briefly before asking her to meet with him one evening after her shift.

Irene, anxious to get home and tired from her busy shift, settled restlessly across from Nolan in the small office where she'd had her job interview.

"What's this about, then? Nothing too serious, I hope."

"No, not exactly serious, just...."

It was unlike Nolan to hesitate or stammer yet he seemed uncertain of how to proceed.

"Oh, out with it, Nolan. It's been a long evening, if you don't mind."

"I know, sorry. Well, there's nothing for it but to spit it out...there's been some talk about Innis going around and I just thought you should know about it."

Irene frowned then sighed in a world-weary manner.

"Always talk. OK, what is it this time?"

"It's been said that he's doing strange things out in the woods in Raven's Back at night. Including devil worship."

Irene's eyes flashed with anger.

"Ridiculous! Who's saying such nonsense?"

"Not one particular person I know of, it's just general gossip, you know, passed around. Look, I don't put any store in it and neither should you. I thought you should know before you hear it yourself, that's all."

"That's all, huh? Of course I don't put any store in such utter shite, except when you're a Kilbride stories like that are especially galling. And hurtful. I get so sick of people sometimes, Nolan. They never bloody stop."

Irene pushed her chair back with vehemence and rose to begin pacing around the small space. Waves of fury seemed to be coming off of her and Nolan remained silent, hesitant to disturb her tirade.

"It must have been neighbors of his, started such malarkey," she suddenly remarked, "that's all I can think of. I didn't want him moving out there to Raven's Back in the first place. The folks out there are full of superstition, most of them huddled out there like hermits. Oh, how did this happen? I always wanted the wide world for my boy--"

She broke off in a sudden sob, collapsing back into the chair while Nolan stared at her in surprise. He'd never seen Irene cry but now the tears and sobs poured from her with an intensity that made him rush around the desk to comfort her. He gently put an arm around her but she brushed it off, wiping her face with the sleeves of her coat and shaking off the surge of emotion like a wet dog. A look of defiance now filled her eyes and she nodded curtly to Nolan.

"Never mind, Nolan. I'm all right now, don't worry about me. I'll get this sorted soon enough and I appreciate your honesty. This sort of thing has happened to my family too many times, is all. Didn't mean to break down like that, guess I couldn't help it."

Nolan wanted to put his arms around Irene to comfort her but sensed she preferred to be left alone as she still practically bristled with anger. She abruptly stood and looked intensely into Nolan's eyes.

"I've gotta get home. I'd really appreciate it if you'd tell anyone who mentions this nonsense about Innis to you again that it's pure rot and ridiculousness. I know it's not my place telling you what to do, Nolan, but I can't have this stuff circulating about my family again. It's been painful enough and hard enough already and I don't know how much more of it I can stand..."

Her voice broke and she fumbled for a handkerchief in her purse. Nolan rose from his chair and went to her, this time putting one arm gently around her shoulders. She leaned against him and cried quietly for a short while and he felt the inappropriate urge to kiss her but instead stood patiently by until her crying ceased. Blowing her nose loudly, she shoved the handkerchief into her coat pocket and patted Nolan's hand.

"Thanks, boss." She offered him a teary smile. "You're a good man. Sometimes I think there's a real shortage of good people on this earth, I truly do."

"Not to worry, Irene. Naturally, I'm gonna let whoever comes to me with these foolish rumors know they're nothing but malarkey. Actually, I already have. Believe me, there's few who'd buy such a tale in the first place. People know your son and wouldn't give such a story any credence, you can be sure."

Irene adopted a wry expression.

"Only takes one or two though, doesn't it? I'm going to talk to Innis about it shortly. Maybe he'll know how this started or who started it. Anyway, thanks again, Nolan."

Nolan watched her leave then sat back down behind his desk. He shuffled a few of the papers he knew he should be reviewing but he couldn't concentrate. The image of Irene's tear streaked face intruded on everything he thought of doing and an old anger that hadn't surfaced since Shannon left rose up in him. Irene was the most appealing woman he'd ever met, strong and competent and kind, yet she found herself at the mercy of careless gossip from fools. Perhaps he should have obeyed his first instinct to move away from the confines of Glenraven after Shannon's departure and start his restaurant somewhere more worldly, more exciting. Unbeknownst to him, he shared such feelings with Irene but his cynical nature allowed that people would be the same anywhere, letting the petty stuff of life overrule their better natures. Locking the office and the restaurant, he headed home with a heavy heart.

Chapter XIII: Piercing the Facade

Innis's continuing research about aye-ayes, both on the Web and what little he could find in libraries, fed his concern about exposing Yaeger to the outside world. The practice in Madagascar of killing aye-ayes and hanging them from trees brought images of his beloved Yaeger coming to the same dreadful demise, and he had a couple of nightmares featuring such a scenario. He began thinking about the people he'd seen in Belfast, homeless beggars who were missing limbs or had unsightly scars on their faces, most of them avoided by passersby whose glances automatically darted away from the deformities. There had been a girl with a cleft lip in his secondary school class who'd been teased and tormented by some of her classmates, and though Innis was proud he'd never participated in such behavior neither had he ever taken her part or confronted the bullies. He remembered homely girls and boys from school who'd usually been considered undesirables and remained outsiders subject to name-calling and ostracism purely on the basis of their appearance.

Yaeger was yet another example of this phenomenon as far as Innis was concerned, and it struck him as ironic that the creature's ingenious physical attributes, such as the long middle finger used for obtaining food, would be perceived by humans as a threatening thing to be annihilated. Looks were merely a facade, he began to realize, even though he knew himself to be a victim of this type of thinking as well. Hadn't he been afraid to approach Yaeger on the beach at first, mainly because of his strange appearance? Didn't his attention usually wander to the prettiest girls he passed on the street or saw in films? It was in the law of nature for a pleasing countenance to attract others for mating purposes, he supposed, yet why should there be such a narrow standard of beauty?

Such thoughts made him even more resistant to the idea of distributing flyers about Yaeger to his neighbors. To him, the aye-aye was a winsome and delightful companion as he'd come to know his ways, but to someone else he was likely to incite fear or suspicion. Would anyone look past the weird eyes and black, bony fingers to comprehend the wonder and beauty of such an unusual creature? Certainly not the neighbors he'd briefly met. Then again, was he failing to give them the benefit of the doubt, making snap judgments based on his first impressions? He decided to make another attempt at contact with a few of them before proceeding with Fin's plan. Perhaps he could manage to persuade someone to his side in advance of exposing Yaeger to neighborly scrutiny.

Remembering Sheena's hospitality he chose to begin his campaign with her. She'd told him she'd been living in Raven's Back for over forty years, so he assumed she might hold some sway with her neighbors, and if she developed a good opinion of him she could prove a valuable ally in acceptance of Yaeger. On one of his days off he made his way to her cabin at mid-morning, the time of day when he'd originally visited, hoping to find her at home again. She opened the door almost immediately after his soft knock and the same open, friendly smile he remembered greeted him.

"Why, Innis! Thought I might never see you again. C'mon in, my boy. What brings ya?"

Innis returned her smile and stepped into the warmth of the cluttered cottage where a fire was once again burning. Sheena wore the same clothing from their previous meeting and exuded the same rough camaraderie he'd found so appealing. He felt at home in the shabby living room as Sheena settled him on the old worn sofa and bustled about in the nearby kitchen preparing tea. When the kettle was on she joined Innis on the sofa.

"We'll wait for the whistle," she nodded toward the kitchen, "and then you can bend my ear for a bit. Sorry, I haven't much to offer you since I wasn't expecting company and I'm due for a grocery shopping. The cupboard's bare, but I do have some soda bread and a bit of dulse if you like."

Before Innis could answer she returned to the kitchen and quickly brought back a large, chipped plate with an array of soda bread and dulse, the seaweed snack which had always been a favorite with Innis.

"How'd you know I'm partial to this stuff?" he grinned, taking both bread and dulse.

"You're a Northern Irelander, aren't ya? Anyway, it's all I've got, good thing you like it."

The kettle began to whistle and Sheena was soon back with two large, heavy mugs of steaming tea along with a pot of sugar and a small carton of milk.

"Want some Bushmills in your tea then? I'm having some, usually do."

Tea with whiskey wasn't usually his way to start the day, but he felt the need for it and was relieved to have Sheena pour a generous helping into both mugs. Sheena and Innis munched their food and drank their tea silently for a few minutes and Innis enjoyed the lack of obligation to speak that sometimes annoyed him in social situations. Sheena finished her bread and dulse quickly, wolfing the food down and wiping her mouth with the back of her hand then placing her hands around her mug to absorb its warmth. Her green eyes fixed on Innis with an almost predatory intensity.

"Well then, Innis, what brings ya?"

Innis instantly regretted not having prepared some sort of speech or presentation about the aye-aye, realizing he hadn't a clue as to how he should proceed. This woman seemed very no-nonsense to him, so he settled on a direct approach.

"First of all, I'm sorry I haven't come back to visit until now. After that first time I wasn't sure if I should be going about introducing myself to all my neighbors. Didn't appear that's the way things usually go around here."

"It's not."

Innis laughed a bit nervously.

"OK, yeah, I see that now. Anyway, you were pleasant to me so I thought I might talk to you about my housemate. I've got a strange creature living with me."

"Mph. Sounds like what I would have said when my late husband was still alive."

Innis laughed and felt the warmth of the tea and whiskey flood through him. Something about Sheena put him at ease and soon he was telling her the story of Yaeger, omitting the beliefs of the Madagascar people about an aye-aye's ominous significance. Sheena listened carefully, reaching for more bread and keeping her eyes fixed on Innis as though hearing an intriguing tale. When he'd finished, she rose from her chair silently and retrieved a bottle of the Bushmills whiskey, pouring it into their now empty tea mugs to a half full level. Innis was feeling quite a buzz, unaccustomed to liquor at such an early hour and hesitated, then bolted back the whiskey, astonished he'd divulged his secret to a relative stranger. Sheena appeared steady and uneffected by the whiskey except for a slight reddening of her ruddy cheeks. She stared at Innis for a moment and broke into a beaming smile.

"Sounds like you've got yourself a bit of a fairy tale, Innis. And seeing as this critter must be of a very few of its kind left in the world I see your need for secrecy. Believe me, some of the fools around here wouldn't get it. Got a picture of Yaeger?"

Thrilled by Sheena's reaction, Innis wished he'd thought to bring his phone with him, though he'd taken only a few photographs of Yaeger for fear a flash would bother the creature's eyes.

"No, sorry, I haven't any pictures with me. Maybe I could get one off the Internet to show you what a typical aye-aye looks like. Nobody except me has ever seen Yaeger since he arrived here. Thanks for believing me, Sheena, and for agreeing with me about keeping him secret. I don't know the people here like you do, so I'm interested to hear it might not be the best idea to expose Yaeger. You think he might come to harm?"

Sheena huffed dismissively.

"I pretty much know he would. Listen, I'm not friendly with most of my neighbors and they're not friendly with me, but I've been around 'em for awhile and my eyes and ears tell me they're more likely to shoot at something they don't recognize than try to learn about it. You keep Yaeger to yourself."

"But the night rambles in the woods, it's wearing me down..."

"I'll help you. Introduce me to the little fella and I'll take him out at night for you, that is if he'll let me. No reason for me to get up first thing in the morning and, as a matter of fact, I can't sleep much anyway. Maybe me and Yaeger can be night owls together."

Innis almost cried, uncertain if it was the whiskey, Sheena's kind offer or the release of the secret he'd been keeping for too long. He realized his first impression of Sheena's warmth and kindness had been accurate and wanted to hug her with gratitude despite her rough demeanor. She'd already risen from the couch and returned their mugs and the empty plate to the kitchen. Turning back to him, she folded her arms and seemed to be sizing him up.

"You're not at all what I thought you were when I first met you, Innis Kilbride. I knew you were Irene and Abbot's boy, a bit of a hellion and a good-looking fella on your own, but I had no idea there was a softhearted ma hiding in you. Seeing as you're trusting me with a secret I'm gonna trust you with one. When your Aunt Bridget moved into Gage's fishing shack after the boat wreck, there was a group of people here in Raven's Back who wanted to burn down the place, whether she was in it or not they didn't much care. I had to stop them at the point of a shotgun. Some of 'em still hold it against me."

Innis was glad he was still seated on the couch as he felt the blood drain from him and became light-headed. The revelation was astounding, far beyond even the cruelty of the writing of 'lunatic' on Bridget's shack. He was certain his mother knew nothing of this insidious threat to her sister and the knowledge of it suddenly colored every one of his Raven's Back neighbors in a darker shade.

"Who was up for it, Sheena?" Anger tinged Innis's voice. "I need to know, I need to be aware of my enemies."

"Now, now, clam down. You'll not be taking revenge, boy. Where'll that get ya?"

"Not revenge, simply knowledge. If there are people living around me who meant my aunt harm, I'd like to know who they are. I have a right."

"Sure you do and I'll tell ya. Keep in mind, this was a long time ago. Some of 'em have moved away since then and the ones that remain have accepted your aunt by now with her strange ways and all."

"Why did they want to burn the shack?"

"Mostly superstition I imagine. Truth told, there wasn't much logic to it as I remember, more like a mob mentality. I only told you because it agrees with what you've been thinking about Yaeger. They can't be expected to accept him and it might be dangerous to try for it."

"The curse of Raven's Back."

Sheena waved her hand dismissively.

"Nah, that's nonsense. More like the curse of people behaving like people. I never believed that curse nonsense and neither should you."

"I haven't until now. I'm just shocked, Sheena. Have any of them told you what they think of me, then? After all, I am Bridget's nephew."

"Very few of 'em talk to me much. I'm a strange old widow lady as far as they're concerned and after I turned my shotgun on 'em they pretty much left me alone."

Sheena chuckled and returned to sit beside Innis on the couch, ruffling his hair as though he was a small boy.

"Don't look so heartbroken, my lad. You'll get used to it. When you've lived to my age nothing surprises you."

"I just had no idea. Are you sure my aunt's safe now? I mean, you've never heard talk about all that since, right?"

"No, but like I said, they don't include me much, never have, figure I'm too old. They don't really include anyone much, keep to themselves mostly, I'm sure you've noticed. Who knows why they got so weird towards your aunt, they never discussed it with me. There's never any guarantees of safety for anyone in this life but no, I don't think they'd try it again. They're used to her now and she's not brought any harm or bad luck down on their heads. Now the aye-aye, that might be a different story."

Innis shook his head in bewilderment.

"It's like I had an instinct, Sheena, I swear. Something told me it would be a mistake to share Yaeger with them. A friend of mine suggested distributing flyers about him just to introduce him, but now I see that would be dangerous. They might even interpret it as a delayed curse due to Bridget and come back at her as well. Ah, fuck me. Pardon the language."

Sheena grunted and shoved Innis's shoulder.

"Off with it, don't you know better than to apologize to me for language? I've the tongue of a sailor, boy, but since I'm usually alone there's nobody to swear at but myself."

Innis smiled and nodded.

"Thanks, Sheena. For everything. Think I might take you up on your offer to help with Yaeger but first I've got to get some sort of plan ready for the future. I see what I'm up against now and it's gonna be more complicated than I thought. I hope we'll be friends, you and me. I need one in Raven's Back."

Sheena clapped him on the back.

"We already are, my boy. You let me know when you're ready to introduce me to your critter and I'll let you know if I hear any rumors or such from our neighbors about anything. Deal?"

They shook hands with Innis slightly taken aback at Sheena's strong grip. He suddenly wondered where she kept her shotgun, or if she still even had it, hoping that she did. Who knows what developments might await in Raven's Back. Returning to his shack, he checked on Yaeger, who was sleeping in the latest nest he'd made atop one of the kitchen cabinets, then sat down at the kitchen table. The whiskey buzz was still with him, though fading a bit, and his thoughts tumbled over the disturbing information he'd received from Sheena. He returned to his previous train of thought about the surface appearance of things and was once again struck by how deceiving they could often be.

He'd assumed the people surrounding him in Raven's Back were rugged individualists and slightly antisocial, yes, but never had he imagined they could band together to form a lynch mob against his aunt. Picturing Sheena with a large shotgun braced against her shoulder, holding back a crowd of shouting, torch carrying neighbors out of an old "Frankenstein" film, he had to smile at the absurdity of it all yet instantly turned sober at the realization of what it meant. None of his neighbors, with the exception of Sheena, could be trusted since he had no way to know which of them had been among the angry mob hellbent on destroying his aunt's home.

He began to wonder if civilization itself was but a thin veneer of control, merely a facade disguising a base and vicious human nature which could never really be obliterated. Piercing that facade, would one find wild, destructive forces within even the kindest and most measured of human beings? He didn't want to believe this, yet Sheena's revelation about their neighbors couldn't help but push him toward such a conclusion. The thing he knew for certain was that his instincts about protecting Yaeger from exposure to others had been right. Regardless of advice from his brother and Fin, he decided to somehow keep his aye-aye secret and now, with help from Sheena, it would be possible to extend his nocturnal schedule with Yaeger until he completed his apprenticeship. Would any of the neighbors notice Sheena's late night visits to his cabin? He dreaded the possibility of bringing any trouble to her doorstep but she'd volunteered for the task and seemed tough enough.

Innis slept badly that night after returning home from his hunting excursion with Yaeger and the aye-aye, sensing his house-mate's troubled demeanor, was restless as well. Instead of climbing to one of his usual spots up high, Yaeger made his way onto Innis's bed and when the human awoke early in the morning, after a disturbing nightmare, for the first time he found the aye-aye curled up on top of the covers beside him. The warmth of the small body comforted him and the sight of the long black fingers slightly gripping the quilt brought tears to his eyes. He drifted back to sleep, his nightmares held at bay by the presence of Yaeger.

Chapter XIV: Magic in the Morning

When Innis's alarm went off the following morning, Yaeger was gone from beside him, back up in the original nest atop the armoire, but Innis felt a lingering feeling of warmth and comfort as he prepared for his day. Although he'd gotten little sleep, as usual, he was refreshed and surprised to find the darkness under his eyes which had betrayed his insomnia to his boss magically removed. Throughout the day he returned to the memory of Yaeger curled up with him, recalling the earthy scent of the aye-aye and the bristly quality of the fur which Yaeger had allowed him to touch ever so lightly. The woodworking he accomplished under Oren's supervision that day was the best he'd ever done, and he reveled in the way the grain and warp of each piece of wood seemed to bend to his every whim, almost as if the wood was communicating with him. Knowing it was nonsense, he still couldn't help feeling that Yaeger had imparted some magic to him.

That evening, Innis opened the door of his shack on his return from work to find Yaeger waiting for him. It was out of the ordinary for the aye-aye to be sitting right by the door, but Innis gathered the harness and rope and picked up Yaeger, tucking him beneath his coat as usual. Darkness had not quite fallen so they made their way more quickly than usual with Innis keeping a sharp eye on his surroundings. Once they reached the far end of the woods where Yaeger was normally set free on the harness, Innis was surprised to feel the aye-aye gripping his shirt as though resisting removal. Innis looked around to make sure no one was nearby but the woods were silent and deserted. He bent his face down toward Yaeger who gazed back at him from inside the coat.

"What's with you, little one?" Innis spoke softly to the creature as though to a baby. "What are you afraid of, Yaeger? I'll let no harm come to you, don't you worry."

Again Innis attempted to remove the aye-aye from his coat to place him on the ground and again Yaeger clung to Innis's sweater, refusing to budge. Innis placed a hand inside his coat to touch Yaeger who was trembling. Wrapping the coat tighter around the creature, Innis felt a cold panic creeping over him. What if Yaeger was ill? Who could he turn to for help with a sick or injured aye-aye? He hadn't noticed anything physically amiss with Yaeger when he'd first picked him up and hadn't felt the aye-aye shivering beneath his coat until now. Yaeger's eyes looked normal except for a hint of fear that Innis had never previously observed.

Forcing himself to relax and become attuned to his surroundings, Innis felt the sense of someone nearby watching him. Was it only his imagination? He didn't think so, and this might explain why Yaeger was acting strangely. Leaving the area he pretended to be walking home then quickly ducked into a particularly dense area of brush and foliage. He waited almost breathlessly with the aye-aye still clinging to him beneath the coat, their hearts seeming to pound in rhythm with each other. After a few moments Innis heard the faintest sound of a twig snapping and became aware of someone walking nearby. Remaining frozen in place, he saw Charlie Halloran pass by only a few feet away, carrying what appeared to be a shotgun. Although he wore a heavy coat with its hood pulled over his head, Charlie was unmistakable and so was his purpose. He'd obviously been following Innis.

After Sheena's recent revelations, Innis now wondered if Charlie might have been a member of the mob clamoring to burn down Bridget's shack, though he doubted that Halloran had been a resident of Raven's Back that long ago. Even more disturbing was the thought that the man was intent on discovering more about Innis's nocturnal wanderings. Innis realized with relief that Yaeger had never been visible from beneath his coat, so at least Charlie hadn't glimpsed the aye-aye. He must have been puzzled by the image of Innis speaking to something hidden inside his coat, though, if he had actually witnessed it.

Glancing around the woods as he walked, Charlie proceeded past Innis's hiding place and was soon lost in the darkness of the woods. Innis and Yaeger remained in place motionless for a short while until Innis felt confident that Charlie was gone, then they returned to the spot where they'd previously been. Innis was relieved to find that Yaeger's trembling had ceased and quickly put him on the ground to begin his foraging.

"Good instincts, little fella," he whispered to Yaeger.

As he followed the aye-aye, collecting nest materials and food items as usual, Innis's mind was racing. The shotgun was especially disturbing and he wondered if perhaps this wasn't the first time he'd been followed by Charlie. Had the man already seen Yaeger on another occasion? Innis reassured himself that he'd always been cautious, but why would his neighbor be stalking him with a gun unless he'd seen the aye-aye? Simple curiosity would hardly warrant a shotgun.

When they got back to the shack, Innis was relieved to see Yaeger acting normal again as he made short work of the food they'd gathered and began to fashion a new nest, this time taking the nest materials to the top of the chest of drawers in the bedroom. Innis smiled, glad to know that Yaeger's fearful behavior had been only temporary and not due to some illness. He was also amused by the multiple aye-aye nests now resting atop almost every high surface in the cabin. His satisfaction was short-lived, however, since the sight of Charlie in the woods kept returning with all its ominous implications. Would it be better to simply confront him or ignore the bothersome and unsettling behavior?

Innis spent yet another restless night and awoke too early. This time Yaeger was sleeping in his new nest and Innis dressed quietly, slipping from the cabin just before daybreak. He felt the need to be close to the sea and walked briskly in the chill morning air. Reaching the shoreline in record time, grateful he hadn't encountered any fishermen on the way, especially Charlie, he was startled to spot his Aunt Bridget standing near the water's edge and gazing out to sea as she used to do in the early days of her madness. Innis halted and watched her for a few minutes, loathe to interrupt her reverie. It had been some time since he'd come to the beach this early in the morning and he wondered if Bridget had resumed her solitary vigil. In the distance a few fishing boats were heading out to the open sea and for a moment he longed to be in one of them.

Bridget, sensing his presence, slowly turned to face him, her windblown black hair, now streaked with silver, partially covering her face. The intense dark eyes, so like Innis's own, caught his gaze and Bridget smiled warmly at him, holding out both of her hands to invite him forward. He went to her, taking her cold hands, examining the beautiful face he'd not seen this closely for quite awhile. Although Bridget's face was now lined and somewhat worn, the whisper of youth had somehow remained and she appeared much younger than her age. Turning back to the sea, she put one arm around Innis's waist and the two stood silently, their bodies touching to provide some warmth against the wind and cold. The worries which had been plaguing Innis since last night drifted away just as they had when Yaeger was curled up next to him. He felt connected to his aunt in an ancient, inexplicable way as though they both were one with the sea.

Bridget's arm dropped away from Innis and she turned to him, her pale face now reddened by the sea air and wind. With that disconcertingly direct gaze that Innis had grown accustomed to, she stared into his eyes for a moment then nodded in acknowledgment.

"I see that something has bewitched you, Innis."

Smiling gently, she tangled her fingers into Innis's long, curly hair and pulled his face closer to hers, whispering in an intimate way so that her words could barely be discerned above the crashing of the waves.

"Has Connla sent an emissary from his kingdom?"

Innis pulled away from her, startled and confused. How could she possibly be aware of the existence of Yaeger? Bridget, oblivious to her nephew's abrupt reaction, casually looked back out to sea. She began speaking quietly to herself, first in Celtic then in an unknown language Innis could not decipher. The volume of her voice gradually rose until she was shouting into the wind, raising both hands to the sky with her eyes closed tightly and her head flung back, abandoning herself to the elements surrounding her and the strange incantations issuing from her.

Innis, frightened yet spellbound, stared at her with mounting concern as her entire body began to shake and sway. He moved to put a hand out and steady her then decided she was better off left alone. Who knew what type of spell she was under. He calmed his nerves and was relieved when the shouted, indecipherable words reached a crescendo then abruptly ceased. Bridget's hands slowly fell back down to her sides and she opened her eyes, a look of ecstatic joy spreading across her face. She took a few steps toward the waterline with Innis following closely behind, ready to prevent her from actually entering the waves. Stopping just as her boots touched the water, Bridget snapped her focus sharply in Innis's direction and she clutched the arm of his coat in a fierce grip. There was a dark fire in her eyes as she hissed at him.

"You must never deny the dictates of Connla! Acknowledge him, learn his ways. He's allowed you to become a part of his kingdom for a reason and you must learn what it is."

Speechless, Innis stared at his aunt, feeling disoriented by the bizarre situation and almost faint from the combination of surprise, cold sea air and wind and the ceaseless roaring of the waves. The fire in Bridget's eyes gradually faded, replaced by a sweet warmth which Innis had never seen from her in the past. Placing a cold hand on Innis's cheek, she clucked to him as though comforting a baby.

"There, there, macushla, don't look so upset my sweet boy. It's going to be all right and I'll help you make sense of it all. Perhaps you didn't completely believe me before when I told you of Connla and his kingdom. I know Irene didn't, not really, though she played along. But you'll believe me now when I explain things to you in more detail. First, you must tell me your secrets and surely we'll have a meeting of the minds. Come back home with me and we'll talk."

"Ah, no, Auntie. I can't right now. I've got work to attend to today. I'm sorry, but what about later this afternoon when I'm finished? Will that be OK for you?"

With a sad smile Bridget turned back toward the water, waving her hand and arm across the broad sweep of the sea.

"Look at this glorious vista, Innis. Is not the sea surely the most magnificent of God's amazing creations? And Connla is master of a portion of it. Whatever he puts before us should never be ignored. How many mornings have you come to this spot recently, so early and alone? Very few, I'd wager. And as for me? This is my first visit in many months. That you and I should be here now, at the same moment, for the same reason of easing our torments with the comfort of the sea? Surely it's destiny, a preordained fate we can scarce deny. That I should know, with a very clear image and undeniable truth, that there is a presence in your life for which you have no preparation, no answer? No, my boy, we are in the midst of a revelation here, at the mercy of magic. And magic comes in the morning. We must talk now and some of your questions may be answered, your fears put to rest. Come, Innis, walk with me."

She gently hooked her arm into Innis's and they silently headed away from the shoreline, back to Raven's Back where Bridget's shack and, perhaps, the resolution to the mystery of Yaeger, awaited.

Chapter XV: A Conspiracy of Three

Trudging back to Raven's Back from the beach, Bridget remained silent, as did Innis out of deference to his aunt, although his mind was racing. Against his better judgment he realized it was inevitable that the existence of the aye-aye should be revealed to Bridget regardless of the possible consequences. Her reaction would be unpredictable but Innis at least was certain she would bring no harm to Yaeger. Seeing him as an emissary from Connla's watery kingdom, and thus an additional link to Gage, she might even protect him. It was problematic dealing with his aunt's fluctuating moods and it gave him pause considering the extent to which she might carry out her belief in Yaeger's connection to the sea; still, she was bound to have insights that Fin, Dalton and Sheena lacked. Innis knew it was pointless attempting to develop a strategy for introducing Bridget to the existence of the aye-aye and watched her face as he struggled to keep up with her long, rapid strides. Gazing straight ahead, she had a slight smile and occasionally nodded as though hearing some inner voice speaking to her. Innis wondered what the purpose of her early morning visit to the sea might have been, but refrained from asking.

When they arrived at Bridget's shack, she glanced suspiciously around before unlocking the front door then unceremoniously pushed her nephew in, slamming the door behind them. Despite Irene's semi-weekly visits and continual efforts to keep the place in some semblance of order and cleanliness, Bridget's shack remained a mess, though much improved from its earlier days. The kitchen was a clutter of unwashed dishes, partially eaten loaves of bread and an open jar which exuded the smell of pickles. Her small living room, musty but somewhat clean, featured piles of yarn stacked on the couch along with books, newspapers and a stuffed toy sheep wearing a sweater with the word "Ireland" and a shamrock emblazoned on its front in green. The shack was chilly and dark, all of its curtains closed and with no fireplace to ward off the cold. A heavy wool blanket was draped haphazardly over the back of the couch and Innis wondered how his aunt stayed warm, though she was usually dressed in two or three layers of clothing which must help, he reasoned.

Bridget briskly strode around the shack, checking behind doors, into corners and even getting down on all fours to look under the couch then bustling into the bedroom where Innis could hear her walking around and moving a couple of things. She emerged with a look of satisfaction and removed her long, heavy coat, tossing it onto the only chair in the living room. He knew, from past experience, not to expect a polite offer of refreshments or even an attempt at preliminary chitchat when visiting Bridget and, true to form, she settled herself on the sofa, pushing aside some of the yarn without requesting that Innis take a seat. Taking off his coat, he draped it on the back of the couch. He had learned to allow his aunt to begin conversation as she otherwise became distracted and went off on a tangent. She sat silently for a moment as though collecting her thoughts then looked earnestly at her nephew.

"So, Innis, to your bewitchment."

Playing to her assumptions, since he knew it was futile to do otherwise, he gathered his courage, suspecting he could be making a colossal mistake yet helpless in the face of Bridget's beliefs.

"Yes, well, there's no other way to put this, Auntie," he began reluctantly, then decided to rush forward. "A creature came out of the sea."

A sudden light of joy appeared in Bridget's eyes and her face broke into a radiant smile. It was almost worth all the weeks of struggle and secrecy with Yaeger to see her this happy, Innis thought. She clasped her hands in delight like a small girl, leaning forward with anticipation.

"Did it though! Oh, Innis, a creature from the sea, of course. Tell me all, dear boy."

Once again Innis relayed the discovery of the aye-aye, describing Yaeger in as much detail as he could manage while Bridget beamed, nodding eagerly and hanging on his every word. When he began to explain the nocturnal hunting excursions, Bridget held up a hand to halt him.

"No, Innis. He mustn't be held on a harness and rope. Yaeger must be free at all times."

"But Auntie, I do realize that would be the best way in an ideal situation, but if I let him free he might wander off and die or be killed by one of our neighbors. The climate is too cold for him here as well and he could get sick. He's used to more of a tropical weather, you know."

Bridget shook her head.

"You're speaking as if Yaeger is an ordinary creature, darlin', but he's not. He's magical, immune to the rules you've read about. He comes from the kingdom of Connla, not from Madagascar. How else would he be here? You needn't worry that he will become ill, he can't. He has come to you for a reason, though, you're right about that, and we must discover what it is."

Innis paused, wondering if he'd just committed a grave error in judgment. Of course Bridget was bound to interpret this strange event as some mystical connection with her imaginary underwater kingdom. Having spent time with Yaeger, he knew the creature to be real, had seen him exhibit fear and hunger, even a sense of humor. For Innis, the simple fact of an aye-aye, with all its odd ways and appearance, was magical enough but Bridget obviously wouldn't accept this. He hoped she wouldn't demand that Yaeger be brought to her since who knew what she might do with him. He didn't want to agree with his aunt's assessment of a magical creature yet didn't dare disagree for fear of incurring her wrath. Her statement about discovering the reason for Yaeger's appearance on the beach, however, was one with which he was in total agreement and had been pondering himself for some time.

"Yes, Auntie, I agree. We do need to determine the reason why Yaeger showed up here and I've been trying to do that for awhile. The only problem is, so far I haven't been able to. Your help would be appreciated, but I have to tell you I'm not sure how magical Yaeger really is. He just seems like a normal aye-aye to me, not that I've got any comparisons."

Bridget offered an impish smile.

"Tell me, Innis, has your aye-aye ever visited the purple woods?"

Innis almost gasped aloud.

"How do you know of that, Auntie? I thought only I knew. I thought I'd discovered it."

Bridget laughed with delight.

"Don't be giving yourself airs, boy. I've been acquainted with the purple forest since before you were born. I spent many an evening there after Gage was taken from me. It was those purple trees that first introduced me to magic. Don't worry, none of our neighbors have been there as far as I know. They're not much ones for wandering, for exploration, not like me and you."

"Yaeger's been there too and I have to tell you he didn't much like it. Once I tried putting him on one of the purple trees and he got all spooked, wanted to leave. I haven't tried it since."

Bridget's eyes narrowed and she sat for a few minutes as though deep in thought. Her fingers clutched and released the bottom of her sweater and her left foot tapped slowly against the threadbare rug. Her mouth moved slightly and Innis was afraid the disturbing incantations in an unknown language would start up again but she made no sound. Finally she sighed, furrowing her brows.

"I'm not sure what to make of it, Innis. The creature you described doesn't sound like anything I've ever been shown by Connla of his kingdom, and if Yaeger is magical, from that realm, he should have been comforted by the purple trees, drawn to them. I certainly was. Unless..."

Her pause in conversation stretched out to an uncomfortably long period of time while Innis waited nervously, afraid of what conclusions her fevered brain might draw. Then she seemed to snap to attention, looking directly at him with her usual disconcertingly intense gaze.

"You must let me meet Yaeger as soon as possible. He was directed to you and so he must remain with you. I've no wish to take him from you but I need to see him, to know what we're dealing with here. We'll go to your home now."

"Oh no, Auntie, not right now. Yaeger will be in his nest asleep, you won't really be able to see him. Why so urgent?"

"I'll accompany you on your hunting trip with him tonight then," Bridget continued without acknowledging Innis's question. "We'll meet at your home after dark and I'll walk with you and the creature. It's not ideal, you know, in the dark. Magic comes of a morning. The nighttime is for secrets. Perhaps Yaeger is keeping a few secrets himself and they might be revealed, especially if we return to the purple forest."

"I don't want to return there, he's disturbed by it. If you agree that he's been given to me then don't I need to decide what's best for him?"

Innis had seldom crossed his aunt but now he saw her eyes flash with a sudden, fierce anger.

"It's not me who's requesting this course of action, you foolish boy! It's Connla! We must obey."

"I wasn't aware you'd had time for a conference with Connla," Innis sniped back at her, undeterred by her vehemence. "Yaeger is in my protection and, with all due respect, I'll decide what's best for him. There is something magical about him but it's because he's simply a bone and blood creature who's incredibly wonderful and special and rare. That's enough for me."

He rushed from the shack, not daring to look behind him, frightened yet also exhilarated by his own actions. It wasn't until he'd settled at his kitchen table, after checking on Yaeger, that the possible implications of what he'd done flooded in on him. He'd never meant to make an enemy of Bridget and hoped he hadn't done just that. More bothersome, though, was that simple word "unless" that she'd uttered before pausing for such a long time. What could her incomprehensible brain be concocting about the aye-aye? Would she simply show up at his door tonight when he and Yaeger left on their hunting trip? If so, what could he possibly do?

Chapter XVI: Between Husband and Wife

Irene left Murphy's in a tizzy after the discussion with Nolan about rumors of Innis's supposed devil worship. Instead of going directly home as she'd planned, she stopped in one of the small liquor stores near Murphy's and purchased a few large bottles of Guinness Stout. She seldom drank, but now she felt the need to do so and hurried back to the farmhouse, hoping to avoid her husband and son who might still be out doing farm chores. The news of the insidious gossip had deeply unsettled her and she uncharacteristically wished to drink herself into oblivion, if only for a short while. She returned home to find Abbot seated on the couch but he instantly rose to his feet and approached her.

"I was a bit worried, it's late."

Clutching the paper bag filled with the clinking bottles of Guinness, Irene brushed him off and went to the kitchen, resigned to the loss of her plan of avoiding conversation with her husband. Abbot came to the kitchen doorway, silently watching Irene who kept her back turned to him while she pulled the bottles from the bag and set them on the counter. Abbot made no comment, as she knew he wouldn't, while she took a glass from the cupboard and opened one of the bottles, pouring a substantial amount.

"Rough day?" Abbot quietly asked.

Irene turned to him, shaking her head vehemently and taking a few big drinks of Guinness.

"You have no idea. You may want to join me once you've heard about it."

Irene knew that Abbot, like her, seldom drank nor did her son Dalton. She also knew, with a certain irritation born of the familiarity of a long married life, that Abbot would wait patiently, silently for her to begin the conversation. Dreading divulging the painful information to him, she continued to drink while he remained in the doorway. In the past, it had been difficult for him to completely understand and accept her issues with the questionable reputation of her sister and its consequences for the family. His own clan, the Kilbrides, had a long history of farming and a scandal-free, solid standing in the community. They were strong, mostly silent people who worked hard and avoided attention. She'd made a point of telling him the details about Bridget before she married him, though he'd already been aware of the community gossip and innuendo. Never one to delve too deeply into discussions about feelings or problems, Abbot instead tried to take concrete, practical steps to handle difficulties and, in his own stoical way, often eventually resolved issues rather successfully.

Despite the appearance of being oblivious to the affairs of his neighbors, he was a keen observer of human behavior and could usually discern his wife's moods with impressive clarity. Like his son Dalton, Abbot had spent the majority of his time in nature, working the crops and the flock, accustomed to harsh weather and physical hardship. There was little sentiment in Abbot and even less tolerance for foolishness in humans or animals. He'd been raised by a strict father and a stern mother who brooked no argument with rules, avoided socialization and abided by their strong Catholic faith. Abbot had always believed more ardently in nature than in God but kept those feelings to himself, as he kept most feelings. His parents had been disapproving when he married Irene, gradually accepting her though never warmly. He'd been glad to leave their house and establish his own home where he exercised a rigorous discipline, though less harsh than that his parents had used. Secretly pleased by Irene's kind and thoughtful ways, as well as her ambition and intelligence, he accepted the value of love for the first time in his life and eventually learned to offer true affection to her. He saw her restlessness as a need to be filled rather than a threat to their home life and encouraged her in her work at Murphy's. Sometimes he caught her expression of longing and excitement while they watched a TV program featuring travel or distant locales and regretted that he couldn't offer her such luxuries which he knew were dear to her heart. Abbot found the world in a field full of sheep or a vegetable patch, looking no further than his little farm in Glenraven by the sea to know what his life was meant to be.

Irene had finished most of the glass of Guinness before she paused and looked at her husband.

"You're not going to want to hear this, Abbot, but there's been some nasty and ridiculous gossip going round about our Innis. I've just heard it from Nolan. I'm so sick of the malarkey and meanness my family's been put through and, believe me, this one takes the cake."

"OK, what is it?"

"Devil worship. In the woods. Is that crazy enough for you?'

Abbot shook his head and sighed. He knew how much this

had effected Irene yet at the same time it was puzzling to him why anyone would allow themselves to be unsettled about a bit of silly gossip. Why did she let it get to her in this way?

"Let it pass, Irene. It's best just ignored."

"Let it pass? That simple, huh? No, Abbot, I'll not let it pass. How can I?"

He knew she was beginning to feel the effects of the Guinness as she'd tossed back the remaining contents of the glass and poured a second. Better to hold your silence, he told himself, although that might also aggravate her.

"What do you intend on doing, then? It's idle gossip. There's no one to accuse. What, do you plan to confront everyone in the town to find out who began it? Even if you knew, Irene, what good would it do knowing?"

Irene's eyes flashed and she slammed the partly empty glass down on the counter so hard some of the Guinness splashed out.

"Oh, I see! Just forget it, let it go. You really are such a farm boy, Abbot. Don't you know how insidious 'just gossip' can be? Next thing we know, nobody in Raven's Back or Glenraven wants Innis working on their homes or boats or anything because he's a devil worshipper! Is that what you want for our son? No, I'm getting to the bottom of this. You can stand back and shake your head at all the drama, like you always do, but I'll not let this pass."

She finished the second large glass of Guinness, rinsed it out and left it in the sink then pushed past Abbot through the kitchen door. He moved aside to let her pass and saw her fumbling with her car keys, cursing quietly to herself. In the slow, steady manner he often used he went to her, firmly taking the keys from her hand and attempting to remove her coat. She pulled away and shoved a nearby chair, knocking it against the dining room table. Stomping around the living room she kicked the leg of a coffee table, the side of the couch and one wall before collapsing into a chair. Abbot folded his arms and watched her, still holding her car keys clutched in one hand. She let out a frustrated growl and rested her head against the back of the chair.

The charged and angry atmosphere in the room slowly subsided as husband and wife both remained silent, each of them gazing off into space, deep in their own thoughts. Abbot was the first to move, replacing Irene's keys next to her purse and going to sit on the arm of the chair where Irene remained. She leaned against his arm, resting her cheek against the comfort of the worn flannel shirt he practically lived in. He thought she might cry but she didn't, merely resting against him as he felt her finally relaxing. After a few minutes she sat up and smiled ruefully at her husband.

"I may have a hangover tomorrow, hope not but all that Guinness that I'm not used to..."

Her words trailed off and Abbot scooped her from the chair, carrying her to the couch where he carefully laid her down, covering her with one of the colorful afghans crocheted by Bridget. Passed out almost instantly, Irene assumed a peaceful expression, her face relaxing into an almost angelic appearance. Abbot sat in the chair and watched her for awhile then went to check on Dalton, who'd eaten his dinner earlier and retired to his bedroom as usual. Knocking softly on the closed door, Abbot waited only a moment before Dalton opened the door, surprised to find his father there.

"Your ma's had a rough night," Abbot spoke quietly to his son, "and she's passed out on the sofa right now. I'll leave her there for the night, she's comfortable enough. She's had a bit of Guinness and probably won't hear a thing, but please don't disturb her. She may be a right menace in the morning though."

"What's happened?" Dalton whispered, glancing over his father's shoulder toward the living room though unable to see his mother. "Is everything all right?"

"It will be. Something I should discuss with you but not tonight. Don't worry, Dalton, it's nothing terrible, I promise you."

Dalton nodded, closing the door quietly as his father left. He'd only seen his mother intoxicated a few times and wondered what might have brought about such an episode and how it could not be something terrible to have created such a reaction. Like his father, Dalton wasn't one to worry for long and he returned to the supply list for the sheep's needs which he'd been working on. The secret about Yaeger and the visit to Innis's cabin, which he'd been keeping from his parents, bothered him and he preferred to keep busy. He had every confidence in his father's ability to handle whatever problems effected the family but this ongoing evasion about such a crucial part of Innis's life felt like a serious breach of trust on Dalton's part and he resented it. If Irene had somehow learned about the aye-aye, what then? Dalton dismissed the thought from his mind and continued with his task.

The next morning, when Irene awoke on the couch, she sat

up carefully, her head pounding but not feeling as dreadful as she'd feared she might. The headache she could deal with and she shuffled to the kitchen to put on the kettle. A strong cup of tea and a few biscuits would do the trick. The house was quiet and, looking at the kitchen clock, she knew her men, husband and son, were already out in the fields. Grateful for the peace and quiet, she sat in the kitchen with her elbows leaning on the table and her head in her hands. She smirked to herself at the thought of blacking out after only two full glasses of Guinness, what a lightweight. The gossip about Innis lurked at the back of her mind like a dark cloud but she ignored it, turning her attention to other ruminations.

After the kettle whistled she made herself a pot of strong tea and brought it back to the kitchen table along with a couple of biscuits she didn't bother to warm. Waiting for the tea to steep while nibbling on one of the biscuits, she thought about her husband and the life they shared. She remembered as a young girl being told by her mother that once married there should be no secrets between husband and wife, that the bond of matrimony was a shared trust, a delicate balance that could be undone by deceit or privacy. At the time, Irene had accepted her mother's advice, but when she married Abbot she came to realize how unrealistic those guidelines could be. It had taken years for her to begin to understand the man she'd married, and even now he was capable of occasionally surprising her. The first few times she'd kept things from Abbot she'd suffered a guilty conscience, her mother's words haunting her. She decided to trust her own instincts instead and, following those initial doubts, never regretted it. She realized there were certain things Abbot was better off not knowing, just as she was convinced he withheld certain information from her.

Unlike her sister, Irene had never been a romantic. She was practical, determined to make a good life for her family, and had never wavered from her choice of Abbot as a husband. He was steady, strong, hard working and, beneath his stoical exterior, very kind. Her desire to travel and see the world had been sacrificed, but for a good cause as she saw it. The wildly intense love her sister had for Gage was alien to Irene's nature and she had always been grateful to have found a man like Abbot whose steady flame would keep her warm for life. Sometimes he drove her crazy, of course, with his lack of conversation and reluctance to show affection, but she'd learned to savor the times when his reserve fell away and she could bask in the rare displays of love and passion he bestowed.

Remembering his response from the previous night to her news about Innis, she wondered if he was right, as he often was. Should she ignore the outrageous claims of devil worship, dismiss them as idle rumors which would eventually die down? She still didn't think so. Although Abbot and Irene seldom took part in the town's organized social functions, she knew her neighbors and human nature well enough to realize that real damage might be done even from something as common as gossip. At times her husband treated her as though she were a drama queen since he was unused to the impassioned emotions that ran in her family. Irene's own passion was mostly reserved for protecting her family and she did so with the power of a mama bear.

Regardless of Abbot's ideas, she was determined to make some attempt at addressing the issue of devil worship and decided her first step must be a talk with Innis. Since his move to Raven's Back she'd waited patiently for an invitation to the new abode but one was never forthcoming. It had been months since Innis had proudly announced the completion of his home yet still has parents and brother had never seen it as far as she knew. She had noticed Dalton acting a bit strange lately but figured it was likely some issue with the sheep.

Irene had the day off from Murphy's and busied herself with reviewing and organizing recipes to be tried at the restaurant and driving to town for a trip to the grocery store and market. When Abbot and Dalton returned home from the fields for their lunch break, a hearty lunch of chowder, pasties and rice pudding awaited them. They had all barely seated themselves at the kitchen table when Abbot uncharacteristically spoke up.

"I think we should all pay a visit to Innis's place this evening."

He proceeded to tuck into his meal with gusto, leaving Irene staring at him in astonishment. Dalton shifted uncomfortably in his seat then concentrated on his chowder. Irene couldn't believe her husband had made such a decision, saving her the effort of convincing him to do just that. She'd spent a good portion of her day developing a strategy and laughed to herself.

"All of us?" she asked.

"Yes, the three of us," Abbot replied, still making quick work of his food. "It's high time we saw that cabin in Raven's Back he's been working so hard on, don't you think?"

Irene smiled and started on her rice pudding in typical fashion as she often ate dessert first.

"It's OK with me," Dalton mumbled with a mouthful of chowder, "but we'd better give Innis plenty of notice."

"I say the sooner the better," Abbot offered, biting into a sausage pasty with gusto. "What's he need notice for? We're his family."

"No, Dalton's right," Irene spoke up. "At least a little notice would only be fair. I'll ring him up today. I'll fix a meal for us to share and take it out there for all of us, he'd like that. The lad's not much of a cook. Sometimes I worry he doesn't see a decent meal for days."

Glancing over at Dalton, she sensed a vague discomfort in his silence and wondered if Abbot had broached the subject of the devil worship gossip with their younger son. No time like the present, she decided.

"Dalt, I don't know if your da's mentioned it to you but one of the reasons we'd like to see your brother is due to some gossip I've just learned about him."

"I know, Ma. Da's filled me in on it this morning before we went out to the fields."

"Good, then you know why it's important we get to the bottom of it as soon as possible. Have you seen your brother lately?"

Dalton quietly set his spoon beside his empty chowder bowl and stared into the bowl as though trying to divine some secret message from it. Evasion was one thing, he told himself, but outright lying was quite another. When his father had told him of the rumors about devil worship, he'd instantly known the story had probably originated with Charlie Halloran and involved Yaeger's nighttime excursions. How could he possibly pretend to be seeing Innis's home for the first time, feign complete ignorance of Yaeger's existence and tell a bald-faced lie about not having seen his brother? He knew himself to be a dreadful liar and was annoyed at Innis all over again for putting him in this position. Still, a promise was a promise and he resigned himself to making good on his word.

"Um, probably not for a little while," he muttered, avoiding his mother's eyes.

"Have you talked at all?" Irene persisted.

"Maybe a bit. He's certainly never mentioned anything about

rumors or devil worship to me, I can tell you that."

Irene, annoyed by Dalton's vagueness, let it pass. She was still marveling at her husband's plans for a visit with Innis and she cornered him after lunch before he could return to the fields for his afternoon's work. Taking one of his large, rough hands in hers, she kissed him quickly on the cheek.

"Thank you, darlin', for deciding about this visit. I know it annoys you sometimes when I create a drama and I wasn't sure how seriously you'd take it. I was prepared to see Innis by myself, but it'll mean much more if we're all there presenting a united front as a family, so to speak. I've been longing to see his new home as well but didn't want to intrude."

"Two birds with one stone, eh?" Abbot squeezed her hand with a wry smile. "I thought about what you said, the possibility of these rumors effecting our boy's reputation and work, and I agree with you. This may be just a drama but it's worth addressing. You do most of the talking though, yeah?"

"As usual." Irene grinned and hugged Abbot who held her closely for a moment before releasing her.

"There's a reason I usually avoid the social life of this town, you know," he said.

"I do know," she nodded, "and this is it."

"Among other things."

"I'll call Innis to set a date for our visit."

Irene rubbed Abbot's back affectionately and watched him heading back out to tend his crops. She recalled all she'd learned from him about the growing cycles of the many different vegetables he cultivated, the mysteries of soil and climate, fertilizers and planting methods. His knowledge had enhanced her own cooking skills and she reminded herself of how lucky she'd been to find and marry a man who truly suited her as a life partner.

There had been a brief period of time, a couple of years into their marriage, when she'd felt the old restlessness return to her, when she'd yearned for a broader, more exciting life than that of a farmer's wife, but she'd let it pass, knowing her love for Abbot was more important than her wild, unrealistic dreams. Although she'd sensed Nolan's attraction to her, it never entered her mind to even entertain the idea of any man but Abbot. The bond between her and her husband was strong, forged from everyday hard work, slow accumulation of understanding each other, the sharing of many joys and disappointments, the raising of their two boys. It had been a challenge for her to trust people after her experiences with the treatment Bridget received, but Abbot had never pushed too hard, said too much or gone too fast. He'd simply become such a vital presence in her life that to imagine existence without him was impossible. It still surprised her a bit that he'd taken her concerns about the Innis rumors to heart, making the push to address the problem promptly before she had to. She knew it must have cost him to impose the family's visit on Innis without an invitation. Abbot was normally loathe to visit others at all, let alone invite himself to someone else's home, even if that someone was their son. He'd also obviously taken it upon himself to speak with Dalton, a task she'd assumed would fall to her. Abbot was seldom in a position to hear rumors and, of course, never gossiped with anyone so his capitulation to her frantic response meant that much more.

Irene was, for the most part, the instigator of most of the actions in the household and always had been. She decided when the family went out for a meal or on the rare vacation trip, planned the meals and prepared them, made the first move when it came to intimate relations with her husband. Nevertheless, Abbot was the undisputed head of the household, disciplining the boys, handling the finances, making the major decisions about budgeting and the operations on the farm. Now his taking the upper hand in the matter of the rumor mill astonished Irene and actually aroused a strong sexual response in her. The couple's sex life was intermittent, mainly due to Abbot's reticence and exhaustion after his hardworking days and long hours. He'd always been awkward in the bedroom with Irene gladly making the first moves, eventually bringing out her husband's passions if not any particular expertise or finesse.

As the couple aged, Abbot's reluctance toward sex increased and Irene felt at times that she was almost pestering him to make love to her. Unbeknownst to her, Abbot had felt such guilt and sorrow about her many miscarriages that the act of sex became abhorrent to him, a cruel reminder of all his wife had suffered as a result. He was flattered by her attentions, never imagining himself to be an object of desire and did his best to please her, but it was seldom a completely pleasant experience for him. Making her happy was the incentive for most of the actions he took in life and the spark of joy he'd caught flashing in her eyes when he'd announced the visit with Innis warmed him immeasurably.

That evening, following dinner and after Dalton had taken his usual early bedtime, Irene hurried through the dishwashing and meal clean-up and the couple retired to their bedroom, both of them in a rare frenzy for each other. They made love with a natural ease which had only existed on a few previous occasions and fell asleep naked in each other's arms like young lovers just discovering the game.

Chapter XVII: A Meeting of the Minds

As the time for Yaeger's night excursion approached, Innis awaited with dread for the possible arrival of Bridget at his cabin. His day at work had sufficiently distracted him from these worrisome concerns, but now at home, as the sky darkened and he waited for the aye-aye to emerge from the nest ready for his hunting trip, the thought of Bridget showing up at his door played at his nerves like a relentless refrain he tried to ignore yet couldn't help hearing. He remembered how easily his wood carving had gone after Yaeger spent the night next to him, how his worries had been erased from his mind. Could Bridget be right, could the aye-aye actually be magic? The situation with the purple grove was the most bothersome aspect of Bridget's involvement. Why had she insisted that Yaeger should return there, knowing it had bothered him on his first visit? He loved his aunt yet couldn't completely trust her when it came to his housemate. Yaeger was real, not some representative from an underwater kingdom. Now that his aunt knew of the existence of the aye-aye, how could he ever keep her away? There was no disputing the odd coincidence of their meeting at the shoreline, however, and Innis's instinct was to agree with Bridget about such destiny, if not necessarily about its meaning. For some reason Bridget was meant to know about the aye-aye.

Yaeger was later than usual leaving his nest to head for the cabin door to request his night out and Innis checked on him with increasing concern while frequently glancing out the window to look for Bridget. There was also the matter of Charlie Halloran to consider, though there'd been no mention of that to Bridget. While Innis was once again peering into the aye-aye's newest nest to see if he was about to roust himself, a soft knock came on the front door. Innis, so startled that he jumped at the sound, hurried to the window to see Bridget standing there in the darkness, her face and form cloaked in the usual long black coat with its hood pulled up over her head.

He opened the door, somewhat surprised and rattled that she'd actually made the trip to his cabin since he knew she seldom left her shack except for visits to the sea and the occasional foray into Glenraven. She gazed at him almost timidly and he saw that beneath the large coat she was trembling. He reached out to place a hand gently on her elbow, guiding her through the door. She let him lead her to the couch where she sank down as if her knees had given way. Innis sat beside her, one arm around her shoulder, holding her just close enough that he could feel her shivering slowly subside. He wished he'd thought to have tea ready for her but he hadn't been certain she would show up at all. Waiting carefully for her to speak first, he glanced toward the bedroom where he knew Yaeger was curled up in his nest but there was no sign of the aye-aye. Would the creature ever make an appearance for company, Innis wondered in frustration. Bridget had raised her eyes to meet Innis's at last and offered him a wavering smile.

"I think I'm all right now," she spoke quietly, her glance taking in the small living room. "It was a frightening trip over to here. I had no idea. These woods are alive with ghosts and maybe a few demons, Innis. I could hear them whispering to me of violence, anger, threat, even a fire. Not a wonder at all that you keep the aye-aye to yourself. It's not safe for him here and probably not for you. Certainly not for me."

Innis gave her a slight squeeze and stood up, disturbed by her mention of fire. He wondered if she was referring to the neighbors who'd planned to burn down her shack, as Sheena had mentioned, but how could she have possibly known?

"I'll get you something to warm you up, Auntie. I'm sorry your trip was so frightening --"

He broke off his words as Yaeger now sat in the bedroom doorway looking directly at Bridget who slowly turned her head to meet his gaze. The look of immediate joy which washed over her face made Innis stop in his tracks. There was an unmistakable light of recognition in her eyes and, shifting his attention to the aye-aye, he saw the same expression on Yaeger's face. Bridget sat motionless, fixated on Yaeger as he made his way toward her with his strange and slightly awkward walk. When he reached her she bent down toward him and he placed his two front hands on her coat, climbing up onto her lap with his long bony fingers clasping the heavy material as he made an eerie chortling sound Innis had never heard from him. Opening her coat so that Yaeger could snuggle into it next to her, Bridget then carefully pulled it back around the aye-aye, enclosing him so that only his golden eyes and a few tufts of dark brown fur could be seen. It was a comical sight that made Innis laugh and Bridget's own laughter, silvery and full of delight, joined his.

She bent her head down to the aye-aye, whispering "Hello, Yaeger," then leaned back against the sofa cushion, softly singing one of the old songs Innis recalled from childhood while Yaeger's eyes periodically closed as though in bliss. Innis felt a flash of jealousy that his aunt had achieved such an instant, strong rapport with the aye-aye but also a huge relief at the sweet bond and the dissipation of Bridget's fear. He could tell from her blissful smile as she sang that she was experiencing that soothing comfort which Yaeger had also brought to him on the few occasions when he'd curled up next to Innis in bed. The aye-aye does have magic, he conceded, and knew he'd be unable to deny Bridget her request to accompany him and Yaeger on this evening's hunting trip.

After Bridget's song ended, she lightly kissed the top of Yaeger's head and once again leaned down to him, talking so softly and rapidly to the contented aye-aye that Innis felt almost intrusive trying to listen in. He soon realized it was the strange and indecipherable language she sometimes used by the sea with which she was speaking to Yaeger and watched her intently. Her expression was sweet and kind without any trace of the sometimes wild, fierce intensity he'd seen her display in the past so he relaxed, enjoying the tender display. Yaeger looked up at her as she spoke, appearing for all the world to be taking in each word with perfect understanding.

Bridget nodded and opened her coat to release Yaeger who slowly climbed back to the floor and made his way to the front door as he always did to indicate his readiness for his excursion. Innis went to the dresser drawer where he kept the aye-aye's harness and rope but Bridget was suddenly behind him, placing a hand lightly on his arm before he could retrieve the items.

"No, Innis. We mustn't restrain him. He'll not run away, I promise you. We've had a meeting of the minds, me and Yaeger, and he's much more than simply a 'normal' creature. You must trust me, please."

Innis turned to look deeply into the dark eyes of his aunt as he'd never done before. He saw unfathomable depths which were impossible to read and glanced over to the door where Yaeger sat watching him. Could he bring himself to trust this much loved, precious creature to the dictates of a crazy woman, even if she was his aunt? Yaeger blinked once at him and gave the weird little chortle he'd uttered while in Bridget's lap, melting Innis's heart, giving him the odd sensation that the aye-aye was directly communicating his agreement. The harness and rope dropped softly from Innis's hand back into the dresser drawer and he closed it.

"Off we go, then," he smiled fleetingly at Bridget, unable to hide his trepidation. "Did you wish to carry the aye-aye? He seems to be rather fond of you."

"No, Innis." Bridget waved him off. "He's more comfortable with you and I'm not as familiar with your pathways. I've not been out in these woods for many years. Lead the way."

Innis bent to Yaeger and the creature quickly settled into his usual position, held against Innis's chest beneath his coat. Bridget kept close to the pair as they hiked through the darkness to the spot deep in the forest where Innis often released Yaeger to forage. For the entire walk Innis's heart was pounding at the thought of Yaeger somehow escaping or scurrying too far up into a treetop to be retrieved. He'd never even considered letting the creature loose and wished he'd brought the harness and rope for insurance. When Innis halted he turned to Bridget.

"This is one of the spots where he often likes to forage for food and nest materials, but I'm still worried about just letting him go. Aye-ayes do live in the tops of trees, Auntie, so I believe it's his natural inclination to climb."

"Has he done so when you've come here before with the harness and rope on him?"

Innis considered, recalling only a few times when Yaeger had climbed into trees and even then he'd kept to the lower branches.

"Actually, no. He's never tried going to the very top of one."

Bridget smiled.

"Release him, Innis. Even if you don't want to trust me, trust him."

Innis opened his coat and lowered Yaeger to the forest floor, running a hand fondly over the bristly back.

"Off you go, little lad. Enjoy."

Yaeger turned and headed off among the trees as he usually did with Innis and Bridget following at a respectful distance. Bridget's amusement as she watched Yaeger locate twigs, bugs and leaves, then wait for Innis to put them into the canvas bag, pleased Innis and he began to relax until the creature reached a tree trunk. Yaeger immediately climbed the tree to one of its lower branches, finding a spot where he listened for activity within then burrowed into the small hollow opening with his long middle finger to quickly feast on the larvae he found. Bridget clapped her hands with delight while Innis smiled, nodding to her.

"This is how he does, it's his natural way. Pretty cool, huh?"

"Marvelous! It certainly explains the long finger, doesn't it?"

Holding his breath for fear of Yaeger climbing farther up into the tree, Innis glanced around, marking sure Charlie Halloran wasn't spying on them then turned back to his observation of the aye-aye. Yaeger had moved to a slightly higher branch to continue his routine and found several more areas of the tree for collecting food. He paused, sniffing the air, his eyes taking on a faraway expression as though he was thinking of some distant memory. Was he remembering the mangrove trees of his native Madagascar, Innis wondered. Bridget, however, had a different idea. She pointed to Yaeger with a smile.

"Look, Innis, he's listening for Connla. He's looking in the direction of the sea."

Innis refrained from scoffing but noticed the aye-aye's gaze was, indeed, focused in the direction of the shoreline though it could not actually be seen from this distance. Yaeger closed his eyes briefly in a contented expression and once again gave out with the eerie chortling sound. Innis couldn't help noticing it sounded as though the creature was talking. Returning to his foraging in the tree, Yaeger secured a few more grubs and larvae then descended to the ground, much to Innis's relief.

Bridget snatched Yaeger up, cradling him in her arms and heading farther into the woods toward the purple grove. Innis hurried after them, tugging gently on Bridget's coat to stop her. She ignored him, walking at a slow, steady pace until Innis managed to get in front of her to block her path. He saw that Yaeger was contentedly lolling on his back in her arms like a happy baby.

"No, Auntie. I can't let you take him to the purple wood. Please, I've already told you he's upset by it. I know that's where you're headed."

Bridget adopted a slightly petulant expression and shook her head.

"You've got to get over that, Innis. I believe I know why he's disturbed by the purple forest but I need to see him there to be certain. I promise you I'll not allow him to be bothered for long. We're going to have a discussion, Yaeger and I, once we get there. You'll see."

Exasperated at his aunt's strong willed stubbornness, Innis shoved his hands into his coat pockets and trudged alongside her, occasionally checking on Yaeger who appeared to have fallen asleep. A discussion with Yaeger? Innis couldn't deny his own curiosity about such a scenario and picked up his pace to arrive at the beginning of the purple grove first. It had been some time since he'd visited here and the quiet beauty of the spot almost overwhelmed him as it had done the first time he'd encountered it. He quickly scouted the area to make sure no one was around then breathed in the earthy, slightly sweet smell of the grove.

Bridget and Yaeger soon arrived but rather than stopping at the beginning of the grove Bridget continued straight into its depths with Innis hurrying after her. He'd never gone this far into the grove and was surprised by its size as well as the unsettling, though not entirely unpleasant, sensation that the trees were closing in on the two humans and the aye-aye in a protective embrace. Innis caught up with Bridget and looked at Yaeger, whose face appeared peering from beneath Bridget's coat. His eyes were alert, bright with curiosity and when Innis placed a hand into the coat to feel Yaeger's body he was relieved to find no trembling or agitation as before. Bridget gave him a caustic glance.

"Ye of little faith," she teased with amusement in her eyes. "I told you it'd be all right. Now will you trust me? He loves it here, I'll show you."

Before Innis could react, Bridget released Yaeger from her coat and he scurried away in the darkness among the trees. Upset at losing sight of his beloved aye-aye, Innis started forward but Bridget put out her arm to prevent him.

"No, Innis, let him go. He'll return to us but he needs the chance to explore."

"What happened to the discussion you were planning to have with him?"

Bridget laughed.

"There'll be time for that when he returns. Is the grove as you remember it?"

Innis glanced around, feeling slightly claustrophobic yet also oddly safe and protected. He didn't recall this feeling from his previous visits.

"Well, somewhat the same but I didn't venture this far into the grove and when I brought Yaeger here we only came to the very beginning of the trees. Do you think that's why he was upset?"

"No, it was another reason, I'm fairly sure, but I need to confirm that with him before I tell you."

Innis couldn't suppress a chuckle.

"OK, Auntie. Would you mind if I listen in on that, or is it a private conversation?"

Ignoring the amusement in his voice, Bridget thought for a moment.

"Sorry, Innis, but it does need to be private. Not to worry, I'll tell you what's discussed."

Innis peered in the direction where Yaeger had disappeared, trying to acclimate his vision to the darkness but it seemed to grow denser and he struggled to calm his nerves.

"How far back does the grove extend, Auntie? Do you know?"

"I've never found the end of it though I haven't really tried. I believe it's a portal to another world. There are such, you know. Just as I found a portal to Connla's world."

Innis looked at his aunt, catching the same faraway expression in her eyes that she often wore when standing by the sea. He knew he was trusting Yaeger to a mad woman yet the certainty with which she spoke of her strange beliefs and ideas gave him pause. Despite his initial stab of jealousy at witnessing Yaeger's instant connection with her, he couldn't deny they did appear to have had a 'meeting of the minds' just as Bridget had stated. Thinking back to the many fantastical tales from his grandfather which he'd loved as a boy, he wondered why it was such a natural thing for children to believe in magic but never for adults. He'd wanted to believe that sheep of all colors, dragons that spat fire and mystical realms on islands in the sea actually existed as he listened to his grandfather's words and now, inexplicably, he found himself wanting to believe Bridget's claims about portals to magical worlds. What if they did exist? He shifted restlessly, still unable to decipher any movement or sighting of Yaeger.

"He's gone awhile. I can't even hear him."

"You worry so, dear boy, but he's only been out of our sight for a short bit. Come over here and sit with me."

Bridget indicated a sizable rocky outcropping beneath a nearby tree and settled somewhat precariously onto it. Innis did the same but squirmed and shifted in a futile effort to relax.

"Its not very comfortable, Auntie."

Bridget ignored him, gathering her thoughts and oblivious to the awkward perch on which she sat.

"Do you believe in the possibility of portals to other worlds, Innis?"

"I don't honestly know. I guess I haven't since I was a kid, but I'd have never believed I'd find an aye-aye on the beach until now so I suppose Yaeger is doing his best to challenge many things I thought I knew or believed in."

Bridget nodded solemnly.

"Yes, I'm sure that's true. And you need to pay attention to what he's telling you, Innis, even though it may not be clear to you at first. I was lost, truly lost, until I knew Connla. Like Yaeger came to you, Connla came to me. He wasn't something I was looking for or even knew existed until he appeared. Same for you and Yaeger, yes?"

"True." Innis turned to face his aunt, almost losing his balance. "When you first saw Connla, did he talk to you immediately? I mean, did you instantly realize all about who he was, the underwater kingdom and all of that? Because that hasn't happened for me with Yaeger."

"Because you viewed him with practical eyes, doing research and trying to duplicate his ideal living conditions as if he were still in Madagascar, right?"

"Well, yeah, but I had to do that otherwise he might not have survived. You didn't see him when he first dragged himself from the sea. I didn't even know what he was."

"You missed his magic, Innis. You bypassed it because it's more important for you to live in the real world, as it were. Think about the magic of the situation, how he came to you. Yes, I recognized Connla the moment I saw him. Then he told me of his kingdom and of Gage. There was no need for me to think about it, I merely listened. Listen to Yaeger, Innis. If you truly listen to him he'll tell you all you need to know. You must open your mind to him as well as your heart."

Innis, who'd continued to monitor the darkness of the forest for signs of Yaeger, registered his aunt's words with a certain amount of regret. It must have been easy for her to allow a fantasy of reconnecting with her beloved Gage to enter her consciousness, he thought, since she was already living in a separate dimension. For him, with one foot still planted firmly in reality, it was quite a different matter. True, he'd sensed a certain magic emanating from the aye-aye many times but he felt lacking in the tools to communicate on the level of which Bridget so easily spoke. Besides, Connla was a picture of a seahorse on a postcard while Yaeger was a living, breathing creature with needs and vulnerabilities, as well as a possible enemy in Charlie Halloran. Innis had never mentioned the episode with the neighbor and his shotgun to anyone and found it unlikely that magic had anything to do with the situation. He almost wished he could find a way to free his mind of all constraints, as his aunt had done, but knew it was beyond him.

Innis checked his watch. It had been half an hour since Bridget had released Yaeger into the forest and serious concern entered his mind. God forbid, what if the aye-aye had vanished? He slipped from the rocky outcropping, heading toward the depths of the grove but Bridget was quickly beside him once again putting out a hand to prevent his progress.

"Wait, Innis. Don't have so much concern. Look up."

She lifted her gaze toward the sky and so did Innis, suddenly spotting Yaeger at the very top of a nearby tree. A faint golden light illuminated the aye-aye, allowing him to be clearly glimpsed despite the surrounding darkness. It was an eerie sight with Yaeger's amber hued eyes reflecting the strange golden aura around him. His gaze seemed to be focused on some distant location as he gazed over the treetops, periodically closing his eyes with an expression of pure happiness and contentment. The top branches of the tree swayed slightly in a gentle breeze and shortly all of the trees in the grove began rustling in unison, their leaves fluttering ever so slightly as though talking to one another.

Innis watched in awe while Bridget, her hands clasped to her heart and her eyes closed, began to hum softly. Innis recognized the old Irish song, "Eileen Aroon" which he'd sung to Yaeger several times in the cabin. A rush of ecstasy began to fill Innis, a wild and exulting joy he'd never felt himself capable of experiencing and he envisioned a painting of Yaeger in the treetop just as he was now, but beneath a brilliant full moon partially hidden by purple clouds. The comfort and solace he'd always felt when painting returned to him, along with the gloriously grandiose and impossible dreams he'd imagined as a young boy.

Yaeger turned his gaze to meet Innis's eyes and Innis heard

the strange chortle from the creature as though the aye-aye was on his shoulder and whispering in his ear. For a moment the physical world fell away and there was only a sense of Innis and the aye-aye, face-to-face, as if Innis had floated up to the treetop beside Yaeger who reached out his bony fingers to gently stroke the sides of Innis's face. The creature and the man leaned toward each other, their foreheads touching while Yaeger's fingers continued to lightly hold Innis's face.

"Go to the wild dreams of your heart," Innis heard a slightly distorted voice whispering to him. "It's only there you'll find your treasure."

Chapter XVIII: Wisdom From An Aye-Aye

Details of that night with Bridget and Yaeger in the purple grove were hazy to Innis, as though it had been a waking dream which he'd conjured from his imagination. He remembered Yaeger climbing down from the tree and the three of them proceeding even deeper into the forest where Yaeger collected grubs and nest materials as usual. He remembered the dense silence and solemn sense of something inspirational as they quietly made their way among the purple trees. And he remembered being amazed at Yaeger's complete lack of fear at being surrounded by the grove that had previously terrified him. What he couldn't recall, however, was the precise moment when he'd realized and accepted that the little aye-aye wandering a few feet ahead of him was, indeed, magical. He'd laughed to himself at the thought of Bridget having a conversation with Yaeger yet now he was convinced that the creature had clearly spoken to him a few minutes earlier.

Bridget seemed to have forgotten about the private talk with Yaeger that she'd mentioned because the aye-aye was shortly gathered up under Innis's coat for the walk back to the cabin. Innis made no mention of his epiphany back at the grove and Bridget remained silent during the entire journey. Glancing at her once, Innis saw a fire of joy glowing in her eyes and wished he could know her thoughts. By force of habit he kept an eye out for Charlie but all was silent except for the occasional call of a raven.

When they reached the cabin, Bridget stopped at the door, leaning in to kiss Yaeger's head which protruded from beneath Innis's coat. She placed a hand on Innis's arm.

"I'll leave the two of you now. You have much to discuss and consider. I have no fear of returning home, no need to see me back. I wasn't sure if you would allow Yaeger to offer his wisdom, but I can tell you've opened your mind to him at last. I hope you know now why he feared the purple grove."

"No, Auntie, I'm afraid I've no idea, although you're right. He did communicate something of great importance to me."

"Good. Then all you need do is think on that and surely you'll solve the riddle. I hope you'll allow me to visit you on the odd occasion, my love. You and Yaeger. I need his magic, just as you do."

"Of course, we'd love to see you. I have the strangest feeling, though, that nothing is real right now."

"Was it ever?"

Bridget smiled and turned away, heading back through the darkness toward her shack at a meandering, slow pace quite different from her usual rapid, purposeful stride. She appeared to be in a day-dream, Innis thought and watched her until she was swallowed by the night. He took Yaeger into the cabin, following their usual routine after an excursion, wondering if the aye-aye would behave differently or if, perhaps, he himself should do so following the visit to the purple grove. Yaeger would normally take his meal first and, despite having consumed more insects and grubs than usual during their hunting expedition, he immediately went to work on the food they'd collected, devouring everything in short order. Innis had taken to providing mushrooms as a supplement to Yaeger's diet and the aye-aye was quite fond of them. Anticipating the treat, Yaeger looked toward the kitchen, pointing his long middle finger toward the fridge. This was something new and Innis guffawed, amazed at his housemate's direct form of communication.

"Oh, is it mushrooms you're wanting, you sly little devil?"

Yaeger blinked his eyes as if in agreement and Innis went to the fridge, collecting a handful of mushrooms which he quickly rinsed in the sink. Yaeger waited right behind him with an expression of delighted anticipation.

"Here you are, my good fellow. Enjoy."

Innis had no sooner placed the food on the floor beside Yaeger than the aye-aye began picking up the mushrooms and slowly munching each one as though savoring them. It always greatly amused Innis watching Yaeger hold each mushroom in his long fingered hands and tear off bite sized pieces with his long teeth. As Yaeger ate, Innis's thoughts drifted back to those delusional moments in the purple grove, for surely they must have been delusional. The aye-aye had spoken to him, the both of them atop a purple-leaved tree, yet how could it possibly have actually happened? Was he losing his mind?

He looked closely at Yaeger, noticing no difference in his behavior from that of his normal actions. He thought of Bridget's parting words and of those which had been whispered to him, supposedly by the aye-aye. The image of the painting of Yaeger also returned to him, but what had it meant? How could he even begin to interpret such events which had no bearing on reality?

After finishing the mushrooms, Yaeger started in on the rest of his food and, after making short work of all the items they'd gathered from the forest, set about collecting the nest materials to begin a new nest in the bedroom. As Yaeger trundled each item out of the living room and kitchen, Innis marveled at the creature's energy and appetite. It's as if he's had a boost of some sort, he thought. Perhaps the incident in the grove had been just as exhilarating to the aye-aye as it had been for him. Once he could hear Yaeger working on the nest in the bedroom, Innis sat down on the couch in an effort to collect and interpret his thoughts.

The most logical explanation was that he'd simply imagined the face-to-face treetop encounter and the whispered words from the aye-aye. He hadn't mentioned any details to Bridget nor had she made any comments to him, though obviously she considered something of great importance to have occurred. A message meant for Innis. The image of the painting, combined with the passionate words of advice about wild dreams, reminded him of the solace and joy he used to feel while creating works of art, before he became a woodworker. There was great pride, satisfaction and enjoyment in carving and building, but he'd been at his most creative when he was painting. The thrill of visualizing a picture then making it come to life, of working with paint and color and his unfettered imagination was light years beyond the work he'd been doing as an apprentice to Oren. He'd learned much about woodworking and had been especially pleased with the completion of his cabin and the items he'd carved from the purple wood, but despite his claims to his mother the he wouldn't abandon his painting he'd done just that. Always too busy and tired from his work and caring for Yaeger, he hadn't even touched a paintbrush nor purchased a canvas for more than a year. Could this be the meaning of the forest epiphany?

As a younger boy just beginning to paint and realizing his own talent for it, he'd indeed had several wild dreams involving fame and fortune, of exhibiting his works in famous art galleries worldwide where celebrities would purchase his paintings and art critics might praise his genius. He'd even imagined living in places like Paris or Venice, inhabiting a charming old loft or studio with perfect light where he'd create masterpieces at his leisure and live among the beauty of those storied cities. Once he'd realized how ridiculous his fantasies were he'd laughed at his own folly and accepted the truth that what brought him the greatest happiness was simply the painting of the pictures. Nothing else, regardless of how extravagant, would top that. Still, he'd abandoned it for the more practical skill of woodworking. Had it brought him happiness? Up to a point, though he had to admit it hadn't given him true joy the way painting and sketching had done.

The discovery of the purple grove had thrilled him but he'd shortly found a way to use the unique, beautiful wood to create items he planned to sell. Perhaps he'd interpreted the magic of the grove in the wrong way, seizing on its financial potential instead of appreciating its mystical qualities. Many times he'd longed to carve more objects from the soft, exquisite wood he'd found there but he'd always resisted this urge, loathe to take any of the wood. Had Yaeger been disturbed by the purple grove because he sensed the ambition it brought out in Innis? Was the aye-aye encouraging Innis to forsake his woodworking and return to being a painter? Far-fetched to be sure, but the more Innis considered it the more certain he became that this was the course of action he was meant to follow.

He decided to begin immediately while the vision of Yaeger in the treetop beneath a full moon was still fresh in his mind. After he'd completed his work the following day, he went to the small arts and crafts supply shop in Glenraven where he used to purchase his painting supplies and bought the largest canvas in the shop, along with some oil paints and a few sketching tools. He'd kept his previous art supplies stored in the garage at his parents' farmhouse and snuck back to retrieve them when he knew the place would be empty with his father and Dalt at work in the fields and his mother in the kitchen at Murphy's. He needed to avoid his mother in particular as her hopes for a return to a painting career for Innis would easily be stoked and he didn't want to disappoint her a second time. Who knew how far this new inspiration would go, how long it would last? There would certainly be no explaining to anyone in his family the reason for this change of heart except for Bridget, who probably already knew. Was this the message about the purple grove that she'd expected to receive from Yaeger? Innis would discuss it with her later. Now was the time for action.

Once he'd organized all his supplies, Innis recognized his approach as similar to Yaeger's gathering of materials for his various nests. In a way, he knew that art was like a nest to him, a true home where he would always feel comfortable and safe, protected from the cares and threats of the outside world, cocooned within a space of his own creation. He'd been observing Yaeger carefully over the two days since their visit to the purple grove but could see no change in his behavior, nor had anything further been heard from Bridget. Considering contacting her to discuss his interpretation of Yaeger's advice about returning to painting, he decided against it. Better to proceed on his own for now without her interference. He had no doubt she would get in touch with him if or when the spirit moved her.

On their next hunting excursion, the night following Innis's epiphany, Yaeger had been content foraging in his usual areas and made no attempt to return to the purple grove, much to Innis's relief. The intensity of emotion he'd felt that night and the strange vision of being in the treetop with Yaeger had unsettled him and he was still uncertain whether the experience was real or an illusion. At some point he intended to question his aunt about exactly what she had witnessed but, as usual, there would be no guarantee that her version of events would be accurate. For now, painting was Innis's priority and he set about making a sketch of Yaeger in the treetop from his vision at the purple grove.

The image easily crystallized and, as when working with the purple wood, the sketch almost seemed to create itself. Innis was merely a conduit to his art, quickly and effortlessly creating the sketch in considerable detail. His expectation of exhaustion after doing his woodworking job, then taking Yaeger out hunting with very little sleep the previous night, failed to materialize. Instead, a welcome, exhilarating energy filled him and he stayed up until dawn to complete the sketch. After a quick call to Oren, who sounded slightly irritated that his apprentice was once again taking a day off work, Innis collapsed onto his bed and fell into a deep sleep without dreaming. The soft touch of something against his cheek finally woke him and he opened his eyes to find Yaeger staring into them. The aye-aye was sitting beside him, tapping him lightly on the face with his long middle finger.

Innis smiled and reached out to stroke Yaeger's bristly fur, surprised and grateful that the creature allowed it.

"Have I overslept a bit, macushla?" he whispered to Yaeger. "If you're up, can it possibly be evening already?"

He sat up, noticing the darkness outside his small bedroom window and was astonished he'd slept the entire day away. Hurrying to take Yaeger out, he bypassed the completed sketch propped on an easel in the living room. When he and the aye-aye returned from their night's hunting, however, the picture accosted Innis almost as soon as he'd stepped in the door. Releasing Yaeger from the harness and rope, which he'd decided to resume using, Innis stared at his creation. There was Yaeger, atop the purple tree and gazing up at a full moon with shreds of cloud drifting across it, just as Innis's vision had dictated. The detail and accuracy with which he'd captured the image astounded him. He had no memory of drawing such a life-like picture that almost vibrated off the paper with vitality. How had he caught that mysterious, otherworldly light in Yaeger's eyes or the veined leaves of the purple tree so brilliantly? Although the sketch was in black and white, the deep purple of the grove was somehow suggested, along with the soft, golden glow surrounding the aye-aye. Even the moon gave off a silver light while the pieces of cloud seemed to be moving along in the night sky. What technique could have possibly produced such brilliant results?

Innis stared at the sketch, aware of the sound of Yaeger's nest building nearby yet feeling in a trance, mesmerized by his own creation. He had no recollection of the actual sketching of the picture, only of a feverish compulsion to complete it. It almost frightened him to contemplate attempting the painting that he'd planned to follow this sketch, as how would he ever make it as amazing?

He returned to work the next day, exhausted and distracted. Oren called him aside after only a few hours of working on a boat they'd been commissioned to repair.

"It's difficult for me to say this to you, Innis, but I feel obliged to. You look as if you haven't slept properly in weeks, and I can see how low your energy level is. You've been an excellent apprentice and now I'm puzzled that you seem to be falling apart. And so close to the completion of your apprenticeship to earn your certificate. It's as if your heart is no longer in it. Much as I value your efforts and like you as a person, I'm afraid I can't risk faulty work. It isn't that the quality of your work has slipped, at least not yet. I don't want it to, though, and I'd rather tell you now before it does. Is there anything you'd like to tell me?"

Innis looked down at his feet, embarrassed and shamed by the truth of Oren's words. Already the woodworking which had brought him so much satisfaction now paled in comparison to the ecstasy of his art. How would he ever explain his situation to Oren? He needed the money from his woodworking and it was true that soon he'd have the certificate allowing him to be a freelance wood-worker. Was he about to throw all of his efforts away, along with his livelihood?

"I dunno what to say," he began hesitantly. "You're right, I've been distracted and the worst part is my heart's not in it like before. You're right about that too. I wish I could explain it to you but, honestly, I'm not sure how. Well, I've started drawing and painting again. You know that was my first love."

Oren stared at the man before him in astonishment, unable to believe what he was hearing.

"So you're saying you no longer wish to do woodworking?"

"I'm afraid not, no."

The words had escaped Innis before he even knew he was going to say them. Oren shook his head.

"Well, I must tell you I'm very disappointed, Innis. You're damn good at this and, to tell the truth, it seems a rather sudden decision. Is this why you've been missing days and losing sleep all along?"

"Not exactly. I know it is a sudden decision. In fact, I've only truly decided right now as we're talking."

"What a puzzlement you are, lad. Don't you think you'd best consider it more carefully? Has something particular happened to bring you to this?"

"As a matter of fact, yeah. A couple days ago. Look, I'm really sorry, Oren. I wish I could tell you more and I know it puts you in a tricky position."

"Yes, it certainly does. We've several contracts yet to fulfill and I'll be hard put to finish them on my own."

"And I'd never do that to you. I'll complete all the work we've contracted for, never worry. I guess this might be considered advance notice. I'm not just quitting. Of course I'll honor my commitments to you and our customers."

"Well, I'm relieved to hear it. And you really should earn your certificate. Perhaps, between finishing these final assignments and a bit of extra work, you'd be able to do so."

"I'm not interested in the certificate any longer. I don't plan to be a woodworker, I plan to be an artist."

Once again Oren peered at Innis in confusion, amazed at the ease with which his apprentice had switched gears. The idea of making a living at art in Glenraven was, at best, hopelessly naïve.

"I've never seen your artwork, Innis, but I know you've shown great skill and talent at working with wood. I hate to see you give it up entirely. I really thought you'd make an excellent wood-worker and would do quite well at it."

Innis smiled almost bashfully at Oren's praise and they shook hands.

"Thanks for everything, Oren. I really do appreciate all you've done for me and under different circumstances I'm sure I could have made a go of it. My mind's made up though."

"Well, I'll wish you the best and we'll finish up the rest of our projects."

When Innis returned to his cabin late that afternoon, he was surprised to see that Yaeger had built his latest nest just below the easel holding Innis's sketch. His nests had always been in elevated spots, befitting an aye-aye's natural habitat in treetops, but this one rested on the floor out in the open in a corner of the living room. Yaeger was still curled up in it, asleep, so Innis went to the kitchen for a snack before Yaeger awakened and requested his hunting trip.

It had become Innis's habit to live, for the most part, on sand-wiches and cans of soup, anything quick and easy. His cooking skills were minimal and, with his apprenticeship, caring for Yaeger and now his art, there was precious little time to spare for meals. Making himself a roast beef sandwich on soda bread with some left-over beef Irene had given him during his last visit home, he took a bottle of Guinness from the fridge, sat at the kitchen table and absentmindedly enjoyed his meal, wishing he'd thought to buy some crisps while he was in town.

I've taken the first step toward freedom, he thought, and although he recognized the sheer insanity of abandoning his future as a woodworker, turning from the careful path he'd chosen and worked so hard to follow, he felt little fear or regret, only an exhilarating vision of creating art, following his muse. Anxious to begin on the painting of Yaeger with the full moon which would be based on his sketch, he checked on the paints, canvases and brushes he'd stored in the small shed behind his cabin. The supplies would be enough for a start, but he knew he'd need to purchase additional items in Belfast.

It had been too long since he'd seen Fin anyway, and he felt guilty at never having issued a formal invitation for her to visit Raven's Back. What would she think of the drastic change he'd just made to his life? How would he explain to her that his decisions had been based on wisdom from an aye-aye?

Chapter XIX: Aftermath of a Death

Shortly after the evening at the purple grove, Innis decided to pay a visit to Sheena. He'd been considering her offer to help with Yaeger and now that he'd begun painting again his time for sleeping was even more reduced. He'd delayed work on the painting of Yaeger until he could find time to go to Belfast for additional supplies but was already making notes about the colors and types of brushes he wanted for the project. The sketch remained on the easel as a daily reminder, and he felt a sense of urgency to begin work on the painting before inspiration evaporated. Making his way early one chilly Saturday morning to Sheena's cabin, he was surprised to see no smoke issuing from the small chimney as usual. He'd waited until 8:00, though he knew Sheena was usually up long before then.

Knocking on the front door but receiving no reply, he called out to her, suddenly spooked by the complete silence. Not even a bird song or rustle of leaves broke the morning stillness. The front curtains over the window to the right of the door were slightly parted, and he peered in, startled to see the figure of Sheena stretched out face down on the living room floor, her feet twisted in an unnatural way. Panicked, Innis desperately tried the front door but it was locked, as were both the front windows. Dashing to the rear of the cabin, he found the back door locked as well with no means of entry. Returning to the front of the cabin, he fumbled in his coat pockets and found an old rag he'd been using for clean-up while working with painting supplies. He quickly wrapped it around his hand and thrust his fist at the front window, shattering the glass on the second try. Climbing awkwardly through the ragged opening, slightly cutting his other hand and tearing his coat and pants, he ran to Sheena, aware with a cold certainty that she was already gone.

The wild, gray streaked hair was fanned out around her head and she wore the same clothes he'd always seen her in. Grasping one of her big boned wrists, he felt desperately for a pulse, though the clammy coldness of her skin had already provided his answer. Gently rolling her over, he found her eyes open, a look of mild surprise on her face. He knew she had no telephone and failed, as usual, to get any reception on his cell phone. He then ran to his cabin to call the emergency service in Glenraven and rushed back to Sheena, breathing heavily from exertion and stress. After briefly considering an effort at CPR he realized it was a lost cause and sat down beside Sheena's body with one of his hands resting lightly on her head to await the arrival of an ambulance and the local police. He hadn't known her well, but still a sharp grief at her demise overwhelmed him and he found himself crying softly as he glanced around the small home where he'd felt such comfort and welcome. Since the rooms had normally been cluttered, it was impossible to tell if anything had been disturbed but everything appeared to be as before when he'd visited her. He knew Sheena was quite elderly despite her robust appearance and wondered if perhaps she'd suffered a heart attack. Regretting that he'd never get to know her as he'd hoped, and that she'd never meet Yaeger as he'd planned, he dried his tears and rose to his feet. Reluctant to go too far from the body, he stood anxiously nearby, finally aware of the arrival of an ambulance and a police car outside. It must have been hell for them reaching this place, he thought, as Sheena's cabin, like his own, was located in an isolated area with no regular roads anywhere near it.

Innis opened the door and was greeted by Michael Carey, the ambulance driver who was vaguely familiar from Innis's childhood in Glenraven. They'd gone to school together though hadn't been close friends. Innis nodded to Carey and to the police officer who was also approaching. The officer was unknown to Innis and struck him as a newcomer to the area. Introducing himself as Officer Tom Sullivan, the man glanced at the broken front window.

"I did that," Innis quickly offered. "I saw her on the floor and I couldn't find any other way in. I thought she might still be alive."

Sullivan turned cold blue eyes on Innis as though assessing him, then proceeded into the cabin without a word while Innis and Carey hovered in the doorway.

"I've checked her pulse," Innis said. "She's obviously been gone for a little while I would think."

The officer knelt down by the body and Carey joined him, checking Sheena's neck for a pulse and manipulating one of her arms briefly.

"Yes, Innis, she's been dead for a bit," Carey nodded. "Never thought this old girl would actually go, truth be told. She was ancient as the Druids."

"Why were you visiting her?" Sullivan rose to his feet, facing Innis. "I assume that's how you came across the body?"

"That's right. I was just coming over to see her, visit and talk a bit, you know. I've only recently gotten to know her at all."

"It's a shame," Carey said. "Her alone out here and all. Not sure if there's even a next of kin to notify. She was a bit of a hermit. Consider yourself privileged to have known her at all, Innis. As I understood it she let very few in."

The tears started back into Innis's eyes and he nodded solemnly.

"I do feel lucky indeed. She was the most welcoming person I met since I moved to Raven's Back and I'll miss her. I'd be interested to know what did her in."

Sullivan, who'd been inspecting the living room, turned to Innis.

"Why the special interest then?"

He peered at Innis in an uncomfortable way, putting him on the defensive.

"No special reason, officer. Honestly, I was just fond of her, that's all. I know she was up in years, but the last time I saw her she seemed perfectly fine."

"When was that?"

Sullivan had taken a small notebook from his pocket and began taking notes which made Innis even more nervous.

"Um, I'm not exactly sure. Probably about a week ago, maybe five or six days, something like that."

"So you visited her in a friendly, neighborly way is all?" Sullivan asked as he continued writing.

"That's right. I went 'round to all my neighbors when I first got to Raven's Back and, to be truthful, she was really the friendliest one so I decided to go back and see her."

"She liked her whiskey," Casey broke in, "I'll tell you that."

Innis laughed.

"That she did, even offered me some with my morning tea once."

"Can't blame her, out here on her own in her old age," Casey added.

"How many times did you visit her?" Sullivan asked.

Innis, growing irritated by the policeman's suspicious demeanor and continual note-taking, remained silent.

"Well, then?" Sullivan prompted.

"What's all this questioning about?" Innis failed to keep the annoyance out of his voice. "You're acting as if I've done something wrong. Why don't you find out why she died before you go making any assumptions?"

Sullivan stopped his writing and looked intently at Innis, a slight tick in his jaw indicating his displeasure.

"Have you done something wrong?" he addressed Innis in a cold voice. "Look, I'm merely attempting to get a timeline here and, of course, the cause of death will be determined. If you're concerned about my assumptions, perhaps you might stop acting guilty."

Accustomed to the familiar local police officers he'd only sporadically encountered and who'd acted in a much more professional manner, Innis bit his tongue and forced himself to shrug.

"Sorry, officer. Only trying to help."

This approach defused the tension in the room and, after asking Innis a few more questions, Sullivan dismissed him, advising that the medical examiner from Glenraven would arrive shortly and thanking Innis for his cooperation. Innis couldn't help pausing in the doorway as he left, casting one last fond glance at Sheena and still feeling partly numb from the shock of his discovery.

"You know, she kept a shotgun," Innis mentioned. "In case you find one, didn't want it to come as a complete surprise. At least she told me she had one, I never saw it."

Casey chuckled.

"She was known for that," he smiled. "Probably one reason few, if any, ever messed with the old girl. Even folks in Glenraven knew about it."

Innis nodded and left quickly before he could mention the incident of the neighbors gathering in a mob to burn Bridget's shack. Doubtful if the police had ever been aware of it, he fumed inwardly. The loss of Sheena weighed heavily on Innis, and he delayed his visit to Belfast and Fin as well as the commencement of work on the painting of Yaeger. For several days following the discovery of Sheena's body, he avoided all of his neighbors and any outside contact, keeping only to his work schedule and his cabin with Yaeger being his one companion. The aye-aye seemed to sense his housemate's sorrow and began curling up in bed beside Innis each night. As before, the nearness of the creature brought peace and comfort and Innis slept well despite his melancholy. He was blissfully unaware that rumors, started by Charlie Halloran, had begun to swirl throughout Raven's Back that Innis Kilbride was somehow connected to Sheena's death.

Charlie had noticed the presence of the ambulance, police car and the medical examiner's van on the morning of Sheena's death and set to work trying to discover as many details as he could. It soon came to his attention that Innis had discovered the body and his suspicious imagination kicked into overdrive. Over a period of two days he visited several of his neighbors in Raven's Back, spreading the news of Sheena's sudden demise and the mysterious connection with Innis Kilbride. Added to the previous tales of Innis's nocturnal devil worship in the woods it made for a damning combination. Charlie had so convinced himself of the validity of his claims that he became somewhat frightened by what he perceived as his 'strange' neighbor and was determined to get to the bottom of things.

Innis received a call from his mother the day following the discovery of Sheena's body. Irene inquired about a visit to his cabin, adding that the entire family was keen to finally see his living quarters and would bring a meal with them. Low and unnerved from Sheena's demise, Innis delayed the visit, surprised at the depth of his mother's disappointment but determined to extend his isolation. He needed to grieve and had become frustrated by the lack of information from the police department when he called to ask about his neighbor's cause of death. Since he was not a relative of the deceased, he was advised, those details were not to be provided to him. He hoped the elderly woman had died of natural causes and wondered what was to be done about a funeral or if any next of kin had been located. It was through Oren at work that he eventually learned Sheena had succumbed to a massive heart attack just as he'd initially suspected. At least it had been a quick way to go, he comforted himself while puzzling how Oren had come by the information so easily.

Innis had noticed that Charlie Halloran was stepping up his surveillance of the evening excursions. Several times during his nocturnal outings with Yaeger, he became aware of a nearby presence, alerted by a twig snap or the rustling of leaves. He'd snatched Yaeger from the ground or a low tree branch and hurried to the cover of trees or bushes, waiting until he'd either seen or heard Halloran moving out of the area. Yaeger no longer seemed fearful of Halloran's presence and sometimes became annoyed by the interruption of his foraging, struggling to free himself from Innis's grip and giving him a withering glance once he was replaced on the ground or in a tree.

"I'm sorry, macushla," Innis would apologize, "but it seems we're being stalked. I don't like it any better than you do."

It began to bother Innis to the point that he grappled with the idea of confronting his neighbor but hesitated for fear of a face-off. Perhaps the subject of Sheena's demise would provide an opening and late one afternoon when he'd returned from work he made his way to Charlie's cabin.

Charlie was outside in front of the cabin clearing away branches and leaves from a recent storm as Innis approached. He returned Innis's wave of a greeting and continued what he was doing until Innis stood beside him. Dropping the rather large branch he'd been attempting to break over his knee, Charlie grinned and offered Innis a firm and hearty handshake.

"Neighbor!" His voice held a slight nervousness to Innis's ear. "What brings ya?"

"If you're busy I can come back another time."

"Not at all. C'mon in."

Charlie swung open the front door of his cabin, scuffing his boots on the door mat and Innis did the same. Innis had only been in the cabin a handful of times but found it unchanged as he'd remembered it. Kept surprisingly neat and clean, considering a single fisherman lived there, the place retained a slight smell of fish in keeping with its occupant's occupation. Innis's gaze darted around the living area looking for the shotgun he'd seen Halloran carrying in the woods but there was no sign of it. He shook his head, clapping a hand on Charlie's shoulder in an overly friendly manner that felt forced to him.

"How you keep this place so clean and nice I'll never know, Charlie. It's a credit to you. Mine's a mess such as my own mother's not even been to see it."

Charlie, obviously flattered by the compliment, beamed proudly as he looked around.

"Thanks, neighbor. I don't do too badly at that. Guess I was brought up that way, being clean and tidy. Will tea do for you or maybe something stronger? Planning to stay awhile or just popping in for a minute?"

"Wouldn't say no to a spot of tea, if you don't mind. I wanted to talk to you about Sheena if that's all right."

Charlie froze in his tracks partway to the kitchen and looked over his shoulder at Innis, a shadow of doubt passing briefly over his face.

"Hmm. Would've never guessed that as a reason for your visit but, of course, fine with me if we discuss her."

While Halloran prepared the tea, Innis paced slowly around the living room trying to formulate his thoughts. Part of him wanted to press his advantage since Charlie was clearly nervous about Innis's presence, probably worried that somehow his neighbor had discovered his strange, stalking behavior. It wasn't in Innis's nature to confront people directly, however, and he decided on a more circuitous approach. Better to draw him out, put him at ease before broaching the true purpose of his visit. Why had Halloran seemed a bit startled by the subject of Sheena?

Charlie returned shortly with two mugs of tea, motioning Innis to be seated on the couch. Innis experienced a flashback of Sheena pouring whiskey into his tea and smiled with fondness.

"Tea brings a smile to your face, does it, Innis?"

Startled, Innis returned to the present.

"Sorry, I was just thinking about Sheena."

Charlie stared at Innis.

"What about her?"

"Well, just the time when I visited her early one morning and she put whiskey in my tea. Had some herself as well. Really sad about her passing, yeah?"

Charlie nodded but seemed uncomfortable.

"Heard you were there," he watched Innis's reaction closely but saw only a wave of sorrow pass across his neighbor's face.

"It was actually me that found her. I was wondering how everybody else in Glenraven seemed to get information about it long before I did. Police wouldn't tell me anything. Who told you about me being there?"

Halloran shifted nervously in his chair, avoiding Innis's gaze.

"I asked around if you must know. Seen the police and ambulance and such that morning so I knew something was up. Don't recall how I found out about you being at the scene."

Innis set his mug of tea, only half full by now, down on the small coffee table in front of the couch. He already missed Sheena's warm, hearty ways, her strong tea doused with whiskey and the welcoming fire in her comfortably cluttered cabin. He felt a sudden ache at the realization that he'd probably never set foot there again. Something in Charlie's implication about Innis's presence at the scene of Sheena's death began to infuriate him and he struggled to keep the anger our of his voice.

"What is it you're trying to say, Charlie? You make it sound as if there was something suspicious about my being there. I simply went over to see her that morning and found her on the floor, gone. Not that it's any of your business."

"Hold up now, Innis. I wasn't trying to imply anything of the sort, I simply--"

"Certainly sounded like you were," Innis interrupted. "That young new policeman, Sullivan, treated me the same way. Have to tell you, I'm getting bloody tired of being treated like I'm some sort of criminal or shady character not to be trusted. Can't say I've done a thing to deserve it after all."

Halloran was silent and Innis picked up his mug to take a few big gulps of tea, barely resisting the urge to confront Charlie about the stalking behavior. This wasn't working out exactly as he'd planned and now he began to wonder if Halloran was only one of many who were speculating about him.

"Look, Innis," Charlie broke the silence, "I'm sorry if you feel that way. I surely didn't mean to accuse you of anything. I didn't even know you and Sheena were friends. How long has that been so?"

"Only recently. I just went to visit her a couple of times. It wasn't like we were good friends or anything, but...I just liked her, is all. What about you? You've been living here a lot longer than me. Did you know Sheena?"

Charlie hesitated, taking a drink of tea before he replied.

""Didn't really know her, mostly knew of her, if you know what I mean. She had a bit of a reputation in these parts, her and her shotgun."

Innis smiled.

"I can well imagine. Feisty old lady, wasn't she?"

"That and some other things. Have to tell you, people weren't always fond of her around these parts. She caused some trouble in Raven's Back in the past, don't know if she told you about that."

Innis wondered if he was referring to the incident with the mob and Bridget's cabin but chose to remain silent, allowing Halloran to continue.

"Yeah, had a bit of a reputation, old Sheena did. Not the best thing, a drunk old woman with a shotgun. She'd been here longer than anyone else in Raven's Back, I'd reckon. Course I've been her going on six years, so there's plenty I don't know about the place or about our neighbors for that matter."

Surprising there's things you don't know, you nosy parker, Innis fumed to himself. Sheena was only a few days gone and here was this fool maligning her name.

"So you didn't really know her?" Innis again gauged Charlie's response, noticing a slight unease in the man's body language and avoidance of eye contact.

"Nah, I didn't really know her," Charlie shrugged. "Didn't really want to. What made you so fond of her?"

There was a brief pause while Innis tried to formulate a reply. It was difficult to put the answer into words.

"Don't exactly know, really. Something about her, guess we just clicked. To be honest, she was more welcoming to me than anyone else here and I liked her rough ways. She was kind to me."

"C'mon now, haven't I been friendly to ya, Innis?"

Too friendly, Innis thought but decided to steer the conversation back to one of the purposes of his visit. Ignoring Charlie's question, he returned to his original line of inquiry.

"How did you come by so much information about Sheena's death then, Charlie? Seeing as you didn't even know her."

"Told ya, I've been asking around. Don't you know yet the way it works here, Innis? You've gotta work the grapevine."

"How long have you known Officer Tom Sullivan? He's new to these parts, isn't he?"

Charlie, unable to disguise his startled expression, rose to his feet.

"More tea, Innis? Think I'll have some."

Innis looked down at the dregs of his not quite empty mug.

"No thanks, I'm good, Charlie."

Innis waited patiently while his neighbor bustled around in the kitchen, the clattering and sporadic cursing a testament to Charlie's nervousness. When Halloran rejoined Innis with a fresh, steaming mug of tea, he made an awkward attempt to divert the conversation back to safer territory.

"Now then, Innis, where were we? Oh yes, the late, shotgun toting Sheena."

Charlie concentrated on his tea for a few moments then furrowed his brows.

"That's right, you were wondering how I know Sullivan but, you see, I don't know him. What makes you ask?"

"My ma works at Murphy's as a cook, maybe you didn't know. Anyway, she's seen you in there having dinner with Sullivan."

Innis stared at Halloran, somewhat enjoying the man's obvious discomfort. Charlie took a large gulp of tea and grimaced.

"Damn it! Burned my mouth. Sorry, I'm not sure...why would your mother mention such a thing to you in the first place?"

"More to the point, Charlie, why would you lie about such a thing? I'm guessing most of the information about Sheena's death you've gotten came from Officer Sullivan. Am I right?"

Charlie set down his mug and looked directly at Innis.

"What's with this interrogation, my friend? Why would you even care where or how I got details? Just because you couldn't, is that it? A bit petty, don't ya think?"

Making a major effort to control his temper, Innis rose from his seat and carried his mug to the kitchen where he rinsed it and left it in the sink. He remained there briefly, forcing himself to be as still as possible until his anger began to subside. Returning to the living room he found Charlie in the same spot gingerly sipping his tea. Innis stood near Charlie's chair, finally catching his eye.

"Look, Halloran, I don't give a damn what you really think of me, which is a good thing because I'll probably never really know. I don't understand why you're being so nosy about Sheena when you didn't even know her, but I was fond of her and I'd appreciate it if you'd keep your bad-mouthing about her to yourself when I'm around."

"But I wasn't bad-mouthing--"

Innis held up a hand to interrupt.

"Don't understand either why you and Officer Sullivan both seem to treat me like you suspect me of something nefarious. Why? And by the way, is Sheena the only person in Raven's Back who owns a shotgun?"

Charlie leapt to his feet, almost knocking over his mug.

"Now wait a minute, Innis. Look who's making insinuations now. Why do you care who has shotguns around here?"

"I didn't so much until I saw you out in the woods one night walking around with one. I assume you don't go out hunting at night, so..."

166

"And what were you doing out in the woods in the middle of the night yourself?"

Both men had begun to raise their voices and Innis let a few minutes of silence pass in order to defuse the shouting match.

"Well?" Charlie continued. "I've seen you going out at night more than once."

"And why are you watching what I do, Charlie?" Innis made a determined effort to remain calm. "What's it to you?"

"The rope, Innis. What about the rope? You were out carrying a long length of rope one night. Remember when we ran into each other? You've been avoiding me ever since and now I'm asking again, what's going on with you? It's not normal whatever it is and that's exactly why you won't tell me. Now you were consulting with the crazy old woman Sheena, plus your crazy aunt--"

Innis was in front of Charlie almost instantly, his face only inches from his neighbor's, his dark eyes blazing with fury.

"I just told you a few minutes ago not to go bad-mouthing Sheena to me," he spoke through clenched teeth, "so you go and not only mention it again but throw my Aunt Bridget into the mix. I'll tell you about the rope if you're so keen on it, but first you're going to explain why you're stalking me with a shotgun."

The two remained face-to-face, Innis with his fists clenched at his sides and Charlie with an expression that was a combination of stubbornness and fear. Gradually the electricity of intense emotion dissipated from the room and Innis turned away, heading for the front door. Before he could open it, Charlie spoke up.

"Let's not part ways as enemies, Innis. I don't know why you think I'm stalking you, but—"

"Look," Innis turned back to face Charlie, "just don't do it any more. Please. I guess we'll have to agree to disagree and try to stay out of each other's way. Can we make a deal on that?"

Charlie nodded and the men briefly shook hands, then Innis returned home with a turbulent heart. Nothing had been resolved with Halloran except now, with more of their cards on the table, a wary truce had been declared. Would Charlie really cease following Innis and Yaeger on their nightly excursions? Innis didn't think so. Perhaps if the aye-aye was taken to the purple grove at night they'd lose Halloran, who might be uncomfortable venturing that far. Then again, if Charlie persisted and discovered the secret, magical woods for himself, what could happen? The loss of Sheena continued to

sadden Innis and when Yaeger approached for his night-time foraging, Innis bundled the aye-aye up in his arms without the harness and
rope, holding the creature close inside his coat, comforted by its
furry warmth and the odd chortling sound that he'd come to associate
with Yaeger's happiness.

Chapter XX: The Landscape of the Imagination

The night following his visit to Halloran's cabin, Innis had a vivid nightmare in which an angry mob of neighbors, led by Charlie, had surrounded his cabin, chanting "Give us the aye-aye!" in an increasing roar of rage. Innis opened his eyes, sweating from the sheer terror of the dream. He sat up abruptly in bed, causing Yaeger, who had settled next to him as had now become their custom, to shift and growl softly in disgruntlement. Innis stroked Yaeger's fur in relief, murmuring softly "It's all right, little fella. Sorry to disturb you." As Yaeger went back to sleep, Innis continued sitting in the early morning darkness of his bedroom. He'd need to get ready for work soon, but the nightmare had rattled him and he couldn't bring himself to rise from the bed.

Earlier that evening he'd taken Yaeger to the purple grove as he'd planned, confident that Charlie was unlikely to risk following him on the very day he'd been confronted about that behavior. The aye-aye had been turned loose to wander, as before, and Innis ventured deeper into the grove, astonished at the depth and width of it. The purple trees once again seemed to be surrounding him closely, almost as though in protection, and he relaxed, letting go of his worries and sorrow for the first time since Sheena's death. As he strolled around in the penetrating darkness of the woods, he sensed a soft murmuring. Was it only the rustling of the purple leaves? There hadn't been a wind when he'd left his cabin and looking up into the forest canopy he saw that all was still. Smiling to himself, he journeyed farther into the depths of the grove when the sound of Yaeger's chortling drew his attention to the top of a nearby tree where the aye-aye was perched, gazing into the distance as he'd done on their initial visit.

"What is it you see, my darlin'?" Innis whispered. "Wish I could see it."

Yaeger's glance turned to Innis as if he'd heard the comment. The golden light seemed to shine from his eyes and Innis once again felt the strange ecstasy he'd experienced during the previous visit. Sitting down with his back against the large tree where Yaeger was perched, Innis envisioned living among these glorious trees, safe from the prying and petty cruelty of the outside world, allowing Yaeger to live free in a natural state. The grove itself seemed to be encouraging him, or was it the aye-aye? All sense of time had vanished and when Yaeger and Innis returned to their cabin, with no sign of Halloran during their journey, it was much later than usual. Yaeger had gathered more nest material and food than in the past but Innis was exhausted, leaving the aye-aye to his treasures and going almost immediately to bed. It was then he'd had the dream.

During his work assignments that day, Innis's thoughts relentlessly drifted back to the nightmare and also the time spent with Yaeger in the purple grove. When he returned home in the afternoon he began work on the painting of Yaeger that was to be based on his sketch. He'd decided to forgo a trip to Belfast for more art supplies, masking do with what he'd already collected. The thought of seeing Fin in his current, agitated frame of mind was too unsettling, and she would surely ask again about a visit to Raven's Back. They'd exchanged a few phone calls and texts, but he'd withheld the discovery of Sheena's body from her and sensed a slight distance developing between them that was more than just the number of miles from Raven's Back to Belfast. He took the fairly large canvas he'd previously purchased at the local craft shop in Glenraven and now began to create the painting of Yaeger in the purple treetop beneath a full moon. Propping the sketch nearby, he worked only loosely from it as the images from those magical moments readily returned to him.

As a woodworker apprentice, most of Innis's tasks had been restricted by the parameters of certain requirements: precise measurements, blueprints, safety regulations, even the warp of the wood with which he was working. Now he needed to adjust to the landscape of his imagination, a wide open and blank expanse he would fill with colors, forms and feelings without rules or guidelines. He'd forgotten the sheer joy and freedom of painting which had so enthralled him as a young boy, but his sense of color and scale quickly returned as he began to mix the limited number of paints he had at hand to achieve the desired effects. The larger canvas on which he was working allowed for more freedom of movement and once again he was transported into a cocoon of creation where time vanished along with the outside world. There was only him, the canvas, the paints and brushes and the images in his mind. An unseen hand seemed to guide him while he painted, making the brush strokes and details of the picture as simple as child's play. Combinations of colors practically suggested themselves to him along with the most efficient ways of capturing the vibrant luster of the leaves in the purple grove, the texture of the soft bark on the trees, the eerie expression in Yaeger's eyes, the drift of the full moon across the sky.

Innis worked over the painting for hours, oblivious to his surroundings or the passing of time. He knew he wouldn't complete the painting in one night but when he finally stopped to rest and looked at what he'd accomplished he was amazed by his own work. The level of sophistication displayed on the canvas was well beyond anything he'd ever done before or even imagined himself capable of doing. The painting was almost a living thing and as he gazed at it he could sense the slight stirring of the tree branches in the soft breeze, the dense but breathing darkness of the forest, the deep sheen of the leaves and Yaeger's vibrant presence.

It took Innis only one more afternoon to complete the painting and on the evening he finished it he felt a palpable relief as though a burden had been taken from him. The painting stood propped on the easel where the sketch had once stood in the living room. Innis had moved the sketch to his bedroom where it rested against one wall, roundly ignored by Yaeger. The large painting, however, was a different matter to the aye-aye. As Yaeger came into the living room for his nightly excursion that evening he stood still, frozen in place in front of the painting. Looking up at it with fascination, he seemed to be carefully assessing it, his amber eyes wandering over every inch of the canvas while Innis watched, cautiously amused.

Yaeger gave his weird chortle and began to climb up the legs of the easel toward the painting. Innis started forward, fearful of damage to his brilliant work but then noticed the aye-aye was carefully maneuvering in such a way that his long claws never scratched the paint. When he reached the top of the large canvas, Yaeger balanced on it and posed in an exact replica of his position and expression in the painting. Innis burst out laughing.

"Ah, macushla, you're too much! What a funny character you are. Now shall we go out hunting? Since you're now such a star, wouldn't want it to go to your head and break our humble routine."

It had become Innis's habit to take Yaeger only to the purple grove now, where he was free to roam while the dense woods provided shelter and a strange inspiration. As Innis wandered among the purple trees, waiting for Yaeger to complete his hunting and exploring, new images for future paintings of the aye-aye began to present themselves, complete with precise details and colors. He realized how quickly and naturally he'd become comfortable again with his own creativity, how vastly more satisfying it was in comparison with the regimented woodworking that had occupied his life for too long. More convinced than ever that the message the magical grove held for him was one of imagination rather than actual use of the purple wood itself, as he'd originally believed, he savored his nights among the sheltering trees, exploring farther just as Yaeger did. His fear of Charlie and the shotgun vanished when he was in the purple grove as he felt protected, immune from fear and danger.

He'd noticed that Yaeger was finding interesting, unidentifiable insects and mushrooms in the grove. The first time the aye-aye had indicated a purple mushroom growing at the base of a tree, Innis had rushed forward to prevent him from touching the exotic fungus, but Yaeger had quickly snatched the mushroom and eaten it, his eyes dancing with delight. Innis had worried the rest of the night about possible harmful effects but Yaeger had been fine and soon the purple mushrooms became part of his regular diet. They seemed to make him more energetic, much to Innis's chagrin and amusement. The aye-aye stayed up most of the night, only climbing into bed to join Innis just before dawn. Yaeger had even taken to dancing. He would stand on his hind legs, taking hold of the handle on a dresser drawer or the leg of the easel and wriggle his rear end from side to side with his long tail swishing in rhythm. Innis found these performances hilarious and laughed uproariously which encouraged Yaeger to shake it even harder.

The creature had also begun to get into things while Innis slept which wasn't quite as entertaining. Kitchen drawers were left open, cooking utensils strewn across the floor and curtains shredded where Yaeger had climbed them. Sometimes Innis was exasperated by the mess he found in his cabin upon waking and left it for the day while he rushed off to his job and Yaeger slept. Certain items began to go missing: a toothbrush, the top to the sugar bowl, a silver ring given to Innis by Fin which he'd never worn. When Innis began to discover items missing he initially became paranoid about Charlie, wondering if the neighbor had actually broken into the cabin to take things simply to pester him. Eventually, after he noticed the amused expression on Yaeger's face once while he made a frantic search for a missing item, Innis realized who the culprit must be. He found all of the missing items distributed among the various nests that were scattered throughout the cabin. There was no sense in punishing the scamp, he knew, since he was never able to catch the creature in the act. Once a stolen item was retrieved from a nest, it was usually replaced with a different one within a matter of days and Innis grew used to the game though sometimes annoyed by it.

As visits to the purple grove continued, visions for new paintings of Yaeger filled Innis's imagination with increasing frequency. He ordered more sketching paper and smaller canvases from the crafts store, spending most of the money from his job on art supplies and avoiding the thought of how he would pay for these things once his apprenticeship ended. The shed behind his cabin soon filled with painting materials and Innis spent every spare moment sketching pictures of Yaeger, usually depicting him in the purple grove. In one he might be holding a purple mushroom in his bony fingers as if about to take a bite, in another he stood on his hind legs atop a tree branch and gripping the next higher branch as if ready to begin a climb, or he was settled among a pile of purple leaves, his long tail curled around himself and his eyes closed as though contentedly sleeping.

Innis knew he was avoiding too many things. His cabin became even more of a cluttered mess with dishes piled up in the sink, grocery shopping neglected, dust gathering over every surface, windows unwashed. His social life suffered as well. He'd continued to put off his family's visit to his cabin along with meeting Fin in Belfast, and he seldom went to the farmhouse for dinner with his family as he'd once done on a regular basis. One afternoon he arrived home to find a note from his mother slipped beneath the door, stating that she'd come by with some food for him and desperately needed to talk to him about something important. If he was never going to invite the family for an official visit to his cabin, she'd written, they would simply drop by some evening soon, adding that he should wash his windows.

Innis ignored all these issues, however, to immerse himself in painting and sketching, amassing an impressive number of artworks in a short period of time. The large painting of Yaeger under a full moon, now completed, held pride of place in the living room where it faced the front door so that any visitor's eye would fall on it immediately. Of course there were no visitors and Innis only kept the painting there for lack of space elsewhere. His cabin was filled with artworks and aye-aye nests and he idly wondered what his mother in particular would make of it should she drop by unannounced. He'd also done a sketch and painting of Sheena from his memory of their last meeting. It featured her in her usual bundled state of dress, a fire blazing in the fireplace of her cabin, a heavy tea mug raised in welcome with an open bottle of Jameson's on a table nearby. It cheered him a bit to recreate his friend on canvas as he'd still been despondent over the loss of her companionship. He'd managed to learn from Oren that no relatives of the old woman had been located and no will or funeral instructions found, so she'd been buried in an unmarked grave in a small cemetery between the town of Glenraven and Raven's Back. He visited the site soon after, able to identify it by the freshly dug plot, and poured some whiskey onto the dirt, singing an old Irish tune he'd heard her humming while she prepared his tea during their final visit. Feeling a bit foolish, he nevertheless told her he was making a painting of her and hoped she wouldn't be offended, promising to do her proud.

The subject of Charlie Halloran had drifted from his thoughts for the most part, and there had been no repeat of the stalking behavior. Innis hoped their discussion had embarrassed the man enough to stop following him and Yaeger's new hunting grounds in the purple grove added to the welcome sense of privacy and security. For the first time, Innis's imagination had become the top priority in his life, along with the aye-aye who'd opened the doors to his housemate's natural creativity.

Once again, as with the carvings he'd made from the purple wood, the idea of showing anyone his paintings of Yaeger gave Innis pause. How could he reveal his art to someone with a sufficient explanation of his subject matter? He immediately thought of Finola. After all, he'd taken a chance going to her with the purple wood carvings and she'd accepted the crazy source of such unusual wood, even keeping the secret as she'd promised. She was also aware of Yaeger, so a painting of an aye-aye might intrigue her more than the average person with no explanation needed. It had been too long since they'd shared a lunch or even seen each other face-to-face. He hoped his sporadic texts and occasional apologetic phone calls had been enough to keep what fire remained between them alive, but the last time he'd talked to her on the phone he'd sensed a distance in her voice that worried him. He missed her though, if he was honest with himself, he hadn't thought about her too often since all of his energy and attention was now focused on his art, his grief over Sheena, his new relationship with the purple grove and, as always,

Yaeger. A text would be too impersonal, he decided, and phoned her one morning at a time he figured she'd be at the shop. Their conversation was brief, but when Innis asked if he might stop in to see her in a few days he heard that familiar, happy lilt to her voice as they set a time and date to meet at The Forestry.

Innis carefully studied the paintings he'd completed, trying to determine which would be best to take to Fin. The one of Yaeger beneath a full moon was much too large, though he considered it the best. Instead, he chose a smaller, whimsical depiction of the aye-aye holding a purple mushroom, about to take a bite. Fin would appreciate the significance of a purple mushroom after her enthusiasm for the purple wood. While he was in Belfast, Innis could pick up additional art supplies as well and he looked forward to telling Fin about the new direction his life had recently taken. Perhaps the dilemma of how to reveal Yaeger's existence to the outside world would be solved using the paintings as ambassadors. Regardless, he valued Fin's advice, craved and missed her support and realized she had become more important to him than he'd cared to admit. It would be like introducing himself to her for the first time, in a way. She'd only known Innis the woodworker but now she would meet the artist, the real Innis who'd taken an unexplored fork in the road just when he'd almost reached his destination on the main path he'd been following through life. And all because of an aye-aye. Would she understand or consider him a silly dreamer who'd diverted his future to chance? He gazed at the painting of Yaeger with the mushroom and smiled, knowing that it was no longer an option for him, taking the safe and steady path, even for Fin.

Chapter XXI: For Love Of Innis

The weeks had dragged by for Fin with only a few texts and the rare phone chat with her beloved Innis. At first she'd been pragmatic about their extended separation, reminding herself that he was nearing the completion of his apprenticeship, probably concentrated on the next step toward earning his certificate as a woodworker. Then there was the physical distance between them. She knew that Innis preferred the natural environment of Raven's Back to the city bustle of Belfast and endured the long trip to spend time with her. Yaeger was another thing undoubtedly taking up Innis's time and when they'd last spoken he'd seemed flustered, scattered and distracted. Innis was probably keeping more secrets from her and she wished he would trust her, would be a bit more forthcoming. It wasn't his nature, she knew, and as time spent together face-to-face diminished she began to wonder if her attachment to the dark-eyed man from the north was really a bad or a good idea. What drew her to him so strongly? Of course there was that face of his with its impish smile, intense eyes and what she considered to be perfect features. And what about the abundance of dark, curly hair in which she couldn't help entangling her fingers while they made love. His kindness and creativity must be added to the list, along with the easygoing way he had of being perfectly happy to sit on a park bench and eat sandwiches with her.

Yes, it was turning out to be more of a long distance relationship than she might have preferred, but their common ground more than made up for that. He was not a romantic and neither was she. They shared a love of wood and the beauties of nature along with a subtle sense of humor that showed itself in small, teasing ways. Sex with Innis was marvelous, especially once they'd become more familiar and relaxed with each other. Even secrets, such as the aye-aye, were shared. Despite trying to prepare herself for an eventual separation from Innis, his absence began to make her think of him more. She wondered all sorts of things about him, silly, pointless things that embarrassed her to think about. Did he ever sing in the shower? What was his favorite dessert and did he prefer his pie and cake with ice cream, whipped cream or standing alone? What sort of books had he read as a child? It wasn't like her to ponder such things about a person yet she couldn't keep herself from imagining all sorts of far-fetched scenarios about her and Innis. They would travel the world together, visiting sanctuaries and zoos where aye-ayes were kept and bred, maybe even making their way to Madagascar to discover Yaeger's true homeland. Or someone might discover the unusual purple wood items Innis had carved and he'd become rich and famous, the two of them buying a small farm near Galway which she still missed more than she cared to admit.

These odd musings annoyed her though, and she chided herself for such childish dreams, sensing that Innis was actually drifting away from her. Before meeting him, there had been a few men who'd caught her eye but only one with whom she'd become more intimately involved. None of them had appealed to her in the way that Innis did and she found herself questioning this unrealistic attachment she'd developed for him. His recent call setting up a visit had transported her to the moon after months of no direct contact, yet how wise was she being, allowing him to effect her in this way? The thought of actually rolling around with him in the small bed in her flat again when she'd been only imagining it for so long sent shivers up her spine. Surely no one should have the power to make her behave in this way, she told herself, but thoughts and daydreams and longings for Innis persisted. After first meeting him, she'd tried to convince herself that she'd been lonely and flattered by his flirtatious attentions. As time went on and she discovered who he was, however, she couldn't deny that things were much more complicated.

Sometimes she'd imagine his life in Raven's Back, researching the area on the Web with little success. It seemed that, while Glenraven had a presence online, there was precious little to be found on Raven's Back. A couple of images revealed the astounding natural beauty of the area but she could learn nothing of its history or everyday details. Innis had mentioned a few things to her about life there but her insatiable curiosity demanded more.

As a girl, she'd been close to her father, spending as much time with him as she could and eventually taking the same livelihood of dealing with wood, though in a different capacity. He'd taught her most of what she knew about wood and also about life. He'd stressed independence and making the most of her affinity for wood, delaying personal involvements until she'd settled into her own profession and established her own life. She'd happily followed his advice, proud to set up her own small business in Galway selling wood products while still living at home. When her father died in an auto accident as the passenger in a speeding truck that claimed five

victims in total, Fin's world upended completely. Left with her argu-
mentative mother, with whom she'd never gotten along, and two sib-
lings who'd never understood her, she struggled to maintain any
equilibrium at all. She closed her shop, sold off all her assets and
shut down emotionally, spending days in bed while her mother
berated her laziness and demanded some of the profits from her business. Fin couldn't see a way to go on with life, but she realized she
missed wood and, knowing that Galway now held too much unhap-
piness, set out for Belfast, as far from her beginnings as she could
get. The beauty and mysticism of her city of birth was replaced by
the darker, more painful history of her adopted city but somehow
this suited her mood and she set up The Forestry as a way of keeping
her father's memory alive and preserving the connection with wood
they'd shared.

Profits from the shop weren't large but enough for her to live
modestly. The occasional windfall from a handful of wealthy customers made it possible for her to save a tidy nest egg. She'd been
content with her somewhat solitary life until Innis came along. Now
she found herself anticipating a phone call or text with what she considered to be a somewhat pitiful enthusiasm. It had always been her
way to get things done, relying on no one, in charge of her life and
glad to be so. Was Innis trying to let her down easy by his increasing absence? Perhaps this planned meeting they'd just scheduled
might be a final goodbye? If so, she began to bargain with herself.
What would she be willing to do to keep him in her life, how far
would she go and what would she be willing to sacrifice for love of
Innis? Certainly not her shop, never that, though she'd entertained
the possibility of relocating The Forestry in Glenraven should she
develop a more serious relationship with Innis. Her own family had
been a turbulent one for the most part, and she had no desire to
become involved with Innis's clan, yet surely that would be
inevitable should something as serious as marriage be an option farther down the road. Getting a bit ahead of yourself, aren't you girl,
she chided herself but couldn't help picturing life with Innis by her
side.

Forcing herself to refrain from buying new clothes or having
her hair restyled prior to Innis's visit, she determined to keep things
as simple and unchanged as possible, strictly business as usual. It
could be a mistake letting this Raven's Back man know just how
much she'd missed him, though she was certain he'd see it in her

eyes. He'd sounded frazzled and tired when he'd called and she wondered if there was some particular reason for the visit. She'd find out soon enough. Meanwhile, every night and every morning she touched the bowl of purple wood which he'd carved, savoring its strange warmth and smooth, soft feel, remembering that morning when they'd first met. She straightened and cleaned her flat in hopeful anticipation of a possible overnight stay with Innis and tried not to get carried away with her fantasies.

The day of the planned visit began early for Fin as she rose, skittish and excited, before her alarm sounded to prepare her usual brown bag lunch and get dressed in one of her usual work outfits. Fussing with her hair and the small amount of make-up she wore, she made a face at herself in the mirror above her bathroom sink.

"Silly girl," she spoke aloud to her reflection. "If you're not enough for him by now you're never gonna be."

She opened the shop early, rearranging a couple of items to calm her nerves and checking her cell phone to make certain there'd been no message from Innis canceling the visit. He was fairly prompt, as usual, which always impressed Fin as she tended to be late for almost everything. She was surprised to see him carrying a covered canvas but the same irresistible smile greeted her and most of her annoyance and resentment at his long absence quickly melted away.

"Stranger!" she called out with irrepressible delight in her voice. "Had almost forgotten what you look like. And what's this, then?"

Motioning to the canvas, she was pleased to see that Innis seemed as happy to see her as she was to see him, though he'd lost a little weight and the darkness beneath his eyes, which she knew was caused by lack of sleep, had increased. He set the canvas down carefully on the counter beside the cash register.

"I've got a surprise for you, Fin my darlin', but first let me have a look at you. It's been much too long, my girl, and you're looking fine, like you haven't missed me even a jolt."

"A jolt, is it? I'll show you a jolt."

Fin came around from behind the counter and threw her arms around Innis, kissing him squarely on the mouth while he stumbled back a little from the force of her embrace. Keeping one hand on the canvas to prevent it from falling, he slipped his other arm around Fin's waist and held her close, returning her passionate and almost frantic kiss in kind. The shop was empty of customers, not that either one of them would have noticed and Fin pulled away first, holding Innis at arm's length to inspect him. She shook her head but continued smiling broadly, unable to mask her delight.

"You're looking fine yourself, Innis, but a bit thin and tired. Sorry for the attack, luv, I just couldn't help myself. Guess I've missed you more than a jolt. And actually, I think it's a jot."

Innis grinned and shrugged.

"Whatever the hell it is, I'm so happy to see you, darlin'."

He hugged her again and she pointed to the canvas.

"So, what's the surprise? Could this be an Innis Kilbride original work of art I have before me?"

Innis mock-bowed with a flourish of his hand and laughed.

"Yes, Fin O'Brian, my dear, it is exactly that. Since we last parted ways I've returned to my first calling. I'm a painter again, I'm afraid."

Fin grinned with joy.

"Marvelous! Let's have a look, then. And what about your woodworking career? You've given it up?"

Innis looked a bit sheepish.

"Pretty much, yeah. I've a few more jobs to finish for Oren and then I'm a full time painter."

"No certificate?"

"I know, it seems crazy, this close and all but, no. I'm a painter so I won't be needing a certificate."

There was a brief silence as Fin studied Innis, her brow furrowed in a way that caused him to jump back in.

"D'ya think I'm crazy?"

She laughed and put a hand fondly on his cheek.

"Of course I think you're crazy. Why else would I be in love with you?"

Both of them looked a bit startled at the unexpected declaration then Fin turned to the covered canvas, embarrassed and wishing to divert the conversation away from her blurted words.

"So, am I going to see this masterpiece?"

"It's hardly a masterpiece. I left that one at home."

They both laughed nervously and Innis drew the cover from the canvas, revealing the image of Yaeger holding a purple mushroom. Fin gasped with surprise and delight, her eyes dancing with happiness and pride.

"Why, Innis, it truly is a masterpiece! Marvelous beyond description really, almost like seeing your aye-aye up close and personal."

She examined the painting, peering closely at its many details and vivid colors, gazing into Yaeger's eyes to find a truly lifelike expression of anticipation of his treat emanating from them. Like the purple wood, a warmth and vibrancy came from the painting, mesmerizing her in an otherworldly yet soothing way. The longer she looked at the painting, the more depth and detail was revealed to her. Barely able to tear her eyes away from it, she finally turned to Innis, struggling to keep her emotions under control.

"It's like magic, Innis, truly. You've captured Yaeger so brilliantly, like he's alive inside the painting. I went online to look at images of aye-ayes, you know, after our discussion about him, and you've really hit it bang on. Even though I've never seen him, it's like I've met him. My God, you really are a painter. Where's this been hiding, your artistic talent, I mean?"

Innis grinned, thrilled but slightly awkward with her enthusiasm.

"Dunno. I've always loved to paint and it's what my ma originally wanted me to do. I didn't paint like this before, though. Only since Yaeger and the purple forest have I been able to do this. It's like some force takes over, Fin, and I'm guided by an unseen hand. I know it sounds insane but that's just the way it seems."

"And the purple mushroom, did you imagine that or is it real? It's a perfect touch, I love it."

"It exists, can you believe it? Yaeger found them in the purple grove, they grow at the base of the trees. He loves them and they've given him an energy boost, I think. Of course I haven't tried them. Can't say I haven't been tempted though."

His eyes sparkled with mischief and Fin pushed his shoulder playfully.

"That's all you need, Innis Kilbride, a magic mushroom. God knows what it would do to you. You seem to be living a charmed life though, I'll say that."

"Yes and no. What am I to do for a living once my gig as a woodworker ends? I've got lots of Yaeger paintings and sketches like this one at home, but do I honestly believe people will be clamoring for pictures of a weird animal they probably don't even know what it is? Not likely. Not for a minute."

Fin held the small painting at arm's length, taking in its wonderful, whimsical strangeness and impressive painting technique. It was all she could do to stop looking at it.

"I don't know, Innis," she kept her eyes on the painting. "It's pretty marvelous."

"Thanks, but then there's the whole question of people asking, even if they did buy it, what made me paint this, who's the model. It all comes down to the Yaeger secret again. How would I possibly explain? By the way, that's yours."

A dazzling smile broke out on Fin's face and she carefully placed the painting on the counter before throwing her arms around Innis in a bear hug. She kissed him passionately and held him while she looked into his eyes, relieved at the affectionate warmth she saw there.

"Ah, Innis, you've made me so spectacularly happy today! I can't thank you enough and I can't tell you how proud I am of you for bringing your dream back to life. And for this brilliant painting. You won't give it to me, though, I insist on paying you for it."

Innis shook his head, holding her even closer.

"Not after the way I've been avoiding you, darlin', I wouldn't take a cent from you. I know you've been wondering what the hell I've been up to and why you've been at arm's length. This is the least I can do by way of an apology. Please accept it."

Fin smiled, kissed him gently on the lips and ran a hand over his curly hair then released him and returned to the other side of the counter, once again eying the painting.

"Very well, and thank you. You're right, I have been worried and, honestly, thinking perhaps you've written me off. I've tried preparing myself for an end to us but I've simply been unable to do it."

Laughing uncomfortably, she turned toward the cash register so Innis wouldn't notice the tears in her eyes. Fumbling to straighten out the money in the slots of the register through her blurred vision, Fin felt the awkward silence growing and kept her head down until there was a soft knock on the counter. She looked up to find Innis watching her with a grave expression. Brushing her tears away she closed the cash drawer and picked up the painting, adopting a cheery voice.

"This little fella is going to keep me excellent company at home and I already know exactly where I'm going to hang him. I assume it will be the same deal as with the purple bowl. No one's to see the picture. Is that it? But Innis, what's the point of art if no one--"

Innis reached across the counter and put a finger against her lips to interrupt.

"You're right, what's the point indeed. No, hang the picture wherever you'd like. This time I don't mind whoever might see it. Not sure how the whole secret of Yaeger is gonna work out yet, but I can't keep hiding it from everyone. I really believe these paintings I'm doing are inspired by some magic in the purple grove, Fin, and also by Yaeger. It's like he's dictating them to me."

The whole story of the past months poured from Innis before he could prevent it. He told Fin of Charlie Halloran and the shotgun, finding Sheena's body and the experiences in the purple grove including his epiphany during his visit there with Bridget. The tale was interrupted several times by the appearance of a customer in the shop but once they'd been attended by Fin and left, Innis would pick up his story, compelled to divulge everything. Fin listened attentively without comments or questions and when Innis had finally finished she nodded with a pensive expression.

"That's the most detailed explanation and, I assume, apology for an absence I've ever heard," she remarked solemnly then burst out laughing at the stricken look on Innis's face.

"I'm having you on a bit, darlin'. I'm sorry, I couldn't help it. You have a charmed life indeed, Innis Kilbride, when, in the space of a few months you've found a dead body, been stalked by a shotgun-toting neighbor, changed your life's entire direction and completed almost a dozen paintings. And here all this time I've merely been running this little shop and wondering what the hell I've done to put you off, waiting for you to call. It's classic, truly."

Innis peered at her, uncertain if she was joking, upset, angry or what. Fin hardly knew herself which it was, possibly a combination of all of them. She picked up the painting and admired it once again.

"I'm glad you've decided to share this art and I'll cherish this, Innis. It's as if I've finally met Yaeger even though I never have."

"I'm really sorry about that, darlin', I know I've put off your visit to Raven's Back, but as you can see--"

Fin held up a hand to halt his words.

"No need to apologize. This painting will do. It's so lifelike, I feel lucky to have it. Look, Innis, I didn't mean to be cavalier about your trying times. It's just a bit overwhelming and I'm sad for you about the loss of your friend Sheena. It's obvious you're quite up against it with your neighbor and your situation with Yaeger, but I don't like being relegated to a sounding board if you won't allow me to be a real part of your life otherwise. And I never pictured myself as a lovelorn female waiting by the phone. It's not who I aim to be. I've got a simple life here, minding my shop, reading my books and taking the occasional trip. I don't want the sort of drama you're talking about. It's not fair that I matter so little to you that you'll put me off like some annoying obligation when I cherish you like a rare treasure. I won't do it anymore, I don't want to."

Innis stared in astonishment as Fin stomped her foot and seemed to be having an argument with herself.

"You stupid girl! Here you've been waiting like a silly school girl with a crush for this day to arrive and now you've gone and made a right mess of it."

She snatched the painting and ran to the back office in the shop where Innis could hear her throwing things around and slamming drawers. He stood frozen in place until a customer entered the shop, the tinkling of the little bell above the door causing the noise from the back to go silent. Innis smiled at the small, middle-aged woman with a camera hanging around her neck who'd just entered and stood gazing around the shop, her eyes bright with curiosity.

"Hello," she smiled at Innis, her American accent and the camera identifying her as a likely tourist. "What a lovely little place. Look at all this beautiful wood. I suppose that's why it's called The Forestry, hmm? I had to find out what that name meant, that's why I came in. Now I understand. Oh, how cute!"

She hurried to a table that held a display of wooden carvings of various forest animals: a deer, a badger, a woodpecker on a tree, a squirrel and a fox. Her hand hovered above the squirrel and she glanced at Innis.

"OK to touch? Can I pick this up to look at it?"

Innis shrugged.

"I suppose so. I'm not actually the owner of the shop..."

Fin suddenly bustled out from the back office, her eyes and nose clearly red from crying but her face dry.

"By all means, feel free to pick up anything you'd like," she hurried over to the customer, holding out her hand. "I'm Finola O'Brian, the proprietress of The Forestry."

She'd made this statement in a jokingly grand way and the women shook hands, both of them laughing.

"Well, pleased to meet you," the customer answered. "I'm Kathleen Miller, from America, as I'm sure you can tell. Pennsylvania, actually."

The two began a friendly discussion as Kathleen examined the little wooden squirrel while Fin told her the name and credentials of the woodcarver who'd made it. Innis remained awkwardly at the counter, reluctant to make a move or say a word with Fin's declaration tumbling around in his head in a flurry of confusion. Had she just told him to get lost, that she was through with him?

He caught Fin's attention, smiling and motioning to the door. She acknowledged him with a brisk nod of her head, turning her focus back to her customer. Innis slipped out the door and found himself walking to the small nearby park where he and Fin had so often shared lunch. Sitting on the bench where they usually sat, he felt despondent, unable to put together a coherent thought about Fin's outburst. There'd been such anger and resentment in it, feelings he'd been completely unaware she was harboring until now. Reviewing the past few months, he could pinpoint times when he'd felt her pulling away from him, a tinge of removal in her voice on the phone or a particularly terse text message. He'd assumed she was annoyed with him, possibly distancing herself, but the vehemence with which she'd just confronted him was something altogether surprising. She has a right to be angry, he reminded himself. After all, he'd procrastinated with everything: her visit to Raven's Back, her meeting with Yaeger, his trips to Belfast to see her.

For a moment he envied his brother and saw the wisdom of Dalton's view that marriages and relationships seemed more trouble than they were worth. It was true, he'd taken Fin for granted, couldn't deny that. Thinking of life without her caused a clutch to his heart that frightened him, yet he also acknowledged to himself the avoidance of complications her absence would bring. Innis was, for the most part, averse to compromise, especially where Yaeger and his art were concerned. He wished to live life to his own specifications, just as Fin obviously did. He'd chosen Raven's Back for his home despite his mother's reservations and decided to chuck his woodworking career apparently on a whim. Smiling ruefully he shook his head.

"Not exactly a prize, are you, lad?" he murmured to himself.

"This whole mess is of your doing to be sure."

"Talking to yourself already?"

Innis's head jerked up to find Fin standing by the bench, her arms folded and an amused smile on her face. He chuckled with embarrassment, tentatively patting the bench next to him and relieved when Fin sat down.

"You knew where I'd go, huh?"

"I made a pretty good guess. Not sure what I would have done if I'd found this bench empty. I'm so sorry."

She threw her arms around him and he returned her embrace, pulling away reluctantly. Fin put her hands in her lap, looking down at them silently for several minutes then speaking softly and hesitantly.

"I'm not sure what brought all that on. Well, perhaps I am, but...I did mean what I said—I suppose I'd been holding it all in for too long...what a right fool I am."

Innis put his hand under her chin to lift her face, noticing the beginning of tears in her eyes.

"I'm the right fool, darlin'," he whispered. "Crazy idiot that I am, to have lucked into the affections of a girl like you and then throw it all away simply because I'm a coward? The very definition of a right fool."

Fin smiled and kissed Innis gently, placing her hand on the side of his face.

"You're not a coward, Innis. Anything but. A bit of a fool, perhaps, but never a coward."

"Nice of you to say, but I'm exactly that. When you said your piece back in the shop, I was surprised at first, but the more I've thought about it the more I realize you're right and I never saw any of it really. I did know I was holding you at arm's length but I was trying to avoid caring about you too much. The bottom line is, I do care about you a great deal but you're right. My life and your life don't exactly compliment each other. I'm not sure it's ever gonna work and, to be honest, I don't think I have the will or energy to make it work right now. I do love you, Fin, but at the end of the day Yaeger is my top priority and will be for the foreseeable future."

Fin gave a short, sharp laugh.

"Ha! I'm thrown over for an aye-aye, am I?"

She took Innis's hands, feeling lightly over the scratches and calluses from his woodworking duties and holding back an ocean of grief at the thought of never feeling these familiar hands again. Somewhere, somehow she'd sensed this outcome was inevitable and she pushed her feelings aside, offering Innis a clear-eyed gaze and a playful smile.

"I understand what you're saying and even though it breaks my heart a bit I've got to agree. I adore you, my darlin' Innis, yet that just isn't going to be quite enough, is it? For us to truly make a life together one of us would have to change too much and neither is willing. I'm afraid that's the bottom line, isn't it?"

Innis nodded solemnly and looked down at the small hands holding his. They were unadorned by jewelry today and he wondered where the silver frog ring had gone. Fin's nails, clipped short without any shaping or polish, suddenly struck him as almost child-like and he raised her hands, kissing each one in turn then placed them in her lap. Feeling a rush of sorrow for all the things he would never learn about her, he took a deep breath and shifted on the bench to face her.

"Would it be asking too much for us to go on as friends? I'd miss your company terribly, you know."

Fin furrowed her brows and was silent for a moment then shook her head slowly.

"No, Innis. I'm sorry but I don't believe that would work. It would simply be too hard for me, seeing you, wondering if we might start back up. I'm at the shop, you know the hours and days, so obviously if you're in Belfast perhaps you could stop by occasionally just to keep in touch. Please wait awhile though. I don't think I want to see you again for a bit. I think you're going to be over me before I'm over you but never worry. I'll get on, and despite my small size I'm sturdy, like the wood I sell."

"Ah, Fin, you're killin' me. I wish things were different, I truly do. Could I just tell you one thing I've been thinking about? Maybe it would change things."

Fin sighed, rolling her eyes and scoffing.

"Always one more thing, eh? All right, mister, hit me with your best shot. Better be good, though, to change things at this point."

"Well, I think it is, at least it could be. Lately when Yaeger and I have been hanging out in the purple grove at night I've felt like the forest is telling me things, suggesting paths of action. One of them is the idea of living there, in the woods. I can't explain it but there's a protection about it, like the trees close in and there's the sense that nothing can harm us when we're there. I know it must sound insane--"

"Well, a bit," Fin commented.

"Yeah, but it seems so true. I've been thinking I'd move my cabin to the purple grove and live there, or else build a whole new home there. The only people who've ever known about the purple forest are me and Bridget as far as I can tell."

"Hmm..and what does that tell you? Sounds a bit too fanciful for me, Innis. Sure you're not indulging in your overactive imagination? So what are you saying, that I might move out there with you?"

"Exactly! You could start a shop in Glenraven and you'd be surrounded by the beautiful purple trees day and night. I'm sure it's a unique offer if nothing else."

Fin smiled sadly at Innis and touched his shoulder.

"I've never received such a proposal before and am unlikely to ever receive such a one again. I'm flattered, truly, that you'd want to share your magical world with me, darlin', but think about it. I long for the world, not just one corner of it. I'm settled in Belfast now but I'm always saving for my trips and going wherever I can. I don't want to be limited to one little area of Raven's Back, charming as it might be. Honestly, I'm not sure you should do that either. You've gone all mystical almost overnight."

"I have," Innis nodded. "And look at my painting. You can't say it hasn't had a good effect on me."

"True." Fin hesitated then sat up straighter, squaring her shoulders in resolve. "I'm a feet-on-the-ground kind of girl I guess. It's not going to work for me, much as we both might wish it could."

They looked at each for a long time, then Fin rose from her seat, leaning down to kiss Innis lightly on the mouth. He remained frozen in place, his heart pounding wildly at the thought of her walking away.

"The best to you always, Innis. Luck, happiness, all the magic you can handle, I wish it all for you. I hope you'll look back on me fondly and I'll always cherish the parts of you I'll keep. The memories, the purple bowl, the painting of Yaeger. They'll remind me of something very special that came my way."

She turned abruptly and marched away without a backward glance. Innis stayed on the bench for some time, fighting tears and the urge to chase after her, thinking with a bittersweet recall of the cycle of their time together which had begun and ended on this park bench in Belfast.

Chapter XXII: The Spy

The confrontation with Innis Kilbride left Charlie Halloran in a state of nerves and fury. The fact that his stalking behavior in the woods was known to Kilbride initially mortified him, but this embarrassment quickly turned to anger as he recalled the righteous indignation on the part of his neighbor. What right had anyone to judge him, let alone Innis Kilbride who came from a notoriously odd family and was new to Raven's Back. The bloody nerve, Charlie fumed as he paced the living room of his cabin after Innis left that day. And what was this implication about the new police officer, Tom Sullivan, and his collusion with Charlie? Yes, he'd gotten some information from Sullivan about the old woman Sheena's death, but he figured what really irked Kilbride was the fact that Charlie had obtained details that he'd failed to get. Why didn't the bloke just be honest about it, he was jealous of Charlie's insider status. And what business had Irene Kilbride, spying on who had dinner with who at Murphy's? The whole family was suspect as far as Charlie was concerned, high and mighty, too good to mingle with town folk, sequestered together like a den of thieves out there on that farm of theirs, circling the wagons around that mad woman named Bridget. He had no use for any of them and especially not for Innis.

When Innis had first moved to Raven's Back, Charlie had tried to be friendly but his overtures had been received with a luke-warm response. The man could have at least made more of an effort. Too good, Charlie decided, that's his problem. Too good for the likes of me. Then when Innis began going out with some of the other fishermen it struck Charlie as pretentious and ridiculous. What sort of bloke does that, riding out in a fishing boat for the fun of it, just for the experience? Hard work, fishing was, and not to be taken lightly in such a manner. Pretty much everything about Innis rubbed Charlie the wrong way, now that he thought about it. That cloying Irish charm, the long hair, the good looks, the secretive ways. He knew he'd stepped out of bounds, perhaps, in starting rumors about devil worship, but it was clear the man was strange and Charlie knew what he'd seen – the man returning from the woods late at night, something bundled in his coat with a long length of rope slung over his shoulder. All those times Charlie had followed Innis and still he'd never succeeded in catching him at whatever it was he snuck out into the woods to do. Why was he hiding from Charlie in

the first place, avoiding his questions, if things were perfectly inno-
cent? No, the fellow was a menace and Charlie was determined to
find him out and bring him down, one way or another.

There was no love lost for Sheena either, as far as Halloran
was concerned. He hadn't known the old woman but had heard of
her through his various sources of gossip, the proverbial grapevine
he had developed to great effect over his years in Glenraven and
Raven's Back. The infamous tale of Sheena preventing a lynch mob
from burning down Bridget's shack had reached his ears long before
it came to Innis's attention. Charlie had no use for Innis's mad aunt
and it bothered him knowing someone who dwelled in the realm
beyond sanity was a neighbor, too close for comfort. The fact that
Sheena had threatened her own neighbors with harm turned Charlie
against her despite never having met the woman. She'd been pretty
much of a hermit, he knew, like Bridget, and he didn't feel comfortable around others who were less sociable than himself. It made him
nervous and although Innis was a friendlier type he was still secretive which put Charlie on edge. He wondered what Sheena and Innis
had in common to have become friendly in the first place. On the
surface they seemed unlikely chums to him. In keeping with his suspicions about Kilbride, he conjured a few conspiratorial theories, all
of them worrisome. The two of them could surely have been up to
no good.

Tom Sullivan, the police officer in Glenraven, had been
recruited partly on a referral and recommendation from Charlie Halloran. The two had become friends a year earlier after meeting at a
festival held in one of the nearby glens. Charlie, always outgoing
and friendly even with strangers, had struck up a conversation with
Sullivan in a restaurant, asking the young man to join him at a table
as the two of them were both seated alone. Over a seafood lunch the
men found they had much in common and agreed to keep in touch.
They occasionally met for lunch if Halloran happened to be in Sullivan's area or attended a special event when the opportunity arose.
Charlie had invited Tom out on his fishing boat once and Sullivan
had taken quite a liking to the village of Glenraven, enthusing over
its small-town charms and the abundance of fresh seafood and scenic
beauties.

Vacancies in the Glenraven police department were rare, as
the town was so small, but when one opened up due to a retirement
Charlie contacted Tom and proved persuasive enough to finagle the

job for his friend. Since this was a fairly recent development, Sullivan had been immersed in learning his new job and the pals had few opportunities for spending time together. When Sheena died, however, Charlie had quickly arranged a lunch with his friend and easily pried some details about the death scene and coroner's results from Sullivan. Charlie prided himself on his impressive techniques for gathering gossip and dispersing it and he had already told Sullivan all about his suspicious encounters with Innis Kilbride. After meeting Innis for the first time in Sheena's cabin on the morning of her death, Sullivan concurred with Charlie's conclusions about this weird and bothersome local character. There was definitely something off about Kilbride, his police officer instincts had told him. The devil worship idea seemed a bit far-fetched but Sullivan nevertheless had a suspicious eye out for Innis Kilbride.

Now that Innis was aware that Charlie was following him, Halloran needed to devise another way of spying on his neighbor. He knew that Innis was out of his cabin most of the day at his job and since Charlie kept very early hours as a fisherman he usually arrived home mid-afternoon, before Innis would have returned. This provided a window of a few good hours for Charlie to do his snooping. If he was lucky, Kilbride was cavalier enough to leave his cabin unlocked as most of the residents of Raven's Back did. Charlie himself, of course, always locked up his own place and obviously Sheena had done the same, judging from Tom Sullivan's report that Innis had broken a window in order to gain entrance.

Charlie chose a day mid-week when he'd seen Innis working with Oren on a house in Glenraven to put his plan into motion. Walking casually to Innis's cabin as though out for a harmless stroll, he was glad that this particular cabin was somewhat isolated, making it unlikely that anyone would spot him snooping about. Approaching the cabin, he knocked on the front door, knowing the place must be empty. He called out Innis's name, announcing himself, then walked the rest of the way around the cabin making sure no one was in the back out of sight. There was a small, windowless shed with a padlocked door behind the cabin and Charlie inspected it closely, detecting a slight scent of paint. He tried the padlock but it was tightly secured. Creeping around this building he discovered nothing of interest but kept wondering what the hell Kilbride had stored inside. There was nothing around the shed to offer any clues.

Returning to the cabin he tried the back door but found it

locked. Peering into one of the windows, thrilled to find its curtains open, he could see the kitchen with what appeared to be Innis's breakfast dishes piled in the sink but nothing out of the ordinary presented itself. There were a few glasses and a bowl sitting on the kitchen table and a white plastic tub with a handle next to the refrigerator, but he was unable to see if anything was in it. Going back to the front of the cabin, he tried the front door which was also locked. Cursing at his luck, he looked into the living room window and came face-to-face with the painting of Yaeger under the full moon, which was propped on its usual easel facing the front door. Charlie gasped and backed away from the window then quickly returned to look again. As he stared at the strange painting, wondering what the hell this weird, unearthly creature could be, the thing's eyes seemed to glow and look back at him with uncanny life. He couldn't believe it. Here was the precise proof of his suspicions. Such an animal was clearly alien, probably from the devil and he shivered at the thought of what disturbing shenanigans must surely be taking place here. He wished he had one of those fancy phones with cameras in them, which he'd continually resisted, hating their high tech implications. Who would believe him, and how would he ever describe this apparition without a photograph? Returning to his own cabin to retrieve his camera would waste precious time and what if Kilbride came home early?

He leaned his face against the windowpane, looking intently at the disturbing painting to memorize every detail despite the hammering of his heart. After a few minutes his attention drifted to something on the floor near the painting and he peered more intently, trying to bring the object into focus. It was difficult to see much detail, what with the distance from the window and semi-darkness inside the cabin, but he could make out what appeared to be twigs and perhaps leaves sticking up from a dark ball of substantial size. A nest? If so it was one of the larger nests he'd ever seen, and what sort of bird would build a nest on the floor of a cabin? Then his eyes drifted back to the painting and he gave an involuntary shudder. Could the nest possibly belong to that godforsaken creature?

He scanned the rest of the living room, most if it visible from the window, and noticed another of the strange nest objects sitting atop a small cabinet against the wall. This one was more easily seen and, like the other, seemed to consist of twigs and leaves with a fairly large hole at the front as a point of entry. It appeared to be empty but he saw bits of what might be shriveled pieces of apple scattered near the nest. What the hell did all this mean, some sort of sacrifice? Or was Innis keeping and tending a monster?

Charlie had brought nothing with him except a small pair of binoculars which he suddenly remembered and snatched from his coat pocket, fumbling in his haste and fear to focus them. Training them on the cabinet, he now saw clearly that the object on it was, indeed, a hand-fashioned nest with an opening against which a few strands of dark fur clung. Switching to the other nest on the floor by the easel, he could see it was almost identical though slightly larger. He resisted turning the binoculars on the painting, terrified of illuminating too much detail and somehow being fixed in a trance by the thing. Lowering the binoculars he stood silently for a moment, trying to process this discovery. Reluctantly admitting to himself that he had started the devil worship rumors partly out of resentment and jealousy toward Innis, he couldn't believe he'd actually been right after all. His neighbor was truly frightening, possibly dangerous. What might he be planning? Should Charlie report his findings to Tom Sullivan, continue this investigation on his own or simply ignore the evidence? No, he couldn't pretend he didn't know. The things in this cabin were too disturbing and could lead anywhere. A chill of terror shook him and, shoving the binoculars back into his coat, he hurried to his own cabin, his mind awhirl with possibilities and scenarios of doom.

As he paced the floor in his bedroom he began to formulate a plan. Better to leave the police out of it for now; after all, what could he tell Sullivan, that there were strange objects and a weird painting in Innis Kilbride's cabin? It was hardly against the law. He needed more evidence. He'd refrained from following Innis on his evening walks to the woods, but at least, due to his previous spying and stalking, he knew the time at which he usually set out and returned. It would give him a perfect opportunity for making a second visit to the cabin, this time with his camera and perhaps some means of gaining entry. Of course it would be dark, though Innis might leave some lights on while he was out on his evening excursion. Worth at least a try, he told himself.

The other part of his plan involved disseminating information to other neighbors who'd been receptive to the devil worship rumors he'd already spread. Charlie knew several of the neighbors who'd been part of the lynch mob intent on burning down Bridget Bahane's shack years ago and had courted their favor. Like him, they were none too fond of Innis and his entire family and had also resented the old woman Sheena for preventing their planned attack. Many of them were longtime residents of Raven's Back, old-fashioned and superstitious in their beliefs and ways, distrustful of anything lacking a rational explanation yet also steeped in the ancient legends and tales on which they'd been raised. Charlic had made himself known to most of his neighbors in the course of the six years since he'd moved to Raven's Back and there were only a handful of them with whom he wasn't on friendly terms. Sheena had been one, as well as the couple who owned the troublesome, noisy donkey Malcolm. Charlie's attempts to rally his neighbors against the donkey's presence and confront its owners with a petition of complaint had been one of his glaring failures, but word of his actions had reached the couple and they were particularly inhospitable toward him from that point forward. Still, he maintained a sizable circle of friends in Raven's Back who enthusiastically supported his unfavorable opinion of Innis and Bridget. Now they would become valuable allies in his efforts to get to the bottom of whatever strangeness was being perpetuated in their midst.

A few days following his discovery of the painting and nests, Charlie returned to Innis's cabin late in the evening when he was certain the man would be out in the woods. Finding the cabin deserted, with all the lights out, he once again checked for open doors or windows but found none. Disappointed, he realized his camera would be of no use unless he could get inside the cabin somehow. He'd brought a tool for picking the door's lock but hesitated, knowing he was no expert on this and might leave evidence that Innis would notice. Perhaps the best plan was waiting, hidden, until Kilbride returned. Surely he would use the front door, Charlie reasoned, so he snuck to the back and hid behind the shed, able to peek around the side of the building from where he'd be able to see the cabin lights come on and possibly hear a bit of anything that was said. Who knows, maybe he'd get lucky and find out what Kilbride was always talking to that was concealed in his coat.

It wasn't long before Charlie heard someone approaching and he cautiously poked his head out from behind the shed to spot Innis nearing the front door of the cabin. Slung across his shoulder was a canvas bag stuffed with twigs and leaves poking out of the top, but the long length of rope that Charlie had previously seen was missing.

Kilbride was talking to something tucked away inside his coat and Charlie caught a quick flash of golden amber eyes matching the creature in the painting. He jumped back behind the shed, rustling a few leaves and holding his breath, remaining as still as possible for several minutes until he was certain Kilbride hadn't heard him. He heard the front door of the cabin close and peered out again to see several lights had been turned on in the living room and kitchen. Creeping slowly forward, his heart fluttering in fear, he advanced until he was crouched just beneath the kitchen window. The muffled sound of Innis's voice reached him and he froze in place. He's actually talking to the thing, he thought, and recoiled at the very notion. In league with the devil indeed.

The night was cold and by now Charlie was feeling a stiffness in his joints from all the crouching and waiting he'd been doing. When he heard Innis's voice moving away from the kitchen and toward the living room he raised himself up enough to look into the cabin. The weird animal from the painting was crouched on the floor of the kitchen, using its long creepy hands to sort through a pile of insects, larvae and what appeared to be purple mushrooms. It raised its eyes to meet those of Charlie and both beings gave a start. Charlie quickly ducked back down, afraid to attempt running back to the shed. He heard Innis re-enter the kitchen and speak to the creature as those to a child or pet.

"What is it, Yaeger? Did you hear something? Why are you staring at the window that way, macushla?"

Charlie flattened himself against the side of the cabin, aware of Innis just above him at the window, probably looking out into the night. If he decided to investigate, Charlie told himself, the jig was up. Holding his breath, Charlie waited for what seemed an eternity then heard a few more unintelligible words from Kilbride to the animal, followed by the sound of the front door opening. Halloran dashed away in a blind panic, racing back to his cabin without a thought for how much noise he was making or how stiff and terrified he had become. As he collapsed onto his sofa panting, safe and sound at home but exhausted from his ordeal, he briefly feared he might be having a heart attack. His heart was racing and he struggled to catch his breath. It took awhile for him to calm down and begin to feel normal again.

He hurried to his front door and locked it, going through the cabin to check that all windows were also locked. What if Kilbride had seen him running away through the woods? What explanation could he possibly give? He'd worry about that later but now he noticed the late hour, knowing he needed to get out to sea early in the morning for his fishing. After a quick cup of tea to further calm his nerves, he went to bed, lying awake for hours awaiting Kilbride's knock on his door and running over the terrifying sights he'd seen that night. Despite a certain satisfaction and surprise that he'd actually been right about his neighbor, he knew he must take some sort of action to prevent whatever nefarious nonsense was being planned by Kilbride from happening. Had Sheena's death really been from natural causes? It wasn't that he doubted the coroner's verdict or the word of his friend Sullivan, but what if the heart attack had been brought on by some unnatural means, a spell or a curse, perhaps merely the sight of that horrible creature he'd seen tucked away in Innis Kilbride's coat?

The first thing to do was kill the creature, Charlie decided, though he'd need to make sure this wouldn't cause any repercussions. After all, the thing was possibly supernatural and certainly frightening with those weird eyes and long, bony fingers. Did it have the ability to cast a spell simply by staring into a human's eyes or pointing one of those creepy fingers at you? If so, he might already be cursed. He'd stared right into the animal's eyes when it lifted its head to look at him from the kitchen. Then again, was it even an animal? A demon from hell seemed more likely. He'd need to proceed with caution. Warning his neighbors and gathering their support would be crucial, but he might also win over a few new believers who'd previously scoffed at his claims of Innis's devil worship. This latest evidence with his own eyewitness account precluded doubt. If only he'd gotten a photograph or two, but now it was clear to him that he'd seen enough. No need to return to Kilbride's cabin or follow him any longer; he had the proof he needed at last. One way or another, he would take action before another tragedy like Sheena's death befell the community of Raven's Back.

Considering the limited time he'd spent with Innis, he still found it hard to believe the man could really be truly evil, though it was likely he'd been somehow mesmerized by the creature to do its bidding, the two of them in thrall to the devil. He'd destroy the creature somehow but couldn't justify killing Innis. Then there was that loony Aunt Bridget of Innis's. She'd been crazy long before Innis moved to Raven's Back, but had the creature been haunting these parts even then? Charlie fell asleep, juggling an avalanche of questions and possibilities, wondering how in the world there could be such a thing as purple mushrooms.

Chapter XXIII: Secrets Unmasked

Yaeger had seen something or someone outside the window that night, Innis was certain of that. When Innis had opened the front door he'd seen movement in the trees over to his right, heard the sound of someone running away through the leaves but darkness had concealed any details. Though the identity of the figure couldn't be determined, there was no doubt in Innis's mind it was Charlie Halloran. Who else would be lurking around the cabin, spying and dashing off? What had he seen? Innis returned to the kitchen where Yaeger had resumed his meal, having polished off the purple mushrooms and started on the insects and larvae. Innis realized with a sense of dread that Halloran might have seen the aye-aye. Leaving Yaeger to his feast, Innis walked around the outside of the cabin and shed, checking that everything was still locked and there had been no disturbance to the property. He noticed an area by the shed where some leaves had been crushed and wondered if Charlie had been hiding out there, awaiting his return. He must have been peering in the kitchen window when Yaeger saw him. It was creepy and infuriating to picture Charlie sneaking around, and the most disturbing aspect of this personal invasion was the possible outcome. Innis didn't trust Halloran and certainly wasn't comfortable with him having knowledge of the aye-aye.

He went back to the kitchen and watched Yaeger finish his meal but the usual pleasure he found in this simple observation eluded him. Thoughts of the break with Fin and the duplicity of Halloran allowed him no rest and he slept badly that night despite Yaeger's presence beside him.

The completion of work assignments with Oren was drawing near with only one more job remaining, the making of some cabinets and a dresser for a family in Glenraven. After months of delaying a visit from his own family, Innis had set a date for the following week, still unresolved as to how he would introduce and explain Yaeger. He longed to call Fin but refrained, determined to respect her request for avoiding contact for awhile. Trips to the purple grove with Yaeger continued with Innis remaining among the sheltering trees for longer periods of time with each visit. It was only here that he found respite from his worries and the positive effect on Yaeger was undeniable. The aye-aye's coat was shiny and luxurious, his energy level at a peak, his appetite robust and his nest building far more adept and sophisticated than it had ever been. He'd become more affectionate with Innis as well and the droll sense of humor that Innis loved was frequently on display.

Sometimes when Innis walked through the purple grove he heard, in addition to the soft creaking of the trees, rustling of leaves in the wind and the calls of the many crows who frequented the forest, what struck him as whisperings, gentle voices that reminded him of the fairies from his grandfather's stories. The words, and sometimes lilting songs, he heard were indecipherable but delighted him nevertheless with their light, sweet, happy sound. His worries about his future, the secret of Yaeger and the troubling behavior of Charlie Halloran were soothed in the dark peaceful confines of the purple grove and he found himself staying longer with each visit. Yaeger too enjoyed their time among the purple trees and Innis had noticed there were fewer nests being built in the cabin lately.

A particularly disturbing event had recently occurred during Innis's work on his last assignment with Oren. While visiting the home of the couple, who'd commissioned a rather elaborate cabinet and chest of drawers, to discuss their requirements, Oren had been drawn aside by the husband for a lengthy private conversation. The wife, continually glancing from Innis to the separate discussion with a nervous smile, was too distracted to answer Innis's questions about the type of wood, design and dimensions to be used for the furniture and their stunted conversation finally ground to a halt.

"Is everything all right?" Innis tried his best to hold her attention. "Perhaps not the best time? We can reschedule."

The woman abruptly stood and left the room just as Oren and the husband rejoined Innis. Before Innis could say a word, Oren motioned to him, quietly requesting that he gather his measuring tools and papers, that the strategy session had been canceled. Puzzled and upset, Innis did as his boss requested, anxious to talk about the sudden change in plans yet sensing Oren's need to leave the house as quickly as possible. He knew his boss well enough by now to detect his angry mood and kept quiet until the two of them were back in their truck, driving away. Innis turned to Oren, unable to remain silent any longer.

"What the hell happened back there?"

Oren stared at the road ahead, concentrating on his driving with a slight shake of his head. He glanced at Innis briefly then returned his attention to the road.

"Is there anything going on with you that I should know about, Innis? Something of importance?"

"Why do you ask?"

"Our contract for doing the work for those people back there has just been canceled. The reason being they're not keen to have you do the work for them. They seem to think there's a certain danger about it, they're not comfortable with you. I tried but I couldn't get anything more out of them, at least not from the husband. Did she say anything to you, the wife?"

Innis, briefly shocked speechless, wound down the truck window to give himself some air, feeling suddenly light-headed.

"I'm so sorry, Oren, I don't know what to say. No, she didn't say a word to me but it was obvious she was worried, distracted. I haven't any idea why they'd feel that way, honestly. I don't want you to lose the commission for the job on my account. Could they have you do it, regardless, without me being part of it?"

"It's not the commission that concerns me. I've already told them I'd rather not work with them, seeing that they've refused the services of my trusted apprentice for no good reason, without even being willing to explain why. I have your back, Innis, but I want to be sure I'm not being a fool. Am I?"

Innis stared out the window, barely noticing the cold air on his face, oblivious to the scenery rushing past. He suddenly knew with a chilling certainty that somehow this was down to Charlie Halloran. Turning to Oren, he made a determined effort to keep the anger out of his voice.

"I really appreciate you turning down the commission on my behalf, but I hope this won't alienate other clients. I have an idea what this might be about but I've gotta check into it." Innis scoffed dismissively. "Me, dangerous? Hardly. I'm glad you don't feel that way, at least I certainly hope you don't."

"Of course not, and I'm surprised anyone does. Yet something's made these people feel that way. If you've got a clue I suggest you pursue it. Glenraven is a small place."

"And Raven's Back's even smaller. I'm fairly sure this has something to do with a neighbor of mine and, believe me, I intend getting to the bottom of it. Guess it's a fortunate thing this was my last job with you. At least now you can be rid of me and my 'dangerous' reputation so I won't be bad on your business. Would've preferred this end on a different note and, again, I'm truly sorry. You've taught me so much, Oren, and I know you've put up with some aggravation on my account."

"You've got real talent as a woodworker, my lad. Wouldn't have put up with some of it if you weren't so damn good at what you do. I still wish you'd think again about giving it up. Seems a genuine waste to me."

"Thank you for the compliment but my mind's made up. After today even more so."

They drove in companionable silence back to Oren's shop where Innis collected his few personal belongings and arranged for his final check to be sent to him. Glancing around the large workshop where he'd spent so many hours, he noticed a few items on which he'd worked and felt a brief pain that he'd never see them through to completion. He and Oren shook hands and Oren placed a hand on Innis's shoulder.

"All the best to you, Innis. Thanks for all your excellent work and keep in mind there have been so many people who've loved your work, whose lives and homes have been enhanced by the beauty of the items you've made. And don't forget to keep in touch. If you ever have need of a reference or a bit of furniture or a boat repair, you know who to ask."

They both laughed then Innis turned away quickly before he could become too emotional. He'd meant to wish Oren best of luck as well but went to his car instead, loathe to go back inside the shop with all its memories. Cut loose from his life as a woodworker, he felt a brief exhilaration that was quickly followed by a feeling of dread. If Charlie was spreading rumors about him, where might that lead? Finally free to concentrate on his painting, Innis realized that his only remaining source of income, the check that Oren would be sending him, wouldn't last all that long. Yaeger's needs were minimal since he hunted for his food with the occasional fruit and regular mushroom snacks from Innis the only supplements he needed. There was rent to be paid on the land where the cabin stood and Innis's own food, utilities and a minimum of clothing expenses but he knew he could live quite cheaply. Still, he'd delayed formulating a plan for selling his artwork, figuring he'd think about it once his job with Oren was finished. Now, unexpectedly, that time was upon him.

It was still early in the day so, rather than head home where Yaeger was bound to be asleep, Innis stopped at Murphy's to see if perhaps his mother was working a shift in the kitchen, gratified to discover that she was. The curt dismissal by Oren's clients, with the claim that he was dangerous and not to be trusted, had rattled him more deeply than he'd let on to Oren, and he felt the need of his mother's comfort and advice as well as one of her home-cooked meals. Seating himself by one of the windows after stopping in the restaurant's kitchen to say hello to Irene, he gazed out at the expanse of sea visible beyond the buildings near the wharf. He tried to understand why Charlie would want to hurt him in this way, the extent to which he might be willing to go to discover Innis's secrets. If he had indeed seen Yaeger, things had greatly escalated and the idea of the aye-aye being in any danger was more than he could bear. Yaeger was alone at the cabin right now, he suddenly realized and jumped to his feet, almost colliding with his mother who was approaching his table with a lunch platter.

"Listen, Innis," she set the plate down and motioned him to sit, "I thought I'd bring your lunch out myself because I seriously need to talk to you. I wonder if I might ask you to stop by again when my shift ends. Where are you off to anyway when you've just ordered your food?"

Innis sat back down, shifting restlessly in the seat and inhaling the delicious aroma of the ground beef and onion pasty and fried potatoes his mother had placed before him. Seduced by his hunger and anticipation of the pleasing meal, he relaxed and gave in. Halloran would be out at sea fishing at this time of day and Yaeger had remained safe during all the other times when Innis was away at work. Mustn't get too paranoid, he reminded himself as he tucked into his meal with gusto.

"What's so urgent that we need to discuss, Ma? By the way," he motioned with his fork toward his partially eaten food, "fabulous as always. I'd actually like to talk to you as well."

Irene paused, a flash of worry briefly crossing her face, and nodded to Innis.

"Enjoy your lunch, darlin'. I'll see you back here when my shift ends, around 5 p.m. Got the earlier shift today. Oh, will that interfere with your job schedule?"

"Nah, that's fine. Catch you then, and thanks again for lunch."

Relieved that this would give him time to run home and check in on Yaeger before meeting his mother, Innis settled in to enjoy his meal, watching the distant sea and thinking it had been too long since he'd visited the shoreline. Without a job to devour his time, he realized he could now do many of the things he'd been putting off, like checking in on his Aunt Bridget, walking by the sea and figuring out a way to make the planned family dinner at his cabin work somehow. His thoughts inevitably turned to Fin and it struck him as ironic that now he'd have the opportunity to spend more time with her, all just a bit too late. The first order of business, though, would be dealing with his bothersome neighbor, Charlie. He needed to make sure no harm came to Yaeger and if Charlie had somehow seen the aye-aye it was imperative to debunk any false, negative assumptions that might have been made.

Innis finished his meal rather quickly, then returned to his cabin to find Yaeger sleeping soundly in the nest by the easel. Worried about what his mother so urgently needed to discuss, he arrived back at Murphy's a bit early, hoping she'd be on time since he'd need to get home for Yaeger's night hunting. As he waited restlessly at the counter, nursing a cup of tea, he wished Fin could have met his family and especially Yaeger. It was completely down to him that she had not. Irene interrupted his musings, tapping him lightly on the shoulder.

"Back to earth, Innis Kilbride," she chided pleasantly. "Where were you, darlin'?"

Innis laughed nervously.

"Sorry, Ma. I find myself doin' a lot of daydreaming lately."

"No matter. Let's get out of here before some emergency calls me back into the kitchen."

They walked to Irene's car, parked at the far end of the small lot by Murphy's.

"We'll have privacy in here," Irene said, unlocking the car.

Seated beside his mother in the front passenger seat, Innis turned to her.

"So, what do we need privacy for? You're making me nervous, Ma."

Irene sighed.

"It's not a conversation I look forward to having, but why don't you go first. You said you needed to speak with me as well."

"You're not gonna like it. I'm done with my woodworking apprenticeship. It ended today and for a troubling reason."

Irene stared at him in shock.

"What? How can you be so nonchalant about this, Innis? Does this mean your certificate won't be happening? Has Oren let you go for some reason? When did you plan on letting the rest of us know about all this?"

"OK, look, I know you're surprised but calm down. It's too long a story to go into right now, but no, Oren hasn't let me go. The thing is..." He hesitated, dreading his mother's reaction to the life changing decision he'd made about returning to painting. "I made up my mind on my own to quit the apprenticeship. I want to be a painter, an artist."

Irene broke into a huge smile, reaching over to crush Innis in an enthusiastic bear hug.

"How wonderful! I'm so pleased. You know it's what I've always wanted for you. I hope you're glad of it as well."

Surprised, Innis breathed a sigh of relief, knowing there were more revelations still to be aired.

"Yeah, I'm really happy about it but that's not everything."

"Will you finally be going to art school, then? Your da and I could help a bit with the cost and I assume you've maybe put a little back yourself from your job."

"Not really planning to go to art school. I don't need to." This is where it gets tricky, he thought, but forged ahead before he could back out. "I've actually been painting for awhile and I'm so much better than when I started out. I've done at least a dozen paintings already, different sizes, and, not to be arrogant, they're quite good. I've given one to Fin and she was very impressed. I know she's not objective but she wouldn't lie to me about something like this."

Irene watched her son's face as he spoke, warmed by the light of excitement she saw dancing in his eyes and the happy lilt in his voice. At last, he's found his true way, she thought.

"Will the rest of us be seeing some of these incredible paintings soon? Or are you waiting until we visit your cabin next week?"

"Well, there's a bit more to the story."

Irene leaned back against her car seat, folding her arms and narrowing her eyes at her son.

"Of course there is. Out with it then."

"I had one more job to complete for Oren because I wasn't about to just leave him in the lurch. When we went to see the people this morning at their house, they told Oren they didn't want me on the job. Something about me being dangerous, although they wouldn't give Oren any details and--"

"Dammit!" Irene interrupted, hitting her fist softly against the steering wheel. "I knew it! I shouldn't have let you put me off. I know exactly what's going on here and I won't have it."

"What the hell are you talking about? I don't even know what's going on, how can you? Well, I suspect what it's about. What are you thinking?"

"That's what I've needed to tell you. It's going around on the grapevine in Glenraven that you're a devil worshiper."

Innis was briefly stunned to silence. He stared at his mother as if trying to interpret her words but she rushed on.

"It was Nolan, you know, at the restaurant, who first told me. This was ages ago and even your da agreed we needed to alert you to this insidious gossip. That's why I was so anxious to visit you, to head off this shite reaching you before I could warn you. Now I've left it too late. I should have insisted, maybe told you over the phone, but you kept delaying our visit. Well, enough. Doesn't really matter now, the cat's outta the bag. This is exactly what I told your da would happen--"

Innis put a hand on his mother's shoulder to stop her rambling speech.

"It's OK, Ma. Don't stress so much. Did Nolan tell you who he heard this gossip from? I'd give odds it was Charlie Halloran."

"Charlie Halloran, the fisherman? Why in the world would he say such things? Nolan didn't know who started it, just general gossip. It's all over Glenraven apparently."

Innis nodded.

"And now it's cost you a job, Innis." Irene placed her hand against Innis's cheek. "I'm sorry, darlin'. Charlie's a neighbor of yours, right? People are so strange out there in Raven's Back, that's one reason I didn't want you living there."

"People are strange everywhere, it's the nature of the beast. You know that better than anybody. Truth is, though, he didn't just pull that nonsense out of a hat. I'm the one who's strange."

Irene cocked her head, giving her son a quizzical look.

"How so?"

This was the moment Innis had been dreading for so long, the fork in the road where he'd either continue his secret life with Yaeger or introduce the strange little aye-aye to the rest of his world. He hesitated only briefly.

"Ma, I've been keeping a secret." Irene leaned forward in anxiety so he hurried on. "I have a weird creature from Madagascar living with me in my cabin. I've been hiding him in order to protect him but I see now it's gotten way out of control."

Irene burst out laughing.

"What in heaven's name are you on about? You have a what from where? This is too much. Are you having me on, Innis? You can't imagine what I've been thinking. You gave me a right fright."

"It's actually true, though, I'm not joking. That's why I've been putting off your visit, because I couldn't think of a way of introducing him to you. Yaeger, that is. He's the aye-aye."

"I've never heard of such a thing. Are you certain you're not pulling my leg?"

Innis drew his cell phone from his inside coat pocket and scrolled through it, holding it toward his mother to present a shot of Yaeger perched on Innis's bed with a piece of apple clutched in his long fingers.

"Yaeger," he announced.

Irene took the phone and held it close to her face, examining the picture carefully then giving out another burst of laughter.

"My God, Innis, I truly wouldn't believe it if I didn't see a photograph. What a weird and marvelous animal."

"Isn't he?" Innis beamed like a proud parent. "He's a wonder. He's changed my life, Ma. It may sound crazy but I know he has. I can't allow harm to come to him, not only because I love him dearly but there are so few of his kind left in the world. It's a critically endangered species. The worst part is that they're killed off, at least in part, by people because of superstitions. Some folks in Madagascar view them as a harbinger of death or destruction and just kill them to ward off danger, even hang them from trees."

"Has Charlie Halloran seen this?" Irene handed Innis's phone back to him and turned in her seat to face him. "Is this the basis for the devil worship nonsense?"

Innis returned the phone to his pocket and shrugged.

"Not to my knowledge he hasn't seen Yaeger, but he's followed me and there was recently an incident where he might have seen him. Look, there's so much I need to tell you but it'll be dark soon and I've gotta get back to the cabin to take Yaeger out. He's nocturnal and nighttime is when we gather his nest materials and go hunting for his food. Ma, I know it's asking a lot, but I wish every-one else could understand that he's got a bit of magic."

Irene nodded and patted Innis's hand.

"You've come to the right place, darlin'. I know a thing or two about magic. I'm a believer if there ever was one. Dealing with your Aunt Bridget has taught me quite a lot about the worlds beyond our normal reality, as you know, and about the value of respecting them. Don't you think it's time I met your Yaeger? At this rate, he may be the closest thing to a grandchild I'll ever have. Is Finola still in the picture and does she know about this creature?"

"She knows but she's not met him. I kept putting her off and now I think I've lost her."

Innis paused, unable to hide the catch in his voice. The enor-mity of losing her crashed over him like a wave and he turned away to hide his tears from his mother. He sensed her shift in her seat then start the car.

"Let's go out to Raven's Back. I'll drive you home and say hello to this fella from Madagascar. Maybe you can fill me in on what's been going on in your life while we drive. Please don't be a stranger to me, my boy. I couldn't bear it."

Innis unburdened himself to his mother during the drive to his cabin, leaving out the detail of Halloran's shotgun and the exis-tence of the purple grove. One thing at a time is enough, he decided, and he sensed that the grove should remain a secret. He made Irene aware of Dalton's visit and his own insistence on his brother's secrecy about it. The fact that Bridget had met and bonded with Yaeger was also kept to himself, along with his knowledge about the lynch mob that had once been intent on destroying his aunt's home. No use to needlessly upset his highly emotional mother, he told him-self. It was enough that the secret of the aye-aye was finally out. After learning of the insidious gossip about him and the rejection by Oren's clients, he figured he'd need all the help he could get with keeping himself and Yaeger safe. It occurred to him that the percep-tion of evil could be almost as dangerous as evil itself.

Chapter XXIV: On The Antrim Coast Road

Despite it being a Tuesday, the sign on the door of The Forestry in Belfast read 'CLOSED, BACK ON THURSDAY'. Fin had made a decision around 8 p.m. on Monday night to drive to Raven's Back and see Innis Kilbride. It wasn't a rash decision; she'd considered it carefully for almost a week, weighing the wildly fluctuating commands of her head and heart, surprised and pleased at the call to action on which she'd finally settled. The discussion with Innis on the park bench had left her much more uncertain and forlorn than she'd expected. Why couldn't she just let him go? She'd examined her own behavior, realizing she'd more or less given up without a real fight, allowed herself to be relegated to a pitiful figure sitting by the phone waiting for something to happen, an image she'd always disliked in others and now despised even more in herself. Of all the many things she regretted about the way things had ended, her failure to meet Yaeger was the one that relentlessly bothered her. Innis's enthusiasm and love for the strange creature, his diligent protection of this threatened and special animal had not only caused her to fall in love with the man but also the aye-aye. She'd developed a fascination with the species and Internet research had provided plenty of intriguing particulars and photos, making her consider attempting a visit to the London or Jersey Zoo where aye-ayes were kept, perhaps even meeting with keepers who worked with the creatures in order to gain information that might be helpful to Innis. While she pondered what the future would look like without Innis in her life, she tried her best to drive him from her plans and thoughts and sometimes succeeded. The aye-aye, though, would not leave her alone and her wish to meet Yaeger continually returned, plaguing her with regret and indecision.

That Monday evening, after she'd finished her supper and cleared away the dishes, she managed to bring all the thoughts, questions, feelings and fears swirling around in her to a standstill. Enough, she told herself. Stop being silly and do what you want to do. The things she most desired came into sharp focus and she smiled with relief. A decision had finally been made. She would drive to Raven's Back, talk to Innis and meet Yaeger at last.

Although those priorities were foremost in her mind, there was another matter of importance to discuss with Innis and she knew it shouldn't wait. Since Innis had declared his new artwork of

Yaeger to be in the public domain, not to be kept secret as the purple wood had been, Fin had decided to hang the painting he'd given her in The Forestry where it could provide company and enjoyment while she worked and be seen by her shop visitors. One of her regular customers, a wealthy man from London who'd been purchasing items from her for years, remarked on the painting and became quite taken with it. He offered to buy it and although Fin wasn't willing to part with it she explained that the artist was a friend of hers and not only had other paintings of the same subject but might be willing to do a custom painting if he were to commission one. The man expressed strong enthusiasm and since Fin already had his contact information she told him she'd get back to him about it. A visit to Raven's Back would not only allow her to view Innis's collection of Yaeger paintings but also to give him news of a possible first sale of his art. Hoping she hadn't overstepped her boundaries a bit, she was excited at the promising prospects of her trip and, although she wasn't fond of driving, she prepared for the visit with great anticipation. She knew she was taking a chance, not even certain that Innis would be around to see her, but she felt the element of surprise was crucial and would prevent him from putting her off yet again.

The most intimidating part of the drive was right at the beginning, navigating through the complex, one-way system of the A2 going through Belfast's City Centre past the Custom House and along Corporation Street. The weather had cooperated and she started out early in the morning, grateful for partly sunny skies and reasonably cool temperatures though the tangle and crush of traffic leaving Belfast made her tense. Once out of the city proper and passing through the northern suburbs she relaxed a bit, marveling at the names of so many places she'd never really visited despite their proximity to her home. Jordantown, Greensland, Carrickfergus, Eden and Whitehead. She drove carefully, staying just at the speed limits or slightly below and made good time, entering the countryside at Larne, a mid-sized town where the Antrim Coast Road began at the town's northern edge.

Fin had seen this stretch of road, running along the coast for about twenty-five miles, before but had never driven it by herself and it had been some time since she'd beheld its many wonders. She passed under the Black Arch of dark stone near Larne, glad for the sparse traffic since the narrow road of only one lane in each direction made her even more cautious about being behind the wheel. As she passed under the Arch, she felt herself leaving the mundane world of hurrying humans, city noises and gray buildings behind and entering an enchanted vista of peace and quiet, green and sea.

As the road followed the shoreline to the north, Fin took every opportunity to enjoy the stunning vistas she was passing through, leaving the car windows down despite the chill so the sea breezes could wash over her. It had been far too long since she'd spent time near the sea and her eyes misted at realizing how much she'd missed it. At times the road ran between the sea on one side and high cliffs on the other. There's no other land on earth as glorious as Ireland, she thought, no other place where one might truly believe that a fairy or unicorn could be peeking out from behind a tree or sheltered in a waterfall tucked away among the green hills. She passed through villages (Ballygalley, Carnlough, Waterfoot) and the legendary glens of Antrim with their breathtaking scenery of rolling green hills, little stone bridges, waterfalls and rugged headlands. Remembering a long ago trip to Carnlough, when she'd trekked to beautiful Cranny Falls, she hoped the charming village with its picturesque harbor on Carnlough Bay hadn't changed too much because she'd heard that renovations to the harbor had recently been made.

Glenraven was farther north than she'd ever ventured and she made a mental note for the future to visit all of the glens, chiding herself for neglecting the awe-inspiring discoveries to be found in her own backyard. Living in the city she'd forgotten how much nature meant to her and she pictured Innis making this drive, wondering if it was possible to ever grow accustomed to such wonders. The sun periodically appeared while she drove, casting sparking diamonds across the distant waves that changed color as light and dark passed over them. Realizing that everything along her path was drawing her back to Innis, not only literally but emotionally, she understood why he'd referred to this part of Ireland as the magical north and smiled to herself. Failing to prevent herself from imagining a life here with him, she allowed herself to dream, ignoring the uncertainties of what she would find once she reached Raven's Back. Would she and Innis reconcile? Would his cabin and the aye-aye be as she had pictured them? Could he be angry with her for taking this decision to present herself unannounced? What did the future hold for her?

Breathing in the bracing sea air, she calmed herself and con-

tinued her journey, excited for the adventure, the sense of astonishment she experienced along the Antrim Coast Road. Part of her
longed to leave the road at each village or glen she passed, to explore
the windblasted and isolated old houses she spotted out in the middle
of nowhere, surrounded for miles by only green hills and trees.
What sort of life went on there, she wondered. Winters must surely
be harsh and pleasures simple, yet there was much to be envied for a
daily existence among such beauty. This was Innis's terrain, all the
more precious to her heart for that.

Glenraven was the most northern of all the glens and at
Cushendall, a small coastal town where three of the glens of Antrim
met, she ignored the point where the A2 heads inland and kept following the coast to take the small, winding Torr Road that climbed to
Torr Head. She knew that, on clear and sunny days, Scotland might
be glimpsed from this area, but she had no wish to interrupt her driving to search for it. Perhaps another time. She continued along the
Torr Road which eventually rejoined the A2 at Ballyvoy. Enjoying
her drive, she marveled at the stunning natural beauty around her,
from cliffs to valleys and glens to the sea. A sense of ancient history
permeated the very ground here and she knew these green hills and
valleys were home to old bridges and monuments, castles and
dwellings now eroded and partially destroyed by time and weather.
It was easy to see how Innis came by the many fanciful tales from
his childhood and she couldn't imagine a more appropriate location
for a painter. Uncertain of his response to the possibility of a first
sale of his work, she hoped he would be pleased but he could be
maddeningly unpredictable.

Once she'd passed through the majority of the glens, she
slowed her pace, worried about getting lost since she'd never driven
to an area quite this far north on the Antrim Coast. There was also a
sudden fear making her hesitate, the fear that this was all a terrible
mistake she might regret. Pulling off the road in a safe spot, she sat
looking out to sea, considering that nearby must be the very spot
where Aunt Bridget had kept her vigil by the waves, where Yaeger
had crawled out of the water, where Innis had been born. A cherished stretch of land and sea, in a way. It's now or never, girl, she
told herself. You're either all in or you let it go.

She saw gulls and seabirds wheeling above the water, heard
their cries and saw a small boat far out on the waves. Casting her
glance over the lush green pastures with their low stone walls and

flocks of sheep, the dense forests dotting the hills, she then briefly closed her eyes and listened to the sea, breathing in its exhilarating scent. Innis's home. Yaeger's home. Could it ever be hers? There was much history here, she knew, and she would always be an outsider regardless of how close she might become to her beloved boy. This wild beauty was powerfully seductive, just like Innis, but was it really for her? Expecting something to strike her like a lightning bolt, for a light to miraculously break through the drifting clouds, a spark to fire her imagination in a way to make her decision clear, she sat motionless with her hands in her lap and her eyes on the water. Then she laughed, shook her head and spoke aloud to herself.

"You've come this far for a reason, you silly girl. Stop being so uncertain. It's the magic you crave and you can't deny it."

She started the car, pulled back onto the road and drove on toward Glenraven.

Chapter XXV: An Eye To Murder

Charlie Halloran drew the line at a lynch mob. Although there would be no old woman like Sheena with a shotgun to stop such nonsense, he didn't feel right about taking such action and, at the end of the day, it wouldn't produce the desired results. He wanted the demon gone from Innis Kilbride's cabin, gone for good. In the few days following his discovery of the weird creature he'd noticed little things going wrong: a smaller catch from his fishing boat, difficulty sleeping with almost nightly dreams of a disturbing nature, minor car trouble. He recognized it was unlikely all these things had been caused by his exposure to the strange demon...and yet. Tales of the curse of Raven's Back returned to his thoughts. Could this inexplicable creature be a continuation of that tradition, the curse made flesh? Even if he were to kill the animal or somehow dispose of it, perhaps take it somewhere far away and drop it off to die, might it still jinx him, extract revenge? He was afraid to get near it, shivering at the thought of those long, black, bony hands clawing at him or the ratlike teeth he'd briefly glimpsed delivering a poisonous bite. This was not a one-man operation, he conceded, and began shuffling through his deck of friends for a suitable conspirator.

There was Tom Sullivan, of course, though being a law enforcement officer would make him resistant to doing anything remotely illegal even if he did share Charlie's view of Innis Kilbride. The somewhat elderly couple who occupied the cabin nearest to him had been friends and supporters of his for some time and he suspected they could have been part of the lynch mob intent on burning down Bridget Bahane's shack. They had little use or respect for the Kilbride clan as a whole and had spent many hours with Charlie bemoaning Innis's move to the area. Mentally he moved them to the top of his list and continued to the next possibility.

This was a bachelor who kept a small flock of sheep at a slight distance from Charlie's place. The man was solitary when they'd first met, but Charlie had drawn him out, detecting a like-minded person who might prove a solid friend. Gradually, over ale and the occasional simple meal at Charlie's cabin, the fellow had divulged his suspicions and dislike of the Kilbride family. He told Charlie about his disapproval of Abbot Kilbride, whose sheep, the inferior Cheviot breed, were pampered and spoiled like children yet their wool was frequently bringing a higher price in the local markets than his own small flock, supposedly a more lucrative breed. The son Dalton was an odd one as well, along with Innis, of course, and that loony aunt. Irene Kilbride had always considered herself above the simple folk of Glenraven, taking on airs and dissatisfied with small-town life, too good for the glens and probably having an affair with Nolan Murphy as well. Charlie had listened to his neighbor's complaints sympathetically and the two became allies, though they seldom saw each other. Charlie placed this man second on his list, doubtful that the somewhat antisocial fellow would agree to be part of a group effort against the threat of a demon.

Charlie abandoned his list making and began to think in terms of strategy, realizing it would be best to approach others with a plan already in mind. At first he'd thought of simply snatching the thing from Innis's cabin and doing away with it on his own, perhaps with a quick shotgun blast way out in the woods where no one would hear or see. His fear of the weird creature, however, prevented this approach. If indeed it was a demon, what might it do to him? The fact that Kilbride was always with the monster when they went out in the evening made things even more difficult. Was there a way of destroying the demon without the animal, or whatever it was, knowing he'd done it? It would keep reprisals away from him but, much as he racked his brain, he couldn't come up with a way. Burn the cabin down with the creature inside while Innis was away? No guarantee the thing would perish, though, and it seemed too cruel to destroy Innis's home in that way. Besides, out in the isolated wilds of Raven's Back a fire out of control could take out a good portion of the area by the time help arrived.

As he thought more carefully about the situation, his dilemma deepened when he reminded himself that Innis was in league with the demon. Those times he'd followed his neighbor it was obvious he was holding something under his coat, talking to it and keeping it from view. Of course it had to be the demon. Could Innis really be trusted? If the demon had already turned the man's mind to evil, what then? Once the creature was dead, would Kilbride seek revenge? It was dreadful considering the murder of a human, and Charlie, horrified at his own thoughts, pushed the idea from his mind. Still, it kept returning, urging him to give it credence, to let it flourish. No, he resisted, Innis was his friend, someone he'd spent a bit of time with, a person with family and friends who'd mourn him. I'm not a killer, he reminded himself. The demon's death was one thing, but doing away with a neighbor could not be part of the equation. Nevertheless, Charlie found it impossible to turn away from these dark thoughts, convinced that if he delayed too long, knowing what no one else knew, any ensuing disaster would land on his doorstep. He couldn't allow it.

If the murder of Innis Kilbride was to become a part of his plan, he knew he'd have to go it alone. Bringing in accomplices to murder was out of the question. The decision to do away with both man and beast made Charlie's strategy easier in a way. Now it would be possible to kill them both one night far out in the woods during their routine excursion with no one the wiser. If I could somehow perch in a tree above them, Charlie reasoned, they'd never even see me. He knew he wasn't a crack shot, but the distance wouldn't be great and a shotgun blast did plenty of damage. The short period of time during which he'd refrained from following them would serve to make Innis less likely to be expecting anything, though clamoring up into a tree once he spotted them would never do. He'd need to find a perch beforehand and wait for their arrival, hoping they'd come his way. It wasn't the best of plans, he knew, but it was good enough.

He readied his shotgun, filling it with ammunition, vaguely wondering if he should do some practice shooting since it had been awhile since he'd actually shot the gun at anything. At one time he'd hunted deer and foxes, but he'd never been an especially successful hunter and had given it up. The first time he'd bagged a deer he'd realized it was too much trouble getting the thing prepared so it could be used for a venison meal, and he wasn't a cook anyway. Nevertheless, he figured he wouldn't need to be much of a shot to hit something right below him from a low tree branch. Time was of the essence when one was dealing with a demon.

While out in his fishing boat that day, he had trouble concentrating on the tasks before him since his thoughts kept returning to his murderous plan. It was hard for him to accept that he was about to kill someone, yet he saw no alternative. Would it be wiser to simply confront his neighbor and get to the bottom of things, face-to-face, and avoid this extreme solution? No, he couldn't take the chance. Now that he'd seen the demon and knew that Innis had been nurturing and protecting it for some time, how could he possibly trust the man? And Innis was aware that Charlie had been stalking him. Surely he'd be out for revenge and might be formulating some insidious plan against him even now. No use waiting, he might lose his nerve. Tonight would have to be the night.

Chapter XXVI: A Wool Cap and a Crossroads

Fin arrived in Glenraven a bit later than she'd planned after getting lost at the turn-off for Innis's village, bypassing it then having to backtrack. Once there, she easily found Murphy's where she knew Innis's mother worked, but remembered that she'd packed her lunch, as usual, and parked her car at a spot where she could sit and watch the water while she ate. Innis hadn't told her much about his birthplace and she was surprised at how small and quaint it was, especially when compared with her Belfast home. Still, there was a certain pleasant bustle to it as fishing boats, people clad in heavy coats and sweaters and small delivery trucks came and went in the seaside downtown area. How had Innis Kilbride ever evolved from such a place, she marveled, although she suddenly recognized a few small-town fishing village traits in him. There was a certain naivete to some of his ideas, a basic trust in the honesty and value of his fellow human beings that was usually missing in the more sophisticated city dwellers with whom she dealt. Accent wasn't the only way Fin could discern a Londoner from a Dubliner or a native of Cork from a Carnlough dweller. She was an astute observer and had discovered all sorts of behavioral quirks and clues over her years in dealing with the public. Customers from all over the world had stopped into her little shop and she'd learned a surprising amount about them simply from watching and talking to them.

After finishing lunch she strolled along what appeared to be the main drag in Glenraven, a street by the water lined with small shops, stores and restaurants. She spotted the 'posh' bakery Innis had mentioned to her, passed by Murphy's again, saw the craft store where he'd mentioned he sometimes purchased his art supplies. Innis references were everywhere, though he'd never mentioned the windswept, awe-inspiring beauty of the place he called home. At times he'd been dismissive of Glenraven, characterizing it as a backwater hotbed of gossip and superstition, a barrier to his artistic inclinations. As Fin walked along, glancing into storefronts and breathing in the brisk, salty air, she realized that people were noticing her, probably instantly aware that she was a visitor, someone they'd never seen on this street. Smiling to herself at this confirmation of Innis's notions about the place, she decided to visit one of the shops, something she liked to do during all her travels as a way of supporting independently owned and operated small businesses like her own.

She chose a place selling clothing, mostly woolen items that were handcrafted and of sturdy quality, charmingly arranged with a sheep figurine sporting a wool cap and scarf in the front shop window. A tinkling bell, like the one at The Forestry, announced her arrival and she was surprised to find a young, freckle-faced boy with tousled auburn hair behind the counter by an old-fashioned cash register. Stacks of sweaters, scarves, caps, mittens and a few coats were crammed into the tiny space and Fin inhaled the soothing scent of wool. Smiling at the boy, who looked uncertain of her, she went to the counter. Before she could utter a word, he spoke defensively.

"Sorry, I'm just sitting in for a few minutes while my ma runs an errand," he said. "I don't really know too much about any of this stuff, she's the one who makes it. Well, most if it. You're welcome to look around if you'd like."

He offered a toothy smile that transformed his face into a sweet, boyish delight. Fin grinned back.

"Thanks so much. Don't mind if I do. You've such lovely things here. Handmade, as you say?"

"Mm hm. It's all local wool she uses." He shrugged. "She asked me to make sure people know that."

Fin nodded.

"Good for her."

She walked among the merchandise, placing a hand lightly on the items to marvel at their softness, quality of craftsmanship and pleasing colors. Wondering if any of the wool came from Dalton's flock, she turned to the boy.

"D'ya know where your ma gets the wool, then? Just curious."

The boy shrugged again.

"Dunno. She can tell ya when she gets back, shouldn't be long. Forgot to mention, there's no prices marked on 'em 'cause it's kind of a bargain deal. You know, you can bargain with her."

Fin nodded, thinking of her own poor bargaining skills and the first time she'd met Innis and bargained for the purple bowl. The shop door opened, interrupting her thoughts, and a woman with windblown straw blonde hair entered, bringing a gust of cold air with her.

"Wind's picking up," she smiled at Fin. "Hope my son's been seeing to you."

Aside from their full, round faces, Fin could see little resemblance between mother and son. Must look like his da, she assumed.

"Yes, he's been quite helpful," she returned the woman's smile. "I understand I'm meant to bargain and I'm quite taken with this cap here."

Fin held up a wool cap of maroon, forest green and black. She'd always preferred the darker colors and figured she'd need the cap to protect her from the sea breezes. The woman bustled to the cash register, carrying two small bags which she deposited behind the counter, then dismissed her son with a thanks and a kiss. He and Fin waved to each other as he left the shop. The woman looked after him fondly then turned her attention to Fin.

"Sorry, I had to pop out for a jiff to run some errands. He's a lovely boy, my son, always willing to pitch in when he's needed. So it's the cap you're wanting? Glad of it, not everyone's favorite colors."

Fin held the cap, turning it over in her hands, impressed by its handcrafted beauty.

"It's quite lovely work you do." She carried the cap over to the counter. "Your son told me you do most of the work yourself. I'm so impressed, all these items are wonderful. I was wondering where the wool comes from. Your son didn't know but said you buy local."

"Interesting question, luv. No one's ever asked me that, most don't care. Yes, I like to keep things local, we need to support each other here in Glenraven. It's small, as you can see, and we haven't the cache of some of the other glens, nor the money. Up from Dublin, are ya?"

"No, Belfast."

"Practically a neighbor then. Well, I get the wool from a farm owned by a fellow named Abbot Kilbride. It's a small, family concern he runs here in Glenraven, just he and his son tend the sheep. He's never gouged me on price so I can pass that savings on to my customers. And the wool quality's the best around here, as you can see."

Fin held the cap against her cheek, suddenly emotional at this personal connection. She'd never owned an article of clothing about which she knew the precise origins. Placing the cap on the counter, she retrieved her small purse from her coat pocket.

"Thanks for the information about the wool, that means a great deal to me. I'm not much at bargaining and I usually buy ready-made clothing, so please just name your price. I wouldn't know where to begin. By the way, I'm Fin."

She reached across the counter, offering her hand.

"Erin." The woman shook hands with a firm grip. "You seem like a sweet lass, I'll give you a bit of a break, I think."

The transaction was completed to the satisfaction of both, then Fin asked for directions to Raven's Back. Erin peered at her as though she'd requested a route to Mars.

"What do you want to go there for? Sorry, none of my business really, it's just an unusual request."

Fin hesitated but a sly smile stole across Erin's face.

"You're Innis's Belfast girl, aren't you?"

Fin, startled by this uncanny acknowledgment, was briefly speechless and somewhat embarrassed.

"Well, yes, I suppose I am," she spoke softly, stumbling a bit on her words.

Erin laughed.

"I'm sorry, darlin', didn't mean to make you blush. As you can see, it's a small world around here and easy enough for me to put Raven's Back, Innis and a lass from Belfast together and come up with the truth. Don't be shy, he's a fine lad, your Innis. You couldn't wish for better."

Slightly uncomfortable with this personal type of conversation, Fin found it impossible to meet Erin's eyes. She presumed the news of a visit from 'Innis's Belfast girl' would shortly be making the rounds in Glenraven. Such a strange way to live, she told herself, and not completely to my liking. Erin broke into her thoughts.

"I've completely embarrassed you, haven't I? Didn't mean to, truly. Anyway, let me write out these directions for you, otherwise you'll be lost for certain. It's a bit complicated finding Raven's Back and you may have to do some searching once you get there. I've no idea which cabin or shack out there belongs to Innis so you're on your own at that point, but I can get you to Raven's Back."

"Much appreciated," Fin smiled, thinking perhaps she'd simply drive back to Belfast.

Erin handed her a roughly drawn map with a longer list of directions than expected. Fin looked at the paper in puzzlement as though trying to decipher a foreign language and Erin laughed.

"Don't worry, it looks worse than it is. You'll have no trouble. Good luck to ya, darlin'. Maybe we'll be seeing more of you.

Stop back any time."

Fin thanked her without further comment and left the shop, pulling the new wool cap onto her head as she walked back to her car, shoving the directions into a coat pocket, slightly annoyed by the friendly encounter with Erin. It's almost as if the woman's already anticipating the wedding and kids, she muttered to herself. The wind had indeed picked up and she was glad to be back in her car, out of the cold. Fishing into her pocket for the directions, she held the paper in her hand without opening it, reviewing what had just happened. Here was small-town life in action with its warmth and assumptions, the personal touch and the insidious gossip. It was a package deal, she now realized, unless it could somehow be stood on its head and how would one do that? She smiled, recalling Erin's kind comments about Innis. You couldn't wish for better. It was true and she knew it with a bittersweet surrender.

Sorting her options she decided there could be ways of having her cake and eating it too, at least up to a point. Assuming Innis would reconcile with her, a strong possibility since she'd really been the one to break off from him, she might finagle a way of holding onto Belfast while including Glenraven. She didn't envision a traditional trajectory of engagement, marriage and babies; the very idea bored her silly. Innis was dedicated to his painting and the aye-aye, she to her city life and her shop. Blending the two wouldn't be easy and hadn't worked to her satisfaction thus far, though she had to admit that neither she nor Innis had really tried. They'd both been drifting along with their relationship, letting the chips fall where they may. Fin didn't know exactly when or how but she'd passed beyond that cove of calm and acceptance out into an unpredictable sea of passion. She wasn't willing to give Innis up, nor was she able to sacrifice her own life to wedge herself into a mold that she'd never fit.

She touched the wool cap, thinking of Dalton shearing the sheep, gathering the wool, of Erin turning the wool into this warm and pretty little item that protected her from the cold. There was a symbiosis here that appealed to her despite the many pitfalls she could identify just as clearly. Was Innis worth it? Of course. How it had thrilled her to hear Erin praising him.

Opening the directions she read over them carefully, following the lines of the map with her finger. She laid the open paper on the seat beside her and headed for Raven's Back, her excitement and nerves increasing as she wound her way along narrow roads through dense woods that seemed to block out the sky. Passing trickling brooks lined with moss covered rocks, the occasional abandoned dwelling with its empty rooms exposed by crumbling walls or a missing roof, she felt the forest growing wilder and more tangled as she drove. In places a low hanging tree branch would scrape across the windshield or roof of her car and she fought back her fear to continue on. This was truly back country, isolated in a way she'd never imagined, although Innis had briefly described it to her. Stopping the car, she rechecked the map directions, making sure she hadn't become lost, but, encouraged by the nearness of a parking area that Erin had indicated, she drove slowly on. She reached the fairly large dirt parking lot soon after, relieved to find several cars and trucks parked there but none were Innis's vehicle as she remembered it.

Her visit had been timed to coincide with an arrival in the afternoon since Innis had told her he was usually back at the cabin from work about that time. She'd killed some time in Glenraven but, checking her watch, realized she was still a bit early. Refolding the map to put it into the glove box then locking the car, she made her way into the nearby woods, following a well-worn footpath she figured must lead to the residences in the isolated area. Not a sign in sight, but then again there were not true streets here, only dirt and gravel trails meandering through the trees. Wishing she could leave a breadcrumb trail behind her in order to retrace her steps to the parking area, she trudged on, glad for the sturdy shoes and warm clothing, the wool cap, as the air was chilly, the terrain rugged. Stepping over a few fallen tree branches and kicking through piles of fallen leaves, she heard the cries of a crow and looked up to see a pair of the large birds circling above.

A small ramshackle dwelling came into sight though she knew this wouldn't be Innis's place. He'd implied that his cabin was in an isolated area and this location was too near the parking lot. She wondered where Bridget's shack might be but pushed on, determined to locate Innis' home despite her growing concern about becoming lost. After fifteen minutes of walking, having passed several more cabins and shacks scattered among the woods, she stopped to sit on a flat rock near the path. Perhaps she was being a fool. Wouldn't it be wiser to simply wait in her car at the parking area until he arrived? Something about the wild isolation of Raven's Back drew her, though, and she rose to continue on, taking time to notice the small pleasures of being in the forest. The smell of the earth and trees, the soft rustling of leaves and branches, the occasional bushy tailed squirrel watching her curiously from a tree, the calling and chortling of the crows. There was a palpable peace but something else as well, an undertow of threat. It was cold among the trees and Fin could suddenly believe that ghosts might dwell here, dark spirits had left their traces in Raven's Back.

The sound of footsteps approaching startled her and she stopped walking as a tall man in a heavy coat with a scarf around his neck walked toward her from farther along in the woods. His rugged face displayed only a brief surprise at the sight of her, then he came to stand beside her.

"Are you lost, luv?" He peered at her as though trying to place her face. "Looking for someone?"

Fin's heart was racing in fear but she calmed herself, relieved to have possibly found assistance.

"Yes, thank you so much." She laughed a little. "I'm quite lost, I suppose. I'm looking for the cabin of Innis Kilbride. Do you know it?"

The man's expression remained unreadable but he nodded.

"I do. I'll tell you how to go, you'd never find it on your own." Glancing down, he looked back at Fin with a small smile. "See you've worn your hiking shoes, that's a good thing. You've a rather big hike ahead of you."

Fin looked at him, realizing she might not be up to a lengthy walk through this tough and dense terrain, also figuring even with directions she could become hopelessly lost and then what? As the man waited with a steady gaze, she made a snap decision.

"Sir, would you mind instead if I follow you to that parking area? That's where I left my car and I assume you're heading there?"

He nodded.

"I am. Wise decision. Kilbride's place is one of the farthest out. Wouldn't want you to get turned around and spend the night in the woods. It'll get dark soon enough."

There was a touch of amusement in his eyes and voice and Fin smiled bashfully, feeling like an idiot and figuring he shared that thought. She turned and scurried along behind the man, his long, steady strides making it hard for her to keep up. She stumbled over branches and rocks a few times but he never altered his pace, glanced back or spoke. When they reached the dirt lot, Fin breathed a sigh of relief at the sight of her car. The man finally turned to her and nodded.

"You OK, then? Is that your car?"

He motioned toward her car and she smiled.

"Yes, it is. Thank you so much, I'm terribly grateful."

She no sooner spoke than he turned away with a dismissive wave of his hand, striding to a dirty black truck with tools piled into its truck bed. Fin watched him leave, waving as he passed her though he never looked her way. Standing by her car she shook her head, talking aloud to herself.

"What a place this is. One's overly friendly, the other's bare bones civil. You're here only a few hours and lost once already. Have you lost your mind, Fin O'Brian?"

The air was cold and breezy and she got back into her car and sat, her attention focused on the road on which she'd arrived. At least this was the only means of entry to Raven's Back so Innis would have to come this way. She'd made the possibly risky assumption that she'd be spending the night here with Innis. If, for some reason, he didn't show up she supposed she'd spend the night in her car. Were there bears and wolves in these woods? What would she eat? Innis has made an idiot of me, she laughed to herself, and noticed with some trepidation that the daylight was fading ever so slightly. Surely he'd be home soon.

Fetching her iPod from her coat she sat listening to The Pogues for awhile and just as "Rainy Night in Soho" had finished she saw a car pulling into the lot. It wasn't Innis's car but she spotted him in the passenger seat and her heart gave a little jump. She'd missed the sight of him more than she'd allowed herself to admit. His resemblance to the woman driving the car was remarkable and she knew this must be his mother, Irene. Same dark curly hair, same dark eyes, same foxy face. Fin took a deep breath.

"Here you go, girl," she whispered to herself and, dropping the iPod back into her coat pocket, she leaped from her car to run over and greet them.

Chapter XXVII: A Glint Among The Trees

Irene stopped the car and stared at the girl with clumps of dark hair sticking out from beneath a wool cap who was running toward her and Innis. Glancing over at her son, she raised an eyebrow.

"Finola, I take it?"

The look of utter shock on Innis's face almost made his mother laugh. He nodded briefly and leaped from the car, meeting Fin in a crushing hug followed by a passionate kiss. Irene drummed her fingers lightly against the steering wheel, annoyed by this unexpected interruption of what she'd anticipated as a pleasant evening alone with her son and his strange new housemate. Innis had talked to her about Fin, though not in the detail Irene craved, but it had been awhile since he'd mentioned his Belfast romance so she'd assumed things weren't going too well. From what little she'd learned about Fin, Irene wasn't thrilled with this selection as her son's paramour. There was the distance to consider, for one thing, and Irene was skeptical about how they'd make that work. Then there was the fact that Fin was a city girl, owning and operating her own business, making vacation trips to some of the places Irene had always longed to see. Embarrassed as she was by the fact that she was jealous of her son's girlfriend's life, she couldn't deny it. Now, as she watched their clearly heartfelt reunion, she grew more resigned to accepting Fin. If Innis was this fond of her, Irene would try to get past her own petty objections. Did mothers usually feel this resistance at losing their sons to another female, she wondered. She had no idea but opened her car door and stood by the car, hands in her coat pockets, looking at the ground and waiting for the kiss to end.

Innis and Fin finally broke away from each other and came toward Irene. Innis's arm was around Fin's shoulders and an unabashed happiness shone in his eyes. Fin appeared wary, approaching Irene with a nervous expression. Irene wished they weren't meeting this way but offered a smile and held out her hand.

"Well, we meet at last. I'm Irene, Innis's ma. Guess you figured that out."

Fin reached out eagerly to shake the offered hand. Irene noticed several delicate silver rings adorning the girl's fingers, briefly self conscious of her own larger, rougher hands.

"Yes, I'm so pleased to meet you," Fin was saying as they shook hands, both of them avoiding each other's eyes. "I'm sorry this is so unexpected for both of you. I took it upon myself to..."

She paused, searching for the right word.

"Just show up," Irene offered.

Fin blushed.

"Yes, exactly. If I'm interrupting--"

"Never," Innis broke in, giving Fin's shoulders a squeeze. "It's a big surprise, but a bloody good one. Yaeger's never had this much company."

Irene remembered that Innis had already told Fin about the aye-aye. She wondered how many other things about her son this stranger from Belfast knew that she did not, but let it go. That's life, she reminded herself, the child growing away from its mother into its own place in the world. Grateful that she still had one son at home, and probably would for the foreseeable future, she walked behind Innis and Fin into the woods of Raven's Back, feeling a bit of a third wheel as the two of them chatted quietly to each other like the closest of friends.

The hike to Innis's cabin, much lengthier than anticipated, tired Irene out but she kept up, determined not to plead age or exhaustion. Innis had finally removed his arm from around Fin's shoulder and the two of them walked close together with Innis occasionally glancing back to check on his mother. When they reached a particularly isolated spot, Irene spotted a cabin that was barely visible among a dense grove of trees and broke into a broad smile.

"Innis!" she exclaimed, coming to a halt to take in the simple dwelling. "You made this, son. I've only seen it briefly from the outside. Now I'll finally be able to enter."

Innis left Fin to stand beside his mother, guilty that he'd been ignoring her and had put off this visit for too long.

"I didn't actually build the cabin, Ma, it was already here. I just renovated it a bit, mostly on the inside."

"It's your home, though. You've made your own home here."

Innis laughed nervously, surprised at the emotion in his mother's voice. He hugged her warmly and kissed her forehead.

"Don't get too weepy. It's only a cabin. Sorry you had to wait but now here you are. I think you should be the first to enter, if that's OK with Fin. Oh, one thing for both you ladies. I'm a bit later getting home than usual so Yaeger might be waiting at the door so enter carefully. I know you've seen pictures of aye-ayes, Fin, but Ma, beware. He's a rather strange creature yet quite a sweetheart."

The three of them headed for the cabin with Innis in front, fishing for the keys in his coat pocket. As they neared the cabin, Irene's breath caught at the sight of Yaeger in one of the front windows of the cabin. He was watching their approach, one front hand with its long, bony fingers placed against the glass. Irene barely kept herself from shouting out in astonishment and merely pointed to the creature.

"Look! There he is," she whispered in an effort not to startle the animal.

Innis laughed and Fin put a hand to her heart in delight.

"My God, Innis, he's so incredible!" she cried. "Oh, Yaeger."

"I've never seen him in the window like that before, the little rascal," Innis chuckled, unlocking the door. "Sorry, Ma, but on second thought I think I'd better go in first. He's liable to be waiting right there."

"Good idea," Irene agreed. "He's already disappeared from the window. It's almost like a dog waiting for its person to come home."

Innis carefully opened the door to find Yaeger right on the other side. Scooping up the aye-aye, he opened the door wider.

"C'mon in, ladies. Welcome to our humble abode."

Fin stood back for Irene to enter first, then closed the door after she'd stepped in as well. She was anxious to see Innis's home but her eyes went right to Yaeger, who was settled in Innis's arms with one hand holding onto his coat collar. The aye-aye's amber eyes gazed directly at Fin and she beamed, standing and watching Yaeger with both hands clasped behind her back. This meeting had been a long time in arriving and she didn't want to do anything to upset Yaeger. Just looking at him, seeing him in the flesh, so to speak, was so marvelous it brought tears to her eyes. The creature, even more amazing in reality that she'd pictured him in her dreams, was holding onto Innis in such a sweet, natural way that it completely captured her heart.

"I see why Innis loves you so much, Yaeger," she whispered to the aye-aye before she realized she was going to speak. "I'm Fin and it's an honor and a thrill to meet you."

Yaeger closed his eyes once as though in acknowledgment of her words while Innis grinned back at Fin.

"He's the best, isn't he? Not quite the drowned rat I found on the beach, I can tell you that."

Just then Yaeger turned his head to look at Innis with a 'What did you just say' expression. Both Fin and Innis burst out laughing. Irene, who'd been surveying the living room, joined them.

"I see he's already entertaining everyone. He's not at all bothered by humans, is he? Not even strangers. Dare I attempt a pet or a touch? He doesn't look the sort of fellow I'd want to cross."

"Nah, he's a sweetheart. Go ahead and try, if you want. Can't guarantee the results."

Irene tentatively put one hand forward with Yaeger watching her, his strange eyes casting such an unrelenting gaze that she drew back her hand.

"Think I'll wait. He's awfully intense, Innis."

Innis laughed.

"He's not had this many visitors and he avoided Dalton completely the time he visited. He's probably hungry as well and anxious for his hunting trip since I'm late. Why don't you two come with us? I think I'd better get this boy out in the woods. You can check out the cabin later."

"I've already noticed how lovely you've made it," Irene rubbed Innis's back lightly. "A real credit to you, son."

Innis retrieved the canvas bag used for collecting food and nest materials and repositioned Yaeger beneath his coat then opened the cabin door.

"I thought you put him on a harness and rope," Fin remarked.

"I used to, but now he just goes loose. I trust him, he doesn't run off. It made me really nervous at first to lose him, but Bridget--"

He stopped, aware that Irene had no idea that her sister had met Yaeger. Irene cocked her head and looked intently at Innis.

"So Bridget's in on the aye-aye secret as well? It's beginning to sound like a very ill kept secret after all. Guess I'm late to the party. And she had advice for you about the aye-aye certainly. I can well imagine."

Yaeger shifted restlessly beneath Innis's coat.

"Can we please discuss this during our walk out to the woods, Ma, or maybe later? He's anxious for his supper."

The three humans and the aye-aye headed out into the night. The darkness had deepened by now and the forest became thicker almost immediately.   Fin and Irene walked silently side by side behind Innis, struggling with the dense undergrowth, occasionally stumbling in an effort to keep up with Innis's rather brisk pace. He glanced back to check on them and wait for them to catch up while Yaeger became more restless under the coat. Fin, astonished by the depth of the forest through which they trekked, listened for the night sounds to which she was unaccustomed: an owl's hooting somewhere among the trees, the rustling of what she assumed were forest creatures nearby, the sharp cry of a bird. She felt herself surrounded by nature and a chill night air that made her shiver yet exhilarated her. Irene, annoyed by the reference to Bridget and the uncomfortably inappropriate shoes she was wearing, trudged along lost in her own thoughts. The fact that Innis was living in this isolated region with a strange animal native to an island near Africa gave her grave concern. During the drive out to Raven's Back from the parking lot at Murphy's, Innis had explained how he'd found Yaeger on the beach, providing details about this aye-aye creature in general and Yaeger in particular. His enthusiasm and love for the animal emanated from him in a way she hadn't observed from anything else he'd ever done, and she assumed the existence of the creature could easily account for the devil worship rumors. Such a crazy, unlikely situation.

Then there was Fin. Irene realized she should probably be talking to the girl as they walked, seizing an opportunity for getting to know her, but something about Fin's demeanor discouraged conversation and they both remained silent. The affection between this girl and Innis was clear, as well as Fin's fondness for the aye-aye. Irene noticed what appeared to be a sharp curiosity coming from Fin and approved of her willingness to go traipsing through the woods with a childlike enthusiasm. She decided she'd give her the benefit of the doubt, wishing Innis had been more forthcoming about the relationship. She had no idea where things stood with this long distance romance but there would be time to talk when they returned to the cabin. Her son's attachment to the strange aye-aye was more bothersome than his girlfriend. Why was he so invested in keeping it secret? He hadn't divulged the situation with Charlie to her, though she sensed there was much more going on than he'd told her.

Innis was also distracted by his thoughts as he headed toward the original forest area where he'd first taken Yaeger. A trip to the purple grove was out of the question since Irene and Fin were present, though he suspected Yaeger would not be pleased. How was he going to explain what had occurred in connection with Bridget and the aye-aye to his mother? Cursing the careless slip of the tongue, he grasped for a strategy but found none. The magic of the purple grove, the epiphany he'd experienced that night when Bridget had joined him there, his aunt's notion that Yaeger was some sort of emissary from the sea kingdom of Connla. All these things would not be easily explained, especially to his mother. Perhaps he wasn't giving Irene enough credit, yet the expression on her face when he'd mentioned Bridget spoke volumes. The night was particularly cold and Innis smiled as Yaeger snuggled closer against his chest.

"Ah, little one," he whispered to the aye-aye. "It's no end of complications you've delivered."

Then there was Fin. The shock and instant joy of seeing her here in Raven's Back had briefly swept all their previous problems away, and as they'd walked to the cabin she'd excitedly related her decision to search Innis out as well as her revelatory drive up the coast. Innis sensed her delight at seeing Yaeger for the first time, yet, in the back of his mind, there was a lingering doubt about the future with Fin. Lately he'd been entertaining the fantasy of going to live with Yaeger in the purple grove, removing himself and the aye-aye from the danger and superstitions which seemed to be increasing around them. He couldn't picture Fin, with her city ways and yearning for the adventure of faraway places, settling down with him in the middle of a forest, basically isolated from the world. She'd mentioned that she'd been doing some serious thinking since arriving in Glenraven and he worried about what it might mean. Would he need to be the one to break off with her this time?

He'd been so preoccupied with his thoughts that he'd almost passed through the area where he'd decided to release Yaeger and came to an abrupt halt, causing Fin to bump into his back and Irene to jostle against Fin.

"Whoa!" Irene blurted. "What happened?"

"Sorry, ladies, I was daydreaming and forgot where I was going. No harm done?"

Fin laughed.

"I'm fine. Doing a bit of daydreaming myself."

"Well, I'll join the party," Irene smiled. "I guess we were all a million miles away."

Inside the coat, Yaeger had shifted and Innis could feel him trembling, almost scrambling to nestle closer against his chest.

"What's up, macushla?"

Innis opened the coat and peered in at the aye-aye, who had his face buried into Innis's sweater, his long fingers clinging tightly to the wool. Softly stroking Yaeger's bristly hair he whispered soothingly to the terrified creature.

"Shh, it's OK, Yaeger. What's got you so scared?"

Innis glanced around, checking the surrounding darkness and listening carefully for any sounds. This was the same behavior Yaeger had exhibited when he'd sensed Charlie and the shotgun. Was Halloran out there somewhere among the trees again?

"What's wrong?" Irene caught the worried expression on her son's face. "Is Yaeger OK?"

"Dunno. He's all shaky like he's terrified of something. He's holding onto me for dear life."

Fin quickly looked around.

"There aren't wolves or bears in these woods, are there?" she asked, suddenly aware of how isolated from civilization they were. If something threatening was out there in the dark, what would they do?

"Nah, nothing like that," Innis continued to survey the woods. "It could be one of my neighbors. He's followed me and Yaeger before and Yaeger sensed his presence before I did. He seems even more afraid this time though."

"Maybe we'd better go back," Irene glanced nervously around. "Why was he following you, the neighbor?"

"Yaeger has to eat," Innis ignored his mother's question about Charlie. "No need getting into all that now. Let's go a little farther and see if that helps."

He wondered if Yaeger could be so upset by being somewhere other than the purple grove that he'd panicked, though that seemed too extreme a reaction. The group moved off, heading a little farther into the woods but Yaeger continued to tremble. Stopping again, Innis looked up into the surrounding trees, watching the slightly rustling branches moving with the night breeze. He caught the glint of something and froze, staring at the spot where it had appeared near the lower branches of one of the nearby trees. The darkness was particularly dense with no moon or stars and the thickness of the woods in the area where they stood made visibility even more limited. Could there be a figure there, hidden in the tree? Innis thought he detected a dark form but couldn't be certain. He pulled the coat closer around Yaeger and held out his arm to warn Fin and Irene.

"Don't move," he whispered. "I might see something in the trees over there. I saw something flash for a second, like a reflection or maybe..."

"A gun?" Irene asked.

Fin, startled, turned to Innis, trying unsuccessfully to keep the panic out of her voice.

"Is someone after you, Innis?" she whispered. "Your neighbor Charlie, maybe?"

"Not after me," Innis spoke between clenched teeth. "After Yaeger."

Continuing to scan the branches above them, Innis saw no movement, remaining frozen to the spot as did Fin and Irene. The aye-aye had to eat, he told himself, but was he putting all of them in jeopardy? Surely Charlie Halloran hadn't become so unhinged as to try to kill Yaeger and, if so, was he himself now a target as well? If the group left this area, would Charlie follow them or, much worse, fire at them as they moved away? No, his neighbor wasn't a madman, after all. Irene interrupted his thoughts.

"Perhaps we'd better leave this area, Innis, if there's a possibility of danger. Is there somewhere else Yaeger can do his hunting?"

"What if whoever's around here follows us, though," Fin put in. "Do you think what you saw could have been a gun? I'm getting scared."

"Let's move away," Innis decided, heading deeper into the forest with Irene and Fin close behind. His ears attuned to any small sound in the vicinity, Innis was relieved to feel Yaeger begin to relax as they walked. Wishing to put as much distance as possible between them and the previous area, Innis picked up his pace, knowing Yaeger must be very hungry by now. The aye-aye was relaxed in his arms and finally poked his head out from beneath the coat, surveying his surroundings with his usual alert interest. They reached a spot where they'd originally found good foraging and Innis bent down to remove Yaeger from his coat. The aye-aye looked around with a brief uncertainty then made his way to one of the nearby trees.

Fin, riveted by the sight of Yaeger in motion, put one hand over her mouth in astonishment at the creature's odd gait and strange physicality. He was slightly larger than she'd imagined with a longer tail than expected and an undeniably otherworldly appearance. Moving quickly to the tree, Yaeger effortlessly climbed to a low branch and began tapping on it, his large bat-like ears moving in a way that made Fin burst out laughing.

"Oh, Innis, he's simply divine!" she exclaimed, her eyes fixed on Yaeger's every movement.

Innis smiled like a proud parent.

"He is, isn't he? He's looking for grubs. Let's hope he finds some. Just wait till you see what happens then."

"He's an odd one, that's for sure," Irene shook her head. "I've gotta say, it's easy to see why a person could be freaked out by the sight of him. What an adorably homely grandson I've got."

Fin and Innis laughed but Innis's thoughts kept returning to the glint among the trees. As they watched Yaeger investigating the tree and its branches, his heart sank at the thought of someone wishing Yaeger harm, someone cowardly enough to wait, hidden, for an opportunity to do what? Kill all of them? They'd need to go back through that same spot in order to return home. If Charlie Halloran was, in fact, the stalker who meant them harm, he'd be well aware of that fact. Innis heard the delighted murmuring from Irene and Fin as they observed Yaeger's grub gathering ritual in the tree, but his attention had shifted and he concentrated his focus on a solution to the problem of the return trip with no success. Nothing sprang to mind and what if they were all walking into a trap by passing back through the area where he'd seen the glint? No, he was certain there'd been a dark figure crouched among the branches. Then again, he wasn't really sure. What with the dense darkness and thick forest, how could he be? In the back of his mind, something began to take shape, softly at first like a whisper then gathering at the forefront of his vision and coming into sharp focus. The purple grove.

Chapter XXVIII: Inside The Predator

Charlie stood in front of the mirror above his bathroom sink, staring at the image he saw there. Was it really him? Dressed in dark clothing with the hood of a black sweatshirt jacket pulled up over his head and his hunting rifle strapped across his chest, he resembled a soldier of fortune or someone going into combat. It was the expression in his eyes, however, that filled him with dread. He saw a focused danger there which he could scarcely recognize, the gaze of a predator. Lifting the night vision goggles he'd purchased up to his face, he fitted the device to his head, glad to erase the clear sight of his own eyes. Vaguely disturbed that he looked like some weird insect in the goggles, he turned from the mirror and walked slowly through the small confines of his cabin, acclimating himself to the night vision with a disturbing sense of foreboding. Tonight he would murder a man, one with whom he'd shared an ale and idle chat, one with a family and a history right here in Glenraven.

After growing more accustomed to the goggles, he removed them, setting them atop a cabinet by the front door in order to remember them when he left. Sinking onto the couch, he sat motionless for some time, contemplating the sobering reality of what he was about to do. He knew he hadn't sufficiently prepared. There'd been no target practice and he'd only donned the goggles for the first time just now. The sense of urgency about ridding Raven's Back of the demon he'd glimpsed through the window of Innis Kilbride's cabin returned and he nodded solemnly, his hands resting on his knees.

"It's got to be done," he spoke aloud. "That thing in Kilbride's cabin is a devil creature and he's in league with the devil himself. It's not only for the good of Glenraven, it's the best thing for Innis, really. There's no coming back from being in the company of the devil. How could anyone ever trust him again? And that animal's surely put a curse on our home here. I may already be too late."

Gathering a box of ammunition he hesitated by the front door. He felt a bit uncomfortable in the hunting jacket which he hadn't worn for some time, not since his hunting days. Placing the ammunition in a pocket of the jacket he readjusted the rifle then realized it was too restrictive trying to carry it underneath the jacket. Fumbling with the jacket he removed it, along with the rifle that was strapped across his chest. He supposed he'd been thinking of concealing the rifle by carrying it beneath his jacket, but who was there to see him anyway? He put the hunting jacket back on, forgetting about the box of ammunition which fell to the floor, scattering only slightly. Impatient and annoyed, he scooped the stray bullets from the floor, slammed them back into the box and shoved the box into the coat pocket. Re-checking the rifle to make sure it was fully loaded and the safety catch was on, he once again strapped it across his chest, this time on the outside of the jacket and opened the door, only remembering the night goggles at the last minute. He decided to wear them as they might increase his speed in moving through the darkness to the spot he'd chosen.

It was a cold night, much to his relief as he was sweating from his awkward exertions and nerves. Remembering the times when he'd tracked Innis on this same path into the woods, he shuddered at the thought that the whole time it had been that demon held beneath his neighbor's coat and whispered to like a beloved child. In a short time he reached the area he'd previously scouted. Feeling better adjusted to the improved night vision the goggles provided, he was impressed by the number of small details he'd never seen while traveling through these woods so often in the past. A few times he caught the reflection of the eyes of small forest creatures and saw squirrels and rabbits or marveled at the marks on the tree bark, the insects scurrying over rocks.

The tree he'd chosen wasn't as deep in the woods as he would have preferred, but it was the only one he'd found that he could easily climb into and perch comfortably at a low enough level where he'd shorten his aiming distance. The leafy branches would do the trick of hiding him as well. For a moment he panicked, unable to locate the tree that he'd only seen in daylight; then he noticed it and quickly climbed to the branch he'd chosen. It was awkward in the hunting jacket and carrying the rifle and he almost fell, cursing under his breath. The goggles were beginning to bother him and he removed them, wiping the sweat from his face and settling into the tree. There was only a light wind, for which he was grateful since he knew his aim wasn't the best. If he shot and missed, he might not even get a second chance. He figured he'd need to take down Kilbride first, then hopefully the demon would come out from beneath the coat and could be picked off as it tried to run away.

He knew he was early, judging from the usual time at which

he'd trailed Kilbride in the past, and he waited patiently, replacing the night goggles onto his head. Realizing he'd forgotten his watch, he tried to gauge the passage of time but it seemed to drag on for an inordinately lengthy period. Surely they should have passed this way by now. Had something happened, was Kilbride going to fail to show up? He couldn't spend the night in the tree and began to grow restless, shifting his weight to accommodate the growing stiffness in his legs. His face had begun sweating again underneath the goggles but he didn't dare remove the contraption at this point.

Suddenly he caught the sounds of movement at a slight distance, leaves rustling as someone walked through them. Raising the rifle to get a bead on his target, he paused as he listened more carefully. There was the distinct sound of several people walking. Kilbride was not alone! Lowering the rifle he watched the area below him, his heart pounding, the sweat running down the side of his face. The group of three, Innis and two ladies, came into view. Charlie almost gasped out loud. Innis appeared to be holding the demon beneath his coat as usual, but who were these two strangers? Peering intently through the night vision goggles he recognized Irene Kilbride but the other woman was completely unfamiliar. Perhaps the girlfriend Innis had mentioned? The idea that others might be a part of this whole demonic activity had never occurred to Charlie but now, cradling the rifle in his arms, he watched and listened as the group paused just a short distance from him.

He wasn't able to hear all their words, catching enough of the conversation to determine that Innis had caught wind of something. The word 'Yaeger' was mentioned several times and Charlie assumed this must be the demon's name. Could the thing possibly have sensed his presence? Innis was looking up into the surrounding trees and appeared to be gazing directly at Charlie at one point. Charlie froze, barely breathing until the group eventually moved on farther into the forest. He could still hear them, their voices and footfalls fading yet close enough that he was still able to see them. They'd stopped and he raised the rifle again, trying to get Kilbride into his sights. This would never work, he cursed his luck. They were too far away and with three of them here he'd have no chance of taking all of them out in time. The thought of killing Irene Kilbride was particularly disturbing to him and without knowing exactly who the other woman was he couldn't very well justify shooting her.

As he watched through the barrel of the rifle, the three people walked out of view and Charlie lowered the gun, remaining in the tree while he considered his options. The group would return by this same route, he assumed, since it was the only way back to Kilbride's cabin without walking miles out of the way. He could attempt picking them off as they returned but the problems of identity and multiple shots at moving targets remained. Odd that Kilbride never even carried a flashlight with him. Charlie'd noticed this in the past while stalking him and wondered if some sort of demonic powers enabled him to see in the dark. Clearly, if this was the case, the two women with him hadn't yet developed that power as they huddled close behind Innis and stumbled comically along through the woods. No matter, it only made Charlie's plan more workable, allowing him to avoid being spotted among the leaves.

The group could be gone for some time, Charlie figured, and he relaxed in the tree, removing the night vision goggles and propping his rifle against the tree trunk. His sweating had stopped, replaced by a slight shivering as the cold night air began to seep into his bones. It occurred to him that it would be much simpler going to Kilbride's cabin one night after he'd returned from his night excursion and shooting him and the demon at close range. There were problems with that plan as well, which was why he'd originally rejected it. An indoor setting allowed for easier clues for police investigators and there was the off chance that someone could spot him on the way to Innis's cabin. It creeped him a bit to admit that he preferred the hunter scenario, to be hiding in wait for his prey, secluded in the tree. The unexpected snag of the women's presence, however, had frustrated him. He'd never be able to explain killing them and couldn't really justify it to himself. Without any proof of their collusion with the demon, it would be cold-blooded murder to shoot them. Innis was a different matter.

Sighing with regret, he put the safety on the rifle and dropped the goggles to the ground, scrambling awkwardly from the tree while holding the rifle and falling into the leaves at the base of the tree. Scooping up the goggles he ran from the site, unconcerned with the noise he made. Innis was somewhere at a distance, deep in the forest, possibly performing who knows what pagan rituals with the two women and the demon. As he hurried back to his own cabin, he smiled wryly to himself. The assassination attempt may have been a failure this time but he would have other chances and now he had the goods on Irene Kilbride. Tomorrow he'd drop another pebble into the lake of gossip he'd begun and watch the ripples spread. Not only was Innis Kilbride a devil worshiper but his mother was as well. Perhaps he'd throw in the Belfast girlfriend for good measure, though he couldn't be certain that was the identity of the second female. He knew he'd never seen her in Glenraven and rather liked the looks of her despite that strange wool cap and the clunky shoes. Best to keep her out of it for now. Who knows, once Innis was out of the way she might turn to Charlie for comfort, that is if she hadn't already been indoctrinated by the demon.

When he arrived home, Charlie poured himself a large portion of Bushmills and sat on the couch, trying to wind down from the strange experience of perching in the tree. He'd been so close to achieving his goal yet fate had intervened on Innis's behalf. The man just seemed to be blessed, or was it cursed? Weary at the thought of going through the whole exercise again tomorrow night, he knew there was nevertheless little choice. The longer Kilbride continued to consult with the demon, the more possibility there was of damage being done to Raven's Back and Glenraven. He didn't dare confide in anyone else and his thoughts turned to the aftermath of carrying out his plan. Once he'd destroyed Innis and the demon, there would be a search for their killer. No one would care about the strange animal, but the murder of a human being was bound to be investigated. He knew that Innis was aware of Charlie stalking him, but had he told anyone else? If so, suspicion would immediately shift to him and he couldn't very well prevail on his friend Tom Sullivan to intervene on his behalf when a murder was involved.

Then there was Innis's mother. Now that he'd witnessed her in the presence of the demon, could she be trusted? Perhaps, like vampires, if the demon itself was destroyed all of its followers would likewise perish. Was anyone likely to even believe Charlie about the demon? If not, he'd be locked away, possibly for the rest of his life. Why had this burden fallen to him? Maybe if he could kidnap the demon while Innis was away from his cabin he might kill it or show it to someone else as proof of his theory. Surely no one who saw the creature with their own eyes could doubt the veracity of his claim that the thing was a demon. He was afraid of the animal, though, and the thought of actually touching it repulsed him. If he was in close proximity to it the demon might work some sort of magic on him, casting a spell of evil just as it may have done to Innis. Where had the thing come from and how long had it been here, he wondered.

The one component of his experience that night which he kept trying to avoid, and failing to do so, was the rush it had given him. That moment when he'd briefly held Innis Kilbride in his rifle sight, knowing with the simple twitch of a finger he had the power to destroy him, had been exhilarating. Nothing in his life had ever felt as thrilling. The many hard and tedious hours at sea fishing, the nights spent alone in his cabin wishing he had someone to talk to, had not prepared him for the possibility of such intense power and joy as he'd felt while perched in the tree tonight. Not only had he suddenly been the master of his own fate but of someone else's as well. He couldn't let that go, even at the risk of surrendering his own freedom. Instead of dreading another night in the tree, he was now anticipating it with an urgency akin to compulsion. He went to bed reluctantly, wishing the following night could instantly arrive. Despite his agitation, he slept soundly and dreamlessly, ignoring his alarm clock in the morning. He'd skip the fishing for a day, he'd decided, in order to be well rested for his second night in the tree. It was going to be a success this time, he just knew it, and he wanted to be alert to savor every minute of it.

Chapter XXIX: A Heart-To-Heart In The Dark

Yaeger was the center of attention, though he was oblivious to the rapt audience watching his every move. Fin and Irene, standing side by side just below the tree where the aye-aye continued his tree tapping activities, gazed up in wonder, straining to watch through the darkness.

"I wish he wasn't so nocturnal," Irene commented. "I'd love to see him doing this in daylight, it's quite the operation, isn't it?"

Fin nodded.

"I'm completely under his spell," she murmured, keeping her eyes glued to the aye-aye. "Reading about this online is one thing, but seeing him do it is something else. How long will he keep this up, Innis?"

"For a little while, then he comes down to look for stuff on the ground."

"He's an impressive climber," Irene noted. "The way he went up that tree was amazing, really fun."

"Trees are his natural habitat but sometimes I wonder if he misses the mangroves of Madagascar. The warm weather there as well. He's a phenomenon, all right. Are you ladies keeping warm enough?"

"I haven't even thought of the cold since watching Yaeger," Fin said. "Haven't thought of much of anything else actually."

"Well, I've been thinking that I'm going to be quite late getting home," Irene turned to Innis. "I'm sorry to rush things, but your da will be looking for me. I did let him know I was coming out here to visit you, but I don't suppose you get much cell phone reception way out here. I don't want him to worry, not that he would but still. And I want time to have a look at your place."

"He must have heard you," Fin laughed, motioning toward Yaeger. "Look, he's coming down."

The aye-aye was climbing down from the tree and immediately began searching the ground for insects and nest materials. Innis and the ladies followed with Innis collecting the items Yaeger selected and putting them in the canvas bag as usual. When Yaeger located an insect he wanted, he stopped to eat it, occasionally looking to Innis to pick up a beetle or mushroom to place in the glass jar kept in the bag. Nest materials were also stuffed into the bag and Fin in particular seemed delighted by the ritual.

"He likes to take the beetles home to have later," Innis explained. "I've become a rather adept bug handler, impervious to all sorts of creepy crawlers."

"You were always that way," Irene scoffed. "Can't blame that on Yaeger."

Innis laughed and turned to Fin.

"That's true. I collected my share of insects as a boy, fair to say."

"I'd have to draw the line at picking up beetles," Fin shuddered. "Although maybe for Yaeger, anything."

"What's on your mind, Innis?" Irene had noticed her son's distracted and worried demeanor, easily reading him as she'd usually been able to do. "Is it what you might have seen back there that's bothering you?"

"Yeah. Not sure if it's safe for us to go back that way, but there's no other route. We can't go walking miles through the woods and take hours to get home."

Fin, still mesmerized by Yaeger, had obviously ignored the conversation, focusing all her attention on the aye-aye. Irene moved closer to Innis, speaking softly so that Fin couldn't hear.

"Do you really think it's possible that someone's out here in these trees with a gun, wishing us harm?"

Innis nodded grimly.

"It's possible. Is it worth taking a chance? I don't see that we've much choice. We can't stay out in the woods all night."

"No, but I've got the light from my cell phone. We could shine it up around the trees once we get back to that spot and make sure no one's there. We'll go as fast as we can, then, to get through that area. Wish I'd thought of that earlier, but it never occurred to me until now."

"And if we shine the light and somebody's up in a tree with a gun, what then, Ma?"

"You watch too many movies, Innis. Then I guess we run like hell. Is it a plan?"

Innis laughed and hugged his mother.

"Yeah, it's a plan. You're a pip, Ma. Anyone ever tell you that?"

Irene placed a hand fondly against Innis's cheek.

"You're the first. Now let's fill Fin in on our intrigues."

The group made their way back toward Innis's cabin after

Yaeger had made everyone laugh by scurrying away from Innis whenever he interrupted the creature's foraging too early. The comical sight of Innis attempting to pick up Yaeger while the aye-aye kept a few steps ahead and cast baleful glances at the human brought a few welcome moments of fun, but the tension coming from the three people was still almost palpable. As they drew close to the area where Yaeger had sensed a sinister presence, Innis raised a finger to his lips to silence any conversation and Irene turned on the flashlight of her cell phone, focusing it at their feet to avoid noisy stumbling. They crept forward as stealthily as they could until they reached the spot where the glint among the trees had appeared. Innis nodded to Irene who swept the light up into the branches of the surrounding trees then surrendered the phone to her son. Focusing the light at the area where he'd seen the glint, Innis breathed a sigh of relief. He moved the light around, illuminating several other trees and switched it off, returning the phone to Irene.

"Good plan, Ma. Thanks. Now we better move out."

They hurried away, though Innis knew from Yaeger's relaxed position beneath his coat, the absence of any trembling, that things were safe. Fin caught up with him, leaning in to whisper.

"I know we haven't time right now, but are the purple woods anywhere near here? I'd love to see them before I go back to Belfast."

Innis smiled.

"Maybe someday. We'll talk."

She nodded and fell back to rejoin Irene. When they arrived back at the cabin, the ladies once again observed Yaeger enjoying the insect treats they'd brought back, then Innis gave them a brief tour of the small cabin which didn't take long. After receiving compliments on his home from Irene and Fin, Innis walked his mother back to her car. There'd been a slightly awkward farewell with a handshake between the two ladies. Irene, loathe to interrupt Yaeger's dining, had blown him a kiss. Mother and son walked silently for a few minutes through the woods on the way to the parking area, then Innis spoke up.

"So what do you think, Ma?"

"Of which?"

"Everything. Yaeger, Fin, my home. I know you didn't want me here in Raven's Back and, to be honest, I'm beginning to see why. And I know your jury's probably still out about Fin, but--"

"Relax, darlin'," Irene cut in. "Your cabin is wonderful, I'm so impressed with what you've done there. I hope you know that. Your da really needs to see it. I'm counting on you to make that happen. As for Yaeger, what can I say? I'd be willing to believe you'd completely made him up if I hadn't seen him for myself. It's very touching, the way you care for him and easy to understand why you've grown so fond of him. Even if he wasn't my only grandchild he'd probably be my favorite."

Innis hugged her.

"Thanks, Ma. I'm glad you get it, not sure everyone would. And Fin?"

Irene paused, considering her response.

"It's obvious the two of you have a special bond, and she's clearly quite taken with the aye-aye. I don't know her at all, Innis, but I'd like to. She seems a lovely girl and I do believe she's going to be a part of your life, wouldn't you say?"

"Yeah, I guess that's fair to say. At times I've thought otherwise, but I didn't realize how much I'd miss her."

"Do you think she'd be happy here? She's a bit of a city girl, right?"

"That's true."

"Love's a strong motivator. It doesn't make all things possible, but much more than you'd imagine. It's difficult for me to accept the idea of someone from Belfast being content in Glenraven. You know how I longed for something more when I was young and even though I'm more than content with the way things turned out it does take a toll, surrendering your dreams, even if you replace them with something of equal value. When I think of Fin, I can't help remembering that."

"But do you like her, Ma?"

Irene laughed.

"So much for the philosophy lesson. Yes, Innis, I do like her."

"Ah, that's a relief."

"You are an adult, my dear. You don't need my approval for anything, really."

"I know, but I'm still glad to have it. You know I care about what you think, your opinion's always gonna be important to me. It does matter."

"Innis, I don't suppose we've time for it right now, but I am

244

wondering about your new job as an artist, how all that's going to work out, especially since you've no intention of taking any classes. The main thing I'm concerned about, though, is this situation out here in Raven's Back with your neighbor. If you and Yaeger are in danger, something must be done. You can't let that go, just ignore it."

"You're right, and there's stuff I haven't told you, but like you said, not enough time. Don't worry, I'm not gonna pretend nothing's wrong. I've got a few ideas and if it is my neighbor Charlie I can't believe he'd actually do something as crazy as shooting me. Yaeger, maybe, and that's what I plan to work on. I'll not let harm come to him, no matter what I have to do."

Innis's eyes grew misty at the thought of the aye-aye getting hurt and Irene saw a fierce, protective anger in his face.

"Don't do anything foolish, son. I know how much you love that creature but you'll be no good to him if you break the law or do something dangerous."

"I'd go to the ends of the earth for him, Ma, but it's not gonna come to that. I've never cared about anything in my life as much as I do him. I can't explain it. When I read how there are so few of them left in the world, aye-ayes, I felt this huge responsibility to make sure he survives. And he's become my best friend. I know it's crazy."

"Well, Fin might have something to say about that."

"I'd choose him above her, though, I truly would. I think she knows that."

Irene shook her head.

"My boys and their pets. You with Yaeger and Dalton with Kieran. Not a dog or cat in sight."

"There's Keeley. I know she's retired from herding now but she's still hanging in there and Dalton still loves her like anything. I believe I've seen you cuddling her by the fire a time or two."

Now Irene's eyes grew teary.

"She's such an ancient girl, not long for this world. It'll go rough with your brother when she passes. With all of us."

"But she's still here now. It's amazing she's reached this age, seeing how hard she worked all her life. I've gotta get over there and see her."

Irene scoffed and pushed Innis lightly on the shoulder.

"Get you, must come visit the dog. Never mind you've not

seen your ma, da or brother for ages."

Innis laughed.

"OK, of course, you lot too. I think Fin should meet every-one as well, don't you?"

Irene glanced at her son then focused her eyes ahead as they continued on through the woods. She'd forgotten the considerable distance between Innis's cabin and the parking area. Why did he want to live in such isolation? It appeared that things were more serious between him and Fin than she'd realized.

"Ma?"

"Sorry. Yes, of course she should meet the rest of the family. Look, why don't you come clean, Innis? This girl obviously means a great deal to you, isn't that true?"

Innis walked along silently for a few minutes while Irene waited patiently until he finally spoke.

"I've got mixed feelings, Ma. She does mean a great deal to me, but honestly when it appeared we'd broken up there was a cer-tain relief to it for me."

"You appeared to be quite happy to see her here, unexpected as it was for you. If the two of you have truly called it quits that was quite an impressive display of acting I saw earlier."

Expecting her son to laugh, Irene was surprised to see him furrow his brows instead.

"It wasn't acting. Yeah, I was thrilled to see her. I suppose she'll be staying the night and I'll be thrilled about that as well." He hesitated, clearly embarrassed at the implications. "Not the sort of thing I'm easy with, discussing this stuff with my ma."

"Ah, leave off. You know you can talk to me about anything. I'm happy to have you bringing me in on things a bit. Go on."

"It's what you said earlier, about Fin being a city girl and all. I've thought about that too and I don't see a way for it to work. She wouldn't be happy here, I wouldn't be happy there, and there isn't really any in-between. So, is it serious?" Innis shrugged. "I've yet to figure that out. Your guess is as good as mine."

"Hardly. You know her far better than I do. It's not some-thing you've got to resolve right away. What's her take on it, do you know?"

"Not really. Suppose we might be having some conversation about that tonight. I guess the sight of her, out of the blue as it was, swept me up a bit. When I get back down to earth, will anything be

246

different? It's still the same situation at the end of the day, isn't it?"

Irene paused and Innis stopped beside her.

"Innis, the girl drove up here to find you even though she'd chucked you out. Does this tell you anything? It tells me plenty."

Innis moved off, Irene following him with her hands shoved into her coat pockets, wishing they'd reach the car park so she could get in out of the cold.

"How do you stand it up here in these woods, so cold and dark? Don't you miss the sea? I know how much you love it."

"I visit it as much as I can." He almost mentioned seeing his aunt there but refrained, afraid to remind his mother about Bridget having met Yaeger. "I like the isolation of Raven's Back. It's hard to explain but something just drew me here, not sure why."

"Well, I hope if you and Fin really are serious about each other that she'll be able to adjust. It wouldn't be for me, but then I'm not the one living here, am I?"

They arrived at the parking area and Irene hugged Innis, holding him closely for a prolonged period of time then releasing him with a kiss on the forehead.

"You worry too much, Ma," he said as Irene unlocked her car door. "And there's really no need to lock that out here," he gestured toward the car. "That's one of the perks."

"I dunno, with a gunman loose and all?" Irene teased, slipping into the driver's seat while Innis leaned down to her to receive a fond pat on the cheek.

"Do be careful," she turned serious. "You and Yaeger both. I'll call you with a date for a visit with the whole family to your cabin and this time we're making it happen."

"Promise. Thanks for everything, we'll be in touch. A hug from me to everybody back home."

He watched her drive away and headed back to his cabin, worried about the inevitable discussion with Fin and the figure he'd thought he'd glimpsed in the tree.

Chapter XXX: The Reunion

Fin was so enthralled with watching Yaeger finish the last of his meal and begin building a new nest in the bedroom that she'd failed to notice how long Innis had been gone. Surprised to hear him come in the front door, she hurried over to greet him, bubbling over with enthusiasm about the aye-aye.

"Oh, Innis, I simply can't tear my eyes from Yaeger, he's too marvelous for words. The poor bloke's probably already annoyed with me for staring at him but I really can't help it. Although, he's actually paid me very little mind."

Innis hugged her then quickly went to the kitchen, attempting to avoid a kiss with Fin. There was too much on his mind for such a distraction and he hoped she wouldn't expect an immediate make-out session.

"Tea?" he called to her while filling the battered old kettle with water. As he turned to the stove he almost bumped into Fin and they both laughed nervously.

"Sorry, didn't mean to sneak up on you like that," Fin said. "Yes, tea's good, thanks. It's OK, Innis, you needn't duck away from me. I won't pounce, at least not yet."

She took a seat at the kitchen table as Innis started the kettle. Busying himself with the tea preparation, he kept his back to Fin, clattering the teacups in his nervousness.

"Are you angry with me?" she asked softly. "For just coming up here unannounced, I mean."

He brought the sugar and cream to the table, spilling the sugar bowl.

"Dammit," he muttered.

Before he could retrieve a cloth to clean up the mess, Fin placed a hand on his arm.

"Innis, please sit down. You're as jumpy as a kangaroo. It's only a little sugar, we can clean it up after tea. Now, will you try to relax? Let's have a little talk and tea, OK? It's only me, Fin. Even if you're cross with me, we're still mates, aren't we?"

Coming around to Fin's side of the table, Innis hugged her then briefly held her, looking into her eyes before kissing her lips softly.

"Of course we're still mates, luv. A bit more than that I'd say."

Fin smiled and disengaged herself from his embrace, motioning to the kettle on the stove.

"Good, I'm glad you've not written me off completely, but I think the kettle's about to whistle."

Innis raised his eyebrows in a provocative expression.

"Indeed it is."

Fin pushed him playfully on the arm.

"Better fetch it then."

Innis poured their tea then poked around in the cupboards.

"Sorry, I haven't any biscuits or anything to have with it. Wasn't expecting company."

"No need, just tea will do nicely. Now please do sit down. You can't avoid me forever."

Innis sat and watched Fin add sugar and cream to her tea. Three spoonfuls of sugar and a generous pour from the little cream pitcher. He smiled, familiar with her ways, feeling himself relax in her company as he usually did. Sipping his own tea, with nothing added to it, he caught her eye.

"I'm glad you're here. And I'm not at all angry with you for showing up. You pretty much had to, didn't you?"

Fin nodded, closing her eyes as she savored her tea.

"Yes, I did. You would have put me off forever. I finally decided I wasn't going to be denied a meeting with Yaeger. I know I've somewhat forced your hand and now I'll have to stay the night, but I can--"

"What a pity. We'll have to manage somehow. Perhaps you'll sleep on the couch."

His eyes dancing with amusement, Innis reached across the table to take Fin's hand.

"I'm very happy to see you, Fin. I hope you know that, surprised or not."

Fin squeezed his hand and picked up her teacup.

"How quickly do you think we can drink this tea?" she archly replied, giving Innis a coy glance.

"Pretty damn quickly," he replied, bolting back the tea with a grimace.

"It's hot," Fin winced. "Careful. Not that fast."

Taking a big breath, she swallowed the rest of her tea.

"Looks like there'll be no tongues for us. They're both too scorched," she laughed.

Leaving the dishes on the kitchen table, they made for the bedroom where Yaeger was already ensconced in his new nest. Fin glanced up toward the top of the dresser where it rested.

"Will we disturb him, Innis?"

Innis laughed.

"It's never been tried. If we're joined by an aye-aye, will that be too much of a buzz-kill for you?"

Fin raised an eyebrow.

"Might be just the opposite."

"Ah, Fin, you're terrible, lass!"

They fell into each other's arms and spent the night devouring each other in the small, rumpled bed while Yaeger slept soundly in his nest, immune to the folly of the humans.

****

Fin awakened to a pleasant morning with the sun creeping through the one small window of the bedroom. Briefly disoriented, she remembered where she was: in Innis's bed, in Innis's cabin in Raven's Back. She snuggled back under the covers, blissfully recalling the intimate moments of the previous night. Innis had been particularly tender with her and she'd been especially passionate with him, quite a reunion. Glancing up at the top of the dresser, she saw Yaeger curled up in the nest she'd watched him fashion himself, tufts of his dark bristly fur sticking out from the nest's round opening. She felt surprisingly at home, she realized, and closed her eyes, picturing the possibilities. The plans she had for her future with Innis were unconventional, she knew, but they might work. Perhaps she was trying to have it all, and why not. Life had taught her to trust her instincts and take chances when they suggested she should. Surely Innis and Yaeger were worth a certain amount of risk.

Rising reluctantly from the bed, she went to Innis's closet and found a plaid flannel shirt to put on, then wandered barefoot into the living room. A veritable art gallery greeted her. Almost every surface contained a painting of Yaeger, some of them propped atop cabinets or on the floor against the couch, others in the window sills or in front of the door. The large painting of Yaeger in the purple grove beneath a full moon had been restored to its usual place on the easel opposite the cabin's front door and Fin gasped at the sight of it. Overwhelmed by the sheer volume of paintings in varying sizes and with a stunning array of Yaeger poses, she walked slowly around the room, gazing at each one in wonder. Innis's work was even more remarkable than she'd imagined and she came to a halt in front of the large painting on the easel. Its lifelike quality, vibrant colors and spiritual essence were stunning.

"Like it?"

She turned at the sound of Innis's voice to find him leaning against the doorway of the kitchen. His hair was still tousled from sleep, he wore a paint-speckled, dark sweatshirt and blue jeans, was barefoot like Fin and impossibly adorable to her. She ran to him, throwing her arms around him in a joyful embrace then kissing almost every inch of his face.

"That would be a yes, I suppose," he laughed, swinging her around then putting her back down.

"My God, Innis, how did you ever? They're brilliant and so many of them. I never imagined. The painting you gave me was marvelous, but I had no idea you'd done all this in such a short period of time."

"Too much?"

"Can there ever be too much Yaeger? You've been hiding them, I suppose."

"Ah, Fin, I've so much to tell you. I'm glad you're here. Well, guess that was obvious last night."

"I've never been so glad to be somewhere as last night," she laughed and placed her hand on his chest. "Too much sexiness, Innis Kilbride."

He put his hand over hers and looked directly into her eyes.

"Back at ya, Fin O'Brian."

They shared another kiss then Innis motioned toward the kitchen.

"Tear yourself away from those aye-aye pictures and have some breakfast, darlin'."

Innis had cleared away the dishes from their previous night's tea and set the kitchen table with scones, small bowls of fruit and a large pot of tea. Fin took a seat at one of the place settings and raised her eyebrows.

"I had no idea you were such a whiz in the kitchen, I'd have shown up much sooner."

Innis sat down opposite her, waving off her teasing compliment.

"Nah, I'm really not at all. I never even had fruit until Yaeger

251

got so fond of it. You're the first company we've had here for breakfast. Thank God I had a few things left. Some guests don't announce their arrival beforehand, now do they?"

Fin laughed and tapped his hand lightly.

"That they don't. Thanks for not being angry. I decided it was Raven's Back or bust. I've tried so hard to go my own way and forget you, Innis, but I've failed miserably. I figured I'd at least get to meet Yaeger, finally, if nothing else. We kept leaving the door ajar and I just pushed it open. Couldn't help myself."

"I'm glad you did. You might not be, though, once I've told you everything. Let's not ruin our appetites. We can talk after breakfast."

They finished their meal, chatting amiably about Yaeger, Innis's painting and The Forestry customer who'd expressed interest about Innis's artwork.

"You really must share your paintings with others, Innis," Fin insisted, "and this fellow has some money. He's been buying from me for some time and once he sees your extensive collection--"

"No, I don't think so. I know it sounds crazy but I don't believe Yaeger wants me to use this sort of creative magic for profit. I didn't paint like this before I met him. It's him who's brought it out in me and he more or less let me know the same thing about the purple wood. He originally didn't want to be in the purple grove because he sensed I viewed it as a way of making money. Once I got past that and appreciated it for its beauty and magic, he loved going there. I won't let him down that way, I can't."

Fin stared at the man sitting across the table from her. She adored him, but how could he be so maddeningly unreasonable? It struck her as sheer lunacy that he was spouting, yet when she considered the way in which his nonsensical mind worked it made a certain sense. Why did he usually require extra effort, complicating matters well beyond the normal?

"All right," she began. "It's ridiculous not to share these beautiful paintings with others. It isn't every day that someone's interested in such pictures of a strange creature they've probably never seen before. I really don't think you should pass up this opportunity, Innis. What if profits from the sale of your Yaeger artwork could be dedicated to aye-aye protection? Then would you be willing to sell?"

Innis rushed around the table to Fin and threw his arms

around her in such a tight grip she almost lost her breath.

"You're a genius, girl! That's exactly it, that's what we must do."

"We?" Fin extricated herself from his wild embrace. "Did I actually hear the word 'we'?"

"Yes, my darlin', you actually did. I can't do without you any better than you can do without me. I think it's a bit like destiny, don't you?"

Fin smiled gently and kissed Innis.

"Yes, it does seem to be that. I've been so longing to be a true part of your life, you crazy man, but it needs to be destiny with some realism, some ground rules."

Innis nodded returning to his seat and turning his attention to Fin.

"I'm all ears, then. Name your price."

Fin laughed.

"Not a price, at least not a large one. I've done a lot of thinking during the short while I've been in Glenraven. I explored the town a bit when I arrived and bought that wool cap I was wearing last night."

"From Erin, I assume? It's quite charming."

"Yes, exactly. That's the thing, you see, I realized what sort of a place it is, how different it would be for me living here. It's too small and personalized for me. I don't think I could do it. I see the charm of it but it's not me."

"So what are you saying?"

"Why can't we simply be long distance lovers? Belfast's not that far and I found the drive quite lovely, at least once I got out into the true countryside. It's not the distance that's the big problem for us, as I see it. It's the willingness to incorporate the 'we' into our lives. That's really all I want, Innis, to be a part of your life. And Yaeger's. It doesn't need to be the main part, even, just a part. It's not a home or marriage or kids I desire. It's simply you."

She was surprised to see Innis's eyes fill with tears and she went to him, settling on his lap with her arms around his neck.

"What do you think? Will it work for you?"

He put his arm around her as she leaned against him.

"Of course it'll work. I just wonder if it'll truly work for you. Before, when you broke things off between us, I thought it was because we never saw each other."

"No, you wouldn't let me in, not really. That's why. We kept that door ajar for so long and I waited for you to open it but you never did. I guess I finally just kicked it open by coming up here on my own. I don't require all your time and attention, I never did. I only want enough of it to keep me happy. Between me driving out here and you visiting Belfast I think we can manage it, yes? All I'm asking is to be included. Maybe we can have our cake and eat it as well."

Innis picked up Fin from his lap, stood and held her close, kissing her tenderly.

"My ma won't like it," he smiled. "Too unconventional. Once she sees how happy I am, though, she'll buckle. Don't know what I've done to deserve you but let's give it a try. I do love you, darlin'."

"And I, you," Fin ruffled his tousled hair. "Probably more than is good for me. And I adore Yaeger. One of the things that made me fall in love with you is the way you care for him. I'm keen to be a partner in that."

"Let me start another pot of tea. There's plenty of stuff you don't know and things have changed for the worse here in Raven's Back recently."

"The glint in the trees?"

"Precisely. We need to have a serious talk before you agree to take all this on."

While Yaeger slept, Innis and Fin sat at the kitchen table for some time, sipping tea as Innis relayed his concerns about Charlie Halloran and Fin offered her newly discovered insights about life in a small community. After checking on Yaeger they took a stroll in the woods, hand in hand at times, at others Fin wandered afield to explore various details that caught her attention. Venturing farther and deeper into the forest, they grew ever nearer the purple grove. Innis had not seen it in daylight for some time and he put a hand on Fin's arm to halt her.

"You asked about the purple woods yesterday," he said. "It's just up ahead if you'd still like to see it. One thing, though. If I show you around there you must keep it to yourself. As far as I know, only my Aunt Bridget and I have seen it or even know about it. Us and Yaeger. So it's very important that it remain a secret. I'm trusting you with something that's crucial to me and Yaeger. We're both at our happiest there."

Now Fin became choked up and clasped Innis's hand, holding it against her cheek.

"Thank you, my love, for that trust. It means the world to me and I'll not betray it, you can be sure."

They approached the purple grove side by side. Once the deep purple hue of the trees came clearly into view, Fin suddenly stopped, staring in awe with one hand held to her heart.

"Why, it's magic, Innis. I can feel it from here."

"Yeah, it is. Took me a little while to accept that. My Aunt Bridget helped me be open to the idea. As a wee lad I always wanted to believe in magic but as you grow up, you know, you eventually accept that it doesn't actually exist. At least not in the way you wanted it to. I haven't been here much during the day since the first time I discovered it. Yaeger and I always come at night. Shall we check it out?"

Fin nodded, taking Innis's hand as they stepped into the purple grove.

Chapter XXXI: The Safe House

The night following Fin's visit to Raven's Back a storm moved into the area. The stroll through the purple grove had been exhilarating with Fin's wonder at the forest's quiet beauty and mystical sense of seclusion reinvigorating Innis's already intense fondness for the place. They'd wandered among the purple trees with Innis pointing out the spots where Yaeger spent much of his time and even the treetop on which the aye-aye had perched, inspiring the large painting. The pervasive comfort and calm provided by the grove was as evident in daylight as it had always been at night, and Innis was thrilled to discover a certain darkness to the atmosphere despite the presence of sporadic sun outside the forest. Once among the trees, a soft darkness descended, shutting out the rest of the world like a tender embrace. Both Fin and Innis were reluctant to leave, and she'd wanted to stay until evening for Yaeger's hunting expedition but needed to return to Belfast to open her shop the next day. She'd left a sign announcing only a two day closure of The Forestry and didn't wish to disappoint or mislead her customers.

Leaving later than she'd planned, after lingering until Yaeger arose from his nest in the early evening so she could wish him farewell with a gentle kiss on the head, Fin also offered a passionate embrace and kiss to Innis. She noticed the dark clouds rolling in over the sea as she drove away from Glenraven, wondering if Yaeger and Innis would beat the onset of the storm for their nighttime outing, and arriving home to Belfast in a pounding rain. Figuring no one would be home at Innis's cabin due to the aye-aye's hunting trip, she left a message for Innis and Yaeger on the answering machine, announcing that she'd arrive back safely and asking Innis to call her when they returned, regardless of how late the hour. Brewing a quick pot of tea, she sat by the window of her small flat, watching the rain and thinking of the many revelations her previous two days in Glenraven and Raven's Back had provided. The sounds of the city outside seemed almost harsh after the stillness of the purple grove and the hush of the forest surrounding Innis's cabin, yet they also gave her the familiar relaxation of being in her element.

So much had transpired since she'd last seen this room and headed north with trepidation in her heart, and the uncertain outcome of her adventure weighed on her mind. She grew nervous thinking of Innis and Yaeger out in the woods in the middle of a storm with the threat of that glint in the trees adding to the danger. Pouring herself another cup of tea to calm herself, she pondered her memories of the sweet reunion in Innis's cabin, the marvelous meeting with Yaeger and the awe-inspiring exploration of the purple grove and smiled, forgetting her fears. There was a real future possible now for her and Innis and she'd obtained his approval to show her wealthy customer the paintings of Yaeger with the caveat that the proceeds of any sales be designated as funds for a 'Save the Aye-Ayes' foundation. She and Innis had touched on the creation of such an enterprise and both were excited to set it up. Suddenly life was full of invigorating new possibilities, a myriad of tasks and the promise of shared times with Innis and Yaeger. Fin decided to celebrate with music and played The Pogues on her iPod while she danced around her small bedroom.

****

Out in Raven's Back, Charlie Halloran was cursing the storm, frustrated by the impossibility of returning to the tree to target Kilbride and the demon as he'd planned. Surely the idiot wouldn't be going out in this weather anyway, he consoled himself, but he'd been anticipating a repeat of the exercise with such excitement and now he was a prisoner of the pelting rain and the cold, harsh wind. There was unlikely to be any fishing tomorrow morning as well, unless things calmed down considerably and this storm didn't strike him as the type to quickly blow through. The area was probably in for several days of heavy rain and Charlie hated being stuck in his cabin, especially when he was itching to carry out his plan to destroy the demon. It would be the perfect time to venture to Innis's cabin, perhaps, and do away with his neighbor and the devil's creature with the rain offering perfect cover and privacy. No one would be out and about so less chance of being spotted on his way to and from the scene of the crime. He wouldn't even need the pesky night vision goggles which had bothered him so much, although tracking mud into Kilbride's cabin could be problematic. He could shoot Innis in the doorway as soon as the fellow answered Charlie's knock, so no need of even entering. What about the demon though? He retrieved his hunting jacket and rifle from the locked closet where he kept them, along with his boots, then hesitated, replacing the jacket with an all-weather water resistant hooded slicker he used in the fishing boat during inclement weather.

Going to the kitchen he took several plastic garbage bags

from a box and wrapped them around his boots, tying them tightly with twine. He wasn't expecting to encounter anyone despite the rather lengthy trek to Innis's cabin and even if he did, though he'd look a strange sight, he'd explain he was merely trying to protect his boots from the mud. The bags would prevent any telltale muddy footprints in the cabin and he was pleased with his own clever solution.

Re-checking the rifle to make sure it was loaded, he pulled on the slicker and glanced around his cabin. When he returned here, he speculated, it would be as a conquering hero, the dragon slain, the village protected. He wouldn't be able to take extra ammo with him due to the rain and the possibility of it getting wet, but he wouldn't need any extra. From close range there was no way for him to miss so he'd have more than enough to take down the demon and Kilbride. Locking the cabin door behind him, he slogged through the mud and wet leaves, struggling to find his way in the dark. He'd forgotten his flashlight. The occasional crack of thunder barely bothered him, so determined was he on his course of action, though he struggled against the strong wind which was whipping the branches and leaves around him, now and then causing a branch to fall to the ground. Almost instantly drenched by the torrential downpour, he needed to continually wipe the water from his face and strained to see the proper direction. He'd placed his rifle in a protective case and clutched the strap to keep it near him.

The distance seemed longer than ever but just as he'd decided he must have lost his way, the dim light from Innis's cabin appeared through the rain and he hastened toward it in a rush of adrenalin. Pounding on the cabin's front door, he fumbled to extricate the rife from its cover and shouldered it, aiming at the center of the doorway. All was silent and he pounded the door again until it rattled. Nothing. The curtains at the front windows were drawn but he tried to peer in anyway, unable to detect any movement or sound within the cabin. Had Innis left with the two women? Might the demon be in there alone? He put the rifle back in the case and walked around the cabin, checking the shed in back which, as before, was locked. Stomping back to the front, Charlie shouted Innis's name loudly, trying to make himself heard through the noise of the storm. No response. The bastard's not here, he muttered to himself, a sudden rage filling him at the thought of once again being prevented from success. If Innis had left, he reasoned, why keep the lights on as though he might return any minute? He kicked the door several times, wondering if he might break it in but it held, its strong hinges and solid wood having been fashioned by Innis himself.

"Goddamn it to hell, Innis Kilbride!" Charlie shouted, the spittle flying from his mouth. "You and your demon creature!"

****

"Stop that, Yaeger! We're not going out in that mess. What's wrong with you?"

Yaeger was scratching desperately at one of the front windows with his front feet, his long tail lashing wildly back and forth while the storm raged outside. Innis had never seen the animal so agitated and wondered if there was something threatening outside. He peered out the other front window, seeing only the driving rain and surrounding trees with their branches tossing in the storm. Returning to Yaeger he watched as the aye-aye continued to claw.

"We've got things for you to eat right here in the cabin, darlin', no need to go out hunting. We can skip tonight. Why are you taking on so?"

Innis went to the fridge, retrieving a handful of regular mushrooms, rinsing them then presenting them to Yaeger.

"Look, one of your favorites. I know they're not purple, but they should do, right?"

He held his hand up to Yaeger who glanced briefly at the offering and returned to his frantic scratching. Innis laid the mushrooms on the windowsill and moved away, hoping the aye-aye would perhaps eat them. Yaeger once again ignored them and butted his head against the window, knocking a couple of the mushrooms to the floor. Snatching the creature from the window, Innis held him aloft and looked into the creature's eyes. There was a hint of fury in them, a belligerent edge he'd never seen before. For a brief moment he thought the animal might bite or scratch him but Yaeger only wriggled from his grasp, dropping to the floor and hurrying to the front door. He began clawing at the door, attempting to reach the handle.

"Yaeger, what the hell?" Innis was growing impatient. "If it's the nest materials you're wanting they'd be all wet anyway and wouldn't do you any good. You've plenty of nests in here already, you don't require a new one every bloody day. We'll go out tomorrow night, I promise."

259

Innis smirked at himself. As if the creature understands a word I'm saying, he sighed. He picked Yaeger up, carrying him away from the door with the aye-aye squirming and wriggling to get free. Placing him near the nest below the easel, which was one of his most frequently used spots, Innis held his hand against the aye-aye's back to keep him in place.

"Please stop it, Yaeger. Calm down. I looked, there's nothing out there."

The instant Innis lightened his pressure on the creature's back, Yaeger left him and climbed back up to the window, resuming his determined pawing and scratching. Knowing well how accurate the animal's instincts had been about the purple grove and Charlie Halloran, Innis conceded defeat. He wasn't about to let the animal wander free in such a storm and pulled out the harness and rope.

"OK, my spoiled little brat, you win."

When Innis approached, Yaeger ceased his activity at once, offering his head for the harness to be slipped over it, his tail finally stopping its wild lashing.

"You love winning, hmm? My God, such a snit. Still, you undoubtedly know something I don't, as usual, so here we go out into a brutal storm. If I come down with pneumonia, will you take care of me, Yaeger? Hmm? I wonder."

Yaeger turned smiling golden eyes on Innis who laughed and took a hooded rain jacket from the closet, placing the aye-aye on the floor while he pulled on the garment. He closed all the curtains in the cabin, hoping this might keep the place warm so they'd return, drenched, to a cozy home.

"Stay under my jacket as much as you can, little one," he cautioned as he tucked Yaeger against his chest in the usual way beneath the coat. "We're both going to get very wet and this is going to be the quickest hunting trip ever."

Bracing himself, Innis opened the door to be confronted by a blast of rain and a cold, howling wind. He moved slowly away from the cabin, grateful for the warmth of the aye-aye's body next to his chest and realizing he'd forgotten the canvas bag, glass jar and lantern he'd thought he might need. He and Yaeger didn't usually travel with a light, but the storm made the woods even darker than usual. Cursing his own stupidity, Innis trudged on, figuring it wasn't worth returning for the missing items. He'd simply make do some- how. As they disappeared into the darkness, away from the cabin, they missed the arrival of Charlie Halloran and his rifle by the slimmest of margins.

****

Why am I struggling through a raging storm, drenched to the bone and cold as hell with an aye-aye clinging to me, Innis kept asking himself. The farther from the cabin he went, the more he began to question the rationale for what he was doing. He heard branches toppling somewhere in the dark and lightning flashes occasionally illuminated the woods around him. There was no trembling from Yaeger, though, and Innis relaxed a bit in the knowledge that no one was likely to be hiding in the trees this time. Reluctant to walk as far as the purple grove, he nevertheless headed in that direction, recalling the especially protective shelter the dense purple trees provided. Once, in the recent past, he and Yaeger had been surprised by a sudden rainstorm while among the purple trees and had barely felt the pelting rain, mostly just hearing the pattering of water on the large, seemingly water resistant leaves above and around them.

It felt like forever until they were finally nearing the grove and Innis arrived feeling like a drowned rat. Making his way among the trees, he was instantly relieved at the cessation of the cold, driving rain and lifted his jacket to allow Yaeger out. The aye-aye, mostly dry with only a slight dampness on his fur, was warm from his time beneath Innis's coat and looked contented and eager to begin his foraging. Innis wiped the water from his face, shook his head and removed the harness and rope from Yaeger.

"You've got it made, you have," he addressed Yaeger, who looked at Innis, closed his eyes once as though in happy gratitude and was off among the trees.

Strolling slowly in the direction the aye-aye had taken, deeper into the grove, Innis listened to the sound of the rain and wind, muted now and seeming at a distance as if the storm was happening somewhere else. He lowered the jacket's hood and tried to ignore the uncomfortable squishing of water in his boots as he walked. He knew Yaeger must be happy to return to the grove and thought of the walk among the trees he'd taken with Fin. Now there were four of them who'd visited here: himself, Bridget, Fin and Yaeger. Once again the grove began whispering to him, folding him into a cocoon of safety.

His plan of living here among the purple trees was revived

261

and he saw a vision of a cabin at the heart of the grove where he and Yaeger might settle far from harm, isolated from the outside world. There was no longer any doubt in his mind that this grove was magical, a wondrous haven from the harsh realities of the vicious and threatening world. Here he could paint, undisturbed, while Yaeger lived free, able to come and go as he pleased, to live in his natural state of being an aye-aye, to thrive among the purple treetops. It would be difficult for Innis to let him go but he was hopeful that Yaeger would visit him from time to time and the idea of the creature being free to roam as he should would be worth the loneliness Innis knew he would feel. Fin and Bridget could occasionally visit but he would somehow avoid others. The more people who discovered the purple grove the greater the chances for danger. He'd leave the grove to see his family, of course, and to see Fin in Belfast. If his paintings did sell he'd retain only enough profit for himself to take care of the most basic needs: food, clothing only when his already spare wardrobe wore out, a nest egg in case Yaeger ever required any medical attention or something aside from his usual diet of bugs, larvae, mushrooms and fruit. There would be no rent to be paid on the cabin once he'd built it so life would be simple and basic, just as he preferred. Maybe he'd eventually branch out from Yaeger paintings to find varying subject matter. It could be a dream come true.

Rousting himself from his fantasy, Innis continued walking through the grove, farther than he'd ever ventured, savoring the peace and stillness that was punctuated only by the soft sound of the rain. The night was almost sacred to him now, the time of his greatest happiness and, like the aye-aye, he had become nocturnal. Amazing to know there was a wild storm raging outside, he reminded himself, yet here things were quiet and comfortable with only a sprinkling of water penetrating the dense cover of branches. Was he mistaken or was the grove actually becoming denser as he moved deeper into it? He'd ceased worrying about Yaeger going astray once they were inside the grove as he and the aye-aye always managed to find one another at some point once it was time to go home. The woods seemed to be drawing him in and he walked as though in a dream, scarcely aware of his surroundings, immune to the outside world.

Innis stopped, then, and stood frozen to the spot. Ahead, nestled among the purple trees, at the very heart of the grove, stood a cabin. Was he hallucinating? He didn't dare move for fear it might vanish. Peering through the darkness he noticed something atop the roof of the cabin. It was Yaeger. Hurrying forward Innis quickly reached the structure, placing a hand against the side of the small building. It was real and he felt the familiar warmth of the purple wood. The cabin was constructed from the purple trees and he laughed with delight. How could this be, who had built this and how long had it been here? He backed away from the building and looked up at Yaeger perched at the top of the roof beside a small brick chimney. The creature was watching him with smiling eyes, still holding a half eaten purple mushroom in one hand.

"You sly devil," Innis shouted up to the aye-aye. "How long have you known about this place?"

Yaeger settled himself against the chimney and nonchalantly began munching on the remainder of the mushroom. Innis, grinning at the image, walked slowly around the cabin, impressed by the efficient way in which it had been constructed. He wouldn't have believed the soft purple wood could be used for a building but the place appeared to be sturdy and well built. Glancing up at the roof, he was pleased to see it too was of excellent quality, sprinkled with only a light dusting of rain drops. Moving his gaze over to the chimney, he marveled at the brick work, noticing it was a bit weatherworn but quite sturdy with vines of purple leaves creeping up along its side.

The cabin itself was larger than his own abode, though still not too big, and full of windows, twice as many as he'd used for his own place. There was a cozy porch in the front, empty except for a small barrel to one side and a three-legged stool, made of purple wood and similar to the one he'd carved himself. Stepping onto the porch he hesitated then knocked softly on the front door. The place appeared deserted so he wasn't surprised when there was no answer. Walking over to look into the barrel, he saw that a run-off pipe from the roof emptied into it, allowing rain water to be collected. The little barrel was almost full, probably from an accumulation of previous storms, he speculated, since very little rain was finding its way down to this point from the current storm. He longed to dip his hands into the barrel and cover his face with the cool, clear water but remained reluctant to disturb anything in case someone was actually living here.

After another soft knock, he tried the front door which opened easily. Calling out "Hello!" as he entered the cabin he slowly walked into a charmingly appointed living room. There were window seats with colorful pillows below each of the front windows and a floor of dark, natural wood without a creak from it as Innis walked around. Strangely, the arrangement of furniture resembled that of Innis's cabin, though with a larger space available there were additional pieces such as a sizable bookcase in one corner and two end tables flanking the couch, as well as a large coffee table made of a slab from one of the purple trees. It was a beautiful piece that Innis stopped to admire, running his fingers over the soft, slightly warm surface, pleased that whatever craftsman had created it had chosen to leave the natural grain and shape of the wood, unpolished and unfinished, just the way he preferred. The couch, larger than his own, held big cushions of robin's egg blue embroidered with fish and waves in a darker shade of blue that made Innis smile at their whimsical reminder of the sea. The table held several books, which he passed over, noting that the bookcase was also filled with books but deciding to look at them later.

The room, less spartan than his cabin, was nevertheless appealing to him, not overly decorated although someone had clearly taken care with it. There was no evident dirt or dust which puzzled him considering it seemed unlikely that anyone had been living here for some time. Or had someone been doing just that? There was a fireplace in the living room, opposite the couch, made of the same brick that had been used for the chimney, with a mantel of dark wood matching the floor. A black iron grate, decorated with whales, fronted the fireplace along with several iron pokers, all of them indicating use though not necessarily recent use. The leavings from a fire were evident but cold ashes told Innis it had probably been some time since a fire had burned here. A small stack of wood, not purple but from some of the other types of trees commonly found in the area, sat nearby, ready for use. The mantle contained only a handful of dried wildflowers which appeared to have been placed there and then forgotten, left to fade and crumble.

Then to the kitchen, where Innis immediately noticed a window was halfway open, letting in the cold night air. It was a small kitchen in comparison with the more expansive living room space and rather minimal, containing the essentials of a somewhat old-fashioned stove, a deep two-sided sink, a table of purple wood with two matching chairs and a narrow pantry whose shelves held only a few cans of beans and some powdered milk. The floor, of worn linoleum, was a robin's egg blue corresponding to the cushions on the couch in the living room. A tin tea kettle sat on the stove with only a couple of saucepans and one small iron skillet, both showing previous use, stored in the cupboard. Whoever lived here, or had visited here in the past, was obviously not much of a cook, Innis observed, then came to a halt.

A scattering of purple mushrooms was spread across the table top, little bits and pieces similar to Yaeger's leavings after he'd finished a meal. Had the aye-aye been here before? Most nights he was free to wander, gone from Innis's sight, so it was well within the realm of possibility the he'd either found a way to open the kitchen window or discovered it already open and climbed in to snack on purple mushrooms. For all Innis knew, Yaeger had staked out this spot on one of their earliest visits and was already familiar with the place. He'd certainly looked quite at home perched atop the roof. Remembering the many times the aye-aye had been reluctant to leave the purple grove, Innis wondered if Yaeger had been trying to tell him something.

Returning to the living room he found Yaeger sitting on the coffee table with a fistful of purple mushrooms, happily pulling them apart with his rodent-like teeth.

"Is this your house, Yaeger?" Innis folded his arms and watched the creature who roundly ignored him. "How long has this been going on, then?"

Innis moved to the bedroom where he found a queen-sized bed covered by a handmade patchwork quilt, its squares depicting a wide variety of sea life: fish, whales, dolphins, crabs, octopus and seahorses. An antique dresser and rocking chair, along with two bedside nightstands, completed the room. Two good sized windows, bare of curtains, both of them closed, allowed views of the purple trees and dark green shrubbery surrounding the cabin. Noticing a small, framed picture on one of the nightstands, he picked it up, astonished to find a photograph of a young, beautiful Aunt Bridget smiling beside her late and lamented Gage. They stood by the sea, their hair whipped by the wind, their arms around each other's waists, looking the very essence of a wildly happy couple in love. Innis replaced the picture on the nightstand and sat on the bed.

"My God," he whispered aloud. "This place must be Bridget's."

Looking back, he remembered several times during his childhood when his aunt had gone missing for several days at a time while his mother, frantic with worry, looked and asked everywhere, only for Bridget to suddenly turn up back at her fishing shack, safe and sound. Where had she gone? No answer was ever given yet this took place perhaps half a dozen times. One of these had been shortly following the vandalism of her fishing shack when the word 'lunatic' had been scrawled there. This is Bridget's safe house, Innis realized. She must have escaped here during those times she'd gone missing as well.

Exploring the bedroom, he saw no other signs of Bridget's presence except for a crocheted blanket draped over an armchair in the corner and bearing the image of a gray seahorse, the sea god Connla. Innis smiled, even more certain his aunt must be the occasional occupant of the cabin. On that night when she'd joined him and Yaeger at the purple grove, was the 'discussion' she'd mentioned wanting to have with the aye-aye centered around this cabin? Innis turned around to find Yaeger settled on the bed watching him with a hint of amusement in his eyes. Wagging a finger at him, Innis chuckled.

"Have you and Bridget been keeping a secret from me? And for how long? No wonder she warned me to let you roam free, off the harness and rope, so you could find this place, right? Well done."

The aye-aye climbed down from the bed, going to a nearby closet door and reaching up as though to twist the knob to open the door. What now, Innis thought, but joined Yaeger and opened the door to reveal a surprisingly large space. It was a walk-in closet where only a few garments hung, several of them recognizable as his aunt's clothing. There was the smell of sandalwood and a bare light bulb with a chain attached. Innis turned on the light, scanning the shelves which were empty save for a heavy fisherman's sweater, neatly folded and unfamiliar to him. Spotting something on one of the higher shelves, he pulled it down, surprised to find himself holding a large pair of worn and weathered overalls, the size appropriate for a rather tall man. He placed it back on the shelf and unfolded the sweater which was also in a large size, clearly too big for Bridget. These must have belonged to Gage, keepsakes from his aunt's lost love.

Feeling a slight tug on his pants leg, Innis looked down to see Yaeger pulling lightly on the material. He shook his head at the aye-

aye.

"You're full of yourself today, aren't you, little fella. What do you want this time?"

Yaeger walked to the back of the closet and sat down, looking expectantly at Innis who saw that the aye-aye was seated atop a trap door in the floor. A large flashlight sat nearby.

"Holy shit!" Innis exclaimed as Yaeger moved aside to allow access to the door. Carefully lifting it up, Innis saw wooden stairs leading down into darkness. There was no light and he lowered the door, looking to Yaeger.

"This is craziness, darlin'. What should we do? Where the hell does this go?"

Yaeger scratched briefly at the handle of the door then looked at Innis.

"You want me to go down there, don't you? Ah, Yaeger, it's a bit scary and more than a bit insane, even for me." He stood silently for a moment, staring at the door. "Still, you've never steered me wrong. Besides, there's seldom been a mischief this Kilbride could resist. But you're staying here. If there's danger to this at least you'll be safe."

Innis tested the door, satisfied that it wasn't too heavy for him to lift from the inside on his return and, snatching up the large flashlight, climbed down the narrow steps. They went farther underground than he'd anticipated and the close smell of earth assaulted him. Resisting a brief claustrophobia, he quickly grew accustomed to the enclosed atmosphere and continued his descent until he finally reached a dirt floor. He turned on the flashlight, illuminating a curving tunnel stretching off into darkness before him. It was a roughly hewn tunnel without lights of any kind but high enough for him to walk upright. After the original curves straightened out, he switched off the flashlight, figuring he'd save it for later.

The complete silence and darkness in the tunnel comforted him at first, but as he walked on and on, occasionally turning the flashlight on to check for a possible light at the end, he began to worry. How long could this tunnel be and where did it come out? He stopped for a moment, trying to decide how much he should commit himself to this effort. With no way of knowing how far the tunnel stretched or where it opened out, if at all, was he on a fool's mission? Confidant that Yaeger would be fine hanging out in the purple cabin for awhile or roaming through the grove, probably pleased with the extra time out, he was determined to follow this path to its end and resumed walking.

Judging by the time and distance from his own cabin to the sea, a trek he'd made many times, he figured he'd been walking for a slightly longer time than that trip usually took when the path began to curve uphill a bit and he switched the flashlight back on. A long stretch of darkness confronted him yet he was certain he heard something in the distance ahead, something that made him pick up has pace and hurry forward. A familiar scent came to him, invading his senses like a jolt of electricity. It was the sound and scent of the sea. He rushed forward, turning off the flashlight as now the faint light at the end of the tunnel could be glimpsed with the crashing of waves and exhilarating salt air scent growing ever more pronounced.

Innis emerged from the tunnel onto a deserted stretch of shore, a vista of dark gray sea stretching before him with black storm clouds hovering above it. The wind-tossed water was crashing loudly, sending up huge waves that showed giant strands of seaweed tumbling within their curves. The tunnel opening was a sufficient distance from the water to prevent any fear of flooding but Innis started toward the wild waves, falling onto his knees in the wet sand, oblivious to the thunder and lightning above him. It had been some time since he'd been this close to the sea and this stretch of shore was unfamiliar to him, though looking through the driving rain he thought he could discern the area farther south where his aunt had frequently stood and where he himself usually visited.

Quickly drenched and shivering from the cold wind, he retreated to the tunnel's entrance and stood observing the turbulent scene play out before him. This was one of the most severe storms in recent memory and he gazed in awe at the power and ferocity of Mother Nature at work. Transfixed by the intense spectacle, he remained in place, losing all sense of time, astonished at this discovery. A tunnel to the sea.

Finally turning away, he walked briskly back through the tunnel without need of the flashlight. His thoughts were racing with all the possibilities this secret passage held. He recalled Bridget's fear at having traveled from her shack to his cabin on that night when she'd met Yaeger, the presence of ghosts and threat of danger she'd sensed in the woods. Perhaps her visits to the sea were sometimes followed by a trek to the purple cabin, using this tunnel to avoid the atmosphere of dread in the woods of Raven's Back. She had already been familiar with the purple grove from long ago. How long had she been visiting here, how many times had her feet led her along the path he was now following? He'd warmed up a bit as he walked and the shivering had stopped, but he felt a chill thinking of his aunt's escape to the haven of the purple cabin in the grove. A portal to other worlds. He recalled Bridget describing the grove in such a way, though he'd never imagined it might be true. Now, as he sensed himself nearing the stairs which he'd descended what seemed like ages ago, another world became clear to him. A life in the purple cabin, both he and Yaeger safe from harm, free to roam, to create their own alternative universe. Bridget would join them, freeing her from the prejudices, cruel behavior and superstitions of her neighbors, able to visit her beloved sea unobserved, no longer lonely. All of them together on this island of purple trees.

Innis ascended the narrow wooden stairs and lifted the trap door, glancing around to make certain Yaeger was nowhere in the vicinity, then throwing the door open to climb out into the closet. He replaced the flashlight in the spot where he'd found it and re-closed the trap door. Heading back into the bedroom, leaving a trail of water behind him, much as the aye-aye had done when he'd crawled from the sea, he saw no sign of Yaeger and continued to the living room. Yaeger was settled on the coffee table, surrounded by an impressive array of purple mushrooms, insects and a few pieces of purple bark. He looked at Innis calmly, as though unsurprised to see the human in such a state of disarray and wetness. Returning his attention to his food, he selected one of the live beetles just before it was able to crawl off the table and popped it into his mouth, crunching happily on it while gazing steadily at Innis, who laughed and put his hands on his hips.

"You've not a care in the world, have you? Look at me, dripping wet, freezing cold and about to burst with the adventure I've just had and here you are, just snacking."

The aye-aye gave out with one of his chortle sounds.

"Ah, Yaeger, I'm so happy to see you. I must dry myself off and warm up before I can join you though. We've much to discuss, my son."

Relieved to find a small bathroom at the back of the cabin, Innis longed for a hot shower but when he turned on the water it was ice cold. He dried himself with one of the two towels then spread it out on the floor to lay his wet clothes on it. Taking the patchwork quilt from the bed, he wrapped himself in it, savoring its soft warmth and returned to the living room. He took a couple pieces of the fire-wood stacked by the fireplace and soon a comforting fire was under-way.

Yaeger, still enjoying his treats, watched Innis with curiosity then crawled into his lap as soon as Innis joined him on the couch. Pushing his face into the folds of the quilt, the creature snuggled close to Innis as they looked at the fire and felt its warmth reaching them. Innis softly stroked the aye-aye's bristly fur and felt a peace that had eluded him until that moment, whispering to Yaeger.

"We're home, macushla."

Epilogue

The elusive, brilliant artist from Northern Ireland by the name of Innis Kilbride became an international phenomenon, famed for his strange and colorful paintings of a weird creature native to Madagascar. Few people had ever heard of the painter or the creature until a wealthy art collector purchased two pieces of the artwork. He displayed one of them in a trendy London club which he owned where they quickly became a conversation piece. Interest in this Kilbride fellow, whose image was impossible to find even on the Web, and the odd animal known as an aye-aye which he obsessively painted, generated additional sales of the paintings with several celebrities even making purchases. Fin O'Brian, proprietress of a small shop known as The Forestry in Belfast, was the sole conduit for all things Kilbride and aye-aye. Sales of the artist's work were handled by her on a personal basis, preventing discovery of the painter's location, personal details or future plans. Requests for interviews were summarily rejected, causing the public to become ever more intrigued, keen to obtain any tidbit to feed their appetite for information.

One intrepid reporter from an art journal traveled to the small fishing village of Glenraven after receiving an anonymous phone call advising that Kilbride resided there, or had at one time. The journalist's visit, however, proved futile. He spoke with many locals, most of them confirming that Innis had indeed been born and raised in Glenraven but seemed to have recently left the area for parts unknown. A referral to Kilbride's family's farm from one of the fishermen the reporter interviewed proved a dead end. He found the farm where he met Kilbride's parents and younger brother Dalton, who were polite and completely evasive, refusing to give permission for their names or words to be used. They provided no details about Innis and closed ranks, ushering the reporter from the premises in a civil but firm manner.

Next, the journalist attempted to glean information from the patrons of a diner named Murphy's where he'd learned Innis's mother Irene worked as a cook. A few people there offered stories of their native son as a child, an apprentice woodworker and an all-around good looking, charming fellow, popular in his community, though none were able to provide pictures of the man. The family, he learned, harbored a dark side which intrigued the reporter who was becoming anxious to develop a story of some interest despite a serious scarcity of details. There was a crazy aunt of Innis's, he was told, and at one point gossip had circulated about Kilbride himself being a devotee of the devil. Thrilled at these disclosures from people he considered to be naive country bumpkins who were excited to see their words in print, the journalist persuaded as much information as he could out of them. It was a bit of a scoop, at least, though he'd hoped for so much more and knew this was only local gossip with nothing substantial as proof.

Oren, the man to whom Kilbride had been apprenticed as a woodworker, was even less communicative than the family had been. He simply ignored the reporter, answering each question with silence while continuing with his tasks in the workshop where he'd been tracked down.

The journalist had learned that Innis lived in an isolated area of Glenraven known as Raven's Back but was unable to learn precisely where the cabin was located and, after traipsing miserably through the tangled woods of the area for miles, finally gave up. He'd become aware during his many conversations with the locals of a reluctance on everyone's part to go beyond a certain point. They were eager to talk yet he sensed there were things here to which he could not become privy. A couple of the old timers had mentioned things of a superstitious nature, curses and such, but became skittish when pressed to elaborate. Based in Dublin, the journalist still recognized the natural suspicions from a small town, the protective way in which they held their secrets closely. He returned to his editor with the peripheral tale of vague Kilbride family scandal and village flavor but no real revelations or details about Innis himself. The article was rejected.

Information about the strange, alien-like animal featured in all of Innis Kilbride's paintings, however, easily came to light. This little known, highly endangered species was thrust into the limelight with many people worldwide learning for the first time about its existence. The fact that profits from the purchase of Kilbride's paintings went to his foundation for protecting and saving aye-ayes gave the public an added incentive for buying the artwork. Prices were kept reasonable despite increasing demand and the foundation's Web site was kept updated with the most current information about the world of aye-ayes. It had been noted that the aye-aye painted by Kilbride was always the same in appearance, though its pose, settings and actions varied. The paintings were titled by their backdrops or situations: Purple Mushroom Breakfast, Trolling For Treats, Watching The Rain. The name Yaeger was known to no one and the large painting of the aye-aye atop a purple tree beneath a full moon hung in the living room of a purple cabin, viewed only by Innis Kilbride, Bridget Bahane, the aye-aye himself and, occasionally, Fin O'Brian.

Charlie Halloran, mortified by his own behavior after learning the true identity of the creature he'd seen through the window of Innis's cabin, moved away from Raven's Back and the entire area, abandoning his occupation as a fisherman and settling in Dublin. He found work as a bartender, a job for which he felt well suited, able to use his penchant for gossip and sociability to great effect. His suspicions and distrust of things beyond the parameters of what he perceived as normal, however, remained. Sometimes, noticing an especially strange face among the crowded city streets or seeing a feral cat whose eyes reminded him of the aye-aye, he recoiled and wondered if the devil really was still abroad, perhaps following him. Innis Kilbride's success as a painter infuriated him and, rather than experiencing relief that he hadn't murdered the man and his freaky pet, he regretted being robbed of that opportunity. He'd kept his hunting jacket, rifle and night goggles, sometimes wishing he might once again find need of them.

When Innis had announced to his family that he planned on leaving his Raven's Back cabin for a different home, there had been confusion and surprise, especially when he'd insisted that no one was to be made aware of his new address. Irene in particular questioned him relentlessly but to no avail. He would be nearby, he assured them, and able to have frequent visits now that he would be a full time painter. Bridget was moving in with him as well, to his family's surprise, though Irene found this situation extremely worrisome. Innis assured her it would work out fine. He told his family about the lynch mob incident he'd learned from Sheena, adding that, in addition to safety, Bridget would no longer be alone. Irene reluctantly conceded the value of the plan and Abbot was secretly relieved that, after watching over her sister for so many years, his wife would finally have help with that responsibility. Dalton secured a firm promise from his brother to visit the farm often, a vow which Innis kept.

Innis's notoriety as a painter followed shortly after his exit from Raven's Back. His family, as well as his previous neighbors, were astonished but pleased, never having imagined their small village would be the birthplace of a famous artist. Innis gave Irene a painting of Yaeger sitting on a purple kitchen table with a slice of apple held in his long black fingers and it hung in Murphy's diner to the delight and pride of the local patrons. Each day when she arrived for work, Irene smiled at the sight of the marvelously strange creature she'd met and kept secret. Both Abbot and Dalton pressed Innis for an opportunity to see Yaeger and, after much persuasion, the infamous aye-aye made an appearance with Innis for dinner at the farmhouse one night.

Life in the purple cabin was sweet and simple, just as Innis had wished. It had taken him little time to make a few adjustments to the place, such as a small hot water heater and a few shelves where Yaeger could build nests. When Innis had invited Bridget to join him and the aye-aye in the purple grove, her emotional and immediate acceptance made him speculate that perhaps she'd been living in fear in Raven's Back for most of her life. Although he would always wonder who had built the purple cabin and what Bridget's true relationship with it had been in the past, he never asked and she never said. He'd learned to allow her secrets to remain unaddressed. Her bouts with madness would still come upon her occasionally but they were less intense and gradually subsided as time went by. Innis was finally able to present her with the small carving of a dragon emerging from an egg which he'd made from the purple wood long ago. She kept it by her bed, sometimes talking softly to it or holding it against her cheek, valuing it alongside Connla as a trusted confidante and communicator.

Yaeger, free to roam the purple grove, grew ever more animated, turning sleek and shiny, even bolder than before. The cabin windows were left open at night, despite the cold, so the aye-aye could come and go as he pleased. He frequently visited Innis and Bridget, sometimes joining them for dinner, and had built a couple of nests on the shelves Innis had provided. During the day, aunt and nephew would sometimes stroll through the grove and might spot Yaeger atop one of the trees in a large nest. It gave Innis great satisfaction knowing he'd contributed to the survival of this fantastic species as well as providing this particular aye-aye with a good life. The tunnel to the sea was often used by Innis and Bridget but Yaeger had no interest in returning there. As Innis lay in bed at night, often with Yaeger beside him, he looked back on the events that had led him to this point with a sense of amazement and a deep appreciation and love for the aunt and the aye-aye who'd taught him never to question magic.

ACKNOWLEDGEMENTS

Many thanks to my sister Sally for her unwavering support and encouragement, astute observations about my characters and much appreciated editing skills. As always, her fabulous sense of humor manages to defuse my crippling self doubts with laughter. Our shared love for critters is an invaluable bond that was especially relevant for me while writing this book. Having been mom to a partially blind horse, as well as seeing two horses through colic surgery to save their lives, she rivals Innis Kilbride in dedication to animal care.

A salute to my sister Debbie for giving a 3-legged cat named Pippin a long, full and wonderful life. In keeping with the theme of my book, I truly believe that caring for animals brings out the best in humans and it's one of our family's cherished traditions.

Special gratitude to Joan Klengler, MaryAnn Marwitz, Lyn Sereno, Jerry Vogler and Diana Leonard for their enthusiasm about reading my book. Knowing I've got interested readers out there is invaluable and much appreciated. An extra thank you to Lyn and Joan, and her husband Ingolf, for rescuing more than their share of critters over the years. A shout-out to Larry Edmonds, the artist in my life, for his friendship and to Adriene Harris, who's gone above and beyond in love and care for critters.

My inspiration for writing this book came from a picture of a marvelous creature called an aye-aye, endangered in its native Madagascar. If I can succeed in bringing this animal to the attention of even a few people who were unaware of its existence my purpose in writing this story will have been achieved. In that spirit, I honor those who put their lives on the line every day to protect endangered species all over the globe, people like Singye Wangmo, a Bhutan forestry officer and tiger protector. That brand of dedication and courage is inspirational, real heroism and I thank all of those exemplary individuals from the bottom of my heart. A world without these unique and marvelous creatures you are saving would be a world without magic.

****

ABOUT THE AUTHOR

Patty Bowman has worked in entertainment and education as well as at a psychoanalytic institute, on a factory assembly line and as a motel room cleaner. She resides in the Los Angeles area. This is her second novel.